Praise for the

"Calls to mind the forensic ~~~~~~~~ Aaron Elkins and Patricia Cornwell. . . . C~~~~~~~~ attempts and harrowing rescues add to this ~~~~~~ced adventure."
                                              —*Chicago Sun-Times*

"Connor combines smart people, fun people, and dangerous people in a novel hard to put down."
                                              —*The Dallas Morning News*

"Outstanding. . . . Connor grabs the reader with her first sentence and never lets up until book's end. . . . The story satisfies both as a mystery and as an entrée into the fascinating world of bones. . . . Add Connor's dark humor, and you have a multidimensional mystery that deserves comparison with the best of Patricia Cornwell."
                                              —*Booklist* (starred review)

"In Connor's latest multifaceted tale, the plot is serpentine, the solution ingenious, the academic politics vicious. . . . This entertaining mystery is as chock-full of engrossing anthropological and archeological detail as a newly discovered burial mound."   —*Publishers Weekly*

continued . . .

ONE GRAVE TOO MANY

A DIANE FALLON FORENSIC INVESTIGATION

BEVERLY CONNOR

AN ONYX BOOK

ONYX
Published by New American Library, a division of
Penguin Group (USA) Inc., 375 Hudson Street,
New York, New York 10014, USA
Penguin Group (Canada), 90 Eglinton Avenue East, Suite 700, Toronto,
Ontario M4P 2Y3, Canada (a division of Pearson Penguin Canada Inc.)
Penguin Books Ltd., 80 Strand, London WC2R 0RL, England
Penguin Ireland, 25 St. Stephen's Green, Dublin 2,
Ireland (a division of Penguin Books Ltd.)
Penguin Group (Australia), 250 Camberwell Road, Camberwell, Victoria 3124,
Australia (a division of Pearson Australia Group Pty. Ltd.)
Penguin Books India Pvt. Ltd., 11 Community Centre, Panchsheel Park,
New Delhi - 110 017, India
Penguin Group (NZ), 67 Apollo Drive, Rosedale, North Shore,
Auckland 1311, New Zealand (a division of Pearson New Zealand Ltd.)
Penguin Books (South Africa) (Pty.) Ltd., 24 Sturdee Avenue,
Rosebank, Johannesburg 2196, South Africa

Penguin Books Ltd., Registered Offices:
80 Strand, London WC2R 0RL, England

First published by Onyx, an imprint of New American Library,
a division of Penguin Group (USA) Inc.

First Printing, December 2003
10 9 8 7

Copyright © Beverly Connor, 2003
All rights reserved

Ⓑ REGISTERED TRADEMARK—MARCA REGISTRADA

Printed in the United States of America

PUBLISHER'S NOTE
This is a work of fiction. Names, characters, places, and incidents either are the
product of the author's imagination or are used fictitiously, and any resemblance
to actual persons, living or dead, business establishments, events, or locales is
entirely coincidental.

The publisher does not have any control over and does not assume any responsibility for author or third-party Web sites or their content.

To Diane Trap

ACKNOWLEDGMENTS

A special thanks to GBI crime scene specialist Terry Cooper for his help—and sense of humor. And another special thanks to Genny Ostertag for her amazing work on my manuscript.

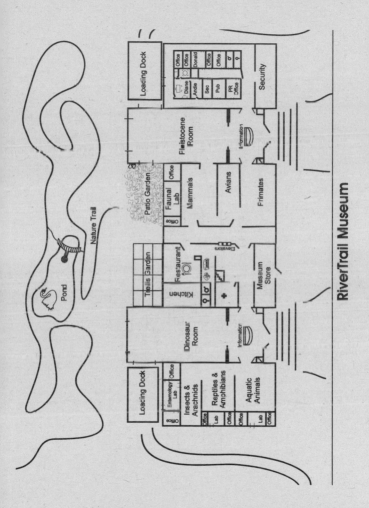

RiverTrail Museum

Loading Dock

Office | Office
Diane | Donald
Andie | Office
Sec | ♂
Pub | ♀
PR Office

Security

Pleistocene Room

Information

Patio Garden

Faunal Lab | Office

Office

Mammals

Avians

Primates

Trellis Garden

Restaurant

Kitchen

Elevators

Dinosaur Room

Information

Museum Store

Entomology Lab | Office

Insects & Arachnids

Office | Lab | Office

Reptiles & Amphibians

Aquatic Animals

Office | Lab | Office

Loading Dock

Pond

Nature Trail

Second Floor

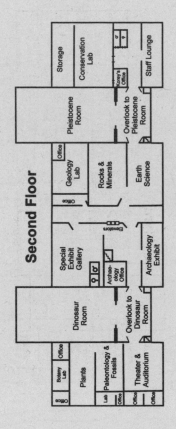

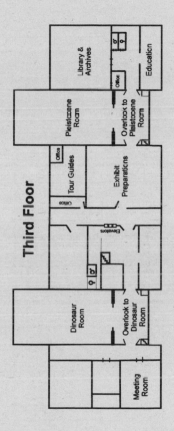

Third Floor

Chapter 1

"His head isn't on straight."

"It doesn't seem to fit. Maybe it's not his."

"Dr. Fallon—"

Diane Fallon, director of RiverTrail Museum of Natural History, looked up from the work she was trying to finish to see the spectacle of Gary and Samuntha, two university students, balancing between a ladder and a construction platform, holding the skull of a giant sloth tilted at an odd angle atop its fifteen foot skeleton. She raked her gaze over the offending skull as Gary was trying to wire it in place. "Wait a minute," she said.

Diane climbed the ladder to the platform to have a look at the problem. She glanced at her watch as she lay down on her stomach on the platform. It was late and she was tired. She inspected the bones and shook her head and pointed to the neck of the giant creature. "You have the atlas on backward."

"Are you sure?"

"Yes, Gary, I'm sure. Bones are like puzzle pieces. When they're put together right, they fit together perfectly. How do you think your head would fit if your neck was on backward?" The other students giggled. "Did you follow the diagram I gave you?"

"Yes . . . I thought we did. I already have it wired in place." He said this as if expecting Diane to say, "Well, then, I guess we'll just have to make the head fit, won't we?"

"You'll have to redo it."

"It's getting late, Dr. Fallon. I've got a big test tomorrow to study for."

"The opening of the exhibit is tomorrow evening. Test or no test, we have to finish this display. You've known the schedule since the beginning of the semester. Lay the skull here on the platform, gently. Unwire the atlas and put it on correctly. Follow the diagram."

"Ah, man," Gary whined.

Samantha looked close to tears. Diane could hear the frustration in their voices, but there was nothing else to do. The exhibit had to be finished and they were aware of the timeline.

Leslie, the third of the student threesome, looked at her watch as Diane stepped down off the ladder. "It *is* getting late," she said.

"I realize this is terribly unfair." Diane pulled loose a piece of packing tape that had stuck to her slacks. "Normally, students get to ask fellow students which teachers are a bitch to work for, but I'm new at the museum and have no track record. You guys can spread the word. Do the work assigned, do it correctly and on time. I give only A's and F's. We miss the opening, it's an F." The three students' eyes widened in surprise. "You've already wired the entire postcranial skeleton and done a good job. Getting the head on straight won't take as long as you think."

"Dr. Fallon, telephone." Andie, her assistant, brought the cordless phone from Diane's office. Diane took it and retreated across the room away from the grumbling students.

"Yes?"

"Diane, how are you?" It was a voice she hadn't heard in three years, and she was surprised that the sound of it made her smile.

"Frank? Frank, I'm . . . fine. And you? It's been a while."

"I'm good." He hesitated half a beat. "I wrote you several letters."

"I didn't receive them."

"I didn't mail them."

"Oh."

"Could I take you to dinner?" he asked. "There are some things I'd like to talk with you about."

"I don't know. This is a bad time, Frank."

He hesitated again. "I hate to ask a favor of you over the phone."

"A favor? What is it?" Diane looked over at her students busily working on the sloth exhibit. She hoped she had sufficiently put the fear of God into them so that they wouldn't mess up again.

"I have a bone that may belong to a missing girl. . . ."

Diane's voice caught in her throat. "A bone? No," she said a little too roughly, almost choking on the words.

"No, what?"

Andie was standing in front of her, holding out two handfuls of artificial leaves. The interruption gave her mind time to think and her racing heart time to slow down.

"Hold on just a moment, Frank." Diane placed a hand over the mouthpiece and raised her eyebrows at Andie.

"They sent the wrong plants, *Archaeopteris*, but Donald insists we go ahead and use them. He says no one will know the difference."

"That's why we're here—to teach them the difference. Tell him this is a museum of natural history, not a B grade movie set—we have to be accurate."

Andie smiled. "That's about what I told him you'd say."

"I'm sorry, Frank. We're opening a big exhibit tomorrow evening and I'm up to my ears."

"What do you mean, *no*?"

"No, I don't do that anymore."

"Don't do what?"

"Forensic work. I don't do it anymore."

There was such a long stretch of silence on the phone that Diane thought he might have hung up. "You still there?"

"But that's what you do," he said.

"Not anymore."

"Look, this is off the record. It's only one bone."

"I don't care. There are other bone experts you can take it to. Get them . . . One bone? You have only one damn bone? There's probably nothing I could do with that anyway."

"It's half a bone, really. You can tell me if it's human."

"If that's all you want to know, any decent osteology student can tell you that." *If you can find one,* she thought, watching hers fumble with the sloth. "But I can't do it."

"It may belong to someone I know. I play poker with the missing girl's father. He's been my best friend since we were kids, and his daughter baby-sat Kevin. The police are treating this as a runaway, but the girl's parents are afraid her boyfriend has done something to her. Her brother found the bone in the woods behind her boyfriend's parents' home."

In the woods, Diane thought. "No."

"Diane . . ."

"I have to go, Frank. I'm working with some students, and if they see me talking on the phone, they'll want to do it too. It's good to hear your voice again. It really is. Come by sometime." She hung up.

Diane stood still for a moment. Hearing Frank's voice was good. The tenor of it brought back past feelings— of warmth and passion. Why did he have to be talking about bones? She filled her lungs with air to clear her head, exhaled and went back to her students.

It was almost ten o'clock before the last person left. Diane was alone in the museum—but not completely alone. Jake Houser and Leonard Starns, the two night security guards, were making their rounds. And somewhere in the three-story structure the cleaning crew was hard at work.

Everything was almost ready for the reception the next evening—just a few odds and ends left. Diane walked among the exhibits representing North America in the Pleistocene. The skeleton of a huge *Bison antiquus* stood, as if on the ancient tundra, against the background of a restored mural of a grazing herd, oblivious to the Paleo-Indians hiding in the tall grass with their Clovis point-tipped spears.

The giant sloth turned out not to be the disaster she had feared. It stood majestic among prehistoric flora, head on straight, looking out at the skeleton of *Mammothus columbi* several feet in front of it. Something in the mammoth exhibit caught her eye. *Archaeopteris* leaves sprouting around the mammoth's feet. Donald, damn him, had put the wrong vegetation in anyway. He was such a willful . . . She stepped over the barrier rope carefully and took up the plants. A loud knock on the front doors brought her head up with a start.

She leaned over to look through the double doorway into the museum lobby. Jake appeared from the direction of the primate room.

"I'll get it, Dr. Fallon," he called out as he pressed the intercom button. "The museum is closed," he said into the speaker.

"Hey, Jake, it's Frank."

Frank Duncan. So he wasn't giving up. Diane heard the clank of keys in the door and their voices.

"Frank, what the hell you doing around here this late?"

"Checking up on your moonlighting. Might try it myself. You get to sleep a lot, I hear."

She heard them both laugh.

"How's that boy of yours?" asked Frank. "In an Ivy League school, isn't he?"

She still couldn't see Frank, but Jake had turned so she could see his face. He was a lean-looking man, at home with a scowl, but a large grin pushed his deep frown lines upward.

"Dylan's great. You know he graduated? With honors. I have this cousin who's always bragging about his boys being first in our family to get a college education." Jake laughed. "The twins went to community college. Dylan went to Harvard."

Diane listened as Jake and Frank talked about Jake's

son. She liked the normalcy of their conversation—so far removed from recent events in her life. Coming here to the museum was the right decision.

"What's he going to do now he's graduated?" asked Frank.

"Looks like he's going to be accepted to Harvard Business School. They don't just take everybody right out of college, you know. Most of the time they wait till they've worked a bit. See who's rising to the top. I'm real proud of the boy."

"What I can't figure," said Frank, "is where he got his brains."

"Not from his daddy, that's for sure. I told Carol it's a good thing he looks like me, or I'd be suspicious. How's your Kevin?"

"Growing. He's in eighth grade now. I'm glad I have a while before I have to start shelling out for college tuition."

"I hear you there."

"Diane Fallon here?" asked Frank.

Jake turned and looked in her direction. "Yes, she's here."

Diane was still standing underneath the huge tusks of the mammoth. She watched Detective Frank Duncan of the Metro-Atlanta Fraud and Computer Forensics Unit set down a briefcase at the door and cross the wide marble lobby into the Pleistocene room. He had the same handsomeness, the same smile, the same familiar face—perhaps just a little older than the last time she saw him.

"Nice," he said, reaching up and brushing the tips of his fingers along the bottom of a gigantic curved tusk. It reminded her of that Celine Dion song—"It's All Coming Back to Me Now."

"Did these things used to roam the neighborhood?" he asked.

"Up until about ten thousand years ago."

"Long gone, eh?"

"A mere blink of an eye in the grand scheme of things."

He stood under the head and tusks of the mammoth

with her, his eyes searching her face. "You look good. Damn good."

Diane brushed a loose strand of hair out of her eyes. "Too much time in the sun. My face is looking like parchment."

Frank shook his head. "A few lines around the eyes and mouth only give you character. You're a little thin, maybe. Didn't they feed you in South America? You're all right, aren't you? Didn't pick up anything?"

"No, Frank, I didn't pick up anything. I'm fine."

Frank tilted his head to one side, inspecting her wrist and arm. "A fellow I know came back from the Amazon and he had this insect bite on his arm that wouldn't go away. Swelled up, started itching and turned black. When he couldn't stand the itch any longer, he went to the doctor. The doctor thought it was a boil and started to lance it. Just as he touched the skin with his scalpel," Frank touched his finger gently to her forearm, "the thing burst open and this big, black, ugly fly crawled out of his arm and flew off. Disgusting." He tickled her skin with the tips of his fingers.

Diane pulled her arm back reflexively, but smiled despite herself. "You haven't changed. What are you doing at the museum this late?"

His eyes were smiling again, searching her face. "I just got off from work. I was passing this way."

"Don't tell me that. You don't pass this place going anywhere." She stepped out of the exhibit, still holding the artificial leaves like an odd bouquet.

"It's been a couple of years. . . ." he began.

"Three years."

"I wanted to see you. How about a late dinner?"

He was wearing jeans and a navy sweater and smelled like aftershave. He hadn't just stopped off from work. Diane wished she didn't feel so comforted by that realization. She lay the leaves next to the exhibit and dusted off her hands, aware that she must have the aroma of the day's accumulation of glue, paint and perspiration. "How about you telling me why you're really here?"

"I really came to see you. Talking with you got me

worried about you. What happened? Why did you give up your career?"

"I changed jobs. People do that." Diane turned away from his gaze and started toward the *Bison antiquus*. "I need to check out the exhibits before I leave. We're having a preopening party for the contributors tomorrow evening."

"Wait." Frank put a hand on her arm. "I want to know about you. What do you mean, you aren't a forensic anthropologist anymore? What happened in South America?"

Diane stopped and looked into Frank's blue-green eyes. "Just one mass grave too many."

Chapter 2

Diane walked with Frank to pick up his briefcase and led him to her office off a corridor to the right of the museum entrance. She moved a stack of books from a chair, pulled it up to her desk and motioned for Frank to sit down. She tore off a piece of butcher paper from a roll standing in the corner beside a tall oak bookcase and spread it on her desktop. "I've been back in town three months."

"I just found out last week. I saw Andie in the grocery store and she told me. I've been on a big computer fraud case for a couple of months and staying in Atlanta, shuttling back and forth to New York. Why didn't you call?"

"I didn't know you knew Andie."

"We met a few months ago in a karaoke bar."

"Karaoke? There is so much about you that I don't know."

"I know, boggles the mind, doesn't it?"

Diane held out her hand for the bone, half dreading to touch it. "If the parents want to know if it's their daughter, they might be able to have a DNA test run." Though when she saw the bone, she doubted that there would be any DNA strands left.

Frank shook his head. "She was adopted."

Adopted. Diane was unsure if she could go on with the examination. She fingered the bone a moment through the plastic bag before taking it out. *Be professional, Diane. This is Frank Duncan asking for your help. Maybe this isn't her.*

"Okay— This is a right clavicle, a collarbone. Been gnawed by rats. See these parallel teeth marks?"

"Rats. Does that mean anything?"

"Just means the body was where animals could get to it. You don't happen to have X rays of the girl's shoulder, do you?"

"No. But I have these." He handed her a large tan envelope.

Diane opened the envelope and removed several photographs of the missing girl and flipped through them. One was of her at the beach with her family. Most were portraits. Diane looked at Frank. "Even you know this isn't a bone from her head. Why the head shots?"

"These are what her parents gave me." He shrugged. "They're all I have."

Diane selected an 8-by-10 studio photograph of the girl wearing a drape, showing a bare, slender neck and shoulders. She turned it over and looked at the back of the photograph, hoping there was a date or an age. It was blank. "How recent is this photo? Do you know?"

"I believe her mother said that one was taken three or four months ago."

"How old is she?"

"Sixteen. Her name's—"

Diane cut off his words. "I don't want to know her name. How tall is she?"

"Five-four or five-five."

Diane raised her eyes from the picture to Frank. "Exactly how tall is she?"

He took a notebook from his briefcase and flipped through a few pages, stopping to read his notes. "Five-five and a half," he said.

Diane took calipers from her drawer and measured the length and breadth of the girl's face and scribbled numbers on the butcher paper. Knowing the measurements of the image in the photograph and the girl's actual height, and knowing that bones usually have a standard ratio to each other, she could make a reasonable guess as to what percent smaller the photograph was, compared to the girl herself.

She made three pencil points along the girl's right collarbone in the picture and measured the distance between each point. "I don't suppose you know if this is a mirror image of the girl or not?" she asked.

"What?"

"Sometimes when the photographer develops the film he—oh, never mind. It doesn't matter that much. I don't even know why I'm doing this."

"To stop me from asking you questions about why you abandoned your career."

Diane picked up the bone and turned it over in her hand, ignoring his prodding. "I don't believe it belongs to her. There's a good possibility it's male."

Frank raised his eyebrows.

"Males have broader shoulders than females. Their clavicles are longer. You guys are also more muscular than us girls. Your collarbones are going to be more robust. The girl in these photographs is relatively small and delicate."

Diane measured the bone and compared it with the math-altered measurements she made from the photograph. She shook her head. "It's not a match. Not even close. This bone is much bigger than hers would be."

Frank leaned forward. "She would be larger than the photograph."

Diane stared at him for a long moment. "Frank, I took that into consideration."

"Well, I've never seen you work. If I knew how to do this, I would have done it myself."

The way he grinned, she didn't know if he was kidding her or not. She shook her head and gave him a lopsided smile, then turned back to the analysis.

"The distal end is broken. It happened antemortem or perimortem and would have been very painful."

Frank frowned. "What would make a break like that?"

She shook her head. "A fall, like from a horse. Hit with something big like a club. Hit by a truck—any number of things."

Diane laid a piece of typing paper on her desk and searched in her drawer until she found a long pair of tweezers. Holding the bone under the desk lamp, she pulled a gossamer wad from the small cavity in the shaft.

"What?" asked Frank, leaning forward.

"Spiderweb."

She put the web in a small wax envelope similar to ones that stamp collectors use. She gently tapped the bone. Tiny dark specks fell from the hollow of the bone to the paper. She examined the detritus with a hand lens. Frank stood and leaned on the desk. The hair on the tops of their heads touched. Diane raised her head and looked directly into his eyes, which were so close to hers she thought she could probably feel the flutter of his eyelashes.

"Bug parts," she said.

"Bug parts? Is this important?"

"It is, indeed. It tells us that during warm weather when these creatures are up and about, the bone was bare and open for them to take up residence."

"Died during the warm months, then?"

"Perhaps."

"How long ago? Can you tell?"

Diane rubbed the tips of her fingers along the shaft of the bone. She was relieved that it was not from the adopted daughter of Frank's friends. "I'd say this bone hasn't seen flesh for several years. How long have the girl and her boyfriend been missing?"

"A couple of months."

"Does anyone know where the boyfriend is?"

Frank shrugged.

"Do you see the roughening of the bone here and here?" Diane touched two areas on the bone.

"Yes."

"Those are where the neck and shoulder muscles were attached."

"That would be here—" Frank traced his fingers down Diane's neck to her collarbone.

"Approximately. Yes."

"I've missed you," he whispered.

"The size and texture of the attachments make me suspect that this was a rather strong lad."

"Lad?"

She pointed to the proximal end of the bone. "The epiphysis has only begun to unite, which suggests an age of between seventeen and thirty."

Frank stood up straight. "So that means that at the place they suspect their teenage daughter disappeared, they found the partial remains of possibly a teenage boy who had been hit with enough force to break his collarbone."

"Yes."

Frank frowned. "I don't like that."

"No. I shouldn't think you would."

"What are the odds that it's just a coincidence that they find the bones of this boy in a place where they were looking for a missing girl?" he said.

"Slim to none."

Diane put the insect parts in another envelope, inspected the original plastic bag for more debris and handed everything back to Frank. "It looks like you have a serious problem on your hands."

Diane was craving sleep as she walked up the steps of the converted old Greek revival house containing her apartment. The dark shadow of herself cast by the dim porch light reflected in the glass pane of the outside door. She looked at her watch—2:10 A.M. She counted to herself. Four hours' sleep, max. She looked up at the sky. Dark clouds backlit by a full moon.

"Don't rain," she commanded the sky. "I don't want to deal with rain tomorrow."

Her fingers, made tender from assembling the exhibits, hurt as she turned her door key in the lock. As she climbed the stairs leading to the second floor, her back muscles burned and her legs cramped from stooping and lifting all day. She fumbled with her keys and opened her door to a dark apartment. She reminded herself to start leaving a light on.

She was bone tired, and, to top off the long day, she had offended Leonard, one of the security guards, by asking him not to be rude to the workers. From the set of his mouth she could tell he hadn't liked being told how to act. She'd figure out something to say to him tomorrow. He'd get over it in time. After Milo, she must seem like an intruder to some of the older staff.

Diane would have liked to soak in a tub of warm water for an hour, maybe two, but settled for a quick shower and crawled into bed and dropped off into the unconsciousness of sleep.

Even in the dark, the foliage blazed a brilliant green. The color was blinding and Diane didn't know how to find her way through it. Fear burned white-hot in her stomach. Off in the distance, a burst of gunfire startled her into full running panic. Everywhere she turned, vines clutched her legs, pulled at her body. Enormous heavy leaves slapped her face. She fought, trying to push them out of the way. Each slap of her hand against the leaves left a bloodred print. The gunfire was deafening—she must be getting closer. Vines grabbed her shoulders, turning into hands, pulling her away from the sound. "No, no!" she screamed, trying to pull the hands off her. The sound of gunfire came so fast it sounded like ringing.

Diane awoke suddenly, breathless, sweating. The phone on her nightstand was ringing. The illuminated radio display read 3:40. She snatched the receiver off the phone.

"Diane. It's Gregory. I'm sorry for calling so late."

Diane sat upright, hearing the familiar British accent, and held her breath. "Gregory. No, it's all right."

"I wanted you to know. They turned us down. They're not going to arrest him."

Diane was silent.

"We're not giving up. I'm going to the United Nations next week—and to the International Court of Justice. We won't stop. We'll never stop."

"Thank you, Gregory." Diane suddenly hadn't the energy to hold the phone. She lay back down on the pillow, propping the receiver to her ear.

"I wanted you to hear it from me, just in case a wire

service might have picked it up. It's not big news. For now we want to keep it that way."

"I understand."

"Are you all right? You sound out of breath."

"I'm better."

"Nightmares?"

"Occasionally."

"How's your weight?"

"Weight? It's fine."

"Are you eating?"

"Of course."

"You know how it is in our line of work. Even now, Marguerite sometimes has to remind me to eat."

"I'm better, Gregory, really."

"Are you?"

"As well as is possible. I miss Ariel every day. I curse myself every day for not leaving in time, and I still break down in tears when I look at her picture." Tears were now streaming down Diane's face. She was angry at Gregory for making her talk about the most painful thing that had ever happened to her, but in a strange way she was relieved to talk about it. No one here knew about her daughter. As painful as it was, Ariel lived on only when Diane talked about her with someone who knew her.

"I know," said Gregory. "I curse myself for not rushing through the adoption papers so you could take her out of the country, or for not arranging to smuggle her out for you. I thought she was safe at the mission. I didn't know Santos' men would cross the border, that he would retaliate. . . ." His voice trailed off.

"What happened wasn't your fault."

"And it wasn't yours. We were getting too close, hurting him, showing the world he's a liar and a cold-blooded mass murderer. I thought President Valdividia was stronger. It was a miscalculation I made, and I have to live with that every day."

"Why is it so hard to have evil men arrested, even with a mountain of evidence against them?" It was a question she'd asked before, and didn't expect an answer.

"We'll keep trying. It's thanks to you and your team that we have that mountain of evidence. You paid a terrible price to get it."

"I am better, Gregory, really. A year away from everything was good for me. I'm completely off the benzodiazepine. I love the museum. It's just what I'd hoped it would be." *I wish I'd gotten out with Ariel before . . .* The thought was too painful to finish. *She would have loved it here.*

"Met any new friends?"

"A great many. Renewed some old acquaintances too. Frank Duncan came by today. You remember, I told you about Frank." She told Gregory about the bone and the missing girl.

"You were able to handle that all right, then? Examining the bone, I mean."

"It wasn't easy, and I don't intend to do it again. I did it for Frank because he knew the missing girl and her parents. If it hadn't been for that, I wouldn't have done it."

"But you were able to do it—that was good. I'll call back at a more decent time and we'll talk again."

"I'd like that. Thanks for the call. Let me know if anything happens."

Diane lay for a moment, listening to the dial tone after Gregory hung up. She swung her legs to the floor, replaced the phone on the nightstand and stumbled into the bathroom. She splashed her face with cool water and stared into the mirror, running her hands over the angles and planes of her face. She did look thin. The result of six months of eating nothing but cottage cheese and yogurt because it hurt less coming back up.

She went back to bed and lay her head on the pillows. She clenched her teeth until her jaw burned, and didn't release the grip even when she escaped into sleep.

Chapter 3

As Diane opened the large carved wooden doors to the museum at 8:10 the next morning, she felt late and tired. The guard on duty at the information center greeted her with a broad smile on her friendly round face. Diane returned the smile as she passed, trying to remember her name. She'd just hired her last week.

Andie was arranging reproductions of large prehistoric plants at the entrance to the exhibition hall. Inside the hall, the folks from CyberUniverse were setting up computer monitors next to each display.

The Pleistocene room looked grand. Murals covering three walls depicted stunning panoramic scenes of the Paleolithic period, perfectly complementing the exhibits. The tall paintings on hardwood panels, discovered during renovation behind a layer of plaster and a layer of wainscoting, appeared to have been part of the original design of the building, a late 1800s museum turned private clinic, and now back to a museum. In the dinosaur room in the opposite wing, more wonderful old murals painted at a time when scholars still thought dinosaurs dragged their tails behind them now formed the backdrop of the dinosaur exhibits.

The current remodeling had removed false ceilings to reveal high domed ceilings with Romanesque molding in the exhibition halls, forming enormous rooms for the display of enormous beasts.

The head guy from CyberUniverse motioned her to

the computer monitor at the sloth exhibit. "You're going to love this."

Diane watched a narrated animation explain how animals can become fossilized after they die. "I do like that. All of you did a great job. The animation is terrific and the explanation is clear and easy to understand."

A young man wearing faded jeans and a blue short-sleeved shirt leaned against the podium and gave her a half smile. "Thanks."

"You're Mike Seger, aren't you? From the geology department at Bartrum University?"

He had the kind of short hairstyle that looked as if he got out of bed and simply ran his hands through the top, then went outside to let the sun bleach the ends—a messy, rugged effect that probably took quite a bit of styling to achieve. He eyed Diane for a second before responding. There was something about him that seemed intense—his light brown eyes, studious expression, or maybe it was simply the crease between his eyebrows, like a permanent frown.

"Yes, I am. You asked Dr. Lymon to work with your education department on the computer lessons. I'm a grad student always looking for a job, so she assigned me."

"You did a good job. I'll write a letter of appreciation to Dr. Lymon, if you like."

Diane thought he hesitated a moment before he said, "Sure. That would be good."

She turned to the computer guys. "Are all the displays ready?"

"We want to do one more check, but it looks like they're ready."

Bang! A loud shot behind her caused her to start. Her breath caught, she whirled around, eyes wide.

"Sorry," said Andie. "The mop fell over. Loud in this hall, isn't it?"

Diane put a hand over her breast, her heart still racing. Ashamed of herself for being so skittish, she headed for the mammoth exhibit to see how it looked. She'd wait to talk with Donald about the vegetation until after the opening.

"Phone, Dr. Fallon." Andie, still holding the mop handle in one hand, gave her the portable.

"Hi." It was Frank. "I'm bringing you breakfast. Egg McMuffin. I know you didn't stop to eat this morning."

"I'm not really hungry. I . . ." She had bent over to rearrange the weeds by the bison's foot and something in the wall painting caught her eye—a tiny figure hidden in the tall grass near the Paleo-Indian hunters. It looked like a unicorn. She moved closer.

"Diane, you still there?"

"Sorry, I was examining this unicorn."

"Unicorn?" He paused. "You mean there really was such a thing? They were here, in Georgia? You have a skeleton?"

Diane took the phone away for a second, stared at it, then put it back to her ear. "No. There's one in the painting."

"Oh." Frank sounded disappointed, and Diane almost laughed. "I'm on my way over," he said. "See you in a minute."

He had hung up before she could protest.

"Andie, have you seen this?"

Andie had her brown frizzy curls tied up in a ponytail on top of her head, making her look sixteen instead of twenty-six. She came over and looked where Diane pointed. "I haven't seen that one," she said.

"There are more?"

"At least two in here. One grazing around the feet of the mammoth herd and another on the edge of the pond behind some weeds, sticking its horn in the water. It's kind of like *Where's Waldo?*"

"How odd."

"I'll say. But nice."

Within five minutes, Frank came through the door, followed by a herd of museum staff. He took Diane by the arm, led her to a bench by the door and produced a still warm egg-and-biscuit sandwich.

A little waft of steam rose from the sandwich when she folded back the wrapper and it had the aroma of breakfast. She took a bite.

"I guess I *am* hungry."

"I thought so." Frank waited until she had taken several bites before he spoke again. "It was a false alarm about the bone."

Diane cocked an eyebrow at him.

"It was part of my friends' efforts to persuade the police to investigate the boyfriend. The bone they gave me came from a deer and not from the boyfriend's backyard." He flashed a gleaming set of white teeth through a sheepish expression.

"You have the bone?"

"Sure." He took it out of his briefcase.

She finished her biscuit and dropped the wrapper into a waste container by the door. "Come with me," she said, leading him through double doors into the mammal exhibit.

"Clavicles are like struts. They keep our shoulders straight and our arms from falling onto our chest." She stopped at an exhibit labeled *ODOCOILEUS VIRGINIANUS*. "OK, here's a deer. Find the bone."

"What?"

"Find the bone on the deer identical to the one you hold in your hand."

He started with the long metapodial bones of the feet, moved to the ribs, walked around the deer and stopped by the shoulder. He shrugged. "This skeleton doesn't have one."

"Neither do any of its kin. Deer don't have clavicles. They don't need them. It doesn't matter if their forelegs fall onto their chest. We primates have them. So do bats and birds. In birds it's called a furcula—wishbone to you laymen."

He looked at her as if not quite understanding, and she dragged him along into another room filled with primate skeletons and stopped at *Homo sapiens sapiens*.

"OK, wise guy, can you find the bone now?"

Frank looked at the skeleton's collarbone. Bingo. It

was identical. He shook his head. "George told me it was from a deer. I've known him for years."

"Maybe he thought it was. You need to find out what pile of bones he took it from. Now, I have a reception to get ready for tonight and I haven't looked at all the interactive media yet."

"About tonight."

Here it comes. Another broken date before we even get started again. Diane stood waiting.

"My son—you met Kevin—he wants to be a forensic anthropologist."

"And you want me to recommend a good child psychologist?"

"Funny, Diane. No. I would like to bring him. I know it's one of these invitation-only affairs, but . . ."

"Fine. I'd like to see him again."

"There's more."

"You have more children?"

"You're real cute this morning, aren't you? No. His mother and her husband would like to come too."

"Family affair?"

"Something like that."

"I'll leave tickets at the door."

"I appreciate this. It's not every woman who would let her date bring his ex-wife."

"We have an entomologist on staff you can show the bug parts to."

"What? Oh." Frank studied the design on the floor, making a face, as if he had just felt a wave of pain. "I—uh—threw them away."

"Threw them away? You threw evidence away?"

"I didn't think it was evidence. The Rosewood police weren't interested. And they were, I thought, bug parts from a deer bone."

"What does your friend do for a living?"

"He's a roofing contractor."

"A roofing contractor. Frank, did you know that before I took the directorship of the museum here, I was an internationally known forensic anthropologist? Did you know that I can give expert testimony in courts of law all over the world about anything concerning the identification and disposition of bones? And you believed a roofer's identification over mine?" Diane threw up her hands.

"I've known him forever. We play poker together."

"What? Is this some kind of guy thing?"

"No. He said it was from the skeleton of a deer, and I believed him."

"He told you he grabbed some deer, skinned him out, and took this bone?" Diane put her forefinger on his chest.

"No. He said he found it with a pile of deer bones in the woods. I'm sure there were probably antlers present," he added, as if that were a reasonable defense, "and hooves."

Diane put her fingertips to her eyelids. "You do know that once an animal is completely skeletonized, it becomes disarticulated—it comes apart. Does the word *comingle* have any meaning?"

"No, it doesn't. I've never worked with a forensic anthropologist. I work with white-collar crimes—paper, computers, ideas and people who at least act civilized while they're stealing from you. All bones look alike to me. Are you going to continue to hit me over the head with this? I'm sorry. He and his wife are best friends of mine. I don't believe he'd lie to me—I mean, I know they lied originally, but they were desperate. Were the bug parts that important?"

"Maybe not. You may be able to extract more from deeper inside the bone."

"How about that spider's web?"

"I'm not sure you could do anything with that anyway."

"So the only damage is to your pride?" He grinned.

"No, to my sensibilities."

Frank laughed. He took her hand in his and gave it a gentle squeeze. "I have to be in Columbus this afternoon to appear in court, but I'll be back in time to pick you up. I promise."

"OK."

"I miss arguing with you." He kissed her cheek.

"Do you?"

"Yeah. I miss a lot of things we used to do."

"It took you a long time to remember."

"Now, that's not fair. As far as I knew, you were still somewhere up a tree with Cheeta," he said.

"That's Africa, not South America."

"You were in Africa?"

She ignored him. "When you find the pile of bones your friend says he got this one from—even if you find a pair of antlers with matching hooves with them—tell whoever's in charge to treat it like a crime scene. Don't let anyone just take the bones and put them in a sack. Their pattern of dispersal will tell you a lot about what kind of agent scattered—or piled—them."

"Did you know you get really pretty when you talk about bones? I mean, you always look great, but there is something about the way your eyes shine when you talk about bones."

"I'll see you tonight. Remember, it's black-tie." She realized she was still holding his hand, and it felt comfortable. It had been a while since she felt so comfortable.

Diane spotted Donald, his thick, square body rigid, glaring into the mammoth exhibit.

"I need to speak with you," she said as he shifted his glare to her.

"You took up the plants." He had a childlike quality to his voice that made her pause a second before she spoke.

"Donald, they were wrong. There is four hundred million years' difference between your plants and the ones that belong in here. Yours didn't even represent the whole tree, only the leaves."

"It won't matter for the event tonight."

"Yes, it will. Donald, this is not a battle to go to the mat for. Leave it alone. We have a lot to do before this evening." Diane turned to go to her office.

"Wait. There are a couple of things we need to discuss."

"Can we do it in my office?"

Donald followed her into her office. He moved a pile of books from the only chair besides hers and dropped them in an empty box. Diane noted ruefully that it was the box the books had arrived in. She took a seat at her desk and pulled out the budget folders but didn't open them. Instead, she gave Donald her attention.

He glanced down at the folders before he spoke. "Some building plans have come to my attention."

Diane started to laugh at the way he made it sound as if he were in charge and speaking to a recalcitrant employee. She forced her face to remain in what she hoped was a frown.

"Came to your attention? How?"

"That's not important."

"It is important. This discussion will end now unless you tell me."

He shifted in the chair as if suddenly off balance. "We can't afford to start a new building project. This building is too big already," he said, leaning forward with his hands gripping the arms of the chair.

Diane stood up. "Donald, I'm too busy for this now."

"I found a copy in the waste can by the Xerox machine," he said quickly. The way the barely articulated words slid out of his lips so fast, she knew he was lying.

Diane narrowed her eyes. "Do you have the adult education exhibit ready for this evening?"

"It's almost finished. The computer people are setting it up. The plans—"

"Go supervise their work."

He hesitated a moment, then stood. "This isn't the end of this. After tonight, you will have this discussion with me and the board."

Diane stared at her closed door for several moments after he left. Maybe she should have talked to him. Milo's plans for the museum weren't secret, but Donald must have thought they were her plans. He must have been poking around in her office. She opened the folder and reread the budget figures. Money would certainly come up this evening and she wanted to be prepared. She could deal with Donald later.

The phone rang. She let it go for several rings and picked up the receiver when no one answered.

"RiverTrail Museum."

"This is the Bickford Museum, confirming an order placed with us. May I speak with Diane Fallon?"

"This is she. What order are you confirming?" Diane searched her memory, trying to remember what might have been ordered.

"Casts of *Albertosaurus, Pteranodon sternbergi, Tylosaurus,* and a triceratops, for a total of 143,500 dollars."

"Oh, yes. We received the items in perfect condition. The display is opening this evening. I'm sure our records show that the invoice has been paid. I reviewed the accounts myself."

"No, you're correct, payment was received. This is a new order."

Diane stared into space, shocked for a moment. "For the same items?"

"Yes, identical to the first order."

"When was this order placed?"

"It's dated last Wednesday. We saw that we had shipped an order for the same items to RiverTrail Museum six months ago, so I'm calling to verify that this is not a duplicate of that order."

"I'm glad you called. There has been some mix-up. How did you receive this order?"

"By fax."

"Please cancel the order, and if you don't mind, would you fax a copy of that order back to me so that I can straighten it out here?"

"Certainly. I'll send the fax right now."

Diane put down the receiver and sat at her desk for a moment, trying to imagine how duplicate orders of a purchase that large and that unique could have been made. She tried buzzing Andie, then remembered that she had gone out to speak with the caterers. She walked into Andie's office just as the fax was arriving from Bickford. The order was as the man had said, placed the past Wednesday. It showed Diane's name—and her signature. She punched in the number code to print the recent history of fax transmissions and tried to make some sense out of the order while she waited. Had she actually forgotten and duplicated the order? No, she couldn't possibly have forgotten; she already had life-sized skeletons of dinosaurs standing in the exhibit hall. In getting away from human bones, she hadn't expected dinosaurs to cast a giant shadow over her life. Diane had expected to find peace here. She scooped up the report from the print tray and went back to her office.

Chapter 4

Frank was late. Diane wasn't surprised. Columbus, Georgia, was a four-hour round trip, aside from whatever business he had to do there. She wrote a note telling him to meet her at the museum and was taping it to the door when she heard a voice coming from the apartment across the stairwell.

"Cats aren't allowed."

"I beg your pardon?" Diane turned, tape and message still in hand, and saw a woman in a blue chenille robe and pink hair net peering out of an apartment door.

"Marvin's allergic to cats. That's why we chose this apartment house. Cats aren't allowed."

There was a distant sneeze. The woman's head retreated momentarily into the apartment, leaving behind a veined hand gripping the edge of the door and a blue sleeve as visible cues that she was still there. After another sneeze and a man's muffled voice from inside, the woman spoke with that tone of impatience and irritability that arises between two companions of long duration.

"I'm telling her. She's right here, and I'm telling her."

Diane waited, trying to think of the woman's name—*Ogle, Ogden, Adell, Odell—that was it, Veda Odell.* When the rest of Mrs. Odell appeared again, Diane spoke.

"I'm sorry for his allergy."

"He doesn't need sympathy, he needs for you to get rid of the cat."

"I don't have a cat."

Veda Odell thrust out her chin. "You heard Marvin sneezing. He's allergic to cats. Nothing else. Just cats."

"Perhaps he has a cold."

Mrs. Odell eased herself a little farther into the hallway, craning her neck as if trying to get a peek into Diane's apartment. "It's a cat. He gets this way around cats."

Diane taped her note to the door and turned to go. "Well, Mrs. Odell, I don't have a cat. Maybe one passed through the yard."

"No . . ." She hesitated, as if just noticing Diane's black sequined dress and the cashmere wrap over her arm. "That's a mighty pretty dress. I hope it doesn't rain tonight."

"I think the weather is supposed to be clear. We're having a party for the contributors to the museum, and I'd hate for the attendance to be low because of rain."

"You work for the museum?"

"I'm the new director of the RiverTrail Museum of Natural History."

"You are? I heard you're a grave digger."

Diane opened her mouth, closed it again and wrinkled her brow. "A grave digger?" she said at last. "No, Mrs. Odell, I'm not."

"Well, I could have sworn," she said, but let her voice trail off. "Marvin and I were hoping you could tell us about the funeral homes here. The inside scoop, you know."

Diane stared a moment before she said anything, trying to imagine the scenario going on inside Mrs. Odell's head. "No. I'm sorry, I can't. I've got to be going. I hope your husband gets better." Diane hurried to her car.

It was a short drive to RiverTrail Museum. It's why she had chosen the apartment, even though they didn't allow pets. *What I'd like to have is a house*, she thought, as she drove slowly down the steep meandering road, *a big house with big airy rooms—that cleaned themselves. No*—she unconsciously clutched the lockct that rested on her chest—*an apartment is better right now*.

At the bottom of her mountain road she turned onto

a stretch of level four lane before starting the climb to the museum. The trees still blossomed with spring blooms, and the days were getting longer. She rounded the curve and RiverTrail came into view. It was a lovely old building, especially with the new renovations. But as the evening grew darker, the outline of the museum would look like an old sanatorium out of a Dracula movie.

She wheeled her Taurus into the parking space between Andie's Toyota and Donald's Lexus, and walked across the pavement to the museum entrance.

The string quartet had just arrived. Diane held open the door for the four college-student musicians. They looked elegant in their long black dresses, carrying their instrument cases.

"Thanks, Dr. Fallon," said the cellist.

"We really appreciate your asking us here," tall, willowy Alix, the first violinist, added.

From the music to the caterers, Diane had used people from the surrounding community. She wanted local support, and thought that giving it in turn would make her job easier.

"My pleasure. Thank you for coming."

Diane peeked into the Pleistocene room on her way to the kitchen. The large vaulted room was now transformed from a work in progress to a rather wonderful exhibit. To make room for a long table of party food, Diane had omitted some of the animals and Paleo-Indian dioramas that would eventually appear in the exhibit. She included only the megafauna, the spectacular big guys, the ancient giant species who always impressed.

The caterers had laid out an appetizing array of finger food on a table decorated with leafy long-blade plants, hard plastic museum-quality replicas of dinosaurs and a magnificent ice sculpture centerpiece of a mammoth with long curved tusks.

The head caterer, a woman in her late fifties, stood back smiling and folded her arms. "I think it looks rather good." She leaned and whispered to Diane, "We found a mold for the ice sculpture. We were quite pleased."

"Well, I like it very much. And the food looks wonderful."

The first of the guests had started flowing through the doors. Among them were real estate agent Mark Grayson and his wife, Signy. As Diane approached to greet them, she overheard Mark Grayson telling board member Craig Amberson that the museum would be better served if they would sell this piece of prime real estate and move into a building closer to Atlanta. Diane greeted him with a smile anyway. Tonight was not the night for fighting.

"Good to see you, Mark. Signy. I'm glad you could make it."

"Wouldn't miss it." His lips stretched into a thin smile.

Model-thin Signy, in a red shiny dress, muttered something and gave Diane a smile that looked more mocking than polite. Diane shifted her attention to the other guests. Kenneth Meyers, CEO of NetSoft, and his wife, Katherine, edged in beside the Graysons.

"Looks like quite a crowd." Kenneth gave Diane's hand a firm shake. He was lean and tan, a contrast to his soft, pale wife. "Tell me, did CyberUniverse do a good job for us?" It was no secret that Kenneth was thinking about buying the budding company.

"They did a wonderful job. I'm very pleased," Diane told him. "You'll have to see their animations."

She welcomed each guest—board members, contributors, the cream of Rosewood society, fashionably arrayed in black, white and diamonds, rich greens, deep blues and dark maroons. Signy stood out like a bright ruby among them. The quartet began to play a Brahms violin concerto.

Frank, looking handsome in his tux, arrived with his son, Kevin, his ex-wife, Cindy, and her husband, David Reynolds.

"I'm sorry," Frank apologized. "I was late getting back from Columbus."

"That's all right." She was actually surprised, and pleased, that he had made it.

Frank's ex-wife was blond, petite and very pretty in a

plain, long black gown with a string of pearls. David—
tall, handsome and friendly—pumped Diane's hand up
and down, telling her how very happy he was that she
had invited them.

"My pleasure."

Kevin, sporting a tux and a fresh haircut, shook Diane's hand solemnly.

"Frank told me you're interested in forensic anthropology," she said.

"I'm interested in bones and detective work. Is that
what you do?"

"It's what I used to do."

"And damn fine at it." Diane felt a heavy arm wrap
around her shoulder.

"Harvey Phelps, how are you?"

Diane gave him a big smile and leaned into him as he
kissed her cheek. Aside from his being a large contribu-
tor to the museum, Diane genuinely liked him—loud
voice, bad jokes and all. He was on the museum board
and had been a strong supporter of Milo and now her.

"I'm better than I have a right to be. I like what you've
done here. Looks good—all of it."

"Oh, Diane you've done a great job." Laura Hillard
was a psychiatrist and Diane's oldest friend, dating from
their kindergarten days in Rosewood. She shimmered in
a dark blue gown. Even her blond hair, done in a perfect
French twist, sparkled. As she gave Diane a light cheek-
touching hug, she whispered, "No matter what Signy
Grayson says." Her blue eyes twinkled as she laughed.
Mark Grayson was Laura's ex-husband. After three years
their marriage had dissolved into irreconcilable differences. The differences being Laura's opposition to Mark's
girlfriends.

Diane managed a genuine laugh along with Laura.
"The staff and students worked very hard to get ready."

"The catering is great. I adore that ice sculpture. I
wish Milo could see this. He would just love to see you
carry on his work." Laura leaned over and whispered in
her ear, "Beware of Mark. He's working the crowd
tonight."

"Milo would be right at home here." Harvey Phelps raised a glass to the mammoth.

As Harvey and Laura looked in the direction of the mammoth, they seemed reflective. "Poor Milo," said Harvey. "He died right here, you know."

"Here, where?" said Diane.

"Where the mammoth is standing," said Laura.

Milo Lorenzo was Diane's predecessor, as well as the one who recruited her to the museum. Most of the renovations and ideas for the exhibits were Milo's. Taking RiverTrail from the old-fashioned model of simple static cataloging and displaying of artifacts into the current concept of museum philosophy—interactive, educational, and research oriented—was his dream. The building plans Donald wanted to complain about were Milo's.

"This is where he had his heart attack?" said Diane. She remembered the last time she had talked to him on the phone. He was in as much hurry as she was for her to finish her job in South America and come to Rosewood to take up her new position as his assistant director. He'd died two days later.

Laura and Harvey nodded. "If the old boy had to die," said Harvey, "this was as good a place as any."

Diane left Laura and Harvey reminiscing about Milo and walked to the giant short-faced bear exhibit, stepped up on the platform, and picked up a microphone placed there for her. She caught the attention of the quartet and gave them a signal to stop playing. With the sudden cessation of the music the crowd stopped talking.

"Hello, everyone. I am pleased to welcome you, our board of directors, our best and most generous supporters and honored guests, to the preopening reception of our Pleistocene room.

"Most of you knew Milo Lorenzo and knew about his dreams for the museum. So it is with great pleasure that I invite you to see what we've been doing to make his dream a reality. Thanks to each and every one of you for your help and support, which have made it possible."

Diane looked at the faces and wondered if she had made any sense. She hated speaking in public and had this vision that halfway through all her speeches, she began speaking nonsense syllables. But they clapped, and considering herself lucky, she quickly stepped down and threaded her way through the sea of tuxedos, fancy dresses and champagne glasses and greeted all the guests.

It was tiring, making small talk and smiling, being political. She felt like a shape-shifter becoming weary of holding the same shape, and the evening was just getting started. At least, everyone seemed to be having a good time, and there was a genuine interest in the exhibits. That was the most important thing: the exhibits.

On her way to join guests who were touring other rooms, she stopped by to speak to Gary, Leslie and Samantha, standing with their proud parents next to the sloth exhibit.

"They all did a great job," Diane told the parents. "It is a fine sloth."

"Does that mean we get an A?" asked Gary.

Diane nodded. "Sure does." She smiled as a father took a photo of her and the students with the huge skeleton towering over them.

As she was making her way out of the Pleistocene room, the quartet started a piece from the *Peer Gynt* Suite. Diane froze in her tracks, her heart pounding against her ribs. She grasped the edge of a huge planter to keep herself from running out of the building.

Chapter 5

Diane's body was crushed by waves of almost unbearable grief and fear. *I'm in the museum,* she told herself over and over as the music taunted her, growing louder and louder until the violins were screaming at her. She wanted to scream at them to stop, but she stood still, making her hands into tight fists, breathing deeply. She caught her breath, stood several moments longer, turned and looked at the faces of the musicians, then at the crowd of guests. Everyone appeared normal. The music ended abruptly and the only sound was clapping. Diane stood still, collecting herself. Finally, she was able to walk on unsure legs to the quartet.

"That piece wasn't on the play list," she said, trying to sound casual.

It must not have worked, because that look of having done something wrong but not knowing what swept across their faces.

"It was in your note," said Alix, the first violinist. She flipped through her music and produced a piece of paper.

Diane took it from her. The hand-printed note on museum stationery said, *Please add "In the Hall of the Mountain King" to the play list.* Her initials were at the bottom.

"It was here when we returned from our first break. Luckily, we knew an arrangement for it. I mean . . . is there something wrong?"

Diane forced a smile and shook her head. "No, nothing's wrong. Someone from the staff probably wanted to

hear it. They often use my name when ordering things."
Apparently, with wild abandon, she thought. "All of you
are doing a beautiful job. I've gotten several compliments, and Mrs. Harris wants to talk with you about
doing a library function."

"That's great. We really appreciate this opportunity,
Dr. Fallon," said Alix, and the other three murmured in
agreement before they took up their bows and prepared
to perform their next arrangement.

Diane turned and took another long look at the crowd.
Everyone was eating, talking or looking at the exhibits.
No one was looking in her direction. She walked among
the guests, the note folded up in one hand, smiling at
each face she met. No mischief-makers or secret enemies
showed themselves.

Frank, his son and his ex-wife were looking at the
computer video depiction of the receding Laurentide Ice
Sheet that brought a close to the Pleistocene period. She
relaxed at the sight of Frank. *Silly,* she thought. *It was
probably nothing. One of the staff just wanted to hear
that piece of music. It's a well-known piece.*

She was starting toward Frank when she thought she
heard her name jump out of the flow of voices around
her. She looked in the direction from which she thought
it had come. Over by *Bison antiquus* a group of board
members, contributors and local real estate brokers,
looking like a clutch of emperor penguins, stood talking
to each other.

David Reynolds, Cindy's husband, was there. Diane
suspected that the reason the pair had wrangled an invitation through Frank was so David could meet with some
of Rosewood's high rollers. She strolled in their direction.

"Diane," said Mark Grayson. "We were just talking
about you. Great party. I've got some good news."

Mark held out his arm as though he intended to wrap
it around Diane's shoulders. She stopped beside Harvey
Phelps, opposite Mark, leaving his arm to gather air.
Donald was there. Diane met his gaze briefly. She wondered if somehow he was responsible for ordering almost

a hundred and fifty thousand dollars' worth of unneeded museum exhibits and signing her name to the order. Donald was a good illustrator. Did that translate into the ability to forge a signature?

"Good news?" she asked Mark. She glanced at Harvey, who raised a bushy eyebrow in her direction. "Tell me."

"The price on the old Vista Building has come down considerably."

"And?" Diane prompted.

"With those picture windows, big rooms, and its central location, it would make a great museum. The board can sell this property for a premium price and have money left over for some of the other things on Milo's wish list."

"I've seen the Vista. It has only one large room. The rest are too small for our needs. The parking is miserable. There is absolutely no place for a nature trail, and I suspect the price is dropping because it's hard to sell, sitting as it is on the edge of a high-crime area. Besides, we've spent quite a bit restoring this place, and I think it's wonderful."

Mark's face hardened. The others looked into their drinks. "This building's much too big for our needs. Besides, it's a steep climb up here in the winter," he said. "It could be dangerous for busloads of children."

Harvey Phelps slapped him on the back. "Oh, I don't know, Mark. We haven't had a decent winter in years."

Diane gave Harvey's arm a squeeze and left them talking about the weather. She sought out Frank and Kevin. "I hope you guys are having a good time," she said.

"Great." Kevin answered for everybody. "Do you have any human bones?"

"Yes, we do. Actually, a great many of our skeletal exhibits are made from casts of real skeletons. They aren't real bones, but they're exact replicas. We have a nice exhibit of *Homo sapiens* and his distant ancestors in the primate room."

"Do you have any bones from murder victims?"

Diane shook her head. "This is strictly natural history.

We have rocks, shells, bugs, dinosaurs, mammals and plants. But no murder."

"Why did you quit investigating murders?" he asked.

"Kevin!" cautioned his mother.

"Yes, Diane, why did you quit?" This was from Gordon Atwell, president of the bank that held the museum's mortgage.

"Traveling all over the world got tiring. I wanted to settle down in one spot. Lead a normal, quiet life, for a change."

"I guess when you've seen one mass grave, you've seen them all, huh?" He patted her on the shoulder. "There's Amberson. I need to talk to him."

Diane was glad to see him go off in another direction.

"What do I need to take in school to learn about bones?" asked Kevin.

"What grade are you in?"

"Eighth."

"You need to be strong in your sciences, especially biology. You need math. If you have any anatomy courses, that would be good. You'll need chemistry later on. And, of course, you have to learn your bones."

Kevin frowned. "Why do I need math?"

"There's a lot of measuring and calculations to do. Bones have a consistent size relationship with each other. You get as much information from the size indexes and ratios as you do from the physical examination of the bones themselves."

"You should see what she told me about a piece of collarbone," said Frank. "Darn near told me what the guy had for his last meal."

Diane started to laugh with the others when a thought flashed through her mind. She looked at Frank. "I think I can tell you what he ate."

Frank looked shocked for a moment. "I was joking. You mean you can? From a bone?"

"Not his last meal, but we may find a bit of information that might help identify him."

"How?" asked Kevin. "How can you tell what he ate by looking at his bone?"

"You have to remove the collagen—that's one of the components of bone—superheat it and turn it into gas so a mass spectrometer can detect the chemicals in the collagen."

"Wow. I really want to be a forensic anthropologist."

"Actually, the person I'm going to ask is a physical anthropologist. He studies bones too, among other things, but without the crime part. This is called stable isotope analysis. It's the same method used to tell us the diet of Neanderthal man. We're going to put one of the computer information programs about it in the primate exhibit."

"How do you tell what he ate?" asked Kevin.

"Have you studied isotopes in school?"

"Sort of."

"Then you know isotopes are like different species of atoms of the same element."

"Yeah . . ."

"You know about carbon fourteen, used for dating objects. Carbon fourteen is an unstable isotope—it's radioactive and decays over time. Because it decays at a constant rate, you can measure the decay to tell how old something is. It's a little more complicated, but that's basically it."

Kevin nodded. Diane was watching to see if his eyes were about to glaze over at all the science, but he listened attentively, so she continued.

"Carbon also has two stable isotopes that don't decay. So does nitrogen. And each has different ratios in the different types of foods—like vegetables, meats and fish. When we eat these things, the same ratios of the isotopes are absorbed in our bones, which means we can measure the ratios with a mass spectrometer and possibly find out what the person ate all his life. Like carbon fourteen tests, it's more complicated, but you get the idea. Using it for this bone is a long shot. Most people in the U.S. have pretty much the same diet, but it could supply some more information about the individual. We might get lucky and he ate only red meat and potatoes all his life."

"Kevin, come here and look at this." David Reynolds

motioned his stepson to another of the computer animations. Kevin was reluctant to leave the conversation, but his mother, Cindy, pulled him away and went over to watch the mammoth animation with her husband.

"That's fascinating," said Frank. "I'll suggest it to the Rosewood police when I give them the bone."

"Did you get in touch with your friends?" asked Diane.

He shook his head. "Not yet. I've been calling. I think George said he was going out of town for a couple of days. He should be back today, though. I'm going over there tomorrow."

They were interrupted by the muffled strains of "Ode to Joy" coming from Frank's jacket.

"Should have left this thing at home," Frank mumbled. He stepped away from the others and answered his phone.

Diane stole a glance at him and saw him drop his arms to his sides, lean on the column and put a hand to his face. She went over and touched his arm.

"Frank?" asked Diane. "Are you all right?"

He shook his head. "I have to go. It's George and Louise. The ones with the missing daughter. The two of them and their son were found dead in their home."

"Dead?" whispered Diane. "How?"

"I don't know. I'm going over there. Look, Diane, I need to . . ."

"It's all right. Do what you have to do." She walked him to the door. "I'm so sorry."

"I'll call later. Tell Kevin I had to leave. Poor kid's used to me taking off in the middle of things." He kissed her cheek, and Diane watched him walk to the parking lot before she closed the door.

Dead—a whole family gone. She put the flat of her palm on the door to steady herself. A missing daughter, and now this. A sudden tap on her shoulder made her jump.

"I'm sorry, Doc." It was Jake Houser, the security guard. "I didn't mean to startle you."

"Is everything all right?"

"Just fine. I wanted to tell you that I've been hearing the phone ringing in your office. I wouldn't mention it, but whoever it is is persistent."

"Thanks. I'll go look at the caller ID."

"Oh, and . . ." He grinned broadly. "My son's here. Guest of Kenneth Meyers. He has a summer job working for him. I'd like you to meet him."

"I'd like that, Jake. Let me check this out, and I'll introduce myself. I overheard you talking to Frank yesterday. You must be really proud."

"Proud's putting it mildly. Dylan's a great kid. It's hard these days to raise a good kid. I'm proud—and lucky. Was that Frank I saw leaving just now?"

"He had to leave. Some friends of his were found dead in their home."

Jake's happy expression dissolved into a frown. "Do you know who?"

"I think their names are George and Louise Boone, and their son, Jay."

Jake backed up and leaned against the wall, his mouth open. "George and Louise. I know them. I play poker with George. Are you sure?" He reached for his cell phone. It rang in his hand and he almost dropped it. "Houser here."

He paused. Diane watched the frown on his face deepen.

"I think so." He held his hand over the mouthpiece.

"My God, it's true. George, Louise, Jay too. They need me down at the station. We're shorthanded. I know you've been very flexible with me. . . ."

"It's all right. Tell Leonard you're going. I think I saw him heading for the upper floors not long ago."

"Thanks, Doc. Thanks." He paused, looked as if he wanted to say more, but instead contacted Leonard on his walkie-talkie.

Diane walked to her office and unlocked her private door. She was just about to punch the play button on her answering machine when the phone rang again. It frightened her. Frank's, Jake's, and now hers—a conspiracy of phones bringing bad news? She trembled slightly as she reached for it.

"Diane Fallon," she said into the receiver.

"Diane. I'm glad I found you. I've been calling your home." It was Gregory. "We've lost track of Santos, and believe his right-hand man, Joachim, may have entered the United States last week. I'm trying to verify it."

Diane's knees suddenly felt weak, and she sank onto her chair. "You think he's coming here?"

"We don't know that. I don't even know if the reports are true. You know how hard it is to verify things. I'll find out. I just wanted to warn you of the possibility. I don't want you to worry, Diane. I wouldn't even have called, but I thought you might hear the news from another source."

"Is the team still down there?"

"I've called them back . . . temporarily. They think they've located two more mass graves, and I don't want to start excavation until things are a little more settled."

So Gregory was more worried than he let on, she thought. "Is something else going on?" she asked.

"I don't know. President Valdividia told some of his friends he's going to take a vacation. You know how unsettled Puerto Barquis has been the past few months." He paused. "He may be . . . what do you Americans say? Getting the hell out of Dodge."

"Something rather disturbing has happened here."

"Something to do with Santos? What is it?"

Diane told him about the museum party, the music and the note.

There was a long pause before he spoke. "Of course, it could be a coincidence."

"It probably is," she said. "But if it isn't, what would be the point? What would he gain?"

"The point might be to put fear into those who took your place."

"Of course, if he shows he can reach any of us, wherever we are, that would be an effective weapon of terror. But it may not be him at all. There are other things going on, things related to the museum." She opened the drawer and fingered the printouts from the fax as she explained the duplicate orders. "I suppose it could be some clumsy attempt to discredit me."

"You don't think that might be related to Santos too?"

"It hardly seems likely. I'm under pressure to move the museum and sell the property to developers. This probably has more to do with that. I just can't see him sending someone up here to make it look like I ordered too many specimens."

The two of them chuckled for just a moment, and it tasted to Diane like fresh air.

"The quartet playing 'In the Hall of the Mountain King.' Could that also be related to the museum situation?"

"Unless it's a simple coincidence, it has to be. I don't know how anyone here would know about the music."

"People can find out things. Do you have anyone from South America working at the museum?"

"Yes, we've had a graduate student and a lab technician, but I've had no reason to suspect them. Besides, they were both from Venezuela."

"I think the music is probably an unfortunate coincidence, but let's not take any chances. We can't allow people like him to take revenge on humanitarian workers, and certainly not in their homes. I'll contact our people who are watching him."

"It's so hard sometimes." Tears brimmed her eyes and almost overflowed onto her cheeks.

"I know. But remember that you have many friends. Call me anytime, even if you just need to talk."

"Thank you, Gregory."

She placed the receiver back on the phone. She could handle whoever it was who had placed the orders. But she wasn't sure she could handle whoever had left the note for the quartet. If the music wasn't an innocent coincidence, then it was something very mean and ugly. She finally stood up to go back to the party when she heard movement just on the other side of the adjoining door to Andie's office.

Diane searched around her desk for a weapon. All she could find was a letter opener decorated with Mayan symbols. She took hold of it, trying to think what to do. Call Leonard? He would still be upstairs. This was foolish. It was probably Andie. She put the letter opener back on the desk and walked out into the hall and around to Andie's office door. If she opened it from the hall side, at least she would have a place to run. From there someone could hear her shout.

She touched the door so that it slowly swung open. A figure silhouetted by the desk lamp was going through Andie's desk drawer.

Chapter 6

Diane switched on the ceiling light and heard a sudden intake of breath as the figure popped up from her stooped position, her hand over her chest.

"Oh . . . Dr. Fallon . . . You scared me."

"That makes two of us. Can I help you?" Diane relaxed, relieved she hadn't brought the Mayan letter opener with her. The intruder was Melissa, the second violinist from the string quartet.

Melissa smoothed a strand of light brown wavy hair away from her face. "Your assistant, Andie, said she had some extra-strength aspirin in her drawer." She held up Andie's keys as if to verify that she had permission to be rambling around in her desk.

"I imagine that playing for hours can bring on a headache."

Her blue eyes looked relieved. "You're not kidding. That, and dealing with people. Do you know someone asked us to play 'Memory'?"

Diane laughed. "I can see it now. Next they'll want karaoke night at the museum."

"Here they are." She poured two tablets out onto her hand and put the bottle back.

"There's a water fountain just outside the door."

Melissa's passage out of Andie's office left a trail of heavy perfume in her wake. She downed the pills at the water fountain and took a deep breath. "We really do appreciate being asked here. We've had several people wanting to hire us."

"I'm not surprised people are impressed. The music's been wonderful."

As Melissa turned from the fountain, Diane noticed that under carefully applied makeup, she had a black eye. A brief glance down at her arms discerned no more bruises, but the dark, floor-length sleeveless dress the young woman wore had a turtleneck. Diane fought an urge to turn down the collar to look at Melissa's throat.

Too much time spent investigating the products of abuse, she thought. She needed to mind her own business, which was now the museum, and not man's inhumanity to man. But it haunted her that she had always been too late to help the victims. They were already decayed flesh and bones by the time she saw them. It would have been nice just once to be in a position to stop some atrocity.

"That black eye looks like it might hurt," Diane said, letting the sentence hang between them.

Melissa was young, shy, and that evening Diane was her employer—powerful stimuli to say something about what had happened, if only to lie. They both stood, paused in the hallway.

"Yes, it does, some. Clumsiness," Melissa said at last. "I was exercising. I have to keep strength in my arms to play the violin. You wouldn't believe how much stamina it takes to keep your arms at that level for hours. I don't know how Lacy manages that viola for so long. Anyway, I accidently hit myself in the face with one of my hand weights. Almost knocked myself out."

Melissa laughed at herself and Diane thought she heard a slight tremor in her voice—and such long, detailed explanations often meant that the teller was lying.

"What bad luck, just before the event. I hope it heals quickly." Diane didn't pursue it. But her friend Laura knew Melissa's family. She would mention it to her.

After seeing that the office doors were locked, Diane walked with Melissa back to the party. Mark Grayson was on his way out.

"Leaving early?" said Diane.

"Signy's staying. I've got an overseas conference call.

Nice get-together. I'm sure everyone's having a good time. I'll see you at the board meeting tomorrow." He punched the air between them with his finger. It could have been a quick, friendly gesture, the way some men talk with their hands, but it seemed to Diane like he was pointing a gun. She was glad to see the door close behind him.

Melissa had taken up her place with the string quartet and they began playing Diane's favorite part of Max Bruch's Violin Concerto in G Minor—the Allegro Moderato. Diane entered the Pleistocene hall where she mingled, talked, laughed at bad jokes and sipped wine. Her feet hurt from the effects of hardly ever wearing high-heeled shoes, and her head ached.

"Wow," Andie said, coming up behind her. "We all did a good job, didn't we?"

Diane turned and nodded as she looked at the guests. "Yes, I believe it's a success. I had my doubts on occasion, but everyone seems to be having a good time. Andie, did you request that the quartet play the *Peer Gynt* suite?"

"Who? No, I thought you were handling the music selections."

"I did, but someone wanted to hear it, and I just wondered who it was."

Andie shrugged just as a good-looking guy tapped her on the shoulder and pulled her toward the murals.

Diane moved toward the buffet. The ice mammoth looked fresh and unmelted. She reached out to touch the trunk and found it cold and dry.

"They just replaced it," Donald said, filling his plate with caviar and crackers. "Apparently, they made several. Someone who works for them must be an ice-carving fool." He drifted away and melted into a crowd of black tuxedos before she could say anything more to him.

Signy was working the room in her husband's absence. She reminded Diane of a mouse cursor trail, the way she and her red dress flashed around the room, flirting with the men, ignoring the women. David Reynolds was Signy's current target. She threw back her head, laughing at something he said. Diane caught sight of David's wife, Cindy, at the bison exhibit looking over the head of her son, frowning at the scene. Diane recalled Frank mentioning how easily Cindy could become jealous.

Kevin was demonstrating the computer animations to a tall elderly woman dressed in a long silk gown as white as her hair, dripping pearls and diamonds. It was the unmistakable Vanessa Van Ross, the museum's best patron, second only to the late Milo Lorenzo as the driving force behind the museum. Diane threaded her way through the crowd toward them.

"Diane, dear. I wondered where you'd got to. I just met the most disagreeable young woman. Flashing around like a red sparkler. Called me by my first name. Mark Grayson's wife. The man has no taste. I guess I shouldn't speak like this in front of the boy. Just ignore what I say, young man."

Kevin cackled. Diane kissed her cheek.

"It's good to see you, Vanessa. May I steal you away from Kevin for a moment?"

"Certainly. Can you pause that thing, young man?" Vanessa Van Ross and Diane stepped away to a private corner.

"I know nothing about real estate," Diane said. "Can you tell me why this land is suddenly so valuable? Why does Mark want it so badly?"

"Did you know Hollis MacElroy?"

"I've heard the name. Farmer, owns a lot of land?"

Vanessa nodded. "*Owned.* He died three months ago. When his will is probated, his heirs intend to put his land on the market. It's considered prime real estate, and it borders the museum property. If they get a good price for it—and they will—this property will increase in value considerably. Rumor has it that a Japanese firm is looking at it for a golf course and country club."

"I'm beginning to see." Diane looked at her watch. It was a little after 8:30 P.M. Mark would be back at his office before 9:00 P.M. for his overseas call. She did some quick calculations. That would make it midmorning in

Japan. So, Mark was talking to Japanese businessmen about the museum property. She looked around the room and wondered how many were on Mark's side.

She turned back to Vanessa. "But there couldn't possibly be enough money involved to pay for moving the museum, setting it up someplace else, and still make it worthwhile for Mark's cronies."

"Not unless the museum is shortchanged. That's the only way I see it working. But I assure you, my dear, I'll never let that happen. Come, take your mind off that for now. Enjoy your party. You deserve it."

Diane tried shoving Mark Grayson's scheming, the incident with the music and the duplicate purchases to the back of her mind. She tried not to think about Frank and what he must be going through—seeing friends, a whole family, wiped out, murdered. The things she tried not to think about were beginning to pile up into an impossible mountain of forbidden thoughts. It wasn't easy to mingle, make small talk and laugh with so much in her head to keep at bay.

She stood watching the party for the thousandth time, scanning the crowd, looking for some suspicious person who might be an enemy. Donald was talking to the students who had put together the sloth. He was number one on her list for the duplicate orders. Signy was by the bar getting a refill of wine.

Laura Hillard was talking with the archivist and one of the new curators next to the refreshment table still heaped with food. Seeing Laura reminded Diane that she wanted to mention Melissa's black eye. She approached Laura and pulled her away with apologies.

"You know Melissa Gallagher's family, don't you?"

"I know them well. Wonderful people."

"I noticed that she has a black eye. It may have been a simple accident, but I'm a suspicious person. A consequence of my previous career."

Laura turned her blond head toward the quartet and back to Diane. "I see what you mean. It wouldn't be her parents. I'd have known. You're thinking boyfriend, maybe?"

"I don't know," Diane said. "People do get black eyes accidently."

"I'll mention it to her parents." Both watched Melissa playing her violin. "I tend to think it's probably nothing." Laura's gaze lingered on Melissa a moment before she turned her attention back to Diane. "Mark Grayson's made headway with some of the board members."

"Won't do any good unless he makes headway with me."

"He knows that. He wants to put pressure on you from all sides."

"Let him. Maybe it'll keep him occupied." Diane hesitated a moment. "Laura, have you seen anyone here you don't know?" Laura was a rare breed, one of the few fifth-generation residents of the area.

"N-no." She glanced briefly around the room. "What do you mean, exactly?"

"Are there any strangers here?"

"No. I don't think so. Some of the catering staff, maybe. Why do you ask?"

OK, now that she had opened this can of worms, what was she going to tell Laura?

"I'm not sure. Some irregularities in purchases. I'll tell you more about it tomorrow at the board meeting."

"That sounds cryptic. What would strangers being here have to do with purchases?"

"It's just a matter of not wanting to believe that the irregularities have anything to do with people we know."

"Now, that does sound bad." Laura knitted her brows.

From the look Laura gave her, she must be sounding completely paranoid. "No, just annoying." She patted Laura's arm. "I'm sorry I mentioned it tonight. I'll talk about it tomorrow."

Hunger pangs had been gnawing at Diane's stomach since she arrived. She headed back to the refreshment table but was caught by Kenneth Meyers, CEO of Net-Soft, with a young man in tow.

"Have you met Dylan Houser?" Kenneth said, introducing the twentyish young man. "He's your security guard's son. Dylan's a sharp boy. Just the kind of hungry lad that'll do well in the computer business. High technology's the thing now." He slapped Dylan on the back.

Dylan shook Diane's hand. He reminded her of a hockey player, the tough, fearless way he carried his youth. His face was a younger version of his father's: dark hair, dark eyes, without the deep rugged lines. He was also charming and looked good in a tux. Every mother's dream for her daughters. She hoped he wasn't Melissa's boyfriend.

Diane mentally shook away the thought. She caught herself weaving a whole story out of that one black eye. She reminded herself that this directorship at the museum was supposed to bring her into a kinder world—at least, one free of violence and death. Just as she was thinking those thoughts, Alix, the first violinist, came up and threaded her arm through Dylan's, and they exchanged a flash of bright smiles. Alix had nary a bruise or blemish on her fair skin.

"Getting pretty good with that violin," Dylan said. "I'm beginning to like that kind of music—though a little bluegrass would be nice." Alix nudged him in the ribs and laughed.

"I never thought this rambling old building would make such a great museum," Dylan said to Diane. "Dad took me and Alix on a tour through the rooms earlier this evening, and it's really impressive. I like those big guys in the other room."

"Thank you. We are all very proud of it." *At least, most of us are,* she mused as she caught a glimpse of Donald talking with Craig Amberson.

"I agree with Dylan." Kenneth took in the room with a sweeping gaze. "It looks good. I like what you've done with computers. I'd like to suggest you use more computer simulations of dinosaurs—maybe something interactive, *Jurassic Park*-style. Some sound effects."

He opened his arms wide and, for a moment, Diane thought he was going to imitate a dinosaur. "This is a computer world now. If you want to hold people's attention, you got to give them high tech. By the way, I've got a nice laptop I'm bringing you tomorrow. My compliments. I'd like you to check it out, see how you like it. I've installed GPS on it. Just the thing for museum personnel in the field—not that I'd use my position as a board member to help my business." He laughed, and Diane had to laugh with him. Kenneth was one of the most shameless people she'd ever met.

Signy sashayed up and neatly slid between Alix and Dylan. "Kenneth's been telling me some good things about you, Dylan. It must be so exciting graduating, ready to make your mark in the world."

Alix rolled her eyes. Dylan smiled politely. "I'll be going to graduate school in the fall, so the world will have to wait while I make another mark at Harvard."

The way Signy eyed her, Diane could tell she was going to say something about moving the museum. Diane started to excuse herself—too late. Signy opened her mouth to speak. However, Craig Amberson came over and interrupted before Signy got out her first syllable.

"Somebody just told me you've been looking at a bone for the police. Going to get back into that business? You think you can do that and run a museum too?"

Signy obviously approved of the question, if the way she beamed at Craig was any measure.

"I looked at one bone for a detective as a favor. As well as director, I'm also the curator of the primate skeletal collection. I believe looking at a bone still falls under my purview."

It just hit her—in light of what Vanessa had said about the rumor of a golf course—that the museum building would make a grand hotel and restaurant for someone like Craig who was in that business. Something must have shown on her face, for his eyes narrowed as he stared at her.

"I think looking at bones is fascinating," said Alix. "Just like that TV show. . . ."

"I agree," said Dylan. "My father's been wanting to write a book. You two ought to get together."

"You talking about the bone Dad showed you?"

"Hush, Kevin. What did I tell you about breaking into other people's conversations?" Cindy and her son had joined the small group. Diane was starting to feel suffocated.

"Dad said you told him a whole lot about it," said Kevin, ignoring his mother.

"Not that much, really," said Diane. "I'd need more of the skeleton. Ah, Mrs. Van Ross is talking to the botanical collection manager. I need to speak with both of them. Nice meeting you, Dylan. Excuse me, please." Diane moved away before anyone else could ask her about that damn bone.

She spoke briefly with Vanessa and went straight to the buffet table. With the affair flowing along on its own, she could afford to feed her stomach before it started growling.

Armed with a plate of raw vegetables, a couple of small triangle sandwiches and a glass of wine, Diane headed for the giant short-faced bear exhibit. She sat down on its platform, set down her plate and glass, and took up the sandwich. Just when she thought she had picked a secluded spot without leaving the party completely, she saw Signy, like a red beacon, gliding toward her, a bright smile on her face and wine in hand.

"Diane. I'm glad you're alone. The party's great, but I'll bet you're frazzled."

It would have been rude to tie her to the bear and stuff an apple in her mouth, so Diane gave her the best smile she could manage.

"I'm holding up. I hope Mark had a chance to enjoy the exhibits before he had to leave." Diane took a bite of sandwich.

"Oh, he loved them." Signy sat down and nearly tipped her wine onto the platform, spilling a few drops, which started to run toward the middle of the exhibit. "Oops, good save," she said, giggling, catching it before losing the whole glass.

Diane wiped up the running spill with her napkin as Signy moved her China plate and wineglass. Diane was wondering if she should have closed down the wine bar. She looked up, wine-stained napkin in hand, as Alix and Melissa approached, offering fresh napkins.

"Dr. Fallon, Mrs. Grayson. You're just the two we need to see."

Diane nodded a thank you and finished the cleanup. The two musicians began a two-pronged conversation with her and Signy. Melissa asked about playing at a Junior League function of which Signy was an officer, and Alix seemed to be inquiring about a summer job.

Diane was grateful to have Signy Grayson's attention diverted from what she knew was going to be a pitch for her husband. As Melissa talked to Signy, Alix picked up Diane's plate and wineglass and handed them to her as the violinist sat down on the exhibit platform opposite Diane.

"We've both had experience working at Disney World." She launched into an animated Disney World greeting, and Diane laughed. "They teach you to be very friendly," said Alix. "Melissa and I would really like to do something with the children's programs at the museum."

"Why don't you and Melissa bring your résumés by this week and leave them with Andie? Disney World has pretty tough standards—that's certainly in your favor—and we're looking for assistants for our docents, the tour guides. With your qualifications, there shouldn't be a problem. You will have to put in some time learning the exhibits."

"Great! You'll have our résumés tomorrow morning."

"It looks like with your music and a job at the museum, the two of you are going to be busy."

"Daddy always said that all play and no work makes one very poor." Alix rose and shook Diane's hand. "Thanks for everything you've done for us. Melissa, I think we'd better get back to our violins."

"Well," said Signy, watching the girls' retreating backs and retrieving her glass of wine, "they are certainly an energetic pair."

"Youth," said Diane.

Signy frowned, as if she'd been insulted, but after a moment her face brightened. "Diane, I wanted to give you a word to the wise. I really think you should give Mark's ideas some thought."

"Signy, do you really think Milo went forward with his plans"—Diane gestured, taking in the room—"without giving considerable thought to the alternatives? He looked into several possibilities before deciding to renovate this location. He considered it to be by far the best, and I agree."

"I'm just asking you to give it some more thought," said Signy. "Mark will win. He always does. That's all I'm going to say on the matter." She smiled and sipped her wine.

I'll drink to that last part, Diane thought, washing down a bite of sandwich with a drink. She managed to avoid discussing moving the museum with any would-be champions for Mark's cause for the remainder of the evening. Toward the end, as the guests were leaving, the string quartet entertained them with a little bluegrass and jazz. It was a good ending to what was actually a successful evening, but one Diane was relieved was behind her.

When everyone had gone and only Leonard, the night guard, and the cleaning crew remained in the museum, Diane climbed into her car, almost too tired to drive home. Despite her exhaustion, she made it home without running her car into a tree, and went straight to bed without even expending the energy to take off her makeup. Cold crisp sheets on bare skin—it felt good. She slept until 7:30 in the morning—when the phone rang.

Chapter 7

"Did I wake you?" Frank's voice sounded like a rasp on sandstone.

"Frank, are you all right?" Diane asked.

"Can I come over?"

Diane hesitated a moment, filled with dread about hearing details of murder. But these were Frank's friends. And so was she. "Sure. I'll fix you breakfast," she said.

"I'll bring it. It's the least I can do for waking you up."

Diane jumped out of bed and into the shower. She had just pulled on jeans and a sweatshirt when the doorbell rang. After slicking her wet hair back with a comb, she opened the door.

Frank was in running sweats, but she could tell from the smell of shampoo that he hadn't been running. He set two sacks on the table. The bulky one was filled with doughnuts; the other with cups of coffee from Vance's Café.

"I'll make us some bacon and scrambled eggs to go with the doughnuts," she said.

She also put on a pot of coffee. Why Frank liked Vance's coffee was a mystery. To say it tasted like dredge from the Chattahoochee River was giving it flattery it didn't deserve.

Diane microwaved strips of bacon while she scrambled three eggs. Frank stood in the doorway of the narrow efficiency kitchen as she worked. "Kevin had a great time last night. It was good of you to let him and his mother come."

"No problem." She took down a couple of plates from the cabinet and warmed them in the oven. She felt awkward, like he had brought a huge gorilla in with him that neither of them wanted to mention, yet it was taking up so much space.

"I think Cindy's husband, David, was the one who wanted to come, to rub elbows with some of the big guys."

"And did he?" Diane asked.

"Must have. Cindy said she wants to invite us over for supper next week."

"Us?"

"You and me."

Diane looked over at Frank through narrowed eyes.

"She's not matchmaking."

"No. I don't think she is. I think Mark Grayson is using David to try and talk me into selling the museum property."

"What's that about?"

"Grayson hopes to make a killing on a big real estate sale he's cooking up involving the museum. I imagine he wants to buy it himself and sell it for a heck of a lot more than he would pay for it." Diane divided the scrambled eggs and slices of bacon—two-thirds on Frank's plate and one-third on hers. "It's all rather complicated, and I'm not sure how he plans to accomplish it without gutting the museum's holdings. He's been trying to push the old Vista Building on me. I wouldn't be surprised if he holds an interest in that."

"Why is he after you and not the board?" Frank took a plate from her cupboard and stacked the doughnuts on it.

"Oh, he's after them all right—to put pressure on me. But even if he gets every member of the board to sign off on it, he still has to convince me."

"You have that much power?"

"I certainly do, thanks to Milo." Diane stood with the plates in her hand, staring at the pyramid of assorted doughnuts. "Were you expecting an army of police-men?"

"I thought you might like a choice."

She set the plates on the table. "Have a seat. I'll get the coffee."

"I brought coffee."

"No, you didn't." She brought two mugs and filled them at the table from her pot of fresh brewed coffee.

Frank sat down and started eating. "You make the best eggs."

"The secret is to not put milk in them, and to cook them slowly until they're just done."

"So how come you have so much more say-so than the board?"

"Do you know Vanessa Van Ross?"

"I know *of* her. Richest old woman in the state, isn't she?"

Diane frowned at him. "I don't know that, but she has money, and she and Milo had a thing."

"She must be one hundred and twenty. He was what? Sixty?"

"He was sixty-five. What is it with you guys? You think women stop being someone you can love when they get crow's-feet?"

"She's got more than their feet."

"She set up the foundation and gave Milo final power over practically everything."

"So the board's only show?"

"Almost. Milo hired me as an assistant while I was still in South America. He fixed it so that not only would I become director if anything happened to him, but all the power would pass to me as well."

"Was he expecting to die?"

"No. But he had a heart condition. It obviously crossed his mind."

"At least he knew it was a possibility." Frank stared into his coffee.

Diane put a hand on his arm. So the gorilla was about to awaken. "How are you?" she asked.

Frank set his coffee down and capped the rim with his

hand. The steam rose through his fingers. It was several moments before he spoke.

"Jay was just fourteen. They found him outside, lying under a tree—shot in the back. George and Louise were upstairs in their bed."

She could see Frank was making a big effort to sound objective.

"Frank, I'm so sorry."

"I can't help but think it's my fault. If I'd taken that bone more seriously."

Diane rose, went around the table and started to hug him. Instead she put a hand on his arm. "It's not your fault. I know it must feel like it is, but it's the murderer's fault." He grabbed her hand and held it. "What do you think happened?"

He pulled away, and Diane walked back to her seat. "I don't know. I'm afraid the detective in charge seems to like their daughter, Star, for it. But as far as I can see, she has little evidence and isn't likely to get any. But. . . ."

"But what?"

"They did find the gun—or at least the caliber of gun they believe was the murder weapon."

Diane sensed there was more. She reached out for his hand. "And?"

"They think it was Louise's gun. George bought it for her several years ago. One of the policemen at the scene thought he recognized it because he gave Louise lessons with it. Last year, Star stole it and took it out to shoot it with her boyfriend. When George found out, he took it and locked it up and grounded Star."

"Do you think their daughter could have done it?"

"She was a handful. Hell, that's being kind. As soon as Star hit fourteen, she turned from this sweet little girl into this rebellious kid." He took a drink of his coffee. "But it doesn't feel right. I can't see her killing her parents, and I sure can't see her shooting Jay."

"If she's into drugs . . . they can change you."

"I know, but her little brother? I don't think she'd do

it. She adored him. The detective in charge is just taking the easy way out."

"What about this boyfriend of hers?"

"They're looking for him. He hasn't been home in weeks. His parents don't know where he is. Right now, it's frustrating, being an Atlanta detective. I have no jurisdiction whatsoever even though I live in Rosewood, and the homicide guys refer to me as just a PC."

"Politically correct?"

"Paper cop."

"Oh." She could see that hurt him. "What about the bone?"

"They don't think it's relevant, especially now that they know George just picked it up in some woods. It could have come from anywhere. Star looks much better to them."

"One human bone's still a body. It's rather a large coincidence, them finding a human bone a few days before they get killed. I think it's important."

"And . . ." He stopped, looked at her and frowned and looked away.

"And what?"

"And I don't know. For some reason they don't believe you."

"You're kidding. In that case, find another osteologist to look at the bone."

"Would you write up a report on it? Please? In the meantime, I'll send a photograph of it to a couple of other forensic anthropologists. They can ID it from a photo?" Diane nodded. "If Detective Warrick doesn't want the information, I can give it to Star's attorney when they find her."

"Bring me the bone back and I'll write a report."

The museum looked big and empty after seeing it filled with people the evening before. Diane was glad the party was behind her as she walked through the rooms looking at each exhibit for any damage or forgotten cups of punch. The cleaning crew did a thorough job. Now it was time for the real task: getting the newly remodeled museum ready for the general public. The thought was uplifting. She felt good. New job, new clothes. She unconsciously smoothed the front of her navy blazer, briefly wondering if she looked like she was more accustomed to jeans and tees rather than the pantsuit and silk shirt she had on.

More of the staff started arriving, and Diane girded herself for a long day. Several faculty of Bartrum University were coming to claim offices in the museum. Her watch said it was only 9:15. She could get about thirty minutes of paperwork done while it was still relatively quiet. She met Andie in the hall on the way to her office, notebook and pen in hand.

"Great party, huh?" said Andie.

"Not bad. Most everyone seemed pleased with what they're paying for. When did you get to bed?" Diane unlocked the door to her office and Andie followed her in and sat down in front of her desk.

"Didn't. Some of us went out. We were all dressed up and didn't want to waste it."

Diane sighed. Gone were the days when she could stay up all night and not feel like she had a hangover the next morning. "Donald put the wrong plants in the exhibit."

"I know. He said you need to learn how to save money. I didn't want to tell you until after the party."

"And he wonders why I don't appoint him assistant director. Any other stuff you were waiting to tell me?"

"Yes. The rock woman and the bug guy are complaining that their offices are too small."

"The geologist and the entomologist?"

"Yeah, that's what I said. Rocks and bugs."

"Their offices are off their respective exhibit rooms. I don't think we can rearrange everything to suit them. Besides, they have offices on campus. They can make do."

"I think they're just bugged because the collection managers have larger offices."

Diane rolled her eyes. "Anyone else?"

"The archaeologist wants to put in an exhibit on ancient Egypt."

"What? She's not even an Egyptologist."

"Not she—he," said Andie. "*She* got a job at some university out of state. The archaeology department offered the museum appointment to one of their emeritus faculty members."

"Jonas Briggs?"

"That's right. Real sweet guy."

"Look, we aren't adding many cultural items yet. We only have exhibits of the Paleo-Indian because of his interaction with megafauna. We'll have to ask them to appoint someone else."

"He really is a nice guy. He knows a lot about Paleo-Indians too. And he's been telling me some really cool stuff about ape archaeology."

"Ape archaeology?"

"Yeah, it's interesting. These archaeologists are excavating sites where apes have lived for centuries."

"Finding anything?"

"Tools."

"Tools? Is this a joke?"

"No, really, he showed me the article in *Scientific American*. It would make a great exhibit."

Diane shook her head. "I'll talk with him. In the meantime, I don't want to see any requisition forms for mummies."

"Got it."

"Next."

"The exobiologist wants to know if he can put a sunroof in the attic for his telescope."

Diane stared at Andie openmouthed. "You mean that the biologist they sent us is—"

Andie held up her hands. "Just kidding. A little bit of *X-Files* humor."

"After the Egyptologist, I thought you were serious. Is that everything?"

"So far."

"Good. If those are all our problems, we're very lucky.

I think we can have this place ready for the general public in a couple of weeks. Let me know when the workmen arrive to move the rest of the paleo exhibits. And if you see Donald, tell him I want to see him—immediately."

"Oh, this arrived for you a minute ago." Andie read the label. "It's from Frank Duncan."

"This must be the bone."

"Bone? I thought you weren't . . ."

"So did I."

"You know, we have room to set you up a lab."

"No," Diane snapped. "This is the last one."

Chapter 8

Diane sat in her office and rolled the bone in her hand, feeling its rough surface with her sensitive fingers. Only four inches of broken bone, yet it *was* a body. If the bone had any distinguishing mark and she had an identical X ray, it could provide an identity. She took the photographs from the envelope and went over the measurements again.

Nothing had changed. The bone appeared to be male, but it certainly didn't have to be. Some females are quite large and very strong. Whoever it was was also young. The young shouldn't die.

Diane closed her eyes for a moment. The image of dirt-covered, tangled bones standing out in relief flickered before her. Dirty little ragged dresses, tiny shoes, broken bones and skulls with bullet holes, all shoved together in one mass grave. Wickedness still caught her by surprise, even though she had looked upon its work so many times.

She opened her eyes and reached for the telephone. She had to call information to get the number, and spell the name several times, but she finally reached Ranjan Patel.

"Ran, this is Diane Fallon."

"Diane Fallon, yes. Good to hear from you. What can I do for you?"

"I have a favor that I hope you can do."

"I will try."

"I have a bone I'd like to have a stable-isotope analysis performed on."

"I see. Tell me about this bone."

Diane explained to him about the bone Frank had brought to her. "I know this is a long shot. . . ."

"But interesting. I'd like to see if it helps you in your investigation. Perhaps there is a paper in it. Do send it along. I only need two grams for the test."

"Is there any chance you can do some oxygen and hydrogen ratios?"

"I was about to ask if you would like those too."

"Do you think they would be useful?"

"I think it would be useful to try. Send another gram."

"I'll do that. Thanks, Ran."

"If you find the rest of him, send along some teeth. Not much work has been done in this area with teeth. Incredible, since they are a protected environment in the skeleton, so to speak. You will do this?"

"I will. I hope we do find the rest of him. Thanks."

She hung up the phone and focused on the bone again. She sniffed it. It wasn't ancient, but she knew that; too much of the internal structure was still intact. She grabbed her hand lens and looked into the opening in the shaft, down into the marrow cavity. Something odd about the shape inside caught her eye, something that didn't look like the lattice structure of cancellous bone— the internal part of bone where the red marrow is housed. Using a set of long tweezers, she pulled gently at the object. A wire-thin curved wisp of bone came out easily. It was almost invisible lying on the white sheet of paper on her desk.

Diane rummaged through her drawers until she found a glass vial for the tiny bone, dropped the bone inside and snapped on the cap. She gathered her bone specimens and her notebook and headed across to the faunal lab, located off the zoological exhibits, where there was a dissecting microscope and a respectable reference collection of numerous species of animal skeletons.

The animal room, as they called it, was a large room that once had rows of iron beds along each side from when it was a hospital. The beds were now replaced by glass enclosed dioramas of animals native to the Southeast. A display of two mounted coyotes in their wooded habitat guarded the door leading to the faunal lab.

A slim, athletic woman in her thirties sporting cutoffs and a tee shirt, with her brown hair haphazardly piled and clipped on her head, stood just inside the lab, blocking the entrance. "Excuse me, but do you know who's in charge here? I need to speak to someone about my office."

Diane remembered Andie telling her about the various complaints of the new arrivals. "Are you our geologist?"

The woman glanced around the room at the animal skeletons lining the room, waiting to be placed with their stuffed counterparts. "No."

Not the geologist. Another who was dissatisfied with her office space. Diane paused a moment, eyeing the woman from head to toe. "How do you do? I'm Diane Fallon, the director. You must be Dr. Mercer, the zoologist."

"Yes. Dr. Sylvia Mercer. What gives? How am I supposed to use an office the size of a shoe box and open to public view?" She pointed to a large window on the left side of the lab that framed one side of her office—ample office space, Diane thought. But then, she was accustomed to having an office in a tent for weeks on end. "Whose office is that?" She pointed to an office across the lab. Also with a picture window, but obviously larger.

"That's the collection manager's office. She's here all day."

"I really need an office larger than this one."

"The arrangement I made with your university was to provide office and lab space to supplement what your department provides you. Your office is off this lab and near the zoology exhibits. The lab isn't open to the public, so you have complete privacy. You're free to put bookcases or storage here in the lab if you have any spillover from your office. I think you'll find the convenience outweighs any problem of size. I also understand you will be spending a few hours a week here, and that

the bulk of your time will be spent at the university."
Diane kept her voice calm and even. She hoped the smile
on her face didn't look fake.

"That's just it. Since I was getting an office here, the
department head took my office and put me in another
broom closet of an office space. Now I have two places
to keep my brooms."

"Oh. That wasn't supposed to happen. I was hoping
to add to what the faculty who come here had, not
take away."

"You're not familiar with universities, are you?"

"Not since I was a student." Diane looked around the
room, searching for a compromise.

"I've got this research I'm working on. I really need
more room. I'm sharing space at the university, and they
want me to move my research here, but it looks like I'll
be sharing lab space with everyone here too. Taking this
position has cut my resources more than in half."

Diane turned back to her. "No, this is your lab."

"Mine? This is my lab?"

"And the collection manager's. He has to use it too.
But as curator of animal collection, you're in charge."

"What about the geologist?"

"She has her own lab."

"And the entomologist?"

"All the collections have their own labs."

Sylvia looked around the room again. "I . . . that's
different. I thought I had to share this space with everyone. They said this was a small museum."

"It is, in terms of the number and variety of collections, but it's a big building. It was decided that providing
lab space would make a smaller museum desirable."

"Don't tell my department. They'll want to send over
some of the tenured faculty to replace me."

"It'll be our secret." Diane handed her the vial. "This
looks like a fish rib to me. Is it?"

Dr. Mercer took the vial and peered at the thin bone
inside. "Yes, it is. I can't tell you what kind of fish. Ribs
are not really distinguishable among fish. Possibly bass or
trout. Where did it come from? Sometimes that's a clue."

"Inside the marrow cavity of a broken human clavicle."

Sylvia Mercer glanced at Diane and back at the fish bone. "How odd. Is it some ritualistic burial practice? I've never heard of such a thing."

"No. This is a modern suspicious death."

Sylvia silently looked at Diane, her brow creased in deep furrows. Diane felt some explanation was warranted.

"Before I became director of the museum, I was a forensic anthropologist." Diane took the bag containing the section of clavicle from her blazer pocket. "A detective asked me to look at this bone that was found by someone. The fish bone was inside it."

"Yes, I think I heard someone say you're an osteologist. I must say, you were thorough if you found it inside that bone."

Not thorough enough, thought Diane, *or I would have found it the first time around.*

"I appreciate the identification. Choose any type of window treatment for your office that will work best for you. Tell my assistant, Andie Layne, and she'll order it." Diane stepped past Dr. Mercer and sat down at a dissecting microscope. She removed the broken clavicle from its bag, placed it on the stage and focused on its surface.

"Will you be using the lab for your forensic work?" Sylvia had come up behind Diane and was looking over her shoulder.

"No. This is a onetime thing."

"Where was it found?"

"That's a good question. It was given to the detective without provenience."

"Is there anything you can tell from just that one piece?"

Diane briefly described what she knew about the bone as she examined its surface under the microscope.

Having missed the fish rib the first time stung, and she wasn't going to miss anything else. But she found nothing on the weathered surface that hadn't been evident with the hand lens. She tore off a piece of butcher paper from a roll hanging on the wall and gently shook and tapped the bone over it. A few flakes landed on the paper, along with a tiny brown oval that looked like a dark flake of popcorn shell. She put the paper on the microscope stage and examined the objects.

"What is it?" Sylvia leaned over Diane's shoulder, looking at the microscope stage with interest.

"I'll have to check with the entomologist, but I believe it's a cap from a blowfly puparium. Its presence inside the bone cavity is as unusual as the fish rib. At this stage of development, the blowflies have moved away from the carrion and burrowed underground. Because this is a cap, we know that the adult blowfly did emerge."

Diane looked at her watch. She had a board meeting in just a few minutes.

The faunal lab, like all the labs in the museum, had a specimen photography setup—a maneuverable camera stand with lighting that allowed the object to be photographed from different angles. Before proceeding with her analysis, she placed the bone on the camera stage and snapped pictures of it from several views.

She found another vial in the lab supply cabinet for the new material. After placing the new material in the vials and labeling them, she took the bone saw, put in a new blade and cut a sample of bone that was more than enough for her friend to test.

Sylvia Mercer looked on as Diane found a specimen bag and box to ship it in. "What kind of test are you going to do on it?"

"Stable isotope. It'll be interesting to see if I can find any useful information."

"It will. I'd think that modern diet wouldn't lend itself to a test like that."

Diane finished addressing the package and started for her office. "I've got to run. Andie has catalogs of office furniture, curtains and blinds and things. She'll help you find whatever you need."

In her office, she locked the vial in her filing cabinet and was putting stamps on the package when she heard Andie go into her office. Diane retrieved the budget figures and the fax information and opened the door between their offices. "I know you just came back from some errands, but I really need you to overnight this package for me."

Andie stood with her keys still in her hand. "Sure. I'll do it now."

"Thanks." Diane looked at her watch again. It was almost time for the meeting. She wondered if Donald had gone up to the conference room yet.

With file folders in hand, Diane locked her door and walked around the corner to Donald's office. When knocking brought no response, she turned the knob. It was locked. Few people in the museum had master keys, but she was one of them. She opened his office and walked in, closing the door behind her.

To Diane, Donald's office did not reflect his personality. His thinking, as well as his work, often seemed disorganized to her ordered sensibilities. But his office was something else, better organized than hers. It didn't seem like him at all. Framed *National Geographic* covers decorated his walls, along with shadow boxes displaying rocks and minerals. A faux zebra-skin rug covered the area in front of his desk. Animals carved from a variety of exotic woods stood between books on his shelves. She would never have thought that Donald had decorated it, had she not seen him carefully measure and hang the pictures and place the books and carvings on the shelves.

She remembered when he had come to her with the catalog showing the desk he wanted—one of the few times his interaction with her was cordial. The polished dark walnut desk with the black ebony inlaid top was one of the most expensive pieces of office furniture they were ordering. The choice defied his characteristic argument for thrift. He had wanted that desk, and she'd agreed to purchase it partly because she hoped it would help their future interactions.

Diane wasn't sure what she was looking for in his office. Some evidence she could confront him with. She didn't approach his desk or his walnut filing cabinet. She didn't intend to rifle though his things. Pangs of guilt gnawed at her for venturing without permission this far into his office.

Nothing stood out to point to his guilt. Maybe it wasn't him. Then who? Not Andie. It could have been Andie, though. Maybe she simply did not remember ordering the duplicate exhibits. No, that was absurd.

Diane assumed that someone ordered the items to make her life difficult. Perhaps she was just paranoid. That thought made her feel better. It would be easier to deal with her own paranoia than with some secret mischief-maker in the museum. Feeling ashamed for her trespass, she turned and put her hand on the doorknob. As she started to turn it, a stack of magazines caught her eye.

On top of the stack was an issue of *U.S. News and World Report*. The cover photograph was of a mass burial. She picked up the magazine and thumbed through the pages. They opened automatically, as if the magazine had been laid open at that point, to an article about a mass burial site she had excavated in Bosnia. There were no pictures of her, nor was she mentioned in the article, but it was her site. She picked up the other magazines and flipped through them—*Newsweek, Time*, more *U.S. News and World Report*s—all had articles about places she'd been.

Only one photograph actually showed her, but she was unrecognizable with the bill of her cap pulled down over her eyes. She and the team always kept a low profile. They avoided mentioning their names for journalists, hid their faces when photographs were taken. No team members went out of their way to make themselves a target. But there were plenty of pictures of open burials in the process of being excavated—skeletonized bodies piled on one another. It made her stomach turn.

So Donald had been reading about her. He knew the places she'd been with her team. How much else did he know? The articles talked about the mass graves, the politics of the region, the United States' and world response to atrocities, but never any personal details about the field crew. Never anything that the forensics team chose to keep private.

Who knew about the last year in Puerto Barquis? Only the people she'd worked with. Only members of World Accord International. Quite a few people, but all were good at being circumspect. She hadn't confided in anyone here. Did someone know? Did someone know what "In the Hall of the Mountain King" meant to her? It wasn't exactly a secret, but to find out, you had to know one of her team—know them well enough for them to trust you.

She returned the magazines to the shelf and looked back over the room, her cheeks burning with anger. She'd a mind to search it, go through his desk drawers, his filing cabinet. But she didn't. This job was her return to a civilization where tyrants are kept in check. She wasn't going to become one after she'd spent the past ten years working to bring them to justice.

She shouldn't have come into his office. First, the mistake she'd made with the bone, and now this. She was getting sloppy. If she couldn't do a good job for Frank, she shouldn't have said she would look at the bone. If she couldn't control her employees without invading their privacy, then she didn't need to be museum director. She left Donald's office and locked the door behind her, got on the elevator and rode to the second floor.

As Diane walked down the hallway to the large conference room, she heard murmurs of restless conversation. Turning the corner, she saw the board members standing in the hallway. Half were looking very unhappy. Donald was deep in conversation with Madge Stewart. He looked up when Diane approached, then down at his watch.

"It's locked," said Madge, tapping her foot, her springy gray hair bouncing with each tap. Madge had missed the contributors' party because she had marked it wrong on her calendar, and she blamed Diane. It appeared to Diane that Madge often blamed whomever was available for everything that the vagaries of life made her do.

"I have other meetings. If I ran my restaurants

like . . ." Craig Amberson was fidgeting with his brief-case. Laura had told Diane he was quitting smoking. He had actually asked the doctor if he could wear two nico-tine patches in the beginning.

Kenneth Meyers was working on his Palm Pilot. "Get yourself one of these," he told Craig. "You can work anywhere."

Diane looked at her watch. Three minutes late. "I'm sorry. I had some unexpected business to attend to."

Even Harvey Phelps appeared curt. "Where's Andie? Doesn't she have a key?"

"Laura went to look for her, just before you got here, Harvey," said Mark Grayson, looking at his watch. "Look, Diane, if this is the way you intend to run things . . ."

Laura rounded the corner. "Couldn't find Andie or Diane. . . . Oh, there you are."

"Andie's running some errands," said Diane. "I have three minutes after eleven. Why is everyone so im-patient?"

"Because we've been waiting for more than twenty minutes," said Mark.

"Donald reminded us last night that the meeting was rescheduled for 10:45," said Laura.

Diane had the key in her hand, ready to unlock the door. She spun around and faced Donald. "Why did you do that?"

He took a small step back. "You said to change the meeting to fifteen minutes earlier."

"No, I did not."

"I have your E-mail."

"I didn't send it. This is going to stop." She thrust the key in the lock. Before she turned it, the door opened, almost knocking her backward.

Chapter 9

Diane and every one of the museum board members took a step backward at the startling sight of a disheveled, droopy-eyed Signy Grayson stumbling into the hallway and almost to the floor, if Diane hadn't held on to her arm. The heavy aroma of metabolized alcohol and perfume wafted over the small crowd.

"I must have fallen asleep. It's, uh, been a long day." She looked at them in confusion.

No one said anything for several beats, shifting their gazes from Signy to Mark, who stood strangely silent and surprised. Diane broke the silence. "Are you all right? Were you here all night?"

"Signy?" Mark found his voice and pushed his way to the door and took her by the arm. "Sweetheart, are you ill?"

"Just feeling a little tired. What does she mean 'all night'?" Signy put her hands to her face and rubbed her eyes.

"Because it's Wednesday," said Diane. "The party was last night."

A look of alarm crossed Signy's face. "Oh, no."

"It must be the cold medicine," Mark muttered to the silent crowd around them. "We won't be long here, and I'll take you home. We can pick up your car later."

"Would you like to go to the first-aid station and lie down?" asked Diane.

"No . . . I'm fine, really."

Diane spotted the head conservator walking in their

direction. She nabbed him as he came past, heading toward the elevators. "Korey, will you escort Mrs. Grayson to the staff lounge?"

"Sure thing, Dr. Fallon. I have the proposal for the conservation workshops." He waved the folder he was carrying. "I'll give it to Andie."

"Good. I'm anxious to see it."

"Come with me, Mrs. Grayson. I was just heading in that direction."

There were some quiet whispers among the board members who stood watching Signy, in her red sparkling dress, walk down the hallway with the much taller Korey, dressed in his khaki dockers and yellow museum tee shirt, his long dreadlocks falling past his shoulders. As the two of them turned the corner to the elevators, Diane heard Korey say: "Lovely dress, Mrs. Grayson."

Diane wondered why it wasn't Mark who was escorting his wife—and how he didn't know she hadn't come home last evening. Laura must have wondered the same thing. She lifted her brows at Diane, who knew what she must be thinking: Mark was up to his same old tricks as when he was married to her.

Signy must have slept on the leather couch at the end of the room. It stood against the wall with two companion stuffed leather chairs arranged in a conversation group. A small glass-and-wood coffee table held an overturned wineglass. It was a comfortable sofa. Signy should have gotten a good night's sleep on it.

They filed around the long mahogany table with Diane at the head. She stared down the length of it as the board members found their seats. Mark Grayson sat to her immediate right. His eyes darted from his watch to the door. As they waited, several board members took quick glances in his direction. They were probably wondering the same thing she was—how come he didn't know his wife hadn't come home last night?

Mark shifted uncomfortably in his chair again as Craig Amberson sat down to Diane's left. She knew that Mark had made the most headway with Craig in his quest to sell the museum and property. They could have been taking up battle positions, surrounding the enemy, the way they seized possession of the chairs and drew them up to the table.

Diane tossed down her papers and glanced at each member of the board. She had decided against bringing up the duplicate orders until she had a chance to question the staff.

The conference room door opened and Gordon Atwell rushed into the room. "Sorry to be late, folks. I didn't get the message about the changed meeting time until a short while ago." He took a seat at the table.

"You're denying you sent the E-mail?" Craig Amberson asked Diane.

"Craig, I didn't send the E-mail."

"I did get it," said Donald. He clamped his mouth shut and stared at her like a bulldog.

"I don't doubt it. Forward me the E-mail when the meeting's over. I'll check my computer to see if that's where it came from."

"All right," said Mark. "I'd like to open up the discussion to moving the museum and selling the property. The monetary gain for the museum would be enormous."

"And what would that be?" said Diane.

"What?" Mark stared at her in surprise.

"What is the monetary gain? Presumably, you've worked out the figures. May I see them?"

"We're talking several million added to the museum's holdings."

"This is a million—or more—left over after we either build or refit another suitable building with the correct spacial, environmental, electrical and security requirements to house the collections, and including relandscaping the nature trails? I think we need to examine your figures line by line before we're even prepared to discuss a change this radical."

"Look, Diane, I called this meeting to discuss the concept. This is a great opportunity to increase the museum's holdings."

"I'll set aside for a moment your odd use of the word *increase*, since all I've heard up to now will decrease the holdings. If we discuss this idea in theory and the figures don't work out, we will have wasted a lot of time."

"I agree," said Kenneth Meyers, fingering his Palm Pilot. "Mark, what's this obsession you have about moving the museum? I can't see how it could work out in the museum's favor. I don't think the land here is going to be as valuable as you seem to believe, and we just remodeled this place, for God's sake."

"With all due respect, Ken, what do you know about real estate?"

"I haven't made any bad real estate investments lately, and I can balance a checkbook. I know we'd have to be getting downtown-Manhattan prices in order for it to pay off for the museum in the way you're suggesting."

"I move we table this until Mark develops a line-by-line detailed budget for the sale of the property and building and moving the museum compared with the current figures for the renovated museum." Laura was smooth and casual in stating her motion. Diane wondered if Mark noticed how detailed it was.

"I second," said Kenneth.

"All in agreement with Laura's motion raise your hands." Laura, Kenneth Meyers, and Harvey Phelps raised their hands. Three votes out of the seven board members present. Mark looked around the room and smirked. His gaze shifted to Diane, whose hand was also raised.

"You can only vote to break a tie," said Madge.

"You're forgetting, I have Vanessa Van Ross' proxy. All those against Laura's motion."

Mark Grayson, Gordon Atwell, Craig Amberson and Madge Stewart all raised their hands, producing a tie vote.

"I vote for Laura's motion," said Diane. "We'll table this discussion until Mark has his figures together."

"Why don't we all just send you a rubber stamp with our signatures, and we won't have to waste our time showing up for these meetings?" said Mark. "I don't know why we even have a board, since you will do what you want anyway."

"Milo intended the board members to offer their expertise for the good of the museum," said Diane. "Why do you consider having to get your facts and figures together a defeat?"

Diane didn't wait for an answer. She stood and took a stack of papers and began passing them out. "Here are the new figures for the opening. They include some workshops we will be offering to the public."

"Stop ignoring legitimate questions for a moment. This is something we need to discuss."

"You mean the purpose of the board? That's covered in the hand—"

"I know, Milo's handbook. Milo is dead, yet every time anything comes up about the museum, you or your friends trot out his name like he's going to show up any minute and judge what we've done to *his* museum. Time goes on, and there are new considerations."

"Milo may not be here with us, but he left us his plans in his will—along with his money. His death didn't change the validity of his plans for the museum. Nor did it change Mrs. Van Ross' commitment to see his plans realized." Diane gazed around at the board members. Most were looking at her handouts.

Mark detected the sudden lack of support and stood up. "I need to get Signy home. Perhaps there will be a future time when this is not such a forbidden topic." The way he left the room reminded Diane of a spoiled child.

There was a moment of silence finally broken by Madge Stewart. "This conservator's workshop, what's that?"

"Korey Jordan, our head conservator, thought members of the community would be interested in learning how to protect some of their family heirlooms," said Diane.

"Oh, I'd be interested in that," said Madge. "I have this quilt. . . ."

Craig Amberson let out a sigh, and Madge glared at him.

"I think the meeting's clearly over," said Diane. "Have a look at the budget I've handed out and we'll discuss it next meeting. Come with me, Madge, and I'll take you to meet Korey. He can give you some acid-free tissue paper and a box to store your quilt in."

"Well, this was a big waste of time." Craig Amberson stood up and stuffed the budget papers in his briefcase.

Gordon Atwell looked at his watch. "I might have just as well stayed at the bank. We should have at least talked about Mark's plan, if nothing else but to get it over with."

"Nothing to talk about without figures," said Diane. "Until we have those, it's all speculation—that's a waste of time."

Craig muttered something under his breath and walked out the door with Gordon. Diane took Madge to the conservation laboratory. It was not a large laboratory. Many of their items were contracted out to be processed. They did have a large storage vault controlled for temperature and humidity, a fume hood for handling chemicals, deacidification facilities, a suction table for treating fragile objects that can't be completely immersed in water, binocular microscopes, and photographic equipment, all managed by a head conservator and five assistants. Diane was negotiating an arrangement with the local technical schools to offer classes for training conservation assistants.

Most of the items Korey worked with were bones, botanical specimens and objects from nature, but he also had expertise in the conservation of historical objects and paper. All the documents that passed through the museum went through Korey's hands first, before going to the archivist.

Signy was leaning over a table looking at water-stained documents, Korey's jacket over her shoulders.

"We found these in an old trunk in a corner of the basement," Korey was telling her. "They contain some of the history of the place. Once I test the ink, I'll know how to clean the paper and separate the pages that are stuck together. I think they'll eventually make a terrific exhibit."

"There's certainly a lot more to this museum business than one would first guess," said Madge.

As they discussed the documents, Diane noticed boxes of supplies, three layers high stacked against the wall. "What's this?" she asked Korey.

He laughed. "Enough supplies to last me into the next millennium. I don't know what's going on. I suddenly started receiving a triple order of everything. I called the supplier and they said we'd ordered it."

"Send me the paperwork that came with it," said Diane. "I'll take care of it. We'll send back all the extras that have a shelf life."

Madge rubbed her bare arms. "How can you stand it so cool in here? I'd turn up the temperature."

"It's best for the stuff we work on if the room is kept a little cool," said Korey. "We get used to it."

"Would you give Miss Stewart a box and some wrapping tissue? She wants to store a quilt."

"Sure thing." Korey went to collect the items.

"I suppose the meeting's broken up, then." Signy took the jacket off and laid it on the table.

"Yes, it has. I imagine Mark will be looking for you in the lounge. I'll show you the way, if you like."

"Thanks, Korey," she yelled after him. "I appreciate the tour."

"No problem, Mrs. G."

"Korey will take care of you, Madge," said Diane. "He can give you advice on cleaning your quilt, if it needs it."

Diane left Madge looking at a tray of resin casts of dinosaur eggs and walked Signy out of the lab to the elevators that led to the staff lounge on the second floor.

"How did the meeting go?" Signy looked at her watch. "You couldn't have gotten much done."

"No. We didn't get much done. Just small business. Did you enjoy your tour of the conservation lab?"

"I did," said Signy. She sounded surprised that she could actually enjoy herself in a museum laboratory. "Korey's a good teacher. Very enthusiastic about his work."

"Mark said you've been taking cold medication. I'm sorry you had to spend the night in the conference room. I'll have to ask the cleaning staff why they didn't notice you."

"It's just as well. I didn't need to be driving, and Mark was going to be at his office half the night talking to Japan."

"I would have been glad to drive you home."

"The couch was very comfortable."

Diane didn't press further, but she found the whole thing very odd. They met Mark just outside the staff lounge. He was frowning and didn't automatically light up when he saw his wife. When he finally did smile, it looked forced.

"I'd better get you home," he said. "You must be exhausted." He nodded to Diane, took Signy by the arm and led her across the emerald green tile floors toward the elevators.

Diane headed toward the elevators herself, but was stopped by Donald. The way he was frowning, she thought she was in for another quarrel with him.

"Diane, I didn't make up that message."

"What?" For a moment she didn't understand what Donald was talking about, for her hearing picked up Mark and Signy's background conversation as they waited for the elevator. Their voices were not much more than a loud whisper, but the words swept her way as if on a breeze.

"Can't you do anything right?" said Mark.

"If it weren't for me, you wouldn't even know about them. I'll drive myself home."

Diane glanced at them in time to see Mark take Signy by the arm. She jerked it out of his grasp and hurried into the open elevator.

"I really didn't. I wouldn't do that," Donald was saying, "and I'm really disturbed that you think I would."

Diane turned her attention back to Donald. "I don't think you did, Donald. I think we both were innocent victims of some prankster." His frown dissolved into a lopsided smile. What she didn't say was that she doubted he would do something that so obviously pointed to him.

"Who do you think it was?" he asked.

"I don't know. Do you have a printout of the E-mail?"

He slipped a page from the folder he was carrying and handed it to her. "It was sent from your computer," he said.

"Looks like it. Will you forward me the message?"

"Sure. I'll do that."

When Donald left, Diane headed for her office. As she crossed the lobby, the guard standing by the intercom stopped her.

"A Frank Duncan wants to see you, Dr. Fallon."

"OK. You can let him in."

The guard opened the door and Frank walked in carrying a large envelope.

"Frank, I didn't expect to see you today. Any news about what happened to your friends?" She gestured toward the hallway that led to her office. They walked through the glass doors labeled ADMINISTRATION and continued down the corridor.

"I know you don't like being involved in any investigation, but I would really like to talk to you."

"Is this about their deaths?" Diane fished her door key from the pocket of her jacket.

"Yes. The detectives have picked up their daughter, Star."

Chapter 10

Diane held her key so tightly in her hand, her knuckles were white. She stopped and turned to face Frank, not even realizing she also held her breath until she spoke. "She's alive, then? She's all right? That's good news. I . . . well, I feared the worst."

"So did I. She's alive, but the kid's in a world of trouble. Her parents and brother are dead, the detectives think she killed them, and I'm afraid the whole thing's being mishandled by the Rosewood police department."

They entered Diane's office by her private entrance, and she sat down at her desk. "Mishandled how?"

Frank drew up a chair and laid his envelope on her desk. "Do you know anything about Rosewood politics these days?"

"Some ongoing disagreements involving the mayor and the city council?"

"And the county commissioners thrown in, just to further complicate everything. It's a hell of a mess."

"I don't know much about local politics. I try to stay out of it as much as my job will allow."

"The short version is that there's a power struggle between Mayor Sutton and the city council. He thinks Rosewood is Atlanta." Frank made a face. "He wants to be governor one of these days and he's using our little city to build his empire."

"A lot of people are moving here. We've had to do demographics for the museum."

Frank waved his hand. "I work in Atlanta and live

here. There may be only sixty-three miles in between, but there's a big difference. The city council's just as bad in the other direction as the mayor is. They don't want any change that might shake up their little kingdom. They have their own fish to fry."

Diane leaned back in her chair. "What does all this have to do with the murder of your friends? Are you saying it was some kind of political hit?"

"No, of course not. That's not what I'm getting at." Frank fidgeted in his chair, moving it closer to her desk. "We finally get a new police commissioner. We needed one. But the mayor wrestled his choice from the city council. The commissioner's been pushing out people who don't support the mayor and hiring new people—most of them old buddies of his, who will, like the chief of detectives, keep a low profile and do what they're told. The chief of detectives, in turn, has been putting his men in. The upshot is that it's all political cronyism, and nobody knows what the hell they're doing."

"The main thing is the crime scene, and the Georgia Bureau of Investigation know what they're doing."

"The GBI didn't work the crime scene. That's what I've been trying to tell you. The chief refused to call them. He's got this hair up his butt that Rosewood police can handle our crime without outside help."

"Can they?"

"No. The best homicide cop was Jake Houser, but he wasn't one of the commissioner's men. Now that he's gone to a desk job, the homicide squad is a bunch of new people hardly older than Kevin."

Diane made an effort not to smile, wondering if Frank was just feeling estranged from officers half his age. "But they might still be competent."

"Whose side are you on?"

"Yours, of course. I think you ought to contact the president of the city council and tell him they were right all along, that the mayor's pricks . . . I mean picks . . . the mayor's picks are screwing up an investigation." Diane didn't know the girl, but she felt a giddy relief upon learning that she hadn't been killed. Jails and trials could be dealt with. But not death.

"This isn't funny."

"No, it isn't. What is it they're doing wrong?"

"Warrick. Janice Warrick—she's the detective in charge—allowed George's mother and stepfather in the house. She let the stepfather tramp around the bedroom before anything was processed."

Diane pressed her lips together. "Did you mention to Detective Warrick that letting anyone on the crime scene was contaminating the evidence?"

"I mentioned it. I hammered her over the head with it. She asked me how a paper detective could possibly know anything about crime scenes. She was going to let them take things out of the house. When I objected, she tried to make me leave. I told her that I was executor of the will, and if anything was missing from the house, I'd sue the department and her personally."

"Were you in the crime scene?"

Frank stared at her a moment. "I stayed mostly on the front porch. Do you have anything else on the bone?"

"Yes." She pulled out a sheet of paper from her desk. "Here's the report. It's on the standard form."

He took the page and glanced it up and down. "Find anything new?"

"Yes."

"You mean you missed something the first time?"

Diane nodded. "Yes, I did."

"Well, does this make us even for me throwing away the spiderweb? What'd you find?"

"A fish rib and a cap from a blowfly puparium in the marrow cavity."

"What? A fish rib and a what?"

"A cap from a blowfly puparium. Do you know about the life cycle of blowflies?"

"Oh, sure, everyone knows about that. . . . All I know about flies is that they're a damn disgusting nuisance."

"If it weren't for them, and a host of other disgusting creatures, the world would be littered with dead, unde- cayed animals. After the third instar of a blowfly . . ."

"Third instar? That sounds like *Star Trek*."

"Bug speak. You know that flies are attracted to dead bodies."

"Yes, I do know that."

"There's a point in the life cycle of a blowfly at which it moves away from the corpse and burrows into the ground. This third skin shedding, or instar, hardens into a capsule and becomes the puparium. From this, it emerges after a period of time in the ground as an adult fly by popping off a cap at the end of the puparium. This cap is what I found. My identification has to be verified by an entomologist, but the significance of these finds is that neither the fish bone nor the puparium cap should be found inside the bone."

"Okay. So, how did they get there?"

"My guess is they washed in. But there are other scenarios. The bone could have already been underground and decomposed, and this fly came from something decomposing on top of it or near it. When the blowfly moved underground, it wound up burrowing into the cavity in the bone. Later the bone was eroded, or dug up for your friends to find."

"Does this help us?"

"It says something about the environment the bone was in—"

"Like in a river?"

"No, the blowfly wouldn't be underwater. Suppose that your friend George thought it was a deer bone because there were antlers, or hooves, or whatever present. So, we have deer bone and fish bone in the same place. I think you might look for the rest of the body—the remaining bones—in a place where animal bones are processed. A hunting camp, somewhere that processes meat . . . something like that."

Frank nodded. "That's something—a good place to start. How is it that you know so much about bugs?"

"Part of my old job. Bodies, bones, bugs and blood."

"All that?"

"It's all connected. Besides, it's hard to find a crime lab in the places I had to go. Those countries often don't want us there in the first place, and their cooperation doesn't extend to lending expert personnel and lab facilities. The team learned how to do everything ourselves."

"So you're familiar with crime scenes?"

"Yes."

Frank stood and walked over to a photograph on her wall of the inside of a cave. He didn't turn around, but spoke to the photograph. "Warrick's finished with the crime scene. I wonder if you'd take a look at it?"

"Frank, I . . ."

He turned in her direction. "They matched the gun with the bullet that killed Jay. It was Louise's gun. Star's just sixteen. Sixteen, Diane. I don't think she did it. I'm getting her a lawyer, but I need to get a handle on the crime scene."

"It's already been contaminated."

"I know, but you said 'bodies, bones, bugs and blood.' You know about blood spatters?"

"Yes. Like other crime scene evidence, blood spatters can be an important element in human rights cases, but . . ."

"That's a place to start. There are spatters. Diane, for now, I'm Star's guardian, until she's eighteen. I've known her since she was a baby. She's like a daughter, and I know she didn't do this, but I need help proving it." He was silent a moment, turning back to the picture. "It looks like you in this cave."

"It is."

"It looks like you're hanging from a rope."

"I am."

"Why?" He turned around and faced her with a puzzled frown.

"The entrance to that particular cave was from above. You knew I was a caver?"

"Well, yeah, you mentioned it, but I thought you visited as a tourist—like Ruby Falls or Mammoth Cave, you know—with a bunch of other people."

She gestured to the photograph. "That cave's in Brazil. I was mapping it."

"Mapping it? Why?"

Diane shrugged. "It hadn't been mapped."

"So that's what you do for fun?"

She leaned forward with her elbows on the desk. "It's very relaxing. Caves are beautiful. The line from Frost's poem—'lovely, dark and deep'—fits caves better than woods. It's like being in the center of a velvet black universe—often as silent as the vacuum of space must be."

"You say it like that's a good thing."

Diane laughed at him standing there with that curious look on his face. "It's a very good thing."

Frank picked up a geode paperweight sitting on her dark walnut desk and turned it over in his hand. "We need to get reacquainted. We hardly knew each other before."

"It seems there's a lot we don't know about each other."

Diane's private line rang and she picked it up, still holding his gaze in hers.

"Diane, how about letting Dylan Houser come down and make an assessment of your interactive computing needs."

Diane hesitated a moment, pulled her attention away from Frank and focused on the caller. "Ken, hi. How are you? You don't waste time, do you?"

"This isn't a business where you can waste time—not like real estate, apparently." He laughed so loud Diane had to pull the phone away from her ear.

"What's up with Mark anyway?" asked Diane.

"Damned if I know. Makes no sense to me, unless he's got his money tied up in it somehow and needs the deal to cover his losses or something. I can't believe he'd put us through all this trouble for commission. How about Dylan? It was his idea. I think his girlfriend wants to work there. He's a smart kid. Already figured out how much money I can make if he talks you into it."

"His father, Jake, is one of our evening security guards. Sure, why not make it a family affair? It won't hurt to see what he comes up with."

"Good. I'll tell him. If I figure out what Grayson's up

to, I'll let you know." He hung up. Ken rarely cluttered up his conversations with hellos and good-byes.

As she placed the phone back in its docking station, her gaze shifted to the envelope on the desk. "Is that the crime scene information?"

"Yes."

Diane regarded the yellow-brown envelope for a moment before she reached for it. She held it tentatively, like it might morph into a snake if she moved too quickly. She knew the envelope held the photographs of a mother, father and their son—dead. Not peacefully asleep, like some people describe the dead, but lifeless, possibly covered in blood, probably limbs lying at odd angles where they fell, stilled when their efforts to defend themselves failed.

Opening the envelope would be opening a door she thought she'd closed and locked for good.

Chapter 11

Diane stared at the envelope.

"Are you all right?" Frank asked after a moment.

"What?" Diane looked from the envelope to Frank as if she had forgotten he was there. "Yes. I was just thinking." She snatched up the envelope, opened it and pulled out the crime scene photos.

Frank dropped into the chair, loosened his tie and leaned forward.

"Have you seen them?" she asked.

"Yes."

"It's hard looking at people you know, murdered. How did you come by the photos? Who called you to the crime scene?"

"A uniform cop friend with the department. Izzy Wallace. He doesn't like the new guys any better than I do. He got them for me. George was his friend too."

"Another poker buddy?"

"Yes. And we all belong to the same hunting club."

Diane grimaced. "Do you know the time of death?"

"Just generally—the coroner thinks somewhere between two and four in the morning. They'll know more after the autopsies."

"Can you get the autopsy reports?"

"Yeah, Izzy can get them."

"Tell me, why do they suspect the daughter? Do they have more evidence than that she may have been a drug user and may have had access to the gun?"

Frank bowed his head a moment, and Diane looked up from the photograph.

"They caught her trying to sell a coin collection. It's one George inherited from his father—very valuable."

"How do the detectives know the collection was in the house at the time the Boones were killed?"

Frank looked like he had just tasted something bitter. "George's mother and stepfather, Crystal and Gilroy McFarland, said they were."

"You don't believe them? They wouldn't deliberately incriminate their granddaughter?"

"You've got to know Crystal. She was a piece of work, even when George and I were kids. Not what you'd call the nurturing type. Nothing like Louise." He paused a moment and glanced down at the spread of photos lying on the desk in front of Diane. "Crystal didn't call Star or Jay her grandchildren. They were adopted, and that didn't count with her."

Diane clenched her teeth and began examining the first photo. Fourteen-year-old Jay lay crumpled on the ground near a large oak tree. He was on his stomach, one arm under his body, the other at his side and bent at the elbow. One leg was straight; the other was bent at the knee. He was wearing a light blue jacket, jeans, and white Nike running shoes. A close-up of his back showed the bullet hole in the jacket and just a small amount of blood. *Possibly small-caliber gun,* she thought. *Just a kid.* She shivered. Even with her experience excavating massacres, it still astonished her that the architects of such atrocities included children in their plans.

"What does Detective Warrick think happened?" Diane asked.

"That Star and maybe her boyfriend came into the house while the parents were sleeping and shot them, stole the coins and jewelry, and on their way out they ran into Jay coming home and shot him. I need to mention that Jay and Star are natural siblings. George and Louise adopted them together when Jay was two and Star was four. She wouldn't have killed her little brother."

"But her boyfriend might?"

Frank shrugged. "I don't know her boyfriend."

"They haven't found him?"

"No."

"You said she was trying to sell the coins. What about the jewelry?"

"Warrick believes they either stashed it somewhere or the boyfriend still has it."

Diane looked at the photograph again. "Why does Detective Warrick think the parents were killed first?"

"Looks as if they were asleep in their beds." He gestured to a photograph half exposed under the stack. "If Jay was killed first, they'd have heard the shot. Neither were heavy sleepers, and George was not shy with a gun."

"What was Jay doing out so late?"

"That I don't know. It wouldn't have been like him."

"Can you find out from his friends?"

"Maybe."

Diane picked up the photographs, stacked and fanned them. "Are there any more of Jay?"

"That's all Izzy gave me. You need something else?"

"The tree."

"The tree?"

"There might be spattering on the tree. I'd like to see it."

Through the door that joined Diane's office to Andie's came the sound of Andie's voice. She was talking with Korey.

"So you didn't order all this stuff?" Andie was asking.

"No. You think I was expecting a run on ammonium citrate?" Korey answered.

"Just a minute," said Diane. She rose from her desk and opened the adjoining door.

"Dr. Fallon," said Andie. "Korey says—"

"I know. We've had some other orders duplicated, too. Did you bring the paperwork, Korey?"

He handed her a folder. "Like you said, I'm sending the chemicals back. We can keep some of the other supplies. Have you had a chance to look at my proposal?"

"Not yet. But I'm sure I'll like it. You already have Miss Stewart interested in the workshop. And thanks for taking care of her and Mrs. Grayson."

"No problem. Always glad to tell people what I do. I was wondering, Dr. Fallon, a couple of my assistants and I would like to work late some evenings on the stuff from the basement. It's like an ancient treasure trove down there. Just yesterday we found a box of Merycodus mandibles."

"What's that?" Andie asked.

"A Pliocene antilocaprid," said Korey, grinning.

"Oo-kay," said Andie.

"Artiodactyl," continued Korey.

"Small fossil deer," supplied Diane.

"I knew that," said Andie.

"I won't say no to such dedication," Diane told Korey. "I'll see about finding you some more help. I think I'll have an intern or apprentice from the tech school within the month. That'll involve you teaching a course once a week for the school."

"I can do that. In fact, that might work out. Don't a lot of people at the tech school have day jobs? Some of them would be perfect for an evening shift here."

"I'll let you know when I've worked out the details," Diane said.

Korey left, happily mumbling to himself about his timetable.

"I wish all my staff were so happy in their work." Diane turned to Andie. "Check with the other departments and see if they've been receiving unusual amounts of supplies or double orders."

"Sure. What's this about?"

"I don't know yet. Let me know if you find any. I'm meeting with Frank. Don't disturb me unless it's an emergency." Diane closed the door, sat down and lay Korey's folder on the stack of eight-by-tens.

"I really appreciate this, Diane. I know you're busy," Frank said.

She pointed to Korey's folder. "Someone's been placing orders for exhibits and supplies we already have. It's like some childish prank, except for the amounts of money involved. Almost a hundred and fifty thousand dollars on one order." She opened the folder Korey had given her. Copies of orders for excessive amounts of supplies for his lab were there—with her signature. "The strange thing is, I appear to have signed all the orders. At least, it looks like my signature."

"But you didn't?"

"Not unless I did it in my sleep. Besides, I wouldn't have signed these order forms, anyway. The department heads would have. It's hard for me to imagine anyone here forging my name. Doesn't that take a certain amount of skill? And whoever's doing it doesn't seem to have been ordering anything out of the ordinary for themselves. It's just the things we normally order, only in huge quantities. The purpose seems to be to annoy—or to make me look incompetent."

"Maybe I can help. Can I see the papers?"

Diane handed him Korey's folder, along with hers containing the duplicate orders she'd discovered. "I received a call from a supplier verifying the order for dinosaur casts. That's how I first found out about it."

Frank took the folders and opened the one on top. "Do you have copies of the original orders?"

"You think you can find out who's doing this?"

"Maybe."

Diane buzzed Andie and asked her to bring the paperwork on the particular museum exhibits she'd ordered months ago.

"Hey, Frank," said Andie, handing Diane the file. "I was sorry to hear about what happened to your friends. I don't imagine you'll be coming to the karaoke bar this Friday. We'll miss you."

Frank shook his head. "No, not for a while, Andie."

"Frank mentioned the two of you do karaoke," said Diane.

Andie nodded. "Frank's a real . . . what exactly was it you called yourself last week?"

"Crooner," said Frank.

"Well, that's a side of you I didn't know about."

His lips curved into a lopsided smile. "I guess we're all full of surprises."

"You should see him in his sunglasses and black suit when he's imitating the Blues Brothers." Andie mimed her impression of Frank's dance moves.

"I can't wait. You sing too, Andie?" Diane asked.

Andie, in her short black denim skirt, glittery chain belt and shiny gray blouse, looked convincing as she pretended to hold a microphone and did a fair imitation of Britney Spears.

"It's a lot of fun. You should come sometime." Andie's bright grin froze as her gaze rested on one of the photographs on Diane's desk. "Oh, God. Is that? Oh, I'm sorry. I shouldn't be dancing around."

"It's all right, Andie," said Diane. "Thanks for bringing the folder." Diane watched Andie return to her office, closing the adjoining door.

Both were silent for a moment. Frank took the file folder and sat down at a table against the wall under a trio of Escher prints: a castle with its endless ascending and descending staircase, an impossible self-filling waterfall, and a tessellation of angels and devils.

"I should have covered the photographs," Diane said.

"It's my fault," said Frank. "You said you came back to find some peace. I shouldn't be bringing this to you."

"It's the fault of the murderer," said Diane.

Diane watched Frank examine two pieces of paper he held up to the bronze desk lamp. "This is it," he said. "They traced your signature from this letter you sent the Bickford Museum confirming an order of . . . whatever these things are."

"*Albertosaurus, Pteranodon sternbergi, Tylosaurus* and a triceratops?"

"Yeah, those guys."

Diane rose and joined Frank to look at the documents through the light of the lamp.

"Don't touch the pages," he said as she reached for them. Frank barely held them at the very edges. "I know your fingerprints are already on them, but there's a chance we can get the perp's prints if we're careful—and lucky."

The signature on the copy of the duplicate order the Bickford Museum had faxed to her matched exactly with the signature on the letter—as did the signatures on the copies of the other orders. They were all exactly the same.

"Tracing is the quick and dirty way to forge a name," said Frank. "Amateurs often do it that way. And profes sionals, when discovery of the forgery after the fact won't matter. It's easy to detect in the original because it doesn't have the smooth quality of a normal signature, among other things."

"I really don't know why anyone would go to the trouble," said Diane, going back to her desk. "It's an annoyance at worst, as long as we return the excess."

"You mentioned that it might be to make you look bad. If you look bad enough, can you be replaced?"

"Yes, but bad enough means some kind of maleficence or gross incompetence. I don't believe ordering too many supplies would qualify."

"But the exhibits—that's one hundred fifty thousand dollars' worth. If they hadn't called . . ."

"That's just it—they would have. These are casts made from fossil bones belonging to the Bickford. Making casts is a big deal. It's not as if they have them sitting in a warehouse with a sign that says, 'some assembly required.' They have to send their preparators here to work with mine. There's a lot of planning and coordination involved."

"Who would know those details?"

She lifted her arms slightly, sighed, and let them fall. "Everyone who works here. At least, all the collection managers and their assistants, and the administrative staff."

"Just the senior staff?"

"Not necessarily. Many people working in lower-level positions are interested in a museum career. They make it a point to learn how we work."

Frank thought for a moment. "The person we're looking for is someone who doesn't know museum procedures but has access to museum files."

That leaves Donald out, Diane thought. *He knows procedures very well.*

"Whoever it is had to order things from purchase orders already on file. They wouldn't know how to choose and order new things. Assuming this is not for personal gain, it must be a grudge of some sort. I'm thinking custodial staff, guards. Didn't you say you have students from the university working here?"

"Yes. But why would they . . . ?"

"That's what we're going to try to find out. Who else works here but wouldn't know much about your procedures?"

"We have new faculty from the university coming in as curators of the various collections. They haven't had any orientation. But they just began arriving yesterday and today."

Frank shuffled through some of the papers and shook his head. "It's probably someone with a key. Your fax records show that the dinosaurs were ordered on Wednesday evening after normal working hours. Who was here?"

"Everybody. Most of us have been working late for weeks, getting ready for the contributors' party."

"Does security log in and log out personnel after hours?"

"Yes. But as I said, that's almost everyone here."

"Would your office have been open at that time?"

"Yes. Andie and I are in and out."

"Do you know anyone who holds a grudge, or someone who might do what a disgruntled board member wants?"

"That might be anyone. And I wouldn't necessarily know."

Frank eyed her for a moment. "Don't get discouraged. I believe I can find out who it is."

"Do you think so? I hope so. It's a pain in the butt right now." Diane looked at him—his sad eyes, the grim set of his mouth. "I know this must seem trivial, in light of . . . of your friends."

Frank shook his head. "Trivial is restful. Besides, it's a small way to repay you for your help."

Diane took a folder from her desk with the note in it about the change in music at the party. "Could you look at this too? It may be related."

Frank read the note without touching it and raised his eyebrows.

"Someone changed the play list," said Diane. "I know that sounds like an odd thing to worry about, but I'd rather not explain right now."

Frank took the folder and added it with the others. "You want it checked for prints?"

Diane nodded. "Thanks."

Diane looked back down at the photographs on her desk that she'd been trying not to think about. She spread out the ones showing the bedroom where George and Louise Boone were killed.

Crime scenes are ugly. Whatever distinction or beauty a room once possessed is displaced by the look and smell of murdered bodies. Bodies. Victims. Not people anymore, not individuals, always something else. She reached for her professional objectivism that had threatened in past months to pack up and leave, and pulled it to the front of her brain.

The floor plan of the bedroom was laid out such that someone entering through the door would be facing the windows. The bed was immediately to the left. The door opened to the right, so that someone walking into the room would have been seen by George, who was on the side of the bed nearest the door, if he was awake.

It's shocking how death takes away all signs of personality. The dead are hard to recognize, even by family members. People's individual looks are due as much to their animation as to the shapes of their noses or the color of their eyes. Even a still photograph of a live face is more recognizable than a real face in death. And dead bodies never look anything but lifeless—not sleeping, not unconscious, just dead.

Diane couldn't tell what George had looked like. His head and chest were covered with blood. He was on his back, his upper torso almost in the center of the bed, lying against his wife. His right arm was stretched out on the bed. The left arm lay across his middle. His legs were all but covered by bedclothes that were pulled halfway down from his body. Louise Boone lay under a blood-spattered sheet with her face buried in her husband's shoulder. A thick mat of blood covered the left side of her head.

"You said they were shot."

Frank looked up from the papers. "That's what I was told at the scene. What are you saying?"

"That I need to look at the crime scene."

Diane started at a sudden knock on Andie's office door. "Dr. Fallon?"

Not Andie. But the voice through the closed door sounded familiar. Diane lay a piece of paper over the pictures.

"Yes?"

The door opened and the first and second violinists from the string quartet walked in, looking very different in their pantsuits than they had in the gowns they had worn at the reception. Melissa's shoulder-length locks were now trimmed short. The hairstyle was becoming on her well-shaped head.

"Alix, Melissa. What can I do for you?" asked Diane.

They glanced at Frank, who rose and complimented their music.

"Sorry to disturb you, but there's no one in the office," Alix said, indicating Andie's office.

"I'm sure Andie will be back shortly. Can I help you?"

They were silent for just a beat, glancing at each other before Alix spoke. "We just wanted to let you know we've been hired to assist the tour guides. We were told we need to fill out some papers."

"Ms. Fielding also asked us to bring you this."

Melissa's sleeve slid up a fraction as she stretched her arm to hand a file folder to Diane. Diane noticed bruises on her forearm. She made a mental note to call Laura, and as quickly dismissed her concern about the bruises as probably nothing, and none of her business.

"Thanks. How do you think you'll like your new jobs?" Diane opened the folder. A note attached to the first page said that it was paperwork for yet more duplicate orders for supplies.

Melissa's smile made her look pixielike with her new cut. "Great. We start tomorrow learning the nature trail."

"We really appreciate the jobs," said Alix.

"The museum needs dedicated staff, so we're glad to have you," said Diane. "Melissa, I see you cut your hair. It looks very chic."

"It looks good now," said Alix. "You should have seen it when she first whacked it off. She looked like she'd been attacked by a weed eater. I had to even it up for her. I told her if she wants anything done right, don't do it herself."

Both girls laughed, and Diane looked forward to having the two of them around.

"I believe I hear Andie back. She'll give you the forms to fill out."

They closed the door behind them and Diane turned her attention to Frank.

"We need to go to the crime scene," she said.

Chapter 12

There were two cars in the drive as Frank rounded the corner and drove up to the freshly painted two-story farmhouse.

"This place is so secluded in the woods, I've hired some security to keep anyone from taking things out of the house. It looks like that was a good plan. That's the McFarlands."

"George's parents?"

"His mother. She married Gil about five years ago."

As Frank parked the car Diane watched the couple arguing with the security guard, a large man who looked as though he should be able to handle himself. Clearly, however, he wanted to back away from the woman yelling at him. Crystal McFarland was a tall woman, cigarette thin, with hair as blond as yellow corn piled on top of her head. She had on snug-fitting coral capri pants of some shiny fabric. Her matching tank top was stretched tight across her chest, which, Diane guessed by the shape and cleavage, was as natural as the color of her hair. Despite her thin frame, the backs of her arms shook— along with her ornate earrings—as she punched the air with her fist in front of the guard.

Her husband, equally irate, was as lean as she and looked about ten years younger. His straight brown hair came just below his ears. He had on tight jeans and a torn white tee shirt. The mild kyphotic curve of his spine caused his long torso to look slightly concave. Diane guessed it was from years of poor posture and not congenital.

Diane and Frank got out of the car and Diane retrieved the suitcase of crime-scene paraphernalia. She'd had Frank stop by her apartment on the way so she could dig the case from the depths of her closet.

They started toward the house and as they neared, Diane noticed Gil McFarland's hands were stained black with grease. Abruptly, as if the sound of closing car doors only now reached their ears, Crystal and Gil turned.

"This is your doing, Frank Duncan." She came at him with her fists raised. "George was my son, my son, and this is my house, my house—do you hear? Mine." She stopped in front of him and put her hands on her hips. I'm going in *my* house and get *my* things." Her body made a slight twist every time she said *my*. *My house, my things, my son.* They were all the same to her, Diane thought; possessions. Her son was murdered in this house and though understanding that grief manifested itself in many ways, Diane saw none in Crystal McFarland.

"This is Star's house." Frank was calmer than Diane thought she would have been. "And you will not take anything out of it. If you do, I'll have you arrested."

"You always was a turd, even when you was a little kid. Star was nothing to George. Those young 'uns was Louise's doing. Couldn't have 'em herself, so she takes someone else's leavings and passes them off as theirs. I'm George's blood. Star ain't blood."

"George loved Star. He left everything to her. I know, because I am the executor of his will, and I'm going to see that Star gets her inheritance."

"You listen here." Gil stepped up to Frank. "My wife's got her rights."

"Yes," replied Frank. "I can't disagree, but they don't include taking Star's possessions."

"You think you're smart, don't you?" said Crystal. "Always a smarty-pants. Well you ain't smart enough to steal what's mine. I'm going to get me a lawyer and have you arrested." She turned to Diane as if she had just now noticed her standing there.

"Who the hell are you?"

If this wasn't so dreadfully serious, Diane would have laughed at the comic pair these two made. It occurred to her what Frank told her about Detective Janice Warrick allowing Gil McFarland into the crime scene. If she had done that, then she also may not have adequately interviewed him. Looking at Crystal and Gil standing there with their faces twisted in anger, the pair looked to her like suspects.

They're off guard—the thought flashed through her mind and before she realized it, Diane made a decision to play a hunch. "I'm going to examine the crime scene for Star and her attorney. Since she's innocent, we intend to find evidence of the guilty party. Considering the two of you don't have alibis, I'd leave here and not cause trouble." Frank glanced briefly at her and back at the McFarlands.

"What do you mean we don't have alibis?" screeched Crystal. "We were together—all day and all night."

"That's what I mean," said Diane, pushing. "You alibi each other. That's not really an alibi, is it?"

"Listen here. Just what are you saying?" asked Gil. "We didn't have nothing to do with this. We . . . we was at a car show."

"Yeah," agreed Crystal, "a car show."

"What car show? Why didn't you tell the police?"

"They didn't ask, Miss Smarty-Pants."

"So you made that up just now." Diane pressed her advantage. "Making something up on the spur of the moment won't do any good. At an event like a car show, many people would have seen you. You won't be able to find any because you weren't there."

"Now just how the hell do you know?" said Gil. "You sure as hell wasn't with us."

"She's right." The McFarlands whirled around at the sound of a new voice in the argument. The security guard Frank hired had come up and stood just a few feet away. He had a thin smile that threatened to break into a grin.

"I'm what my wife calls a car nut. I go to and organize car shows, and I know there wasn't any in the Southeast then."

"There's that 'un at Gatlinberg that's year round," said Gil. "That's the one we went to."

"No, sorry. Closed for renovations." The guard now grinned broadly.

"Well, ain't you the la-dee-da know-it-all," said Crystal. She spun around to Frank and Diane. "We don't have to tell you nothing. We didn't do nothing, and you can't prove no different."

"That's what the lady is here for," said Frank.

"Now, just a minute. That's my son's house. I've been in there."

"And I was there with the detective looking to see if anything was stolen," said Gil.

"To carry stuff out," said Frank. "How will that look to a jury? You should never have been allowed in the crime scene. It looks to me like you were trying to cover up the fact that your prints were in the bedroom already, and I don't think either George or Louise would have ever invited you into their bedroom."

"You ain't going to find nothing, 'cause there's nothing to find," said Crystal. "Come on, Gil, darlin', we'll go get ourselves a lawyer who'll tell them a thing or two." She and Gil headed for their car. Crystal suddenly turned to Frank. "Tell that Star she can't inherit a thing if she's convicted of George's murder. And she will be. That brat did it. You mark my words—his property and everything will be mine." She raised her chin high, daring Frank to disagree.

"No, Crystal, you won't. Even if Star is convicted of her parents' murder, you aren't in the will."

Crystal stared openmouthed for a moment. "What? You telling me all this goes to somebody else? Who?" Frank didn't answer. "They can't cut me out—I'm the closest blood relative George's got. It's not legal. Gil's cousin's daughter's a paralegal, and I know for a fact you can't cut blood out of your will. We'll just see about this."

The three of them watched the McFarlands get in their '92 Lincoln and drive off, white smoke billowing from the exhaust.

"Well, that was interesting," said the guard.

"It was something," said Frank. Frank introduced Diane and started to lead her into the house.

"I'd like to take a look at the spot where Jay was shot before it gets dark."

He led her to the place where Jay was found, near a live oak with a thick trunk and broad canopy. Diane wondered how old it was—decades older than Jay.

"Here," said Frank, squatting next to a place where someone had dug into the ground.

Diane squatted beside him, scanning the area. "This is where they found the bullet?"

"I believe so."

The sun was sinking behind the tree line; however, a remaining flicker of sunlight reflected on something. She took a pair of tweezers from her pocket, along with an evidence bag and picked up the object.

"What is it?" asked Frank, looking at the curled piece of clear plastic about the size of two postage stamps.

"Plastic."

"Is it important?"

"Might be." Diane put the fragment into the bag and planted a ribbon and nail in the ground. "The pictures aren't clear about which direction the body lay." Frank stood, hesitating for a moment before he spoke. "I know this is hard," said Diane.

"Yeah. I just remembered, today's Louise's birthday." Frank pointed to the house. "Jay's head was pointing toward the house."

"Do you know if they found any gunpowder residue on his jacket? I didn't see any, but . . ." She let the sentence hang as she backed up from where Jay had fallen. "If Detective Warrick's saying he was coming home and was surprised by his sister, why was he shot in the back?"

"I guess she'd say she couldn't face her brother."

"But she'd just killed her parents in their bed." Diane

looked around the grass where she stood. She squatted and scrutinized the area again. Just a couple of feet in front of her she found another plastic fragment smaller than a postage stamp. She bagged it and marked the place.

"Did the crime scene find more of these pieces? I don't see any tags. . . ."

"I don't know what they found. I'll see if I can find out. You think it means something?"

"Possibly." She handed him the bag and he put it in his jacket pocket. "We need to have it analyzed." Diane glanced over at the guard sitting on the porch, watching them. The cost for Star's defense was mounting and it had just begun. Unless the murders were solved soon, there wouldn't be much for Crystal McFarland to fight over.

Diane examined the tree trunk, but saw no obvious blood spatters. She also looked around for more pieces of plastic, but found none.

"OK. Let's go to the house now."

"I think I'll tell Harry he can take a break. How long will we be here?"

"All night."

Chapter 13

Diane stood in George and Louise's bedroom and stared at the bare bloodstained mattress. It had been new; now it was ruined. Before it was a crime scene, their bedroom probably had an airy brightness, with its light pine furniture, green iron garden bench at the foot of the bed, and floral-patterned wallpaper. It was the wallpaper that drew her attention away from the bed and created a frown on her forehead.

Frank stood next to her, his gaze darting from the chest of drawers to the dresser covered with family photographs, to a new green wrought iron headboard still in its box leaning against a wall, and finally to the bed and the bloodstained wall next to it.

"Louise was redecorating the bedroom. You should have heard George complaining on poker night. Said he had to win big just to pay for the new headboard. It's all unfinished. Jay's too—unfinished."

Unconsciously, she grasped Frank's hand and squeezed it. He squeezed back.

"This is going to take all night?" he asked.

She nodded, her thoughts focused on the scene before her. The room smelled of death. It emanated from the mattress, the curtains, the walls. And the house was hot. She felt her scalp prickle with sweat, and she hadn't even begun yet. It was going to be an unpleasant night. She took two pairs of latex gloves from her kit and handed one pair to Frank. He took the gloves but looked at her quizzically.

"You think we still need to protect the crime scene, after all the people that have trampled through here?"

"The gloves are not to protect the crime scene," she said. "They're to protect us from the crime scene."

"It is pretty ripe in here," he said.

"You'll get used to it."

She looked in dismay at the wallpaper as she pulled on her gloves. Antique red roses, gold buttercups, baby's breath and green leaves against a background of tiny flecks of color—and overlain by blood spatters.

She gestured to an area of fine spattering. "See this fine mist pattern here?"

Frank studied the wall, squinting. "Yes."

"This is high-impact spatter from a gunshot. But where the drops are larger—here—these are places of medium impact. And this line of spattering that leads upward to the ceiling. That's castoff from whatever was used to strike them."

"I sort of see. Kind of hard to see on top of that wallpaper."

"That's going to be a problem. It's difficult enough, but the pattern on the wallpaper makes it like a hidden-picture illusion."

"You saying they were shot and beaten?" He asked, as if he had just realized what she had said.

Diane nodded.

"The autopsy will give us the details of that," he said.

"But the autopsy can't tell us what this spatter can. Up on your trig?"

"Trig?"

"Trigonometry."

"Oh. Yes, math I understand."

"Analyzing blood spatters is mostly geometry—you take the two-dimensional pattern from the wall and project to three dimensions."

Diane looked over at Frank. This was the blood of his friends that she was at the moment being so dispassionate about. He was already getting a five o'clock shadow and, though most of the time it made him look sexy, it now made him look more melancholy. "Are you all right with this?" she asked.

"I'm fine." His voice was a little too sharp, but Diane took him at his word and continued.

The only way to do a good job is to find your objectivity and hang on to it like an anchor. That was one of the things that Santos took away from her—for a while.

"What I'll be analyzing is the medium-impact spatter, and I have to measure the two axes—the length and width—of the drops."

Frank turned his face to her, his dark eyes startled. "You're kidding. All of them?"

"Not all, but a significant enough number to make sure I get reliable results."

"I guess that will take all night and then some. Damn, how can you even see them?"

"It'd definitely be easier if she'd chosen plain white wallpaper. I'll use a magnifying glass."

She picked up the glass from her case and showed Frank magnified spatters of blood that had hit the wall.

"A spatter that hits the wall head-on at a perpendicular angle will be round. As the angle of impact gets smaller, the more elongated the drop becomes. See the little tail on most of these drops here?"

"If I hold my head just right and put my tongue between my left molars."

"Now you're getting the idea. The drop goes in the direction of the tail, like a comet. If you've ever spilled anything that has any viscosity at all, you've noticed that phenomenon. Ever have a bottle of ketchup blow up on you and spatter across the table?"

"As a matter of fact, that happened in a restaurant once. Covered me and the people at the next table. I impressed that date. But I don't recollect observing the shape of the drops of ketchup."

Diane watched his face as he smiled. He was trying hard. The thing she had remembered most about Frank was his smile—it made his eyes squint with a mischievous twinkle that made you think he was sharing a joke with you, and it never failed to make her smile back at him.

This one was short-lived. She wished she was someplace else, doing anything else.

"If I were to draw a line along the longest axis of the drops, I'd have the two-dimensional point of convergence."

"Which tells you what?" he asked.

Diane hesitated a moment, biting her lower lip.

"Go ahead and tell me. I'll have to explain it to Star's lawyer—or maybe throw it in Warrick's face. No way you can make it any harder for me than the fact that they're dead."

"I know. I'm sorry. OK. When the perp strikes a blow on a victim, blood is spattered on whatever surface is near. All of those drops in that spatter are part of a set that defines that particular blow. For analysis purposes, they all belong together. When the perp swings his . . . his weapon, it will have blood on it, and that blood will be cast off, making a trail across the wall, the ceiling or whatever, depending on how he swings it. The victim, if he isn't unconscious with the first blow, will move around. When he is hit again, it will leave another set of spatters, but at a different angle, with a different point of convergence. Finding the different lines of convergence can tell me how many times the victim was struck and where the victim was located at the time of each blow."

Frank nodded. "That makes sense. So if you know that the more elongated the drop, the more acute the angle of impact, then you can compute the angle. What is it? Something like, the sine of the angle equals the width over the length?"

"You *are* good at trig."

"I was going to get a degree in math until my father asked what kind of job I could get with it. I went into accounting instead."

"And that led to crime?"

"I was determined to make as little money as possible."

Diane took out a calculator, a protractor, and a roll of trajectory string.

"What's that? Fishing line? What else you got?"

Diane watched as he poked around in her blood-spatter analysis kit.

"I'll attach this string to one end of a drop with a push pin, compute the angle, align the string to the angle, and anchor the other end of the string. After I do several drops that way, the strings will cross at the point of origin of the blood source. I'll probably end up with several points of origin, all at different heights and distances from the wall. I should be able to do a fair job of reconstructing the scene when I'm finished."

Diane hoisted her case up on the nightstand and opened it. "I'll start by marking off sections of the wall and taking pictures of each section. After that, I'll start measuring and recording."

She took out a small laptop computer. "Kenneth Meyers says he's going to give me a new laptop. Some top-of-the-line model he has."

"Ken's as much a go-getter as Mark Grayson, though not as obnoxious. He's been trying to get me to recommend his computers to the Atlanta PD," said Frank.

Diane shook her head as she reached down and plugged in her computer. "Are you going to do it?"

"I told him I'm not the one to ask. I have a tough time just getting pencils."

"Hand me that flashlight," she said.

"You find something?"

Diane took the light from his hand, wondering if the batteries still worked. "This is new carpet, you said. When was it laid?"

"George started complaining about it about a month and a half ago. About that long ago, I guess. What did you find?"

"A round imprint in the carpet between the nightstand and the bed."

She angled the flashlight until it showed the depression. It was hard to see, barely there. In another day or so the new carpet would spring back up and it would be gone.

"Hold the light and let me take a couple of pictures."

Diane laid a small ruler next to the depression and snapped several photographs with her digital camera. She checked the images in the viewer to make sure she had gotten a clear picture.

"Did George keep a baseball bat by his bed?"

"I don't know. I'll ask Star. That does look as if the business end of a baseball bat stood there, doesn't it? I wonder if Warrick found it."

"I'm having a difficult time grasping the idea that she was so completely incompetent here." Diane took a pair of calipers, measured the indentation, and recorded the information on her computer.

"I'm not saying she doesn't have potential. She just doesn't have the experience."

"But letting McFarland in the crime scene. Even inexperienced criminalists know better."

"I know. I got the impression Warrick knew Crystal— that they were friends or something. Hell, maybe Crystal did her hair."

Diane used her digital camera and markers and began the process of photographing the bloodstained wall.

"While you're in here, I'm going to search Jay's room. I'd like to examine his computer, if Warrick didn't take it. Maybe I'll find some clue as to what he was doing out late that night."

Diane had prepared a small maze of string when she realized it was getting dark outside. Subconsciously, she heard muted sounds of Frank in a far bedroom moving things around. Other than those muffled noises, she was aware of nothing but numbers. Tuning out the grimness, the gore on the walls, the smell of the room—there was nothing but the silent crunch of numbers creating lines of trajectory.

"How about a break?" Diane started at the sudden voice coming from the doorway.

"Oh, hey. I lost track of time." She looked at her watch. "A break's probably a good idea. I could use a

couple of minutes out of this room." She anchored the
end of the string she was holding and the two of them
went downstairs and out on the porch.

It had gotten dark and there was only a sliver of a
moon. Out here the stars shone bright in the night sky.
The light from the living room windows gave off only a
dim glow, so the two of them sat mostly in the dark on
the top step. Diane watched the fireflies and listened to
the crickets.

Beside her, Frank patted his pocket. "Wish I hadn't
given up smoking. I could use a cigarette about now."

"Did you find anything in Jay's room?" she asked.

Frank didn't say anything for a moment, and Diane
looked over at him. She could see his eyes were misty
with tears.

"His fishing gear, soccer uniform, his CD player—all
the things left of his life. Jay and I used to go fishing a
lot. George liked to hunt, but Jay really didn't like the
idea of shooting things. But he liked fishing. He was
good at fly-fishing, too. You know, that's not easy. On
weekends during the summer, me, George and Jake
Houser would take our sons and go up to my cabin.
George, Jake and Dylan would go hunting. Jay, Kevin
and I would fish. I was thinking as I went through his
things, at least it's easier on George and Louise. I'd go
crazy if I lost Kevin—especially like this."

Diane hugged her legs to her and lay a cheek on her
knees, listening to an owl in the distance.

"They'd taken his computer," Frank continued. "I
guess I should be glad that Warrick at least made like
she was collecting evidence. But I'd sure like to take a
look at his hard drive."

"Maybe your cop friend—Izzy—can tell you what's
on it."

"I'd like to examine it myself. It's like you and blood
spatters—you have to know about computers to be able
to extract all the evidence that's on them. You have to
know where to look and how to look. Besides, Izzy's a
uniform cop and there's a limit to what he can get for

me from Warrick's investigation. Izzy's gone out on a limb as it is."

Diane didn't say anything for a moment. She imagined that the police department had somebody who could look at the hard drive. Then she remembered that Frank was an expert in computers and computer fraud. "Maybe they'll let you look at it."

Frank looked over at her. "Yeah, right."

"You can ask."

"I searched Star's room too. Nothing helpful. Except it seemed to be empty of current personal things—it was more like looking at her past. I've been thinking about George and Louise being both shot and beaten. That usually means two perps, right? Two different weapons." Frank seemed to be struggling for words. "I can't help but wonder . . . I mean, there's Star and her boyfriend . . . on drugs. It's just, I can't imagine Star with that much hate. . . . You have to have a lot of pent up hate to overkill. Isn't that right?"

"Don't go reconstructing the crime scene before we've collected the evidence. We don't know anything right now. We know that they were shot. The coroner did say that at the scene, didn't he?" Frank nodded. "And at least one was also hit. We don't know if both were beaten, and we don't know how many people were involved. Now we just have a crime scene. Let me finish processing it. Tomorrow we'll sit down and talk about it."

"You're right." Frank stood up and pulled Diane up with him. "Look, neither of us has had anything to eat. There's a Krystal down the road. You like those little square cheeseburgers, don't you? Why don't I go get some food and bring it back."

"Sure . . . that's a good idea." Diane stretched the kinks out of her back. "And bring back plenty of coffee too." She opened the screen door and started back inside. "I'll be upstairs, working."

Chapter 14

Before Diane began again with her grim work, she picked up a silver framed photograph sitting on the dresser and looked at it. It was a studio shot of the family. Family portraits rarely tell the whole truth. They always show a happy family. That's their job, and they do it so well that all who look upon the smiling faces of a family touched by tragedy never fail to be astounded that this terrible thing could have happened to them.

The Boone family portrait was like that. They all looked happy—and so different from the only other photos she had seen of them. George and Louise were in the center of the picture, their bodies slightly facing each other and their faces turned toward the camera.

George's tanned face testified that he spent time outdoors. His short dark brown hair was receding slightly. His dark eyes, staring at Diane from the picture, looked friendly. Louise had what might be called a perky face. Her smile was big and crinkled the corners of her hazel eyes. Her shoulder-length brown hair and bangs made her look carefree and young.

Jay's forearm rested on his father's back, as if casually leaning against him, a broad smile illuminating his face. He looked so young. He and Star looked alike—dark hair, dark eyes, same slender straight noses. Star's hair was a short cut with one side combed over and longer than the other. A blond streak on each side framed her face. She had the same charming grin as her brother. It was hard to imagine that Star could turn on her family. But family portraits aren't meant to show the dark side.

Diane set the picture down beside the other photographs of various family members— cousins, aunts, uncles, grandparents? She noted that there were none of Crystal McFarland.

She disengaged herself from thoughts about the family, glad she hadn't known them, and began again with her task of measuring their drops of blood, computing angles, stringing trajectory lines. The work had such inherent tedium and required such focus, it was easy to keep her mind on the task and not try to analyze the data before all of it was in. But she did have a few ideas forming. An interview with Star would be good. Perhaps Frank would arrange it.

As she measured and computed in the quiet house, sounds subtly began to ease into her consciousness —the owl she'd heard earlier, the house settling. *House settling*—what did that mean exactly? What was actually settling? The wood framing? And why was it starting now?

She stopped a moment, as she often did when stray thoughts began intruding too far into her task. A straying mind makes mistakes. She put down her tools, stretched, and kneaded her tired shoulders. Her stomach growled, and she looked at her watch. Frank seemed to be taking his time. Probably buying several of everything so they could have a choice. She smiled at the memory of the stack of doughnuts he had brought to her apartment.

There it was again—a creaking, like one board rubbing against another. Now that she wasn't making any noise, the settling sound was louder. She listened, wondering if all old houses make sounds. *Creak*. She walked around the bed to the doorway and listened. Nothing. *Silly,* she thought, mentally reminding herself that it had been Melissa in Andie's office and not some intruder, and that she was apt to become crazy and paranoid if she didn't watch herself.

She had started to pick up her measuring tools when she heard it again. From her vantage point by the door, it seemed to be coming from the stairs. It reminded her of the jump tales told around campfires—the ones where the ghost keeps saying: "I'm on the first step. . . . I'm on the second step. . . ." Now she *was* being silly.

Of course, it could be Frank coming back and setting up in the kitchen or somewhere before he called to her. *This is ridiculous,* she thought. She headed for the stairs. From the top she peered down the stairway into the darkness. Hadn't the lights been on downstairs?

"Frank?" she called out. No response. It wasn't him. It was probably nothing. She turned to go back to work, determined to keep her mind on what she was doing. There it was again; another creaking sound. A hand clasped on her arm from behind.

Diane jumped instinctively and pulled away, but the hand stayed, the grip biting into her upper arm. She grabbed at the fingers as she was pulled and shoved, trying to turn around to see who it was. She was pushed forward through a doorway and fell on her shoulder, skidding on a rug across a hardwood floor, bumping her head on some piece of furniture. She saw the butcher knife looming over her before she saw the face of the person who held it.

"I'll cut you with this. I will."

Diane looked into the twisted face of a boy of about sixteen, his tangled brown hair falling into his eyes. His clothes looked as if he'd been living in a cave. They were wrinkled, dirty and covered with cobwebs.

"You're Star's boyfriend, aren't you?" Diane found herself saying with more resolve than she felt.

"Shut up!"

She clutched the dresser she had landed next to and pulled herself to her feet. Her gaze darted around the room. Cedar bed and dresser, buck head mounted above the green-and-red plaid-covered bed, no personal items. The guest room? Had he been living here? No. It was too neat. Her mind was a whirl of questions and her head hurt.

He stood a few feet away. Holding the knife toward

her. "I heard you and him talking. You want to pin this on me—me and Star."

"No, that's not true."

He waved the knife. "Don't lie. I heard you talking. I heard what he was saying."

"What you heard was fear that maybe Star did it. You heard fear, not certainty. You heard when he talked about Star, he couldn't even make a complete sentence. Frank loves Star. She's the daughter of his best friend. He's her guardian now, and he's scared to death for her. If you were listening, you had to have heard that." Diane thought she saw a subtle change in his features. "Do you know who did this?" she asked.

"I didn't. Neither did Star."

"Why, then, are you standing here holding a knife on me?"

" 'Cause . . . Look, shut up. You don't know nothing."

"Why don't you tell me?" She heard the high-pitched sound of her phone ringing in the other room. "That's my phone. He'll expect me to answer it."

"He'll just think you went to the bathroom or turned it off."

"At any rate, he'll be back soon."

"I know." He paced back and forth between her and the door. "I got to think."

"What are you doing here?"

"Don't talk. I got to think."

"What's your name?"

"Look, what do I have to do to get you to shut up?"

"Why did you pull me in here? Why didn't you just hide out until we left? You must want something."

"I thought you were going to search the house, and I'd get you first. And maybe you have some money."

"Okay, now that you have me first, what are you going to do?"

He took a couple of steps toward her. "I could get rid of you."

"If you didn't kill Star's parents, why start now? Look, let me help you. What's your name?"

"Dean! It's Dean. Are you satisfied? Don't you think I know you just want to turn me in?"

"Turning yourself in might not be a bad idea."

"It sounds like a bad idea to me. You people are all alike. You have to have control, tell me what to do."

"No. You have control over what you do. You make up your own mind. I'm just suggesting you do something that works. This isn't working for you. Look at yourself in the mirror. Unless rheumy eyes and snot running out of your nose is a new fad like green hair and body piercing, you're not doing that well. You're hungry, you're alone, the police are looking for you—it's not working."

He wiped his nose on the sleeve of his jacket. "Yeah, and just what do you think turning myself in will do?"

"It will be a start in solving this. It will look really good for you if your lawyer can say to the court that you turned yourself in because you're innocent and want to help find out who killed your girlfriend's parents."

"Like they're going to believe that. Besides, I can't afford a lawyer. They'll just give me one of those free ones that don't know nothing."

"Do you know how to make a silencer?"

He looked at Diane as if she were the one on drugs. "What? A silencer? Like a hit man uses? That metal thing you screw on your gun? No, I don't know how to make one. How would I know how to make one of those?"

"How did you and Star get her grandfather's coins?"

"Why are you asking me all these questions?"

"I want to help. Right now, that's why the police are holding her. They think she took the coins after she killed her parents."

"That's a load of crap. She came back here and got them a couple of weeks ago. Been hanging on to them like they meant something."

"Crystal McFarland told the police that the coins were in the house until the Boones were killed."

"That's a lie. How the fuck would she know anyway? Like Star's father didn't hate her worse than me."

"Dean, why don't you tell me everything? I'm trying

to find out who killed Star's family. Right now, I don't believe it was Star or you. Won't you put the knife down and talk to me?"

"I'll hold on to the knife."

"Make yourself look innocent. You think I'm going to jump you if you put it down?"

"No, but he will when he comes back."

"No, he won't. Not if you don't have a weapon. Look, if I know him, when he gets back he'll have enough food for an army. We'll all sit down in the dining room and talk."

As if on cue, Diane heard a car door slam. Dean gripped his knife tighter and looked at her, wide-eyed.

Chapter 15

Diane held her breath as the door opened.

"Hey, I called . . ."

"Frank, this is Dean. He's going to eat with us and tell us about himself and Star. I hope you brought enough food."

Frank stood in the front doorway, two large sacks of fast food in his arms, and stared at Diane and the teenager standing beside her.

"Hello, Dean," he said, stepping inside and kicking the door closed behind him. "Shall we go into the dining room?"

The dining room, between the kitchen and foyer, was a bright yellow. Wilted parlor palms and peace lilies stood in the corners. Diane made a mental note to water them before she left. The round oak table had been dusted for fingerprints. She went into the kitchen to get something to use to wipe it off.

She stopped for a moment to look around. All the appliances, including the mixer, were pink. The floor was a checkerboard of black-and-white tiles. The countertops were a classic fifties design of squares with rounded corners and tiny antennae—the iconic symbol of the popular new and powerful innovation of the time, the television screen. Louise Boone had loved her home, she had loved to decorate it and loved to make it fun. Diane wet some paper towels, took some all-purpose squirt cleaner from under the sink and went to the dining room to remove the detritus left from collecting evidence of Louise's murder.

They sat around the table and Frank pulled out the

mounds of food he had brought back—cheeseburgers, corn dogs, chili-cheese pups, French fries, Cokes and a thermos full of coffee.

Dean downed four Krystal cheeseburgers and was on his second corn dog before he said anything. "We were in Atlanta when her parents were killed."

"Is there anyone who will alibi you?" asked Frank.

"Not anyone the police would believe."

"You said Star took the coins about two weeks ago," said Diane. "Is there any proof of that?"

He threw a French fry on the table. "I knew you wouldn't believe me."

"That's not it," said Diane. "Star was arrested because of the coins. If we can show the police proof that she already had them, then we'll have a better chance of getting her released."

"And proving that McFarland bitch is a liar? I don't know. We came in when her parents were gone. She knew where they kept them. Said they were hers anyway, for her education. What would be proof? It's not like she signed them out."

"Did anyone see them?"

"Are you kidding? To Star they were the family jewels. She hid them, and even I didn't know where they were." Dean kicked his chair legs as he talked and fidgeted in his seat. He grabbed hold of a Coke and drank down half of it. "Is it true they used to be made with real coke—you know, cocaine?"

"Early on, it was made with trace amounts of the coca leaf," said Frank.

Dean giggled. "I wish they still made it that way." He pushed on his forehead with the heel of his hand. "Do you have anything for a headache?" He wiped his nose with a napkin.

"I think I can probably find something," said Frank. He left the table and came back in two or three minutes with a bottle of aspirin and gave Dean a couple.

"Man, I need more than that."

"Start with that and I'll give you some more later. Where have you and Star been living?"

"Different places. I got this cousin in Atlanta."

"What's his name?" Frank asked, picking up a chili-cheese pup and taking a bite.

"Her. Why do you want to know?"

"Anything we can get to verify where the two of you were, the better for you and Star," said Diane.

"She'll get all mad if I bring trouble to her. The only way she'd let us stay was if Star'd clean her house and take care of her baby."

Diane raised an eyebrow and took a bite of her cheeseburger.

"And you," said Frank. "How did you contribute?"

"I got odd jobs."

"Were you there when Star's parents were killed?"

He shook his head. "We'd moved on by then."

"Where to? I thought you said you were in Atlanta?"

"Places. Around Atlanta. Why you asking so many questions? You're just like Star's parents. Always wanting to know our business."

"You may know things you're not even aware are important," said Frank, pushing another cheeseburger in Dean's direction. "Where did you and Star stay after you left your cousin's?"

"We camped out some. That was fun."

"How did the two of you eat? What were you living on?"

"Odd jobs. I told you."

"What kind of odd jobs?"

"People pay for stuff. No big deal."

Both Diane and Frank let that rest for now. "Why didn't Star want to come home?" asked Frank.

"Her parents were too hard to get along with. They'd gotten into some kind of tough-love crap someone at their church was feeding them. They didn't understand me or Star. Them folks think by calling something love, it's good. They kicked Star out. I bet they didn't tell you that."

From the look on Frank's face, Diane guessed Dean was right. That might account for their desperate attempt to lie about the bone in order to get the police to look for her—guilt and fear that their tough love might have driven her to her death.

"Tell me, Dean, do your parents have a pile of animal bones behind their house?" asked Diane.

"Lady, you ask the weirdest questions. Silencers and now bones. No, not that I know of, they don't. What would Mom and Dad be doing with a pile of bones behind the house?"

"Why don't you go back to your parents?" asked Diane.

"Dad's always drinking and Mom's always fussing and crying. They don't want me back, and I don't want to go back."

"Dean, can you think of anyone that saw you about the time Star's parents were killed?" asked Diane.

"I don't know. I think we were with some friends in Cherokee County. They don't want anything to do with the police."

"They don't have to get involved with the police. All they would have to do is say you were there," said Frank.

"Trust me. They wouldn't make a good alibi."

"Dean. I have a son," said Frank. "He has this dog—a lab who loves to play keep-away. She gets a stick, or one of her toys, and brings it to you. Just as you reach out to get it, she pulls it away and runs. I think you like that game too. I know you think you're being pretty smart, keeping information from us while you get to scarf up our food, but it's not smart. And you aren't doing yourself a favor."

"Look. These guys are probably gone. Anyway, they'd just say we weren't there, and that'd be worse."

"Do you know anyone who might have killed Star's family?" asked Frank.

"No. I just know we didn't. Star's been going crazy, especially about her brother, Jay." Dean took another drink of Coke and got another corn dog. "What are you two doing upstairs?"

"Looking for clues," said Frank. "How did you get in the house?"

"The back way."

"It's locked."

"Star showed me how to get in when we got the coins."

"Show me," said Frank.

"No. I told Star I wouldn't tell anybody."

"Look, son—" said Frank.

"I'm not your son. I'm not anybody's son, so don't you call me that."

"OK, Dean. Let me take you down to the police station. We'll tell them you want to clear your name."

"So you're going to turn me in anyway."

"I know it doesn't seem like it to you, but it would really be best if you went to the police yourself. They will find you eventually," said Frank.

"Not unless you turn me in, they won't. I've got friends."

"No one has enough of that kind of friends. You've already said your friends won't give you an alibi. Your own cousin made you work in order to stay at her place. You'll just get into more and more trouble unless you start getting your life together now."

"Look, it was nice of you guys to feed me and all, but . . ." He jumped up from the table. "Gotta go. . . ." he sang as he ran to the front door and threw it open.

"Hey, young fella, where you going in such a hurry?"

Diane had jumped up after Dean. Frank followed. A barrel-chested man in a Rosewood policeman's uniform held Dean by the arm. "Drove by and saw some lights on. Thought something might be going on. Frank Duncan, what are you doing here?"

"I'm having Dr. Fallon take a look at the crime scene."

"Is that a fact? This young fella here helping?"

"He was on his way to turn himself in," said Frank.

"Was he now? In a bit of a hurry to do that, it seems. What's he doing here?"

Frank shrugged. "Looking for some kind of help, I suppose. We've been having a late meal." Frank pointed from the foyer into the dining room. "And he's been telling us about where he's been and how he'd like to clear all this up. Weren't you, son?"

"Sure."

"Well, then, we'll go, and you can tell the detectives why you and your girlfriend were trying to sell her parents' coin collection."

Dean looked at Diane and Frank. Diane guessed he wasn't sure whether or not to go along with what Frank had said or to protest. He looked at Diane again and she held his gaze, cocking an eyebrow, silently reminding him of the butcher knife and his attack on her. Dean's shoulders sagged, and the policeman led him away without protest.

Diane didn't say anything until Frank had closed and locked the door. "You called the police when you went to get the aspirin, didn't you?"

Frank nodded. "That was Izzy Wallace. I knew he was on duty. I called his cell phone so I'd get through quickly and told him to come in about fifteen minutes. I knew the little punk wasn't going to give himself up."

"What did I just witness? Your version of good cop, bad cop?"

"Yeah. I told Izzy I want to remain on good terms with the kid if I can." He smiled and motioned toward the dining room. "I brought some apple turnovers I was saving from that little bio-vac. Now that he's gone, why don't we have them with some coffee?

"Sure. Then I have to get back to work."

They sat down and Frank fished out the apple turnovers and poured two cups of coffee in a couple of Styrofoam cups.

"I wonder how he got in here. I'll have to look for a key to the back door. The little creep may have pocketed it."

"He came in through the basement," said Diane. "Did you see his clothes?"

"Ah, I'll bet you're right. I'll have to secure the windows. Very observant of you."

"Look for any bones while you're down there. You might check the garage too. If both Jay and his father got the bone from a pile, Jay might have taken some more he thought were cool. We might get a clue as to where they came from."

"Good thinking. I'm glad you're working on all cylinders this late."

"I was refreshed by the adrenaline rush I got from Dean."

"How did you find him?"

"He surprised me upstairs. Knocked me on my ass and threatened me with a knife."

Diane said it so calmly it took Frank a second to respond. When he did, it came out as an explosion.

"What! Why didn't you say something?"

"I thought he had a lack of resolve."

"Lack of resolve? Are you crazy? The kid's probably on or coming off drugs, and he's desperate. You can't take chances like that."

"Like what? We were alone in the house. He had a knife. I talked him down. Was that dangerous? Yes. However, I didn't really have a choice."

"You should have said something to me."

"He was disarmed. I thought we might get some information from him. As it was, he didn't know anything. Or won't tell. The knife's up in the guest room on the dresser, if you would like to have a look, get some prints or something." Diane took the last bite of her pastry, wiped her hands on a napkin and stood up. "If you clear up our trash, I'll water these plants. Then I have to get back upstairs."

Chapter 16

The sun had been up a couple of hours when Diane finished. The last thing she did was to collect blood samples. She had photographed, drawn and diagramed the impact and cast-off spatters. She had measured and located the point of origin of the medium-impact spatters, so that now the trajectory string displayed an eerie blow-by-blow scene of the events that took away George and Louise Boone.

"It looks like a giant cat's cradle." Frank stood in the doorway with a box under his arm.

"Do I look as tired as you?" Diane asked.

"Not a bit."

"Liar."

Frank surveyed the crisscrossed string from different angles. "What can you tell me?"

"Can you get me the autopsy reports first—and get these samples analyzed at a crime lab?"

"I'll get you the reports tomorrow. About the samples, that'll take longer."

"I'm going to plug my numbers into a computer program." She gestured toward the bloodstained wall. "It will show us a three-D image of what the string is showing us. Come to my office tomorrow with the report and we'll talk. What's in the box?"

"You were right. I found a couple more bones in the garage."

"Let me see."

Diane took the box from him, set it on the dresser

and opened the flaps. Inside was a deer skull and what she thought was a racoon skull—items Jay probably thought were cool enough to keep. The Boones probably believed the bone they showed Frank belonged to this deer.

"Let me take these back to the museum."

"Sure. Diane, I know this has been a pretty big favor. I appreciate what you've done for me."

You have no idea, she thought.

Diane stopped by her apartment and took a long shower—as hot as she could stand it. She soaped up and just let the water run over her body. She didn't realize how long she had stayed until the water started getting cool. She stepped out of the shower, dried off and went to the closet to select clothes, giving the bed a longing glance as she passed by. Damn Frank and his favors. Her dreams would probably recur after this. She selected a maroon pantsuit and pulled it onto her still-weary body.

Out in the hallway, Mrs. Odell came charging out of her apartment. "I want you to know, I took Marvin to the hospital today. Allergies. If you don't get rid of that cat, I'm going to sue you for every penny you've got."

"Mrs. Odell, I don't have a cat. Have you talked to the landlady?"

"Humpf, a lot of good that does. She refused to let me search your apartment."

"Good for her. Do you think maybe someone else here has a cat?"

"There's the upstairs people, the downstairs people and us. It has to be on this floor, and we are the only ones here."

"I can't help you, Mrs. Odell. I don't have a cat, but I do have to get to work. I hope Mr. Odell gets better soon."

"Poor man. I got some funeral home brochures for him to look at while he's there. It was the only thing that cheered him up."

Diane started to say something, but kept her mouth

shut. She didn't even want to know. She headed for
the stairs.

When she arrived at the museum parking lot and got
out of her car, she saw two spaces over that Alix Nils
seemed to be involved in an argument with Mike Seger,
the geology student who supplied the content for the
computer animations.

She heard Mike say, "Why don't you get a life, Alix—
or help—and leave us alone?"

Alix fixed a stare on Mike that would have killed him
had it been bullets. "Don't . . ."

"Is there a problem, Alix?" said Diane, stopping next
to the car.

Both of them turned abruptly and stared at her.

"Problem?" said Alix, recovering her composure. "No.
Just having a word with Melissa's boyfriend."

Melissa's boyfriend. Diane looked over at him sharply.
He must have noticed her expression, for he narrowed
his eyes very slightly. It was then she noticed that both
he and Alix were wearing museum tee shirts.

"Are you working here?"

"Part-time," he answered. "Dr. Lymon is my major
professor, and she asked me to assist her here."

Alix and her boyfriend—and his father, and now Melissa and her boyfriend. This was getting to be one big
family affair.

"I guess I'll be seeing more of you around, then,"
said Diane.

"I guess so."

"Are the two of you coming or going?"

"We just arrived," said Alix.

Alix and Mike avoided looking at each other as they
walked into the museum with Diane. Alix stepped into
the elevator to go to the third floor where the docents'
office was located. Mike watched the closed elevator
doors for a moment, then turned to Diane.

"Dr. Fallon, Dr. Lymon wanted me to ask you about
the office space."

"What do you think of the office space?"

"Me? I, uh, I like it. It's near the rock lab and the exhibits."

"Good. Then perhaps you can persuade her of its good qualities."

Mike made a pained face. "She was thinking maybe a larger office is available."

"No, one isn't."

"All right, I'll try to sell her on the one we have."

"I would appreciate it."

Mike took the stairs to the second floor, and Diane headed down the hallway to her office. Instead of using her private entry, she went to Andie's office.

"Andie, how is everything this morning?"

"Great. Some more of the Bartrum faculty curators are moving in today. So far, most of them like the facilities, especially the lab space. So did you and Frank go out last night?" Andie sat behind her desk, grinning, her hypercurly hair held on top of her head with Japanese hairpins.

"In a manner of speaking. He asked me to examine the house where his friends were murdered."

"Oh, great. Dinner and a crime scene. I'm going to have to give him lessons on romantic evenings. He did at least feed you, didn't he?"

"We had takeout from Krystal."

"Lessons, definitely needs lessons."

Korey burst into Andie's office looking winded. "Dr. Fallon, we had a break-in in the lab."

"A break-in? What was stolen?"

"Nothing—that I can find. The drawers are pulled out, things scattered. It looks more like a vandal, or someone looking for something."

"Have you called security?"

"I thought I'd call you first."

Diane had a pang of guilt for having not yet hired a chief of security. It was time she did that. She and Korey walked up the stairs to the second-floor conservation lab. On the way, Diane stopped at the security office and asked the guard on duty, Chanell Napier, a slender, round-faced black woman, to come with her.

"Do you know who was on duty last night?"

"Leonard and that new kid, the skinny one with the red hair."

"Bernie," said Korey. "He's the one scared of the skeletons in the primate room."

"Yeah, that's the one."

Oh, great, thought Diane.

Diane examined the lock on the second-floor lab door. It indeed had tool marks all over the brass plating. However, any tool the size of a screwdriver or larger would have gotten them into the room. Her guess was that they got in with a key.

Inside she was greeted by a sullen group of Korey's assistants, who stood in the middle of the room with their arms folded, angry that someone had violated their space and was now keeping them from their work. The room was in disarray—mostly open drawers and cabinets, supplies pulled out and dumped on the floor, equipment moved. A box of latex gloves lay with its contents scattered across the floor, along with packages of photographic paper, pens, exhibit forms. It looked to be mostly a mess, with no real destruction.

"Any damage?" she asked.

"I haven't tested all the equipment, but I think it's all right," said Korey.

"What about the vault?" Diane walked to the back of the room to the environmentally-controlled storage vault. Someone had pried at the handle, marked up the door jam, but it appeared that they were unsuccessful in gaining entry. Only she and Korey had a key to the vault.

"Someone was looking for something." Diane glanced around the room.

"It doesn't look like they found it. I checked the vault," said Korey. "They didn't get in."

As she walked around the room looking at what the intruder had done, her gaze stopped on one of the work-tables. A handprint was visible on its polished surface—or rather the terminal and intermediate phalanges of four fingers, as if someone had gripped the tabletop and squatted down to pull out the drawer.

"Does this belong to any of you?"

They all came over to look, but all shook their heads.

"I doubt it," said one of the assistants. "The last thing we all do is clean the surfaces before we leave."

Korey nodded in agreement.

"Don't we have a fingerprint kit in the security office? Would you mind getting it for me?"

The security guard nodded and left. Diane turned to Korey.

"I wonder what they were after."

"I've no idea. Most of the really valuable stuff is in the exhibits."

"Was anyone working late last night?"

"Barbara and I were here until nine. Nothing strange happened, no strangers hanging around."

"How about people who weren't strangers?"

"No. It was pretty quiet. Bernie came in and looked around on his rounds, but that's all. That was a little after eight, I guess."

Chanell Napier came back with a black carrying case about the size of a small suitcase. "I called the police while I was down there."

"Good." Diane set the case on a stool, opened it, and began searching through the materials for the things she needed.

"Shouldn't the police be doing that?" asked one of Korey's assistants.

"They won't," answered another assistant, before Diane could say anything. "My dad's house was robbed a year ago. They took the television, Mom's jewelry, and my brother's computer. The police told them they probably wouldn't get any of their stuff back. They didn't even look for fingerprints or canvas the neighborhood."

"I thought they always tested for fingerprints," said the first assistant.

"No. And Dad was really pissed. When this fracas with the city council and the mayor started, he wrote letters to the editor about how sloppy the police were. If they won't take fingerprints for a burglary, they sure won't when nothing was stolen."

As they spoke with each other, Diane examined the print on the table, determining which of the various methods of obtaining a good impression would be best. She closed the case and asked Korey to bring her a camera.

"You're not going to take it after all?" The guard sounded disappointed.

"I think the best method will be to photograph it and enhance the photo. Check the trash for any latex gloves that might have been thrown away. Whoever made this had on gloves."

"Then you can't get a print anyway," said an assistant.

"For any of you contemplating a life of crime," said Diane, taking the camera and tripod Korey handed her, "I'll tell you a little secret. Surgical gloves fit like a second skin. Fingerprints can show through them."

Diane mounted the camera on the tripod Korey set up, set it for greatest depth of field and took several shots. "Korey, can you get that light and shine it under this ledge? If I'm not mistaken, there should be a thumbprint."

She and Korey looked under the edge of the table, but saw nothing.

"Nothing visible," said Diane. "You have a UV light, don't you?"

"Yeah, for detecting microorganisms," answered Korey.

"There's one in the fingerprint kit," said the security guard. "In the leather pouch." She pulled out the pouch and retrieved the light. "Battery operated." Diane looked at her. "I went through the kit."

Diane laughed as she reached for the orange goggles. "Okay, you guys without goggles step back." She turned on the light and looked under the table. There it was: a large thumbprint—faint, but she could enhance it.

"We don't have any of that superglue stuff," said Chanell.

"Cyanoacrylate. I guess we're going to have to make sure we have a better supplied security office." Diane grinned at her. "I'll use powder. I think that should do."

"Were you a crime-scene expert in another life?" asked one of Korey's assistants.

"Forensic anthropologist," Korey answered for her.

"Cool."

"Where I worked, it was a good idea to learn everything," Diane said.

She chose a magnetic powder and brush from the case. Holding a piece of paper under the table edge to catch the powder that fell, she dusted the print and removed the excess with a magnet. It was faint, but usable. Diane lifted it with tape, which she placed on a backing card.

Just as she finished, the door to the conservation lab opened and Andie came in with two policemen and another man in a gray suit, matching hair and a sour expression.

The mayor, Diane thought. She wondered why a little break-in at the museum rated the mayor's assistance.

Chapter 17

One of the policemen was Izzy Wallace, whom she'd met the evening before. The other one she had caught a glimpse of on the porch when he came with Izzy to the Boone house.

Diane had an uneasy feeling in her gut, but didn't know why. Something about Izzy's demeanor the previous evening and the mayor's expression now.

"Will you develop this, Korey?" Diane handed him the camera and slipped the fingerprint card in the pocket of her blazer. "Chanell, take the fingerprint kit back to the office, please."

"Sure, Dr. Fallon."

Diane washed her hands at the sink and turned to greet the police. "Thanks for coming." She held out her hand.

"Nice to see you again," said Izzy, giving her hand a firm shake.

"How's your guest?" asked Diane.

"Not a happy camper, but at least he's tucked away safe and sound."

Izzy was courteous, but not friendly. She turned to the mayor.

"Mayor Sutton, nice of you to come visit the museum," she said, taking his offered hand. His handshake was a little too hard to be polite. He'd have to work on it if he wanted to campaign for governor.

"I thought it would be a good time to meet you," the mayor said. "I'm sorry I couldn't be at your . . . event the other evening. Pressing matters. But perhaps we can talk now, privately."

"Of course. Korey, fill the policemen in on the break-in."

She started to escort the mayor to Korey's office, but it had a large window open to the lab.

"This way," she said, and they stepped out into the hallway.

As they emerged into the hallway, an older man, about five foot seven, if he weren't slightly stooped in the shoulders, stopped to greet her. "Dr. Fallon. I wanted to thank you for the opportunity to work here." With his white hair, bushy eyebrows, toothbrush moustache and crystal blue eyes he might have been a wizard dressed up in modern, albeit well-worn clothes.

"Jonas Briggs." Diane clasped his outstretched hands in hers. "My pleasure. This is—"

"Mayor Walter Sutton," Jonas said. "Yes, we've met, after a fashion. Crossed verbal swords in the city council meetings. Democracy is a wonderful thing, don't you think, Mayor?"

The expression on the mayor's face suggested that he didn't think democracy was wonderful at all. "Yes, yes," he muttered.

"Jonas, may I use your office?" she asked.

"Certainly. It's unlocked. I was just going to the staff lounge. Introduce myself to some of the people in the museum here."

Jonas Briggs looked like a man who had found a home.

"His office is on this floor," Diane told the mayor. "We'll use it, rather than going downstairs to mine."

Jonas' office was across from the archaeology exhibits, the smallest section in the museum. In the back of his office was a small workroom. Through its open doorway Diane could see pieces of broken pottery sitting on worktables.

In his outer office he had already moved in large book-cases and filled them to capacity with his books. On the wall were enlarged photographs of archaeological excavations. From their dress, the archaeology crew looked like they were from the thirties. In one corner of the room was a table flanked by two stuffed chairs. A Staunton sandalwood chessboard was set up on the table and a painting of bold, bright slashes of color hung on the wall.

Diane sat behind the desk and indicated one of the stuffed chairs for the mayor.

"What is it you want to talk about?" she said as he pulled the chair nearer the desk and sat down and leaned forward, resting both elbows on the arms of the chair. If Jonas was a wizard, the mayor was a toad.

"I'm going to be blunt, Ms. Fallon. I believe in speaking plainly and getting to the point. It saves time, and time is money."

"Please do, Mr. Sutton."

He twisted and sat half upright. His frown deepened and he stared hard at her. She kept a pleasant expression on her face and held his stare. She was tempted to ask him if this was a contest.

"There are two things I want to talk with you about. First, it has come to my attention that you are interfering in police business."

Come to my attention was an unpleasant weasel phrase that annoyed Diane. She raised her brow and cocked her head. "I believe you're misinformed."

"Misinformed?" He leaned forward. "I have this from the police chief himself."

"He is misinformed."

"Let's not dance around this, Ms. Fallon. You were seen by two policemen at a crime scene—the George Boone house."

"Detective Janice Warrick had released the house before I was asked to take a look at it. As far as the detectives were concerned, it was no longer a crime scene."

"You were asked there by an Atlanta detective who has absolutely no jurisdiction in the case."

Diane was beginning to wonder just how good a friend Izzy Wallace was to Frank. "Again, you have been misinformed."

"Frank Duncan is an Atlanta detective. He's in the fraud division, not even homicide. He has absolutely no business interfering in a Rosewood matter."

Walter Sutton leaned farther forward and placed a hand on the desk. For a moment, Diane thought he was going to pound it. She had never met the mayor and was becoming increasingly puzzled by his hostility. She'd learned from her friend Gregory that you only show anger in diplomacy when it gives you an advantage, and that most of the time, calm in the face of anger gives you the most advantage—so Diane remained outwardly calm.

"Mr. Sutton. Frank Duncan is executor of Louise and George Boone's will. He is now, on their deaths, guardian of their minor daughter—who has been arrested for murder. It is most certainly his business to protect her interests and secure for her a defense. I'm shocked that you would think otherwise. A responsibility of that nature is a sacred trust."

The mayor glared a moment before he settled back on the seat of the chair. "There's another matter that's of the utmost importance to this community."

Diane knew what was coming and she almost laughed. Instead she picked up a pencil lying on the desk. Another of Gregory's little bits of wisdom: Put a desk between you and the subject and trifle with a writing instrument. It works mainly in Western cultures, he had told her. There are so many authority figures that it's subconsciously associated with—teachers, principals, doctors, psychiatrists, lawyers . . . just one more little thing that can give you a psychological edge.

"And what would that matter be?" she asked, absently rolling the pencil between her palms.

The mayor shifted in his seat.

"We've been working hard to build a community with a strong economic base," said the mayor, straightening up in the stuffed chair.

"I know," said Diane. "We at the museum are proud to have contributed to that base by being able to hire more than a hundred employees, not to mention offering two business opportunities—the restaurant and the mu-

seum shop—to local entrepreneurs. And, of course, there
are our liaisons with the local schools, technical colleges
and university."

"Yes, well, there's an opportunity to enhance the museum's contribution." *By getting us to fall on our sword,*
thought Diane. "I understand," the mayor continued,
"that you have refused to consider an opportunity that
would not only be good for the museum, but bring much-
needed jobs to the community."

"Mr. Sutton. You have me completely bewildered.
You came in here under the impression that I was interfering in police business. However mistaken that impression was, you were correct in condemning that as
inappropriate behavior. So you can see why I'm now
puzzled that you're interfering in museum business,
which is my business."

Mayor Sutton's face reddened slightly. Gregory always
said she would make a terrible diplomat, because she
took such a perverse pleasure in making the other person
mad. She had to confess he was right.

"When it is something so important to the community,
as a leader it's my business as well. Look, Ms. Fallon,
we've gotten off to a shaky start. It was not my intention
to make you defensive, but to ask you to see reason. It's
not fair to the people that you use a position you fell
into by the merest chance."

"Chance?"

"I have no desire to embarrass you, but you know
Milo Lorenzo hired you because he was a friend and had
compassion for you. Losing your job, being out of work
for a year. That's hard on anyone, and I'm not condemning you for it. However, had Milo known he was going to
die so soon, he would have changed the way the museum
governance was set up. You shouldn't use this accidental
power you have to make bad decisions. You are in over
your head."

Diane laughed out loud. "Yes, we have gotten off to
a bad start. Part of the reason is that from the first you
have all these assumptions that aren't true. However, to
explain, I would have to go into a whole history that,

quite frankly, is none of your concern. Be that as it may, what you and some members of my board have to learn to deal with is that I do have the power. And I will use it to benefit the museum."

"There are other alternatives for the museum. Do you realize how many jobs are at stake?"

"No, and neither do you. Not only are the other alternatives for the museum inadequate, but they will take it out of the county. Many of the current employees won't be able to move with it. The county will not benefit from any of the tourism the museum brings or the taxes generated. What jobs would come our way from the sale of the museum land is merely speculation. What we have is solid."

"There are things about this you don't know."

Diane sighed—that old shoe. "Yes, there are, and it would be foolish of me to make decisions of the magnitude that you are suggesting until I have all the facts."

"I have learned it's impossible to reason with a person who thinks she has all the answers. Let me just say this— there's a lot of money involved, a lot. Right now, sitting up in your ivory tower, you seem to think you're invincible, but you aren't. There are ways to unseat you, despite what you believe, and when you fall, it will be hard."

Diane set the pencil down and leaned forward. "If all else fails, try to scare me? Mr. Sutton, I have been threatened by men who will go to far greater lengths to obtain my cooperation than you are even willing to think about. You're not scary." She stood up. "I think it's time this meeting ended."

Mayor Sutton stood, looking for a moment as if he were searching for something that would be the last word. However, he turned on his heels and walked out the door. Diane watched him through the open office door as he headed for the elevators and punched the DOWN button over and over.

When Jonas Briggs came in, Diane was still standing behind the desk, scowling. She couldn't shake the notion that had taken hold of her, that there was another, hidden piece to this. Despite the trite old excuse politicians and bureaucrats were wont to drag out about there being things unknown to mere plebes, this time she believed there were.

"I have to hand it to you," said Jonas Briggs. "I thought I was good at making him red faced, but you're so much better than me. I've never seen him quite so agitated."

Diane turned her attention to Briggs and smiled. "Thanks for letting me use your office."

"It's only my office at your discretion." He made an elaborate bow. "While you're here, I've got an exhibit idea I'd like to talk to you about." He sat down in the recently vacated chair. Diane sat back down behind his desk. "I don't know if you've heard about the archaeological excavations in West Africa at the chimp nut-cracking site."

Chimp nut-cracking site? It sounded like a lampooning of a Christmas musical. "This is a joke, right?"

"No. Since Jane Goodall, we've known that chimpanzees use tools. Well, a primatologist and an archaeologist got the perfectly reasonable idea that an excavation of an area where they were seen carrying out that activity might yield some interesting information. So far they have excavated at least six wooden anvils and debitage—waste flakes—from pounding their hammers to crack nuts. There's a remarkable resemblance to stone waste flakes found at some early human sites. It's all quite fascinating."

"And you want to do an exhibit on—what did Andie call it?—ape archaeology?"

"Not exactly. See that painting?" He pointed to the colorful painting hanging over the chessboard. "Do you know who did that?"

Diane shook her head. "I'm not very well versed in modern art."

Briggs beamed at her. "But do you like it? You see it as art?"

"Yes, I do."

"It was painted by Ruby."

"I'm not familiar with modern painters, either."

"Ruby was an elephant housed in the Phoenix zoo."

"An elephant?" Diane stared at the painting for a moment. "I think I have heard of elephants that are trained to paint."

"Ah, but are they trained? Some animal behaviorists say so, but Ruby's handler gave her a brush and paint because she saw her doodling in the sand with her trunk. If we see a child doodling in the sand and give him crayons, is that training or nurturing a talent?"

"Where are you going with this?"

"Did you know that elephants play music? Have you heard of the Thai Elephant Orchestra?"

"Actually, I have their CD. However, I do have a hard time wrapping my brain around the idea that it's the elephants and not their handlers that are composing the music."

"What I'm suggesting is an exhibit designed to look at animals in a little different way than a collection of instinctive behaviors. Making the familiar strange and the strange familiar, if I may paraphrase T. S. Eliot. That makes good poetry, good anthropology, and good museums."

Diane's face turned up in a grin. "I think I like that idea. Go ahead and start working on it. Discuss it with the exhibition planner and designer—she's up on the third floor. Let me see what you come up with."

Briggs's head bobbed up and down happily. "I'll do that. I haven't been up to the third floor yet. Thanks for listening to an old man. I'm happy to have a home here."

"I had a hard time getting the archaeology department to send anyone," said Diane.

Jonas Briggs studied the subtle leaf pattern woven into his bronze-colored carpet. "A little bit of snobbery, I'm afraid."

"Snobbery?"

"I probably shouldn't say anything, but hell, it's never stopped me before. The physical anthropologist has some issues with your appointment here."

"I don't even know him. What issues could he possibly have?"

"My dear, I see you are unfamiliar with the subtle

workings of the academic mind. You're a forensic specialist. You don't do research, you apply research, which means you are a mere technician of the art of studying bones. And thereby have no real qualifications for a position of this kind."

"I see."

"Willard quite put everyone off, then Julie decided she liked the idea of an extra office. Of course, later, she got a job out of state. They weren't going to replace her until I said I would like to come. They jumped at that, so here I am. They were glad to get rid of an emeritus faculty member. For all their love of old things, they aren't much fond of old faculty."

"I rather think the geology department had the same feelings." Diane's eyes sparkled in amusement.

"Well, we'll just have fun without them."

Diane rose and headed for the door. "You play chess, I see." She nodded in the direction of the chessboard.

"A little. I'm not very good, but I was hoping I could con somebody into a game with me now and then."

She walked over to the board and moved the white pawn to king four square before she went out the door.

Chapter 18

By the time Diane got to the lab, the police were ready to leave. From the frowns on everyone's faces, they hadn't given the conservation team much satisfaction.

Izzy Wallace turned to Diane. "Not a lot we can do, really. Sort of a nonstarter. Got in with a key, didn't take anything, not much messed up, really." He glanced over at one of the assistants and back to Diane. "No use in taking any prints. There's not a lot we can do with them. It was probably someone who works here, and their prints would be here anyway."

Diane folded her arms and looked at him a moment, wondering if he had anything to do with the mayor's misinformation. "That's all right, Officer Wallace. We didn't expect a lot, but we did want it on record in case it happens again and they do take something."

"We're real sorry, ma'am," said the other policeman, "but there's nothing to be gained by pursuing this. The DA would just drop it."

"I appreciate your coming."

It was a second or two before Izzy's eyes left Diane's. "Is the mayor downstairs?" he finally asked.

"Presumably."

He nodded. "We'll be going, then."

As soon as they were out the door, the staff began complaining.

"They hardly did anything. They even so much as implied that we left the lab in a mess."

"I'll alert the night guards to keep a lookout. Don't

worry too much about it." Diane left them grumbling and took the stairs back down to her office.

On her desk was a note from Andie to call Frank. She picked up the phone and dialed his number.

"Diane, I have the autopsy report. It will be a while before I can have the blood samples you collected analyzed. Would it be all right if I come over around quitting time and discuss it? I'll bring Italian."

"Sounds good. If the restaurant were open, I'd treat you to a meal at the museum."

"You guys have a restaurant?"

"We will have one in a couple of weeks. I'll see you around six-thirty."

Diane took out her laptop and memory stick from her digital camera. After she printed out the photos she took of the crime scene, she called up a program she hadn't used in a while. One that computed directional trajectory and gave a three-dimensional animated image of the scene when the information was plugged into it. If she hurried, she could have a rough set done by the time Frank arrived.

"What's this you have here?" Frank pointed to a corkboard on the table leaning against the wall. Pinned to it were two rows of computerized 3-D images of the crime scene.

"It's a storyboard depicting the events at the crime scene. I find it helps me see the sequence of events and what's missing from the sequence." She looked at the bags in his hand. "You think we can eat all that food?"

"You never know who might drop in—like a murder suspect on the lam. Besides, it's just a few appetizers to go with the main meal."

"I thought we might eat out on the terrace, then come back here."

"Suits me." He glanced again at her storyboard before following her out the door.

The terrace was an open patio in the rear of the museum looking out onto the nature trail. She spread their meal on a wrought iron table. It was hotter outside than she'd realized, but the sun was going down and the table was in the shade. The air had a sweet, hot fragrance of some shrub. She made a mental note to find out its name. Here in the rear of the museum it was quiet. Road noise sounded so distant they could have been deep in a glade.

Neither spoke about murder or autopsy reports. Diane didn't tell Frank about the break-in or her talk with the mayor or her uncertainties about his friend Izzy Wallace. Instead, they looked out at the nature trail, and she told him about the various plants located on the trail and the pond with a family of swans. He laughed as she told him about Jonas Briggs, ape archaeology and elephant fine arts.

"Elephants actually make music?"

"Apparently. Jonas is going to look into it. Speaking of music, what's this karaoke thing you and Andie have going? You're a crooner?"

"Was last time. I might be Elvis next time. It's just a fun thing I do occasionally. Turns out Andie's a big karaoke fan, too. You'll have to come sometime. Do you sing?"

"Not for any amount of money."

"Oh, we don't get paid."

Diane laughed and looked out into the woods. It was getting dark—and late—and she hated the idea of going back to her office to examine what awaited her there. But better to get it over with.

"I think that's about all I can eat." She looked over the quantity of leftovers. "How many carts do you fill up when you do your grocery shopping? Why do you always buy so much food?"

"Actually, I don't keep much in my house—except when Kevin comes over. I'm in Atlanta most of the time, working. Which I'll be getting back to in a few days."

Diane thought that getting back to his job would probably be a relief for him. It would be hard enough if he only had to arrange the funerals of his friends, but all the crime scene analysis must be hard for him to handle. Frank helped pack up the leftover food and pick up the trash. "Have any idea what we can do with the left-overs?" he asked.

"We'll put it in the refrigerator in the staff lounge. You can take it home with you when you leave."

In Diane's office Frank handed her an envelope from his jacket pocket. The autopsy report. She opened the envelope reluctantly and removed the contents slowly, as if there might be the possibility that if she just held off long enough, some intervening event would make it unnecessary for her to look at them. But there they were. Autopsy reports for young Jay and his parents.

Jay was shot once. The bullet went though his spine and lodged in his heart. There was no gunpowder residue on his clothing. Melted plastic was present in the wound. Diane stopped for a moment and thought about the pieces of plastic she had found in the grass. It's what she had suspected. Attached to Jay's autopsy report was a mention of other plastic pieces. They lifted a partial fingerprint from one, but the expert was of the opinion that they couldn't make a match, especially with the new federal court ruling that fingerprinting didn't meet the U.S. Supreme Court's standards for scientific evidence.

George and Louise's were more complicated. Just as the blood spatters showed, they both had been bludgeoned and shot. The bullet entered his upper chest, went through his spleen, traveled downward through the small and large intestines and out his lower back. The presence of gunpowder and smoke on his clothes indicated that it was a close shot.

There were contusions on the left side and front of the scalp, depression fractures in the left parietal and frontal bones. His left zygomatic bone was crushed, and his nasal bone was fractured.

The left parietal bone of Louise's skull was fractured, and she was shot through the same part of the head at close range. Jay, George and Louise had no alcohol or drugs in their systems. From the drawings by the medical examiner, Diane noted that the fractures were consistent with a baseball bat.

While she read over the autopsy reports, Frank was looking at the computerized 3-D pictures pinned on the corkboard. He held the photo of Jay lying face down in the grass in his hand.

"I've talked to Jay's teachers, his friends, his soccer coach. . . . I have no idea what he could have been doing out that late."

"I don't think he was," said Diane. "That is, I don't think he had left their property."

In her hand she had a stack of index cards which she laid on the table along with the photographs she had taken of the crime scene. She sat down at the table and motioned for Frank to take the seat beside her. He eyed her a moment as he sat.

"You think Detective Warrick's scenario is wrong?"

"Yes, I do, and so will she when she examines the evidence closely."

"What do you think happened?"

"Warrick thought Jay was shot last because she believed that George would've been awakened and armed himself, and therefore would not have been shot in his bed. I think he was awakened, armed himself with a bat, but simply did not have time to get out of bed."

Diane laid Jay's autopsy report on the table. "First of all, Jay had no alcohol or drugs in his system," she continued. "Though it's certainly not automatically true, a kid who sneaks out of the house at night often will at least drink a few beers. But the important thing is the plastic. We'll see when the report comes back on the plastic pieces I found, but I believe it was a silencer."

"A silencer? Out of plastic?"

"I asked Star's boyfriend, Dean, if he knew how to make one. He didn't. He may have been lying, but he did seem puzzled by my question. You can take a plastic liter soft-drink bottle and put it over the muzzle of a gun and have a onetime-use silencer that is moderately effective. Jay had plastic embedded in his skin. I think the killer used a plastic bottle silencer and Jay was killed first."

Diane took the card with a sketched picture of Jay

being shot by someone holding a gun with the silencer and pinned it as the first in the line of pictures.

"Since it doesn't completely silence the noise, George and possibly Louise may have heard enough to wake up, but it was not loud enough to get them out of bed. They may not have even known why they woke up. But when the intruder came up the stairs to their bedroom, George was roused to action."

She took her photos of the string reconstruction of the blood spatter trajectory lines and laid them in front of Frank.

"Where the strings cross is the origin of the blood spatters."

"Amazing," said Frank.

"Math," said Diane. "The computer program drew these 3-D depictions. I fed the spatter measurements into the program and it computed the origin of the blood source, just as the trajectory strings do. The pictures are crude because I was rushed, but the math is right. I've placed the head of the victims . . ."

She glanced briefly at Frank. She hesitated to use their names because it made it too personal, but she hated to call them *the victims*.

"It's all right," he said, putting a hand on her arm and squeezing it.

"The different positions of their heads are the sources of the blood spatters."

She was glad now that the drawings were of crude artist-doll figures. It helped keep things distant.

"I don't have the blood analysis that will help me know which blood belongs to Louise and which to George, and the superimposition of the spattering is difficult to determine at best, so new information may change things slightly. However, this is what I think happened:

"George was partially awakened by the muted noise of the gunshot outside. When someone came up the stairs and into their bedroom, he became fully awake, probably put one foot on the floor, grabbed the bat by the bed and swung at the intruder. At the same time, the intruder fired the first shot, hitting George in the chest and traveling downward. George hit the intruder, possibly knocking the gun out of his hand. The intruder grabbed the bat from the injured George and hit him on the left side of his head. This is that first strike."

Diane pointed to the crossed collection of strings closest to the side of the bed George was on. She then pointed to the picture of the figure partially raised up in bed.

"See this castoff here that hits the chest of drawers? The intruder swung the bat again, hitting Louise before she could get out of bed."

Diane pointed to the farthest crossed string and matching picture on the storyboard. The picture showed that the figure representing Louise had moved, trying to get out of bed and away.

"Louise fell, probably unconscious, and he swung the bat again. Here's the castoff going up the wall and across the ceiling. This time he hit George again, fracturing his forehead and nose. He swung again, crushing his cheekbone. Notice these two points of origin are close together and nearer to the pillow of the bed.

"The last thing the intruder did was shoot Louise in the head where he had struck her. She was probably moaning or was attempting to rise. After that, he left."

"Warrick's thinking that because there were two forms of attack, then there were two people involved—Star and her boyfriend," said Frank.

"It's possible there were two people involved, but I think this is a reasonable scenario that fits the evidence."

Frank sat back and looked at the storyboard. "Why was Jay outside?"

"That's the key. He didn't have alcohol in his system. He didn't show signs he had been anywhere. He might have just left the house on his way to meet someone. If he were meeting friends, perhaps you can find them."

"I've talked to his friends of record. Jay was a busy kid—soccer, Boy Scouts. He didn't have much time to get into trouble or have secret friends."

"Kids that age are good at keeping parts of their lives

secret. But someone out there knows. Perhaps Star does."

"Star? You think he was meeting her? That wouldn't look good for her," said Frank.

"Ask her. He might not have been meeting her, but if he was doing things his parents didn't know, he may have confided in her."

"It's hard to get her to talk to me."

"Get her lawyer to talk to her. Keep in mind too that the intruder did not break in. Warrick thinks that fact points to Star. However, Jay could have inadvertently let the killer in. It could be someone Jay knew and trusted."

Frank looked back at the storyboard and photographs of the trajectory lines. "You're pretty sure about this analysis?"

Diane stood up and stretched. "The math, yes. Any explanation will have to fit that geometry."

"That's interesting about the silencer. Warrick doesn't know that."

"Maybe that's one thing she's keeping back. I would have thought she'd have collected the plastic."

"Izzy would know."

"Would he have told you?"

"Of course."

"Is he one of your poker buddies?"

"And fishing."

Diane looked at her watch—7:42. It was getting to be dusk outside. Time to go home. Lack of rest was catching up with her. She looked at Frank.

"Would you like some coffee at my place?" she asked.

Frank's face brightened. "Sure. You don't make it like Vance does, but that'd be great." He grinned as she made a face at him.

"Let me check my E-mail. By the way, any prints on that letter or the invoice to the Bickford for the dinosaur exhibits?" Diane went to her computer and called up her Internet connection.

"I'm sorry, I meant to tell you. No prints."

"Not even mine?"

"No, none."

"Well, that's interesting. Shouldn't there have at least been mine?"

She had several messages. One from the archaeologist Jonas Briggs. One line: Pawn to king three. She E-mailed back: Pawn to queen four.

"I would have expected it; however, it doesn't necessarily mean the letter was wiped clean."

The next E-mail was from Laura, her psychiatrist friend and friendly board member. It was about Melissa and the bruises Diane saw at the museum party. Laura had talked to Melissa's parents—discreetly, she said. They told her Melissa was always getting bruises, ever since she was a kid. That didn't sound particularly good to Diane, but Laura knew her friends and she was a psychiatrist.

Her other E-mails were from department heads and the newly arrived faculty-curators—the botanist thanking her for his lab and office space. She E-mailed him back, but decided to wait until tomorrow on the others.

Diane's apartment was sparse. She'd directed all her energy into the museum and hadn't spent any time decorating it. The beige carpet throughout came with the apartment. She'd purchased a large burgundy-and-gray striped stuffed sofa that converted into a bed. She hadn't even tried to find one that went with the carpet. Instead, she bought an Oriental rug to go in front of the sofa and pretended the carpet under it wasn't there. In front of the sofa she had a cherry wood coffee table. The only other pieces of living room furniture were a black leather stuffed chair and a stereo. Not an elegant room, but one her mother would have said had potential.

Diane headed for the kitchen to make coffee. Frank followed and began stuffing her refrigerator with Italian food.

"It'll just spoil in mine," he said. "And I'll have to clean it out, and I hate cleaning out the refrigerator."

She filled the coffeemaker with water and turned around into Frank's arms. She had forgotten what a good kisser he was.

Chapter 19

"I missed you," said Frank. "I should have mailed you all those letters I wrote. I should have come to find you in the jungle."

Diane looked into his eyes; they were more blue than green at the moment. "It's good to be back. It's good to be standing right here, right now," she said and kissed him again.

"Can I stay the night?" he whispered against her ear.

"I told myself if we ever got together again, I was going to go slower this time," said Diane. "Go places with you, get to know you . . ."

"So can I stay the night?"

She giggled as the kitchen filled with the aroma of coffee. How long had it been since she actually giggled?

"What the hell? Maybe we'll get tired of each other—then we can go on dates and get to know each other."

"I can tell you my deepest, darkest secret right now—you know that and you'd know the worst about me." He rubbed her back under her shirt and his touch both chilled and warmed her skin.

"What's that? What's the worst thing to know about you?"

He pulled her closer and nuzzled her ear. "I know how to play the accordion."

Diane pulled back and looked him in the eye. "No, you're kidding. That's not true."

"It is." He put his forehead against hers.

"I'm not sure I can handle that," she said. "What if

some evening I find you playing a polka under my window?"

"You don't have to worry. I have it under control."

He kissed her again, and Diane felt the strains of "Ode to Joy" vibrating against her breasts.

Frank stepped away, pulled out his phone and looked at the display. "Cindy," he said, pushing the ANSWER button.

"Hey," he said. "How's Kevin?"

While he was talking, Diane filled two cups with fresh coffee and took them into the living room on a tray with cream and sugar.

Frank came out of the kitchen holding his hand over the phone. "She wants us to come over for dinner this Saturday." He raised his eyebrows and shrugged as he said it, smiling, perhaps at Cindy's bad timing.

Diane felt the hand of Mark Grayson at work. "Tell her I'd love to and I've got a bottle of wine I've been dying to open, but it'll have to wait until I get some museum business resolved that's hanging over my head."

Frank put the phone back up to his ear and repeated almost verbatim what Diane had said. He listened for several seconds. "I'll give her that argument, but this thing at the museum really has her tied up right now. She's not been able to go anywhere." He paused. "I'll do that and get back to you. Can I speak with Kevin?" The pause was shorter. "Homework, in the summer?" Pause. "Yeah, I'd forgotten about that. I'll give you a call later." He pushed the END button and put the phone back in his pocket.

"I suppose you heard that. It looks like you're right— David must want to pressure you. She was pretty insistent we come for dinner."

"She was asking you to convince me?"

"Yes."

"Not being able to talk to Kevin wasn't a part of it, was it?"

"I don't know. I hope not." Frank was pensive for a long moment. "That wouldn't be like Cindy—unless she's under a lot of pressure from David. I can tell her no. It's not a problem."

"I don't mind going. But let's wait a few days and see how much pressure comes our way over it. You know, it could just be her way of letting you know that it's OK with her if you and I are together."

"That wouldn't be like Cindy either. So where were we?"

"Drinking our coffee?" Diane handed him a cup she had dressed with cream and sugar.

"Was that it? I thought we were going to drink it in the bedroom."

He took Diane's hand, backed away and led her into the bedroom.

A long while later, Diane lay her head on Frank's chest, and gently stroked his skin with her fingertips. "Why didn't you mail the letters?" she asked.

"I wanted to—I wanted to a little too much, and it scared me. I'd been divorced from Cindy for less than two years. I'd been through some rough times. I didn't trust myself anymore. I didn't know what I was feeling. Why did you stay gone for so long?" he asked.

Diane didn't say anything for a long time. Instead of answering, she kissed his chest, then his lips.

"If this is a way of getting out of telling me, it's very charming." He slid both arms around her and pulled her on top of him. "And it will work." He kissed her again.

It was dark in the jungle. One bright spotlight illuminated a circle of the dark gray-green foliage, then another, darting around like the eye of a predator. The music crept in from the distance. Diane heard it and ran toward it. She kept running, and it grew louder and louder until she was surrounded by the engulfing, deafening strains of "In the Hall of the Mountain King." Where was it? She had to find it. She stopped, looking around her everywhere for the source of the music. The ground; it was coming from the ground. She knelt and dug in the hard jungle soil with her hands until they were bleeding.

Fingers dug into her shoulders, dragging her back. *No,* she screamed. *No!*

"Diane, Diane. Are you all right? Diane."

It was still dark, but she could see the bright moon shining through an opening. She sat up, confused for a moment before realizing she was in her bed—with Frank.

Frank reached over and switched on the lamp at her side of the bed. "Are you all right? You were crying in your sleep."

"I'm fine." She was cold and shivering. She hugged the bedcovers around her body. "It was just a nightmare."

He cleared his throat to get the sleep out of his voice. "You want to talk about it?"

"I just need to get a drink of water." She slipped out of bed and grabbed her silk robe hanging on the footboard.

She took a bottle of water from the kitchen and went into the living room with it and sat on the sofa, pulling a soft faux zebra throw next to her to snuggle up against. Frank came in wearing jeans and an open white shirt. He sat down on the couch beside her.

"I know something bad happened in South America," he said. He hesitated, as though looking for words. "Something you haven't wanted to talk about, and I understand that. Sometimes mistakes happen. . . ." He trailed off, as if the words he finally found were inadequate.

"Mistakes?" Diane watched him and took a sip of water.

"I've heard," he started uneasily, "that there was some mistake that led to a tragedy, and you lost your job. Whatever happened made it difficult to find another one for almost a year."

Diane's heart was still pounding from the dream. "You heard that from your friend Izzy?"

"He heard things. I think he just wanted to give me some kind of heads up."

"I saw him the other day. We had a break-in at the museum. I felt then that he had some issue with me."

"He just wanted me to know everything."

Diane shook her head. A smile that felt more like anger than humor played around her lips. "That couldn't be true. If he really wanted you to know everything, he would have checked his information. It's what I would have done for a friend. And you believed him. Is that why you kept asking me if I was sure about my calculations?"

"If I had any serious doubts about you, I would have never asked for your help. I told him he probably didn't have the whole story."

Diane looked at Frank for several seconds, his mussed hair, sleepy eyes. Last night was the first really happy moment she'd had in a year. Maybe Gregory was right; she should at least confide in Frank.

"He didn't have any part of the story right. There was a tragedy last year—a massacre at a mission across the easternmost border from Puerto Barquis in Brazil, in the Amazon. It happened not because I made a mistake, but because I did my job too well. A job I didn't lose, but resigned. Wait here a moment."

She went to her nightstand in the bedroom and opened the drawer. It contained only photographs, some in frames, others loose. She brought them back to the living room and curled up at the end of the couch, holding the pictures to her chest.

"Puerto Barquis is a country not many here are familiar with. Early in its history the border started on the west coast and stretched eastward into the Amazon jungle. The coastal port has since been claimed by another country, so it's now landlocked. The population is composed of Spanish, Portuguese, Germans, Native Indians and various mixtures. It's been ruled in recent history by a series of strong men, the latest one, Ivan Santos."

His name felt like a sharp rock in her mouth and didn't slip easily from her tongue.

"During his rule he massacred thousands of the native population, along with hundreds more who either disagreed with him or were in the way. I won't go into the whole history, but he was deposed and Barquis had its first free election, watched over by the United Nations.

Xavier Valdividia became the first legally elected president, and he had a very good chance of holding on to power. But Santos and his henchmen and his spies inside the government were waiting and plotting for any opportunity to retake control."

Frank sat silently on the couch facing Diane, listening to what she was saying, a deep crease between his eyebrows. He took a sip of the water she'd left on the coffee table and passed it over to her. She took a long drink.

"I worked for World Accord International. My team collected evidence—we excavated mass graves, interviewed witnesses, discovered and photographed and examined secret torture rooms. We amassed a mountain of evidence about atrocities that Ivan Santos was claiming never occurred, and we were connecting it to him. World Accord was hoping he would be tried and imprisoned so he would no longer be a threat to the elected government of Barquis.

"While I worked there we often stayed at a mission just across the border in Brazil. Our World Accord team shared food, blankets and medicine with them in exchange for their hospitality. Over the years the mission had taken in countless refugees from Puerto Barquis."

Diane stopped talking. Her eyes filled up with tears. Frank reached for her hand and squeezed it, but didn't speak. That was a trait Diane admired in him; he knew when not to speak, when to just be there. She took a framed photograph, looked at it a moment and handed it to Frank.

"That's me and my daughter, Ariel."

Frank looked at the photograph and back at Diane. He opened his mouth to speak, stopped and looked back at the photograph.

"I didn't know you had a daughter," he said. "Where? . . ." he started to ask, but stopped. Diane could see the confusion in his eyes.

"I have to tell you about Ariel—then you will understand."

Chapter 20

It was several moments before Diane could continue her story, Ariel's story. She stared out the window at the dark tree line. Beyond, she could see the glow of the city lights—not bright, but enough to know something was there.

"Let me make us some coffee," said Frank. "We could both use some." Diane nodded.

She listened to him in the kitchen—pouring the water, opening the cabinets, turning on the coffeemaker. It started to rain. Diane hadn't remembered rain in the forecast. The drops spattered against the window, blurring the bright moon. The sound on the roof drowned out the few road noises present at that time of night.

Frank came into the living room carrying two cups of coffee. He'd added cocoa to hers, and it tasted rich and sweet. She took several sips, not thinking about anything but the taste of the chocolate-spiked coffee.

"About four years ago—this was after we were together . . ." She started to say *after we broke up,* but they'd never really broken up. She went to her job in the jungle, and he stayed at his in the city. When they parted it could have been for a weekend or forever. Neither of them said any of the things people were supposed to say to each other when they were parting. They'd had an odd relationship. No, not odd. Purely sexual? Not exactly that either, but Diane smiled inwardly at the thought.

"We used the mission as an unofficial base," she said.

"I was there making plans for our investigations. There were several possible mass grave sites that I wanted to look at in Barquis. Outside the compound one day, I came upon this little three-year-old girl on the edge of the forest. She was dirty and crying. That wasn't a particularly unusual occurrence. God knows there were too many orphans, but she was different. When she looked at me, she smiled the biggest smile you've ever seen and had the prettiest velvet black eyes. I picked her up and carried her into the mission. The sisters tried to find parents or relatives, but no one came forward. I spent all my free time with her, and as time passed and they were still unable to find her parents, I decided to adopt her."

Tears welled up in Diane's eyes and spilled onto her cheeks. "I should have just taken her out, smuggled her to the United States or somewhere safe. I had the connections, I should have done that. But I was going to do everything legally. That's what we did—follow the rule of law. We were so self-righteous. If I'd been a good mother, I'd have gotten her out." Diane collapsed in tears, spilling the photographs onto the couch and floor.

Frank picked them up and put them on the coffee table then sat closer, pulling Diane to him.

"Diane, I'm so sorry. These past few days must have been a nightmare. If I'd known . . ." He was silent for several minutes. "Please . . . can you tell me about her?" he said at last.

After a moment, Diane straightened up and reached for her coffee. It was lukewarm and tasted sweet mixed with her salty tears. The photographs lay on the table and she picked them up, shuffling through them, pulling some out to show Frank.

"She was the sweetest little girl and very smart. The nuns named her Anna, but when she was four she told me she wanted to be named Ariel, you know, after the Little Mermaid. She said she wanted a brand-new name—Ariel Fallon.

"I kept her with me when I wasn't going to dangerous places. I took her for a short trip down the Amazon River." Diane cast a glance at her stereo. "Ariel loved music. I bought her this CD player." She smiled, remembering the steady supply of batteries. "Batteries don't do well in the jungle and it was hard keeping her in batteries. I burned a CD of her favorites. She liked 'The Mighty Quinn,' 'The Lion Sleeps Tonight,' the one by the Tokens—she was very specific in her musical tastes. But her favorite was 'In the Hall of the Mountain King.' She'd turn up the volume so loud you could hear it all over the compound and into the jungle.

"I watched her grow, watched her little personality blossom. We'd made these plans. I told her all about the United States, about snow and Disney World, the Grand Canyon, the Smoky Mountains. I ordered these mother-daughter dresses. It took so long for them to arrive, I thought she'd be too big when they came. But hers fit perfectly. We're wearing them in the photograph." She showed him the silver-framed photograph of the two of them, hugging, smiling in identical dresses.

"At the time, I was corresponding with Milo and agreed to accept his offer to come to the museum. I thought it would be the most wonderful place to raise her. During that time, I didn't visit the U.S. When I came back, it was going to be with her."

"What happened?" asked Frank.

"What happened." Diane sighed and rubbed her eyes and pressed her forehead with her fingertips. "We'd been there three years, and my team and I had made a lot of headway collecting damning evidence against Santos. We thought President Valdividia would arrest him. We overestimated the president's power. He was afraid. We were coming back from the capital, and about three miles from the mission we heard gunfire. There's no going fast on those roads. As we grew closer we heard 'The Hall of the Mountain King' wafting through the jungle."

Diane stopped, unable to speak for several moments. "When we finally got to the compound, Santos had . . . he had . . . had killed everyone in the compound, including . . . There was blood everywhere. He had already taken most of the bodies. That's the way he liked to do things—bury his atrocities in hidden mass graves.

We found Ariel's CD player in the middle of the compound, set on repeat so that it played 'In the Hall of the Mountain King' over and over. He'd left her . . .'' Diane's mouth quivered and fresh tears spilled down her cheeks. "He'd left her bloody little shoes with the CD player. She must have been so scared, and I wasn't there for her.''

Diane curled up in a ball, clenched her fists, trying to breathe through the sobs. Frank pulled her against him again and stroked her back. It was several more minutes before she could speak again, several minutes of trying to breathe deeply, trying to stop the flow of tears. When she began again, her voice was a tremor. "All that death was aimed at me because I'd nailed his lies—but I hadn't counted on his vengeance. I thought maybe Ariel had run and hidden in the jungle. There were often survivors from his massacres. That's how we found eyewitnesses. I ran through the bush yelling for her, looking everywhere until they—my friends—dragged me away.''

Again they sat in silence. Frank rested his chin on the top of her head as they sat intertwined on the couch. Diane listened to the rain's steady drive on the roof.

"I said some insensitive things about how I'd go crazy if I lost Kevin, especially like George lost Jay. I'm so sorry—I had no idea.''

"You didn't know. Very few people here do.''

Diane shifted and lay her head on his shoulder and looked through the photographs of Ariel. Besides grief, the worse feeling was the regret at not just taking her and leaving. Why did she wait for the damn paperwork? Ariel could be here, right now, with her.

"Gregory—he was my boss—changed out teams. My objectivity was compromised along with everyone else's on my team. I took a leave of absence for a year.''

"What did you do?''

"For a while, nothing. I came back to the United States and hid out in my apartment, taking benzodiazepine to try to deaden the pain, until some of my caving friends talked me into exploring a few caves. Caves are very peaceful places—like being in a womb, I suppose.

Caving helped. Milo asked me to come here. I almost said no, but I spent a few months learning about museums in general and RiverTrail in particular."

"Why didn't you call?"

"I wasn't really fit company for anyone. I was very bitter, angry at the drop of a hat. I had to work my way through a lot of stuff before I wanted to see anyone."

"I would have understood."

"I didn't want anyone's understanding. I didn't want to feel good for a long time. I didn't deserve to feel good." Diane fought back the tears. She was so tired of crying. Her head hurt and her eyes were sore and swollen.

"The museum has been good for me," she said, "even with all its little problems with the board." The rain increased and lightning streaked across the sky, illuminating the tree line for a second. The crack of thunder rattled the windows. "Ariel wasn't afraid of the thunder and lightning. She thought it was a great show, and she was really into loud noises. I worried about her little ears. I wouldn't let her have earphones, no matter how much the nuns begged me."

" 'In the Hall of the Mountain King' was written on the note you gave me to analyze."

"Yes. Someone, I don't know who, left the note for the musicians to put it on the playlist."

Frank pushed away and stared at Diane. "A coincidence?"

"Perhaps." Diane told him about her conversations with Gregory and about the possibility of one of Santos' associates being in the United States.

"Diane, why didn't you tell me? This is serious."

"It's also a long shot. He's run the president out of Barquis. I doubt it'd be worth the effort to come after me. These days the U.S. is in no mood for terrorists. I'm sure Santos is aware of that. I've suspected that it has something to do with Mark Grayson trying to get me to sell the museum property."

"That would be a cruel thing to have done. Is he that mean?" asked Frank.

"I believe he, like a lot of dictators, wants what he wants."

"Have you confronted him?"

"I have no proof whatsoever. But I'm getting pressure from all sides." She told him about the unpleasant visit from the mayor. "So I've heard that rumor about me before."

"I'll tell Izzy. He didn't know. . . ."

Diane stood up and began gathering the pictures. "He didn't know. I wonder why, then, he felt justified in re-laying the rumor."

"He was looking out for me. I'm sure he'll apologize."

"I suggest he doesn't come around me for a while, or he won't like the consequences. The mayor didn't."

Diane looked at the clock on the wall. "It's almost four A.M. Maybe we can get a couple of hours' sleep before we have to get up. You don't have to go in to work tomorrow, do you?"

"No. I've had some time coming to me. I'm using it to try to take care of things." He stood up and gathered the coffee cups and took them into the kitchen. When he came out, he caught Diane going into the bedroom and put his arms around her waist and held her close.

"Diane, you've been a big help to me. I didn't realize the cost."

"I guess I'm just a sucker for hard stories."

Chapter 21

The grounds personnel were hard at work cleaning up the broken limbs and debris when Diane arrived at the museum. Storms are good at cleaning out the dead wood of a forest, and apparently this one went to work along the nature trail and the larger trees around the museum.

"Much damage?" she asked the head gardener, a small silver-haired man who'd retired from the university grounds department a couple of years ago.

"Not much. Mostly in the nature trail. We did have a tree limb fall against the west wing, but, fortunately, no windows were broken."

As Diane walked up the steps and into the museum she heard voices raised in anger coming from the stairwell.

It sounded like Melissa Gallagher quarreling with some man.

"Don't be like this, Mike. You don't understand." Melissa sounded close to tears.

"No, I don't, and I really can't deal with it anymore." It was Mike Seger, the geology graduate student.

Diane hurried up the stairs in time to see Mike close his hand around Melissa's arm.

"What's going on?" said Diane.

"Nothing," said Melissa.

"It doesn't look or sound like nothing." Diane held Mike in her gaze. "You're going to bruise her arm, the way you're holding it."

"I'm not holding it that hard," Mike said. But he let her go.

"Really, he wasn't," said Melissa. Diane thought she saw fear in Melissa's dark eyes as she glanced from Mike to her.

"Your argument is spilling from the stairwell out into the museum. It would be better if you take your disagreements off museum grounds."

"Oh, I didn't know. I'm sorry, Dr. Fallon. Really. It won't happen again." Melissa hurried up the stairs and out of sight.

Mike remained, however, and turned to face Diane. He was a few inches taller than she, so she moved up to a higher step to face him.

"I don't want anything like what I just saw occurring in the museum."

"We were having an argument. That was all. I know we shouldn't have been arguing here, and we won't again. But that's all that was going on."

"I've noticed Melissa has had bruises in the past few days."

"They haven't come from me. That's what you're thinking, isn't it?"

"If I find they did, you're out of here."

"Look, Dr. Fallon, I need this job. Assistantships in geology are hard to come by, and this has been a fortunate opening for me. I don't want to be fired because of something I didn't do."

"Then do we understand each other?"

"Yes." He turned and headed up the steps, then stopped and came back down to Diane's level. "Korey Jordan said he found old maps, rocks and fossil collections in the basement dating from the mid- to late-1800s?"

"Yes. This was a museum, then a clinic and now a museum again. There are some exhibits left over from that earlier time."

"Were any of the maps geologic maps?"

"I'm not sure."

"What's going to happen to them? I mean, is there any chance I can look at them?"

"Korey will have to assess any damage to the materials and stabilize them first. Perhaps do some repairs, if that's possible. After that, they can be examined."

"I have an interest in old geologic maps. They could make an interesting exhibit, especially if the rock and fossil collections can be matched up with the maps."

"I don't know if we have any provenience on the rock collection. Many of the things Korey is finding in the basement and attic were stored without much thought to organization or archiving."

"I'd be glad to take a look at the rock collection. I may be able to determine where they were collected."

"I'm not sure if it would be worth the time it would take. We currently have an extensive collection, as I'm sure you've seen."

"Yes, I know. But I might find something interesting. Sometimes a specific kind of rock can get mined out and disappear. And who knows about the fossils? Sometimes new species have been discovered in museum collections."

"By all means. Take a look at them."

"Thanks."

He disappeared up the stairs. Diane stood for a moment wondering about him and Melissa before she went back down to ground level and to her office. Through the adjoining door of her office, she heard Andie talking to someone.

"Yeah, they'd rather chase down somebody trespassing on some taxidermist's place or some dog peeing on Mrs. Crabtree's flower bed than investigate anything really illegal," Andie was saying.

Diane opened the door between the offices and saw that it was Korey talking to Andie.

"We didn't have another break-in, did we?"

"Oh, hi, Diane," said Andie.

"No," said Korey. "Just telling Andie about the non-action posture the police took. And I was delivering these." He handed Diane an envelope. "They turned out pretty good."

Diane opened the envelope and took out photographs of the fingerprints. "How about your office, Korey? Was anything missing?"

"It had been searched, but nothing missing. Somebody was looking for something, that's for sure."

"I'll see if I can get these prints run through the system. Korey, do you know Mike Seger very well?"

"Just met him. He was looking around in the conservation lab the other day, and I showed him some of the geology stuff we found in the basement."

"What kind of guy does he seem to you?"

Korey shrugged. "He seemed an all right guy. You don't suspect him of breaking into the lab, do you?"

Diane was taken aback for a moment. She'd been thinking about Melissa and not the break-in. "No, not at all. There are a lot of new people coming in from the university, and I just wondered what your take on him was."

"Fine. I like him. Seems to know his business."

"Thanks, Korey. I'll let you know if I find out anything about the fingerprints."

Diane went back to her desk and pulled out her calendar, skimming over today's schedule. There was no urgent business. Dylan Houser wanted to meet about her computer. She could put that off for another day.

She called up her E-mail. Jonas Briggs had sent his next chess move, pawn to queen four. Diane thought a moment, visualizing the chessboard in her mind's eye. The beginning game moves weren't hard to remember, but before long she would have to go up to the second floor and look at his board before she moved. She E-mailed him to move her knight to the queen's bishop three position.

It hit her suddenly. She jumped up from her computer and hurried into Andie's office.

"Andie, what were you saying when I came in?"

"Hi, Diane?"

"No, before that. When you were speaking with Korey."

"Oh, he was telling me how the police weren't the least interested in finding who broke in to the lab, and I said they were more interested in finding out who peed on Mrs. Crabtree's flowers—oh, and finding trespassers."

"You were more specific than that about the trespassers."

"Some taxidermist?"

"Why did you say that?"

Andie shrugged and looked wide-eyed. "I don't know, I was just making conversation."

"No, I mean why did you use those examples?"

"Oh. I like to read the sheriff's incident report in the paper. Sometimes they're real funny, like this woman who reported that someone broke into her house, messed up her bed and left an unused condom on her dresser. Why?"

"Can you tell me more about the taxidermist and the trespassers?"

"Let me see." Andie rolled her eyes upward, thinking. "It began as a complaint from a woman. Her neighbor was shooting off a gun. The neighbor—a taxidermist—said he heard someone trespassing. Apparently, they were disturbing the cows in his pasture, or something like that, and he fired a shot in the air. That's all there was to it."

"When did you read this?"

"Just a few days ago. Why?"

"Do you know his name?"

"Something sort of funny." Andie thought a minute. "Luther, Luther Something? Why are you asking me all this?"

"Tell you later." Diane went back to her office, closed the door and dialed Frank's cell phone number.

"Diane, how you doing this morning?"

"I'm fine, really."

"That's good. I was worried."

"It was good to share Ariel with someone. She was special."

"Yes, I can see that she was."

There was a distance in Frank's voice that puzzled her.

If she hadn't known him better, he sounded like someone who didn't want to hear from a one-night stand. As she started to speak, she heard a pinging in the background, then an intercom voice calling for a doctor.

"Frank, where are you? Is everything all right with you? How's Kevin?"

"Kevin's fine. But I'm at the hospital. I got a call when I got home. Star tried to commit suicide this morning. She's not good."

"Oh, Frank." Diane's voice trembled. *This is not the time to collapse,* she scolded herself.

"I didn't want to tell you, I mean, after last night, but . . ."

"Do you know what happened?"

"It was after they picked up her breakfast. She used a corner of her bed to cut her wrists. God, she had to be desperate to go through that. They said she lost a lot of blood."

"An otherwise healthy person can lose up to forty percent of their blood volume before they even require a transfusion." After she said it, Diane realized that it must have sounded so technical and cold. She wanted to be comforting. "I can come over."

"I don't know what to do," he said.

So much sadness. Diane felt guilty. Last night her story, and now this.

"Find out who did this to her family. It won't heal her overnight, but it will help."

"I know, but right now, I don't know what else to do," he repeated. "We got all this information, but what does it leave us with?"

"That's why I called. I think I know where to look for the rest of the skeleton."

Chapter 22

The other end of the phone was silent except for the hospital sounds in the background.

"The skeleton?" Frank finally said. "You mean the one the collarbone was taken from? You know where it is?"

"Maybe. I'm not certain, but it's a good lead. Remember I told you that it might be someplace where animals were processed? Andie told me about an item in the sheriff's incident report about someone trespassing on land belonging to a taxidermist."

Sheriff's incident report. Diane just realized that probably meant it was in the county and not the city limits—not the jurisdiction of the chief of detectives but in the jurisdiction of the county sheriff. She hoped that boded well for their investigation.

"I remembered the mounted animal heads in George's house, and that sounded like a good lead. This was just a few days ago. The trespasser could be someone looking to recover a body he left there several years ago, hoping it would never be discovered."

"That does make sense."

Diane could hear relief in his voice. Hope is a powerful thing.

"Do you know the taxidermist's name?" he asked.

"It might be Luther."

"Luther Abercrombie. He's mounted a fish or two for me. Did some work for George too. You too, as a matter of fact."

"Me?"

"If I'm not mistaken, Milo Lorenzo bought some stuffed animals from him for the Georgia collection."

"Can we make arrangements to go see him?"

"Yeah. We can do that. I want to visit with Star first, when they let me in."

"Would you like me to come to the hospital? Could you use some company?"

"No, but thanks. I'll be all right, especially now we have this lead. Maybe I can hold out some hope for her. Look, thanks, Diane. This . . . just, thanks."

"So," said Sheriff Bruce Canfield, "you're asking me if I can help solve one of the biggest murders here in decades and at the same time make a fool of that new chief of detectives in Rosewood?"

Sheriff Canfield was a large man in his late fifties. He had a full head of hair the color of brown that comes from a bottle, and a uniform that looked like it might have shrunk a bit in the wash. He laughed out loud.

"That's not exactly the way we'd put it," said Frank, grinning at the sheriff. "But yes, that's what we're asking."

"Well, who can pass up a deal like that? Let's go." He stood up and guided them out of his office. "How is George's little girl?"

"Right now she's sleeping and sedated." Frank told him about her trying to kill herself.

"Poor thing. Maybe we can do something here."

Diane and Frank followed the sheriff's car out to the Abercrombie farm, which consisted of three hundred acres of woodland and pastures, a white farmhouse and a garage with a sign that read ABERCROMBIE'S TAXI-DERMY. They parked their cars on a gravel drive and walked up to the gate. The sign on the gate read: I'LL GIVE UP MY GUN WHEN THEY PRY IT FROM MY COLD, DEAD FINGERS.

The sheriff opened the gate and hollered, "Luther, you got company."

A man much younger than Diane had imagined came out of the taxidermy shop wearing a leather apron and wiping his hands on a towel. He pushed his straight black hair from his eyes and smiled. His teeth were white against his neatly trimmed, short black beard.

"Frank Duncan, what you need with a sheriff's escort?"

"Hey, Whit. How you doing? This is Diane Fallon. She's the new director of the RiverTrail Museum."

"Come for more business, I hope." He grinned.

"We want to take a look at where your father dumps his carcasses," said the sheriff.

"Now, sheriff, you know he disposes of his waste legally—since he had to pay that fine a couple of years ago."

"This would be an old dump," said Frank. "We think there may be a body in it. It could be why your father had a trespasser the other night."

Whit gave a long whistle. "This is serious. I guess you need me there too."

Diane raised her eyebrows and looked at Frank.

"Whit's the county coroner," said Frank.

"Well, that makes everything convenient," said Diane.

"Can I ask why you are interested?" he asked Diane.

"I'm a forensic anthropologist."

"I see." He looked at the sheriff. "Do you know where you want to look?"

"A site that was being used from about five to ten years ago," answered Diane.

"Let's see. I covered most of them up for Dad."

"Do you have one that could have been visited by George Boone or his son, Jay?" asked Diane.

"Dad mentioned George was out here with his son a couple weeks ago for target practice. That's just awful what happened to that family. Is this about them?"

"Maybe," said Frank. He explained about the bone.

"There's one place I had a hard time getting to. I just lightly covered it, so it might have eroded out. Let's go take a look." He hung his apron and hand towel on a post, and led them back out the fence. He looked at the sign as he was closing the gate and shook his head. "Some folks think that's clever, but I told Dad it looks like an invitation to me. Let's go in my Jeep."

It was a bumpy ride down an infrequently used dirt road. The sheriff rode in front beside Whit. Diane and Frank rode in back, which made the ride for her even more like a buckboard. The rough ride through the woods was too much like the ride through the jungle. Diane gripped the seat until her fingers cramped. When they stopped with a lurch, Diane thought she would throw up her scant breakfast.

"You OK?" whispered Frank.

Diane nodded, but accepted his help in getting out of the vehicle.

"We have to walk from here," said Whit. He sprayed himself with bug spray and tossed the can to Diane. "Lot of deer ticks in the woods, not to mention mosquitoes."

After the four of them sprayed themselves, they set out through the woods. The North Georgia woods are quite different from the jungles of the Amazon and Diane found herself missing it. The rain forest is far more dense and so green, lush and full of oxygen it made Diane happy just to be breathing. The trees are tall, with leaves big enough to curl up in. The thick rain forest canopy doesn't let much wind down to the understory, so the stillness there is palpable.

Here a breeze fluttered the leaves and ruffled Diane's short hair. The smell of insect repellent traveled with them and masked the natural scents of the forest. As the trail became more overgrown, the woods threatened to become as thick as the jungle, and Diane was glad she had dressed for it. Shortly, they came to another dirt road intersecting the path they were on.

"We keep going on this overgrown path," said Whit, to Diane's dismay.

She stopped in the middle of the road. "Where does this road go?"

"From the main road to the upper pasture. We use it to bring in hay."

"How long has it been here?" asked Diane.

"Couple of years for the part leading to the pasture. That's when Dad bought the new land. It used to turn here and go back to the house."

"So at one time it went to your house but not the pasture?"

"That's right."

"They got lost," said Diane, looking up and down the road.

"Who?" asked the sheriff and Whit together.

"The intruders. They were looking for the way to the dump site, but the terrain has changed since they were last here, and in the dark they couldn't see this overgrown path. They didn't know the new road leads to the pasture. That's why they disturbed the cows."

"You pretty sure there's going to be a body up ahead?" asked Whit.

"No. Maybe just a wild goose," said Diane.

Whit grinned and led the way through the thick brush. The trail was interrupted by a large gully about fifteen feet deep with a stream flowing in the bottom.

"There used to be a earth bridge and culvert here," said Whit, "but it got washed away last spring."

"How do we get across?" asked the sheriff.

"There's an easier way down the bank down yonder."

As they were discussing the easiest way to descend to the bottom, Diane scrutinized the walls of the ravine. It was solid rock face with jagged cracks caused by roots and weather. She positioned her pack on her back, stooped down and eased herself over the side and climbed down using the cracks in the rock face for hand-and footholds. She was crossing the narrow creek when they noticed her. Frank and Whit looked at Diane then at each other with that "now we have to do what she did or look like a wimp" look.

"Which way did you say is easier?" asked the sheriff.

"Down the bank about a hundred yards. There's a kind of path down to the bottom," said Whit before he and Frank began climbing down the side.

As they were descending, Diane started up the other side. This side wasn't a rock face like the other, but there were large boulders and rocks weathering out of the surface. She climbed, testing each rock before she put her full weight on it, pulling herself up. On top she waited for Whit and Frank. When they reached the top she held out a hand to help each of them up on the bank.

"You do that real well," said Whit.

"Thanks." It was an easy climb, but from their panting, she decided not to mention it.

"She explores caves and does some rock climbing," said Frank, dusting off his hands.

"A woman of adventure. You dating anyone?"

"Yes, she is," said Frank.

Whit laughed. "I may give you some competition. By the way, why do you think there's a body here?"

Diane explained to him about the clavicle Frank got from George and her analysis of it.

"And that led you here? Amazing."

"That and the item in the paper about your trespasser," said Diane.

"Adventurous and clever too. You're definitely going to have some competition, Frank." He slapped him on the shoulder.

The sheriff made his way around to them, wheezing and breathing hard. "I sure hope we find a body. I'd hate to come all this way for nothing."

"It's just a short ways now," said Whit. He led them through more undergrowth to a depression that was once a small gully. It was now covered with leaves and detritus. Protruding from the ground here and there were the unmistakable shapes of bones.

"Here it is," said Whit. "Dad used to dump his carcasses here. He plugged up that narrow end with stumps and branches from where he'd cleared a pasture so the carcasses wouldn't wash into the big creek. He was a little sloppy about covering them up, but hell, it's out of the way."

"I can see where someone might have thought it would be a good place to hide a body," said the sheriff. "But weren't they taking a risk that your father would see a body when he threw more carcasses in?"

"Sometimes Dad would throw a little dirt over them, especially in the summer. Maybe that's what they did—if there's a body here."

Diane stepped carefully around the depression, inspecting the ground as the men discussed the relative merits of hiding a body one place or another. Another mass grave. She'd vowed never to dig another one. The side of a deer skull showed partially through the dirt and leaves. Not human. This was not a mass grave for humans. Though she had a hard time understanding how anyone could shoot a beautiful, healthy animal. . . . On the other hand, she did enjoy fishing. Her brain was hopping from one thing to another—trying to deal with the prospect of excavating a mass grave.

"What's your opinion, Doc?" said the sheriff.

Diane stood and looked over at them, surprised at how she had completely tuned out their conversation. "I'm sorry, what are you asking?"

"Where do you think is the best place to get rid of a body? Whit thinks this place, Frank votes for the foundation of a building, I say a wood chipper."

"In a pigpen," she said. "Pigs eat everything, including the bones."

Chapter 23

Diane stooped down and took a small crime-scene evidence flag from her pack and stuck it into the ground.

The three men stood staring at the flag for a moment.

"Mr. Abercrombie, I believe we need your permission to excavate," said Diane.

"You found something?" said the sheriff, surprise in his voice.

The three of them came walking across the dump site past protruding bones and suspicious lumps beneath the ground to where Diane was crouched. There, about the size of half a golf ball and stained brown like the surrounding dirt, a small, odd-shaped squarish bone lay on the ground next to the flag.

"That's a human bone?" asked the sheriff. He glanced around at the other bones peeking through the surface of dirt and leaves. "How can you tell it's human among all these animal bones?"

"Every bone is distinctive. It's a human talus—a bone of the foot."

"You're sure about that?" asked the sheriff.

"Yes."

"OK, what do we need to proceed?" asked Whit.

"It must be excavated as a crime scene—not dug up by untrained hands."

"You can do that?"

"Yes, but you don't have to use me," said Diane, hoping he'd say something like, "My cousin's a forensic anthropologist—I'll have her do it."

"Why not?" said Whit. "You're here."

"All right. I have an archaeologist at the museum, and I'll get some experienced excavators from the university's archaeology department."

Diane sat in one of Jonas Briggs' stuffed chairs studying the chessboard as he called his former archaeology students. He had moved his knight to the king bishop three position—only three moves for each of them. They were still in the beginning of the game, battling for early control of the board. As he hung up the phone, she captured his pawn and stood up.

"I've gotten four of my best excavators. They are very enthusiastic." He rubbed his hands together. "This is certainly an unexpected turn of events." As he stood, he looked at the chessboard. "Will you capture your pawn, please?"

Diane took his black pawn and captured hers. "Shall I pick you up at your house early tomorrow morning?" she said.

"Yes, please. The crew will meet me there, and they can follow you." He took his jacket hanging on his coatrack and followed Diane out the door.

"You know, the terrain is a little rough. There is a substantial gully to traverse."

"I have traversed many a substantial gully in my time. You do not need to worry."

"Anyway, Whit Abercrombie said he would see about arranging for a temporary bridge across the creek. He thinks perhaps the county will do it."

"A creek—is that all we're talking about? A creek?"

"The creek is in a fifteen-foot-deep gully."

"You don't need to worry about me."

"I'm not. But it would look bad for me if I killed one of my curators on a field expedition."

"Then I'll do my best to make you look good."

They rode the elevator to the ground floor.

"Here." Diane handed him one of the three laptops she had been given by Kenneth Meyers to field test.

"This looks nice." He rubbed a hand over the metallic case.

"I think it is. I haven't looked at mine yet, but I believe it's the top of the line and good for field work. It works with a cell phone, so you can send any information to the museum. Let me know how it works."

"If the anthropology department knew how many perks this job came with, they'd send someone else over."

"That's what Sylvia Mercer said. I'm going to ask her to work with you on the faunal identification. She's the zoologist."

"Does she get a computer too?"

"Not one of these. She gets one for her office, like your other one."

"I get two computers. Well, this is just dandy."

Diane laughed at him and sent him on his way. Jonas Briggs went home to prepare, and Diane went to the faunal lab and Sylvia Mercer's office. Sylvia was in the lab rearranging the equipment.

"Dr. Mercer, I have a favor to ask."

"Shoot, and call me Sylvia, please. I hope you don't mind me rearranging the lab a little."

"No, whatever works. Remember that clavicle I was looking at the other day?" Diane didn't wait for an answer, but told her how she'd found the probable place it came from.

"The site is filled with animal bones. I was thinking that if I could match the taxidermist's records with the animal bones above and below the human remains, it might help establish the approximate time of death. I'd like you to identify some of the animal bones."

"Sure. If you've found a clavicle and astragalus, aren't the bones probably pretty much comingled?"

"I'm sure there's a lot of mixing, but I'm hoping enough stayed in place to give me a lead."

"Do you need me to come to your site?"

"It would help, but I don't want to take you away from your research."

"I can manage a few days. This sounds rather interesting."

Interesting, Diane thought to herself. Jonas Briggs, his students and now Sylvia Mercer all thought this was interesting. They saw the science, the puzzle. They wouldn't be so fascinated if they had seen it through her eyes, the dreadful tragedy of it. If they'd dug grave after grave after grave filled with the bodies of people who once had life and who had loved ones who still mourned them.

Diane thanked Sylvia and left for her own office. In the hallway outside Andie's office, she was surprised to run into Frank's ex-wife. Cindy had her blond hair pulled back into a loose twist and was dressed casually, with little makeup.

"Hi. I was just looking for your office."

"Good to see you again. I hope you and your husband had a good time at the reception."

"It was great. We really appreciated your invitation."

Diane directed her through Andie's office into hers and offered her a seat. "What brings you to the museum today?" She wondered if she sounded too harsh. She hadn't meant to, but she thought she knew why Cindy was there, and she was growing weary of the pressure.

"I thought it would be more polite to invite you to dinner in person than through Frank. Men often get things muddled."

"Thank you for your offer. I would like to come, but I've had something come up that's going to take me away from the museum most of the time for a while, so I'm not making any plans."

Cindy shifted in her seat and gave Diane a wan smile. "I understand. But you have to eat."

It occurred to Diane that Cindy herself must be under a lot of pressure from her husband for her to be here doing something that so obviously made her uncomfortable.

"I'll probably be eating here at the museum in the evenings. I'll be putting in overtime, since I'll be gone during the day."

"Of course. Perhaps next week, then."

"Perhaps, but I'm doing something that will take quite a while."

She hated to sound so cryptic, especially since it made her sound like she was lying.

"Something rather important has come up and I have to attend to it." She got out her calendar. "How about next month? Saturdays are usually good for me."

Cindy's face hardened. "That will be too late."

Diane cocked an eyebrow. "Too late?"

"Look, Diane, I'm really no good at this, so I'll be blunt. I'm sure you've guessed anyway. David wants to talk to you about the museum. This . . . this . . . . "—she searched for words—"opportunity has come his way. It means quite a sum of money. It could pay for Kevin's college education and then some."

"He's been approached by Mark Grayson."

"More likely, he approached Mark Grayson." There was such bitterness in her voice that Diane suspected they had had harsh words over it. "He tells me there are plenty of great places for the museum other than this building. I've been in the rooms here. None are filled. You could house the entire contents in a much smaller, more modern building."

"I know what the argument is. It's the one Mark's been telling everyone, and it's wrong. Do you know why Mark is so keen on this?"

Cindy shrugged her thin shoulders. "Something to do with Japan—hotels and golf courses. Mark wants to purchase the building and land through another company and sell it. That's about all I know. He promised David a substantial commission if he could influence you."

Through Frank, thought Diane. And through his son? Surely, Cindy wouldn't allow that. "Unless the numbers add up to something fantastic for the museum—and right now they don't—it isn't going to happen."

Cindy looked away. Her eyes rested on a photograph of

a stalagmite-and-stalactite formation, but Diane doubted she was seeing it. When she brought her head around again, her soft brown eyes were now as hard as flint.

"This is just a job for you. There's nothing you lose by agreeing to sell, and there is everything to be gained for other people—for us, for Kevin. If you had children, you would understand. You do things for your children. If you care about Frank, you should care about his child."

Cindy Reynolds' face suddenly transformed from hard and angry to startled and frightened. Diane realized her own anger must have taken over her face as well as her pounding heart.

"Mrs. Reynolds, I did have a child." She clutched the locket around her neck. "She's now dead. Murdered by a man who was willing to kill thousands just to get what he wanted. I am weary and sick of men who think that what they want is more important than anything else in the world. I am singularly unsympathetic to people who are collaborators with that kind of man. If you indeed are a good mother, you won't use your son to get what your husband and Mark Grayson want."

Cindy gripped the arms of the chair and stood on shaky legs. "I . . . didn't know. Frank never said anything." She paused, apparently searching for words. "David doesn't know I came here. I hope you will not mention it to him, please."

"I don't have any reason to ever speak with your husband."

"Thanks . . . I . . . I can see my way out." Cindy left through Andie's office, looking defeated. Diane followed, watching her go out the door.

Andie sat, wide-eyed, at her desk. "Diane, are you all right?"

"I suppose you heard our conversation."

"I didn't mean to, but yes. I didn't know. . . ."

Diane took off her locket and opened it. On one side there was a miniature of the photograph of her and her daughter. On the other was a small picture of Ariel's dimpled pixie face. She handed it to Andie.

"This is my daughter, Ariel. She died a little over a year ago."

Andie looked at the photograph with tears in her eyes. "She was a pretty little girl. Look at all that black hair."

"Yes, she was." Diane took the locket and put it back around her neck. "I would have told you about her, but it's been hard to talk about."

"I can understand that. I'm so sorry." Andie took a Kleenex from her drawer and blew her nose. "I don't understand why Grayson is so set on selling the museum. What's that about?"

"Money, apparently." Diane shrugged. "I have a feeling something else is going on, but I have no idea what it is." She started for her office, but turned back to Andie. "Do you remember me asking you at the party if you knew who asked for the 'Hall of the Mountain King'?"

Andie thought for a second. "Yeah, I remember. . . . It wasn't on the playlist, you said."

"No, it wasn't. Someone left a note for the quartet and signed my name. That piece of music was Ariel's favorite. She played it all the time on a CD player I gave her."

Andie's eyes widened again. "Oh, no. You think someone . . . ? That's mean."

"Yes, it is. It could've been a coincidence."

"But what a coincidence. You want me to try and find out who did it?"

"How?"

"I can kind of ask around. See if anybody saw someone leave a note. I can be discreet."

"Don't go out of your way, but if there is an opportunity . . ."

"Sure. I'm really sorry about your daughter. That's so sad."

"I was hoping to raise her here, occasionally bring her to the museum. I was thinking about asking Milo if we could put in a staff day-care center." She forced her mind away from that lost possibility. "It's why I quit forensic work. I couldn't face the work anymore. But now I find that I need to use my skills to help Frank and his friend's daughter." She told Andie about the pit of animal bones and the human talus.

"You're kidding. You found where that collarbone came from—a clavicle?" She said *clavicle* carefully, as if she were trying to learn a new word. "What was the other bone you said. A talus?"

"Yes. It's a bone in the foot. The tibia—the shinbone—sits on top of it. It has a pulleylike structure where the tibia rests that allows you to move your foot back and forth. It's also called an astragalus."

Andie swiveled her chair around to look at her feet and moved her foot up and down. "So, wow, you think you've found the guy?"

"It seems likely. I'm going to be excavating. Jonas Briggs and Sylvia Mercer will be joining me."

"Didn't I tell you he's a nice guy?"

"Yes, you did, and you were right. I'm going to be in and out for the next few days or weeks, depending. You'll be able to reach me on the cell phone if you need to."

"OK. Maybe I could go some time and watch?"

"The process is very slow. It could be boring watching."

"I'd like to see it anyway."

"Sure. When we get a substantial portion uncovered, you can come take a look. In the meantime, would you have a table put in . . ." Diane thought for a moment. "The room across from the docents' offices. That's still empty, isn't it?"

Andie nodded. "We may have a few things stored there, but not much. You need a place to work?"

"Yes. Better yet, you know that corner room on the third floor, west wing? That's completely out of the way. Set up something there. And don't mention this to anyone. I won't be in tomorrow morning. I'll be at the Abercrombie farm, excavating the dump site."

Chapter 24

Whit Abercrombie, with the help of the county road crew under the direction of the sheriff, had constructed a small footbridge across the creek at the point of easiest access in the gully. They'd widened the narrow path that led down one side of the gully and up the other, anchoring stepping-stones every few feet. It was serviceable enough to carry equipment from vehicles parked along the roadway that led to Luther Abercrombie's cow pasture. Whit had also brought in his farm tractor with a brush hog and mowed a better path from the road to the creek crossing.

It was still relatively early when Diane and her crew finished setting up a tent to serve as a field office and had inventoried the cameras, mapping equipment, digging tools and other assorted equipment. But the early-morning Georgia sun had already heated the air to over ninety degrees. It would only get hotter as the day progressed, and the section they were working in had only saplings for shade.

To Diane's relief, Jonas' former students were experienced archaeological field crew, just as he'd promised. They'd brought three more people than the promised four—a total of four men and three women, dressed in cutoffs, tee shirts and sneakers. One of the women was interested in examining a model for taphonomic processes—the study of what happens to human and animal remains after death. For archaeologists, the knowledge means finding cultural clues to people's lives; for forensic anthropologists, understanding the fate of human remains can mean uncovering clues to their death.

In particular, the student was interested in looking at the differences in bone damage from butchering and from wild-animal scavenging. In the archaeological context, her project translated into the ability to tell human activity from natural phenomena. Diane didn't mind allowing the archaeologists to conduct research on the animal pit. Whatever information they discovered would be useful to her field too.

"We'll start by making lanes in the search area. The pit will be the center of the area, but we'll search all around it first, using a line search pattern. Are you familiar with that?" They all nodded, giving her their full attention.

"Isn't this method also called a strip search?" said one of the guys, to a round of laughter.

"In a manner of speaking," said Diane, trying not to smile too much. "It's called the line or strip method. OK. Look for signs of bone and mark them with a flag—red if you suspect it's human, green if animal. Yellow if it's some other object." She'd feared that some might have a don't-tell-me-what-I-already-know-how-to-do attitude, but their expressions were attentive and interested.

"Like a ground survey," said a woman.

"Exactly. I've been told that a light layer of dirt was used to cover each load of animals that were dumped— or at least, most of the time. So if we can, I'd like to use those dirt layers to mark different strata. Notice that I've tagged some of the trees growing in the pit. Excavate around them. I need to know where the roots go. And we may be cross-sectioning the trees when we're finished." Diane paused and looked at the pit. "The human remains here may be linked to a recent homicide. The more time that elapses after that crime, the harder it is to solve. It's important that you work as quickly as you can and still do a thorough job."

"We'll do a good job," said Jonas.

"Thanks. And I appreciate the willingness of all of you to do this."

Marking the search lanes didn't take long. The pit, as Diane called it, was a plugged-up erosion ditch about seven by ten feet. Whit said the runoff had been diverted at a place several feet up from the ditch, and as far as he remembered, this area hadn't seen much washing out. Diane was glad for that. Digging in a soggy pit that had been filled with animal carcasses didn't bear thinking about.

When they finished marking the search lanes, the search area was about sixty feet by sixty feet, with the pit in the center. The north section was down a slope through thick underbrush terminating in another erosion gully, which took most of the runoff that used to go into the dump pit.

Starting at one end, they walked slowly down the strips with Diane setting the pace, scrutinizing the ground, using long sticks to gently move away leaves and other detritus to uncover bare ground. Diane wanted to finish this search before they stopped for lunch. She didn't expect to find any clues dropped by the perpetrator, but did expect to identify bones scavenged and dragged out by animals.

The temperature climbed quickly. It was forecast to reach a hundred today. It felt like it had already topped out. Diane's tee shirt was wet and her skin hot. She took a drink of water from a boda bag she had slung across her shoulder. She came upon the end of a long bone. It wasn't human. She sunk a green flag in the ground beside it.

A searcher let out a short laugh. "I found an arrowhead." His colleagues laughed with him. Under the circumstances, the archaeologists thought such a find to be ironic.

When they reached the end of the marked lines, they had completed half the search area. Switching to the remaining search lines, they began the slow search process again, looking and setting flags into the ground.

"I found a patella," said one of the guys.

"Human?" asked another.

"Do animals have them?" he asked.

"Damn straight," said a third guy. "My dog's kept jumping out of place and he'd be all stiff-legged. He had to have surgery to tack it down. Cost me a fortune, but he's fine now."

"Go ahead and put a red flag beside it," said Diane. "I'll check it out later."

There was more conversation during the last half of the search. But as Diane glanced at them, they never took their eyes off the ground. When the last leg of the initial survey was finished, there were small patches of flags around the pit from five to twenty-six feet—marking places where, in all probability, animals had dragged carrion from the pit. There were very few yellow flags. Diane wondered in passing if the guy had marked the arrowhead or simply picked it up.

"Let's break for lunch," she said, rubbing her sore back. "I know it's sort of a late lunch. And I thank you for the good job you're doing."

They had all brought packed lunches and now looked for comfortable shade to sit down in and eat. The only shade was in the surrounding woods several yards from their search area. Diane found a rock beside Jonas Briggs and sat down with her peanut butter sandwich, apple and bottled water. She was more tired than she thought she should be. *Must be old age creeping up on me,* she thought, but there was Jonas, looking as refreshed as when he started. She took a long drink of water.

When she was in the jungle digging, on those occasions when she was close enough to get back to the compound in a reasonable amount of time, she'd sometimes drive a couple of hours or more and arrive so hot and tired she'd collapse on the cot in one of the two rooms she rented from the mission school. Ariel would come with a bottle of water, pat her arm and snuggle up to her. As hot as Diane was, Ariel's warm little body was always a comfort. She'd tell Diane everything that had happened at the mission that day or what she'd learned in school. Diane would tell her a story, and before long she wasn't tired anymore. Sometimes the worst of her feelings was regret—that terrible wishing that more than anything she had taken Ariel out of the country. The wish sucked at her heart, hurting all the way to her throat, filling her eyes with tears.

"The Abercrombies are letting the crew bed down on the floor of their den," said Jonas, jolting Diane from her thoughts. "Mrs. Abercrombie's a very gracious woman. She's fixing us all supper this evening."

"That certainly is nice of her."

"It seems as though she likes to entertain, but her husband doesn't. This is her chance. Lucky for us."

Diane tucked away her sad thoughts and asked the crew members what each of them did. Two were looking for positions at universities, three were professional archaeology field-crew members, and two were working on their doctorates. During lunch she got a summary of their interests, which ran from taphonomy to pottery types and debitage, which was explained to her as the waste flakes from projectile-point production. Another of the doctoral students was about to explain behavioral-chain analysis when Frank and Whit arrived with the sheriff. Diane got up to greet them, feeling guilty at her relief for not having to listen to the explanation.

"How are things going?" asked Frank, looking out over the terrain of flags and string.

"Got a good start. After we eat, we'll begin excavating."

"I appointed a couple of deputies to stay at the site," said the sheriff. "Maybe some of the guys would like to help them with guard duty. A couple of them said they always stay with their archaeology digs to warn off pot hunters. I didn't know there were people out in the woods actually looking for the stuff. Seems to me you wouldn't want to come upon somebody's patch."

"I think they mean people who steal artifacts," said Diane.

"Oh, well, that makes more sense. Got a call from your-all's chief of detectives yesterday." The sheriff laughed. "He's not real pleased with this project here. Thinks we're interfering. I asked him how locating the rest of a body to go along with that foot bone you found in my jurisdiction is an interference in anything he's doing in his city."

"And?" asked Frank.

"Came down to he didn't want me mentioning it to the newspapers that some of us think it might be connected to the Boone murders. God forbid facts might get in the way of his theory on the case."

"What's the deal with them?" asked Diane. "Why aren't they anxious for leads? Even if they don't lead anywhere, you don't know until you investigate."

"As far as they're concerned, they've got the killers in jail and the case is solved. This is the first big test of the mayor and his new chief of police's ideas for better police work. It's the mayor's chance to show the city council and the rest of Georgia that he's a man who gets things done in a big-city way. I'm sure he's making his campaign signs for governor right now."

"So," said Whit. "You have a collarbone and a foot bone. That's at least one, maybe two people." He suddenly laughed uneasily. "Two people buried here would look bad for us, wouldn't it?"

Frank and the sheriff looked askance at him. "Yeah," said the sheriff. "It sure would. One could be passed off as an accident. Two would be downright carelessness."

"Lady," Whit addressed Diane. "I really hope you don't find more than one person here."

"Right now we have a minimum number of one," said Diane, almost smiling at his sudden discomfort.

"Oh," said Frank, taking a large envelope from under his arm and handing it to her. "Here. I called your office, and Andie asked me to come by and bring this to you."

Andie had written on the envelope: *Fax from Ranjan Patel.*

"That was quick. It's the results from the stable isotope analysis."

Chapter 25

The phrase *stable isotope analysis* must have leaped out of their conversation and over to the crew, for suddenly they stopped talking and came over to Diane, carrying their sandwiches and drinking water.

"You had an SIA done on some material?" asked one of the doctoral students.

"On the original bone that started all this." Diane looked at the fax transmitted by her friend, Ran. It wasn't a particularly good copy, but she assumed he sent her an original in the mail. The first page had a list of numbers in a table. The other pages were Ranjan's conclusions, written in his typical pedantic manner.

You're in luck. Your fellow was a vegetarian—note the values in the table. However, I don't think your person was a vegan, nor did he, I think, consume an abundance of legumes. Interesting. The delta numbers and the levels of the trace element strontium suggest that he ate fish and shellfish. I am most excited about this. Another interesting possibility to think about: You said the fellow was young, perhaps an older teenager. This would mean he had these eating habits from childhood. Is vegetarianism in children common? You must identify the fellow so we can test what the values seem to indicate. Also, I would say death took place five years ago.

Ranjan's report went on to explain the numbers in detail and listed all the caveats associated with them. Bottom line, however, was that this analysis could be a clue in identification. His last paragraph explained the oxygen-hydrogen stable isotope ratios.

"Your person grew up in a climate that is cold and humid," he wrote. "See table."

"Cool," "great stuff," and "let's find the guy" were the sentiments of the excavation crew.

"Ain't that something?" said the sheriff.

"Damn. You did it," said Frank. "You not only told me what the guy had for his last meal, but where he had it."

"Ranjan's warnings weren't just cover-your-ass warnings. The conclusions aren't written in stone," warned Diane. "There are many variables."

"Sure," said Frank. "But it's several damn good leads. We have a young man, perhaps in his late teens, perhaps a vegetarian, may have disappeared five years ago and may have grown up somewhere in the North. That's enough to start looking at the missing person database."

"Would the database have their eating habits?" asked one of the crew.

"Sometimes," said Frank. "Particularly if there's some kind of medical condition or distinguishing trait. The family usually tries to give as much information as they can."

"Do you think he lived on the coast—maybe Maine or somewhere on the East Coast?"

The crew was getting into the spirit of the hunt. They liked the idea that their science might solve the mystery.

"Maybe," said Diane. "He could just as well be from Michigan, North Dakota, Washington State or Canada, for that matter. If you guys are finished with lunch, we'd better start digging. Ranjan's going to be calling me every day to see if I've found him—or her."

"I'm going to go over and watch the digging for a while," said Whit, following the crew.

The sheriff watched Whit's retreating back and gave a half-hearted chuckle. "I think ol' Whit's a little nervous.

Be funny if he and his family turned out to be serial killers."

Frank laughed. "Yeah, that'd be just hilarious."

They were joking, but as Diane watched the crew gather their tools and remembered that they were staying in the Abercrombies' home, she said, "You don't think?" She let the question hang.

"No, of course not," said Frank. "Whit and I went to school together."

"Everybody went to school with somebody," said Diane. "You didn't go to school with his father, did you?"

"What's this about?" asked Frank.

"Nothing. It's just that the crew is staying in the Abercrombie house."

The sheriff laughed. "Boy, wouldn't that be funny."

"It might be Mrs. Abercrombie," said Frank. "Maybe this vegetarian fellow was a guest, and he insulted her by not having any of her pot roast."

"This isn't funny at all," said Diane.

"Yes, it is," said Frank. "I know these people. Do you think Whit would lead us right to the dump site if it'd been him? I think you—and the sheriff," Frank glared at him, "are letting your imaginations run away with you."

The sheriff chuckled again, clearly enjoying letting his imagination run away with him. "I'm going back to the office. I'll tell my deputies to keep an eye out if they see one of the Abercrombies wielding an axe. Seriously, Ms. Fallon, I've know'd ol' Luther all my life. He's a good ol' boy and wouldn't hurt a fly. Neither would Whit. They're good churchgoing folk." The sheriff took a deep breath before he started back to his car. "I do wish the perp could have picked a more convenient place to dump the body," he was saying as they watched his stout body disappear through the trees and underbrush.

"Maybe you're right," said Diane. "How's Star?"

"Angry. Angry at the guards who found her before she bled to death, angry at the police for arresting her and not looking for whoever wiped out her family, at her parents for dying, at herself for not dying with them.

I think she's afraid if she gets over the anger, the grief will be more than she can stand."

Like all the people who couldn't find anything to say to her, Diane couldn't think of any comfort for Frank. She couldn't say that Star would get over it, because that would be a lie. Or that time will heal—it hadn't healed her. She'd learned to get by, day by day, but that was hardly a comfort.

"Maybe anger's a good thing right now. It takes up space," she said.

"I'm going back to see her this evening. I've been staying with her at the hospital as much as I can—to let her know she's not alone. Why don't you come with me tonight to visit? You can tell her what you're doing."

Diane hesitated a moment, not wanting to watch someone else's grief when she had no comfort to offer her, but in the end relented. "Sure, if you think it will help. When do you have to get back to work?"

"The end of next week. Think we can solve this thing by then?"

Diane offered a weak smile. "I don't see why not."

Frank shook his head. "I can't help but wonder"—he gestured toward the pit where the crew were laying grid lines to start excavating—"what if this is not related to what happened to George and Louise and we've wasted all this time and energy in the wrong direction?"

"This is someone who needs justice too. Besides, what are the chances that your friends find a human bone, then get murdered within the week? My gut feeling is that someone didn't want this site found. Have you talked to people they might have told about the bone?"

"Some. So far, looks like they either told no one or no one is admitting it."

After arranging with Frank to pick her up at the museum later on, she went back to digging. The crew had laid out a grid of string and stakes. One of the guys was setting up the tripod and transit for mapping. Another guy and one of the women were setting up a screen to sift out the smaller objects from the dirt they removed. The remaining members of the crew were either driving stakes around the outlying bones or beginning excavation of the grids. It was going well; they didn't seem to need her. How tempting to just leave in their hands this thing that looked too much like a mass burial.

Let's just do it and get it over with, she told herself, squatting down beside a grid containing exposed bone. There was a row of teeth that looked like a deer's. Not human; that was good. She took her trowel and began removing the dirt from the bone. Before long she'd uncovered a deer skull. The top skull plate had been sawed through to remove the antlers and a portion of the skull. Normal find for a taxidermist's pit.

By the end of the day, a large portion of the first layer of the pit had been uncovered, leaving a tangle of exposed animal bones standing out in relief.

"We'll call it a day," said Diane, standing up, observing the completed work. "You guys are doing a good job. Fast too." She carefully walked among the grid squares, surveying the bone. All animal that she saw. A little easier than a pit of all humans, but it was death just the same. She didn't think she could be a hunter. As she started to step out of the grids so they could cover the area with plastic for the night, she spotted the end of a bone just about to be uncovered. Diane walked over and squatted down beside the woman who was working on that square.

"See something?" the young woman asked.

"It's been gnawed on by one of the canine family, but it's the distal end of a human humerus—the end that fits with the radius and ulna, the bones of the forearm," said Diane. She had expected to find an arm and perhaps a shoulder girdle close to the surface, since the original clavicle had made its way to the surface. She liked it when her expectations were met.

"Think the rest of him is close by?" asked the woman.

Diane shrugged. "Maybe. Or an animal could have separated the arm from the torso and dragged it here, or it may have percolated to the top."

"Grim stuff," she said.

"Yes, that's the word for it. *Grim.*"

*   *   *

Diane went from the site to the museum to check the day's activities before meeting Frank. Andie had left notes on her desk. Nothing urgent. She showered in her private bathroom off the conference room of her office. She slicked back her short wet hair, put on her minimalist makeup, and changed into denim pants, a black tee and maroon shirt jacket. It was good to feel clean.

There were more people in the museum after hours these days; the closer they got to the public opening, the more people stayed late. Her absence today reminded her that she needed to find an assistant director. She hadn't liked any of the applications that had come across her desk and wasn't sure she wanted to promote anyone in house.

She took the stairs to Jonas' office. Inside, she studied his chessboard. She had started the game to make Jonas feel at home, and was surprised how much she enjoyed it. It had been a long time since she had played her last game with Gregory. He nearly always won, except that time she had beat him in forty-six moves. She moved her other knight to the bishop three position and left the office, locking it behind her, and went down to meet Frank.

The museum seemed to be looking gentler—not quite so harsh as her first images of it—perhaps due to the good work of the groundskeepers, who were constantly planting, landscaping and manicuring.

"Dr. Fallon."

Diane turned from looking at the building to two girls coming up the steps—Emily, the cellist, and Lacy, the violist from the string quartet.

"Hello. You here to meet Melissa and Alix? Are they working late?"

"No. We came to see you," said Emily.

"Maybe we shouldn't," said Lacy, grabbing her friend's arm.

"You want a job?" asked Diane, smiling at them. "We can always use energetic workers."

"No, it's not that," said Emily. "It's something else."

She looked up at the windows as if looking for a spy. "It's kind of personal."

"Would you like to go to my office?"

"That would be better."

As Diane led them to her office, she called Frank and told him she would be running a little late. Entering her office from the private door, she led the two young women to her conference room. The stuffed sofa and chairs in the corner were more comfortable and less forbidding than her main office. She sat in one of the chairs and motioned for Emily and Lacy to sit on the sofa.

"Now, what can I do for you?"

"It's about Melissa," said Emily. She hesitated a moment, and Lacy interrupted.

"We're friends with Mike Seger, her boyfriend, too." She stopped a moment and took a breath. "This is really hard for us. We promised."

"Go on." Diane sat, waiting for a revelation. She couldn't have been more shocked when it came.

"I know you think Mike is hitting Melissa," said Emily. "He's not. It's Alix."

Diane opened her mouth, closed it and opened it again. "Alix? I don't understand. Did Mike tell you to say this?"

"No," said Lacy. "He doesn't know we're here, and we don't want him or anyone else to know."

"Please explain it to me."

"Melissa and Alix have known each other a long time. I think they were even in day care together. The two of us met them in first grade, so we know both of them well. Alix has a temper and she hits. She always has. She hit me once in second grade, and I knocked her down. She didn't do it again."

"That's true," said Lacy. "She tried to hit me too, and I slapped her face hard. If you fought back, she backed off."

"All kids hit now and then," said Diane.

"Yes," said Emily, "but Alix was different. She always hit with her fists—or whatever she had in her hands— and she never grew out of it. She and Melissa have been best friends for a long time, and Melissa is totally loyal to her—and never fought back."

"Are you saying it's Alix causing the bruises on Melissa?"

"Yes. Her parents think she's just clumsy. Mike thought it was her father until he saw Alix punch her hard in the arm. Melissa made us promise not to tell. She says it's not Alix's fault."

Diane stood up and walked around her desk and looked at the two of them sitting side by side on the sofa. They looked sincere. "I'm having a hard time grasping this."

"We thought you would. But it's true. Alix will hit anyone who will put up with it. She even hits her boyfriend, Dylan."

"Yes," said Lacy, "Emily and I both saw how she bruised him. He's crazy about her. I don't know how she commands such loyalty. If I beat up on my boyfriend, he'd be out of here."

"We didn't want you to blame Mike, or we wouldn't have said anything," said Emily. "Something like this could hurt him. Not just with you, but with Dr. Lymon."

"It's true," said Lacy. "If we were lying to protect him, we'd have come up with a more believable story. Look, we promised Melissa we wouldn't ever tell."

"So don't tell anyone, please," added Emily.

"The two of you are adults now, and you know that there are some promises you shouldn't make."

"I know, but we don't want you to get the wrong idea. Alix really is nice. She's quick to give you help with your music if you need it. You can count on her in a crisis, and most of the time she's real sweet."

"I won't tell who told me, but I will mention this to a family friend of Melissa's."

Emily and Lacy looked at each other and back at Diane. "I suppose that's all right."

"It is all right. It's not all right for Melissa to be abused by anyone, and it's not right that innocent people be blamed. And if Alix is truly a nice person other than this, she needs counseling, not secrecy."

Emily wrinkled her brow. "Does this mean you believe us or not?"

"I don't disbelieve you. It's just hard to wrap my brain around."

"Well, I can understand that," said Emily. "It is weird."

Diane escorted them out of the museum and watched them get into their car. Alix? Could that possibly be true? She walked back to her office and called Laura.

"I find it hard to believe," said Diane. "I've never heard of such a thing."

"It's rare," said Laura, "but not unheard of. Melissa's obviously dependent on Alix and their friendship. You can't tell me who told you?"

"No. And I don't want to spread rumors either. I don't know for sure if this is true, but the source seemed very sincere, and is in a position to know."

"So you're putting it all in my lap?"

"Yes."

"Thanks."

"Don't mention it. How about lunch at the museum sometime? We're opening the restaurant in a few days."

"You're on. What's this I hear about you digging again? You found a body?"

"I'd prefer not to go into that right now. Where did you hear?"

"On the TV news. Something about the Abercrombie farm. I just caught the tail end of it. Wouldn't have caught that, but your name jumped out at me."

"Oh, great. I suppose Grayson and his bunch heard it too."

"So what? I think it would be good for the museum to have a forensic anthropology unit."

"Don't even think it."

"Talk to you later."

Diane hoped this was the last of her involvement in the Melissa saga. As much as she wanted to stop any abuse, this was turning out to be an odd can of worms. She locked up her office and walked out of the museum just as Frank drove up.

"Thanks for coming," he said. "Maybe we can have a late dinner after we see Star."

"Maybe, but I need to get in bed early. I'm working two jobs now."

"I appreciate that too."

"I guess you heard we were on the TV news," she said. "What? You mean . . ."

"Digging at the Abercrombie farm," she said.

Frank groaned. "We'll have to ask the sheriff to double security around the clock. The place will be crawling with TV newspeople. It goes with the territory, I guess."

Frank called the sheriff on his cell phone. The sheriff had already heard the news. Diane could hear his cursing coming from Frank's phone.

On the way to the hospital, Diane explained what they had accomplished at the animal pit. "The last thing we found before shutting down was another human bone—an arm bone."

"Another one? Are you sure?"

"I wish you wouldn't keep asking if I'm sure. Yes, I do know the bones of the human skeleton."

"I wasn't doubting you. I'm just—surprised, I suppose. I'm still surprised at this whole thing—George, Louise, Jay. It still doesn't seem possible."

They parked in the visitors' area at the hospital and entered the building. Diane didn't like hospitals. She didn't suppose many people do. She didn't like the antiseptic smell, nor passing rooms where people lay sick with their relatives around them. On a primal level it was frightening, like a dark room or hanging your arms or legs off the bed at night. She saw Star's room up ahead—the only one with a guard sitting outside the door. As they drew nearer, they heard a raised voice inside the room, apparently directed at Star.

Chapter 26

"Don't try this passive-aggressive shit with me, girl. It won't work. I'll let you sleep all night in your own urine."

Frank shot ahead and entered the room before Diane. The guard, a policeman that looked to Diane like he might still be in high school, let him pass unchallenged. He stopped Diane.

"I'm with Frank Duncan," said Diane.

He lay the book he was reading under his chair. "I'll have to search your purse."

"Sure."

Diane opened her purse, which was basically a large billfold with a shoulder strap, and the policeman looked around in the zippered areas. Diane couldn't imagine what kind of weapon he thought he would find in the small spaces.

"Have anything in your pockets?"

"Only this."

Diane pulled out a small leather card case with her drivers license, one credit card, two fifty-dollar bills, and a small picture of Ariel. After spending years traveling, she developed a habit of carrying important identification on her person, not in a place that was easy to get separated from.

"That's fine." He motioned her in.

Inside, Frank was trying to find out what was going on. Star and a nurse's aide were both talking at the same time. Star's black hair, which was short in the family photograph, was almost to her shoulders and fringed on the ends. The blond streak that had framed her face was now a purple-fuchsia and had grown out to the ends. Her pixie face was as pale as the pillowcase, even in anger, and her dark brown eyes were made to look even larger by the dark circles underlining them. Star looked small in the hospital bed and pitiful with bandages on both her wrists, halfway up her forearms. Restraints on her upper arms fastened her to the bed.

"I rang for the nurse over an hour ago. You can't tie me to the bed and leave me here without any bathroom breaks."

The nurse's aide, a woman in her mid-forties dressed in a stained white pantsuit, looked as if she were trying to stare Frank down.

She turned to Star. "There's a lot of sick people on this floor. We don't have time to run to you every five minutes."

"Wouldn't it have been easier to let her go to the bathroom than change her sheets?" Frank was having a hard time remaining calm and polite.

"She can hold it until we have time to get to it."

The stubborn set of the woman's face angered Diane. This was a health-care worker, for heaven's sake.

"Are you aware," said Diane, "that 'holding it,' as you put it, can lead to a bladder infection?"

"No worse than she deserves," muttered the woman so low that Diane almost didn't catch it.

Frank shot out of the room so suddenly that it startled even Diane. The woman looked at the door, then at Diane, a stubborn frown setting around her mouth. "Where's he going?"

"I imagine to the head nurse or to the hospital administrators."

As the woman started out the door, Diane called after her, "Star needs help," but the aide didn't look back.

Diane walked out the door to the policeman, who spoke before Diane had a chance to say anything. "I just guard the door—I don't change bedpans."

"Of course you don't," said Diane with her best sweet

voice. "And you shouldn't have to. But I need you to undo her restraints so she can go to the bathroom and clean up."

He sighed and rose, putting his book down again. Diane noticed it was a Western. He stepped into the room long enough to unlock the restraints. Diane thanked him and helped Star out of bed. There was a large wet place on the sheets and the back of her gown.

"So you're Uncle Frank's girlfriend," said Star as she went into the bathroom.

"We date," said Diane.

"Are you sleeping with him?"

"None of your business," said Diane pleasantly and heard Star give a faint laugh.

"I'm going to take a shower," she said.

"Should you get your bandages wet?" asked Diane.

"I'll just turn on the shower and rinse off my body. I won't get them wet. God forbid that bitch should have to change them for me."

"You have some more pajamas?"

"In the dresser drawer. Some underwear too."

Diane was glad that Star was concerned with cleanliness and dignity. People in despair give up their pride first—"pride goeth before the fall," a meaning of the aphorism that made more sense to Diane than the one more often attributed to it.

Of course, Star might not have meant her injuries to be life threatening. She could have only wanted to get out of jail or to get attention. But Diane noted that her bandages covered half of her forearm, a serious sign. Often people bent on suicide slit their wrists lengthwise up the arm, along the vein, to insure a bleed out. That looked like what Star did. *She must be in tremendous emotional pain to have done that with a dull cutting tool,* Diane thought.

Diane retrieved a pair of cotton pajamas and panties and stood outside the door. An orderly entered with clean sheets and began stripping the bed. Diane watched him take off the soiled sheets, clean the plastic mattress cover and remake the bed. He worked quickly and said nothing, merely nodding at Diane on the way out. By the time he finished, Star was ready for her clothes and reached out the door for them.

When Frank arrived, Diane had Star tucked into a clean bed and the policeman reentered to lock her restraints.

"Why don't you leave those off, as long as we're here?" asked Frank.

"They told me not to," he said and went back to his post.

Frank shook his head. "When this is over . . ." He was interrupted by a nurse entering the room.

Diane expected another angry nurse, but this woman was friendly. Slim, in her early thirties, with light brown skin and short hair, she looked efficient and spoke to Star like she cared. Her name tag said LORAINE WASHING-TON, and she was a registered nurse, not an aide.

"How are you feeling?" she asked as she took Star's blood pressure and pulse.

"I'm okay," said Star.

"Your blood pressure's a little low." The RN took her temperature. "And you're a little hot. The next time you have to go, I want you to collect some urine for me." She set a specimen cup on the nightstand.

"I'm OK, really," said Star. "It's just that when I have to go, I have to go."

"How many times have you been kept waiting?"

Star shrugged. "Just in the evenings. That nurse doesn't like me. In the daytime, or when Uncle Frank is here, things are all right."

"They'll be all right from now on. I want you to drink lots of water."

"That'll just make things worse."

"No, it'll make things better."

"Then you think you can talk that policeman into coming in every thirty minutes and giving me a sip?" Star tried to lift her arms against the restraints.

Nurse Washington smiled. "I see what you mean. Someone will come and check on you more often and give you a drink. Do you like juice?"

"Orange juice."

"How about cranberry?"

"I don't know."

"I'll see you get some of that too. It'll be good for your bladder." She patted her arm and left.

"Well, Uncle Frank, you must have ripped somebody a new one."

"I had some words with a few people. I don't think this was the first complaint about that particular aide." He reached over and grasped her foot through the covers and shook it. "You doing OK?"

"Sure. I did a number on my arms and they hurt and itch like hell, I've just peed all over myself, my family is dead and the whole world thinks I killed them."

"Not the whole world," said Frank.

"They said they was going to try me as an adult. All my life people's been telling me I'm just a kid, and now they decide I'm an adult because that makes me in worse trouble."

"I doubt it will even get to trial. We'll find out who really did it before then," said Frank with such conviction that Diane believed him.

"Will it matter?" said Star. "They'll still be dead, and people like that bitch nurse will still believe I did it."

"It turns out that the nurse's aide is a friend of Crystal's," said Frank. "I thought I'd seen her before."

Star rolled her eyes. "That explains a lot—for starters, why she's as dumb as dirt."

"How have you been treating the people around here?" asked Frank.

"Better'n they treat me."

"Why don't you try just being polite to the people here and not cursing. You don't have to make friends with them, a little politeness will do—after all, they're armed with needles."

Star gave Frank a half smile and turned to Diane. "Frank tells me you met Crystal and her husband. Aren't they a kick? Crystal's so proud of Gilroy the boy toy. He's about fifty years younger than she is, you know."

"More like fifteen," Frank said.

"She parades him around like he's some prize she won

If he was the big prize, I'd hate to have come in second in that contest."

Diane had to laugh at Star. So did Frank. She could be a charmer. Diane tried to visualize her in a killing frenzy, but couldn't imagine her doing what it took to kill her parents.

"I heard on the TV that Dean gave himself up. Did he really?"

"He had help," said Frank.

"That figures. How was he?"

"In need of a good meal and a place to sleep," said Frank.

"Serves him right. He ran out on me, you know. As soon as he heard about my parents, he got scared, even tried to steal my coin collection. We was supposed to go to California. He said he knows somebody that could get us on as movie extras. You know, people in a crowd. That would be fun."

"Star," said Frank. "Can you tell us anything about Jay's friends?"

She turned her head away and stared out the window at the night sky.

Diane took her hand. "Star, we need your help, if you can give it. We want very much to find the person who did this to your family."

Star shifted her gaze to Diane. "You don't believe I did it?"

"No."

"Why?"

"Frank believes you, and I trust his judgment—and you aren't tall enough."

Frank jerked his head around to Diane. Star's eyes grew round. "Not tall enough? What's that supposed to mean?"

"The person who shot your brother was taller than either you or Dean."

"How do you know?" asked Star.

"The trajectory of the bullet. It was from a taller person, and you couldn't have been standing uphill, because there isn't a rise in the vicinity where Jay was shot."

"If you know that, why don't the police?" asked Star.

"Because right now, they don't want to, and they will no doubt try to explain away the discrepancy. However, it's there. Star, I can't give you any words of comfort about the loss of your family. It's a terrible thing that's happened to you, but you can get though it and have a life. It'll be slow progress and hard, but you have to keep your sights on the things you loved about them, not their deaths."

Star looked away again, but Diane took her chin and turned her face back.

"Frank's right—we'll find out who did this. And even if you have to go to trial before we discover the real killer, you won't be convicted. The detective made too many mistakes. She allowed the crime scene to be compromised and she's overlooked important information. All they have is the fact that you took your mother's gun a year ago and you had some coins in your possession, and that can be explained."

"They were mine. You know that, don't you, Uncle Frank?"

Frank nodded. "Your parents were holding them for your education. But yes, they were yours."

Star's face brightened. "They don't really have anything, do they? I mean, the coins are mine and I took them weeks ago. Crystal's lying about me like she always does. The gun too. Mom and Dad took the gun back a year ago and they locked it up."

"No, they don't have anything. But we need to ask you a few questions so we can help you. Will you answer them?"

Star nodded.

"Star," said Frank. "We need to know why Jay was out that night. Do you know any friends he may have been meeting?"

Star frowned. "I don't understand him being out either. He didn't do things like that. He was mad at me because, since I was always the one in trouble, the burden was on him to be good. None of his friends that I know of would have been out either. But . . ."

"But what?" asked Frank.

"Jay liked to hang around older boys. He was really impressed by them. I mean, what kid isn't? He may have friends that none of us knew about. I just don't know. He was in the Scouts, he went to school, to church, and played soccer. His friends were in those places."

"Jay never confided in you about who he liked to hang around with?" prodded Frank.

"I wasn't around much lately to confide in. He liked to hunt and go camping. That kind of thing. Maybe his friends will talk to you."

"If you think of anything, let me know," said Frank.

A disembodied voice announced the end of visiting hours. Frank kissed Star on the cheek, and he and Diane left.

"You didn't mention before about the height of the perp," said Frank.

"It just dawned on me. I guess I'm slipping. I remember seeing the trajectory information on the autopsy report, and the lay of the land around the body suddenly dawned on me. Neither Star nor Dean is tall enough to have fired the shot that killed Jay."

They left the hospital and Frank drove Diane back to her car at the museum. As she moved to open the door to get out, Frank leaned over and kissed her. "Let me take you to dinner tomorrow evening. They'll be taking Star back to the jail. And, well, both of us need a break."

"That sounds good. Let's wait and see how things go at the pit tomorrow. Maybe we can order in a pizza and watch TV or something."

He kissed her again. "That sounds good too—maybe better."

Diane got in her car and drove to her apartment and pulled into a parking space in front of the entrance. She got out, feeling like she'd left something undone at the museum and wondering how she was going to explain to the board about this current museum project. Community relations, perhaps. The thought made her smile. As she approached the steps and took out her key, she was hit hard in the stomach.

Chapter 27

Diane fell to the ground, gasping for air. She tried to rise to her hands and knees and simultaneously catch her breath. A blur of motion carrying a heavy shoe with it kicked her hard in the side. Lightning pain shot through her body and the force knocked her backward off the sidewalk. She fell helplessly into a roll down the grassy slope into the dark. She couldn't stop the momentum of her fall, tumbling until she crashed into bushes. Pushing herself to her feet, she tried to yell out. Her voice wouldn't come out of her throat. Desperation and fear rushed over her as the sound of muffled footfalls ran toward her in the dark. She was consumed by the overwhelmingly urgent need to get away, to run—anywhere.

Two steps, she stumbled and rolled farther down the hill. Footsteps coming faster toward her. She pulled herself to her feet again and started running, looking for a weapon, anything, but it was too dark to see. Running, trying to go faster; something caught her clothes from behind, jerked her backward. Her legs collapsed under her. A strong arm slipped around her throat. She pushed up, kicked the legs behind her and grabbed at the arm around her neck, pulling at thick gloved fingers, prying them loose. She heard a muffled cry of pain close to her ear as she pulled a finger back hard. She tried clawing at eyes, but got only a handful of wool. She held on to it, hoping to blind him. She kicked and stomped at the legs behind her, twisting and turning, trying to free herself. She hit her mark half a dozen times and heard suppressed yelps. She bit down hard on the arm and got punched in the back.

A car door slammed—twice. Witnesses. Help. She tried to scream for help but was pushed to the ground, her face held hard in the grass for five seconds . . . ten . . . Then he was off her after one last knee in her ribs, and running away.

She staggered to her feet, almost blinded by pain, but ran after him, watching him run past parked cars, down the street, and turn up another street before she could resist the pain no more.

Help. She needed to find help. She stayed in the light and made her way, stumbling, holding her arms tightly folded across her stomach, back to her apartment building.

She made it to the door. Climbing the stairs, trying to get to her apartment, she realized her keys were in her purse and it was gone. Damn that son of a bitch. Her cell phone was gone with it. She stepped, half stumbling, back down the stairs to the first floor and banged on the landlady's door.

"I'm coming, I'm coming. Keep your pants on," came a muffled voice inside. The door opened tentatively. "Oh, it's you, Ms. Fallon. My, what happened?"

"Someone mugged me outside the building. My purse is gone, and my keys. I have an extra set. Would you let me in my apartment, please?"

"Why, sure." She went away for a moment and came back with a master key. As she closed the door, Diane thought she saw the tail of a cat swishing. At least she solved one mystery.

"Someone attacked you here?" said the landlady. "I don't like that one bit. I've asked the police to drive by once in a while, but do they listen to me? No, they get on the television and talk about what a good police department the mayor is putting together. Well, I don't see it." Diane followed her upstairs. "I've been afraid something like this would happen. I was telling Dorothy—she's a friend at the beauty shop—I was telling her that it's just a matter of time, with all the growing

Rosewood's been doing the past few years and all the young people moving in from Atlanta, that we'll start having crime. I supported the mayor in the beginning when he was talking about us having a professional police force, but I haven't seen it. I see the talk, and they sure take out the taxes. Do you want me to call the police?"

"I'll call them from the hospital. I just need to get in my apartment and get my keys."

"The hospital? You are hurt, aren't you? Well, this just won't do." She opened Diane's door and followed her in. "Do you want me to drive you? I can do that, or I can call my nephew."

Diane found her keys and started back out the door. "No. But thank you. I can drive myself. I just need to make sure I don't have any broken ribs."

As she closed the door she heard movement in the apartment across from hers. She hurried down the stairs as quickly as the pain would allow. The last thing she wanted was to get into a conversation with Mrs. Odell about Marvin and his allergies. The landlady followed, streams of conversation still flowing from her. Diane thanked her again when she was able to get a word in. She made it to her car, got inside, locked the door and sat in the driver's seat, trying to breathe normally. After a moment she put the key in the ignition. She knew she was hurt more than she wanted to believe.

As Diane drove the distance to the hospital, she wondered several times if she should have let the landlady drive her. But after what seemed like too long, the lights of the hospital finally came into sight. She left her car in the emergency room parking and made it to the intake desk. In gasps, she told the nurse what had happened. After giving her name, address and insurance carrier, Diane sat in the waiting room. She wanted to call Frank, but he had too much on him already. She didn't want to bring him more worry.

She watched the other people waiting. A man with a bloody rag around his hand, a child with a cough, a woman with an ice pack on her ankle, others she couldn't tell what was wrong. Some watched her too, and she wondered what she looked like. If she looked like she felt, she looked awful. Her back was killing her. She had some serious throbbing pains in her stomach and ribs.

Who attacked her? she wondered. A mugger? Or did it have to do with the bones she was excavating? She lay her head back against the wall.

She jerked awake and noticed some of the people had switched out with newcomers. The child was gone, and so was the man with the bleeding hand. She jumped when she felt a hand on her shoulder.

"Diane Fallon? Come with me, please. Can you walk, or do you need a wheelchair?"

"I can walk." *Barely,* she thought.

She followed a nurse into the examining room, where another nurse asked her to remove her shirt. There were broken blood vessels, welts and bruises in perhaps a dozen places she could see.

"You were attacked?" The nurse listened to her heart and took her blood pressure.

"Yes. Hit in the stomach and kicked in the ribs and the back. That's all I remember right now."

"Um hmm. Somebody worked you over good. What kind of pain are you in?"

"I hurt pretty bad."

"We need to get some X rays for the doctor, and the police will want to talk to you. You can put your shirt back on right now."

"Okay." Diane started to put her shirt back on. Her locket was missing. "My locket, it's gone. I've got to go look for it."

"The police will take care of that."

"No, you don't understand. My daughter gave it to me. It was a surprise. She worked sweeping out the schoolroom when I was away and got the nuns to order it for her. She picked it out from a catalog." Diane started crying.

"She was only six years old. I have to find it. You don't understand, she . . . she died, and she gave it to me." Out of context, she knew her story didn't make much sense, but she couldn't find the words to explain it any better. The woman probably thought she was crazy.

"I'm sure the police will find it." The nurse's voice was calm and soothing.

She must deal with hysterical people in the emergency room all the time, Diane thought.

After almost an hour and a half, she was taken to be x-rayed; she waited another half hour to see the doctor. The doctor on call told her nothing was broken but he was concerned about her right kidney. He thought it was only bruised, but would like to keep her overnight.

"Fine," Diane told him, and after another hour she was taken to a private room. Coincidentally, on the same floor as Star. All during that time, no policeman showed up.

The floor nurse gave her one of the nightgowns with no back, and as she removed her bra, the locket fell to the floor. She snatched it up and cried. The fastener was broken, but it could be fixed. When she got in bed she put it under her pillow in the small case that held her driver's license.

In about an hour, another nurse came in to take her blood pressure. It was Loraine Washington, the nurse who had helped Star.

"Didn't I just see you in here visiting a while ago?"

Diane explained what had happened.

"Right after you left here? That's terrible. Right at your own front door?"

"Thanks for taking good care of Star. A lot of people are pretty down on her right now."

"I always say a person is innocent until proven guilty, and if they do turn out to be proven guilty, then how you treated them is about the kind of person you are, not the kind of person they are."

"Those are nice sentiments. Can I quote you?"

"Certainly." She handed Diane a couple of pills and a glass of water. "These will help with the pain and help you sleep."

Diane swallowed the pills and lay back on the pillows. "I could use a good night's sleep."

She expected nightmares, but as far as she remembered, she didn't even dream. She woke up in the morning almost too sore to move, but she managed to make it to the bathroom. She took a quick shower but had to put back on yesterday's underwear. If she'd been thinking, she'd have grabbed a change of clothes while she was at her apartment. But they'd probably release her today.

Breakfast arrived while she was showering. Cereal, eggs, toast, orange juice and coffee. She ate the cereal and drank the juice. As she finished, a policeman, Izzy Wallace, arrived with his partner. He walked in the door looking sheepish.

"I wanted to apologize, Dr. Fallon, for the misunderstanding. Frank told me . . . well, about your experience. We're sorry too, we didn't get here last evening. A lot of things going on in town last night."

Diane felt too sore to argue with anyone at the moment. She merely nodded.

"Can you tell us what happened?"

Diane explained about the attack, and no, she didn't see a face, but he was male. Why? Because she saw him running and it was a male and he was strong. "He was around six feet tall," she said.

"How do you know that?" asked Izzy's partner.

"He was taller than me. He ran past the cars. I could tell where the top of the cars came to on him."

"Did you hear his voice?"

"No, he didn't say a word. He did make sounds when I kicked him, pulled his finger back and bit him, but nothing I'd recognize."

"How about smells? Did you notice anything distinctive?"

Diane thought for a moment. "No. No, I didn't."

"You say he took your purse?"

"I assume so. It was gone."

"What was in it?"

"My checkbook, keys, about twenty-five dollars, lipstick, a notepad."

"Credit card, driver's license?" prompted Izzy.

"I carry them separately in a pocket. A habit I picked up from traveling."

"A wise thing to do. We'll probably find your purse dumped somewhere and empty. I doubt we'll find the guy. Just nothing to go on."

"What if it wasn't a mugging? What if it was connected to the bones?"

"Bones? Oh, the bones. You think it might be?"

"I don't know. It's a possibility."

"Has anyone threatened you?"

"You mean, besides the mayor? No."

Both Izzy and his partner looked sheepish again.

"Or it could be related to the break-in at the museum. Have you found any leads there?"

"No. That's a dead end right now. Since nothing was taken . . ." He let the sentence trail off. Diane knew they weren't following up, but she couldn't resist making him feel uncomfortable.

"We'll do what we can," he said. "I'm supposed to be going off duty, but I'll go over to your apartment house and look around. Maybe he dropped something or somebody saw something."

"I appreciate it."

"Be a good idea if you have your locks changed," he said.

After they left, a doctor, a gray-haired, athletic man who looked to be in his early sixties, came in.

"Dr. Fallon, I'm sorry to see you under these conditions."

Diane recognized him as one of the contributors to the museum.

"Dr. Renner, isn't it? You were at the museum contributors' party."

"Yes, I was there with my wife, and we thoroughly enjoyed it. We can't wait until it opens to the public so we can take our grandchildren. This town needs a place like that. I understand there will be a restaurant too."

"Yes."

"That's just grand." He looked at her chart a moment. "I see things went well last night. That's good. You have some bruised ribs and a bruised kidney. It's not serious. Some bed rest and control of your fluids will take care of it. I'm going to prescribe some pills for your pain." He gave her a packet of papers. "We've discovered it's better to give out a sheet listing what we want the patient to do, as well as tell them. Just follow the instructions."

"Thank you. Does this mean I can go home?"

"Surely. But I'm serious when I say rest. And don't get dehydrated. Don't overdo the fluids either. I'll be looking forward to the museum's opening, and I want to see you in tip-top shape. When will that be, by the way?"

"In just a couple of weeks."

"That's great. You'll probably be seeing a lot of me. Take care of yourself, and if you have any problems—blood in your urine, pain that the pills can't take care of, nausea, headaches—call me. My number's on the card in your packet."

"Thanks for your help. Oh, Dr. Renner. I have a question. It's related to something else. Is it very common for children to be vegetarians?"

"More common than I like to see. Growing children need a balanced diet, and you have to be a good vegetarian to be a successful one. It's not a matter of eating only vegetables. Of course, some children are allergic to various foods and sometimes have to stay away from meats. True food allergies aren't that common. What many people call allergies are really sensitivities. However, some children—and adults—are allergic to cow products, for instance. That includes beef."

"Allergies." She hadn't thought of that. That could be another thing that might help identify the remains. Perhaps her bones had a food allergy.

"Thanks, Doctor. Please let me know when you're coming to the museum and I'll give you and your family a tour."

"I'll do that. Maybe we can see some of the areas where you put things together."

"You would probably enjoy the conservation lab. I'll be sure you get to see it."

When he left, Diane got dressed, wishing again she had clean clothes. While she waited for the nurse with her discharge papers, she walked down the hall to Star's room. She wasn't the only visitor. Crystal was there with her husband, Gil.

Chapter 28

"Guard," Star yelled. "Get them out of here."

But the guard was not on duty. Diane walked into the room. Crystal stood by Star with a sheaf of papers, trying to force a pen into Star's hand.

"You'd better leave," said Diane. "If you don't, you'll be in more trouble than you want."

"Well, if it isn't Frankie's bone woman. Heard about you on television digging in ol' Abercrombie's carcass pile. Just what do you think you're doing here?"

"Running you out of Star's room."

"This is my granddaughter." She almost choked on the word.

"She's trying to get me to sign over Mom and Dad's property," said Star.

"I am not. This is just something to let me keep her money safe so the lawyers won't get it all. I explained that to her."

"Even if you could coerce her into signing, it wouldn't be legal. She's a minor."

"Not no more. They're going to try her as an adult." Crystal nodded her head with emphasis.

"That's not a shortcut to majority. You're attempting to coerce a minor. Now get out of here before her guardian comes and throws you out."

"I have more right to be here than you."

"You have absolutely no right to be here at all." Frank stood in the doorway glaring at the McFarlands.

As Crystal turned to Frank, Diane saw a phrase on

one of the pages Crystal held. Diane snatched the papers from her hand without thinking.

"Why, you damn bitch! What do you think you're doing? Give those back."

Diane darted past her and made it to Frank, avoiding both Crystal and Gil grabbing at her. "This isn't just to sign over property, this second page is a confession."

Star screeched. "You fucking sorry bitch. Take your boy toy and get the hell out of here."

The guard, an older heavyset man, rushed into the room. "What's going on in here? Who are all you people?"

"These two slipped in here and were trying to force Miss Boone to sign a confession," said Frank, showing the new guard his badge. "I'm Miss Boone's guardian."

"We're just visiting our granddaughter."

"She's not my grandmother. She's just an old whore who can't get anybody to fuck her except some no-butt moron."

"Star," said Frank. "That's enough."

"It's true. Look at him. He's so skinny he looks like somebody sliced off his butt. He can't even fill out a pair of tight jeans."

"That's enough," Frank said again.

"You're going to fry, little girl, you're going to fry, fry, fry. . . ." sang Gil McFarland, screwing up his face and bending his lanky frame in her direction.

"All right, you're out of here." Frank took Gil by the arm and propelled him out the door. "You too, Crystal."

"You've not heard the last of this," Crystal spat out, marching out of the room, joining her husband.

"We can hope," Star yelled after her.

The guard stood for a moment as if waiting for someone to tell him what to do. "I just got here an hour ago," he said. "They must have been watching for me to take a break."

"I'm sure," said Frank.

The guard took up his post at the door and Frank turned to Star. "What did I tell you about that mouth?"

"They started it. Crystal's mouth's worse than mine."

"One of the nurses said something very wise to me about behaving according to your own principles and not someone else's. Think about the kind of person you want to be when you open your mouth," said Diane.

"You're not my mother."

"Star!" said Frank. "Diane's gone to a lot of trouble on your behalf. You can treat her with some respect."

The way Star sat back on her pillows, her lips in a pout, hair mussed, and tied to the bed, she looked like she should be expecting an exorcist to arrive any minute.

"Don't you get it? Nothing's going to do any good. Nothing. If I go to prison, at least I'll have a place to live."

"Star, you have a place to live."

"Where? In that house by myself? I never want to set foot in it."

"With me—and Kevin when he's with me. You have a home. When this is over, you're going back to school and graduate and you can decide if you'd like to go to college. I'm going to get your life back for you. I need your cooperation."

Star stared at him for a long time. "You mean you'd let me live with you?"

"Of course. We've known each other for a long time. Your father was my best friend. You're like my niece—my daughter. Now, can you calm down a little?"

"Did you see his face when I called him a no-butt moron?"

"Star."

"Oka-ay."

"How are you feeling?"

"I'd feel better if I weren't tied to the bed. I'd like to get up and walk around. I get dizzy every time I get up."

"I've talked to the detectives in charge, and they consider you a flight risk. I'm sorry. I know it's not fair."

"Did you tell them my arms are much too tired to attempt flight?"

"Didn't think of that. Star, when you're feeling better, I want to talk to you about getting counseling, and getting off drugs."

"I don't do drugs." Frank looked at her. "I don't. I smoke marijuana sometimes, that's all."

"Marijuana's a drug."

"No, it's not, not like cocaine or ecstasy. It's just a smoke. Did you know they used to call marijuana Mary Jane? I learned that in school."

"It destroys your brain cells. Did they teach you that?"

"We'll just have to agree to disagree."

"We'll just have to stop smoking."

The nurse came in holding some papers. "They said you'd come down to visit Miss Boone," she said to Diane. "I have your release papers. If you come with me, I'll get a wheelchair and you can go home. Do you have someone to drive you?"

"I have my car here," she said.

Both Frank and Star stared at Diane.

"What's she talking about?" asked Frank.

"I stayed in the hospital last night. Someone mugged me outside my apartment. I'm fine, just a few bruises."

"Why didn't you call me? Are you all right?"

"Yes, I'm fine. I'm going home right now. I've got to call Jonas and tell him I'll be late."

"You'll be staying home and resting," said the nurse. "That's what the doctor ordered."

"I'll drive you home," said Frank.

"No. I'm fine, really. Stay here with Star. I'll talk to you later." Diane started to follow the nurse out.

"I'll come by your apartment in a few minutes," said Frank.

When she was almost out the door, Diane thought she heard Star say she was sorry.

Diane managed to get home, but the steps up to her apartment were uncomfortable and she longed for an elevator. Inside, she locked and chained the door, took a pain pill, changed clothes and made herself comfortable on the sofa. She looked up Jonas' home phone number and dialed. After several rings, the answering machine picked up. She hung up without leaving a message. Next she dialed his cell phone.

"Briggs, here."

"Jonas, this is Diane. I'm going to be late getting to the site today, so you're in charge."

"That's fine. We're getting started now. You sound a little weak. Are you feeling all right?"

Diane went into the explanation of what happened to her last evening, trying her best to downplay the event.

"Are you sure you need to come out at all? Shouldn't you just stay home and rest?"

"I'm OK, really. A few bruises here and there."

"If they kept you all night at the hospital, you got more than a few bruises."

"The bruises were on a kidney. But it's fine."

"Oh, is that all? A major organ. I think that calls for bed rest. We can manage. We have your excavation plan and we're all experienced."

"I know you are. How did things go last night at the Abercrombies? No one came after you with a knife in your sleep, I hope."

"What? No. Were they supposed to?" Diane laughed and it hurt. "They were great. Hospitable folk. Mrs. Abercrombie makes a great pot roast and pecan pie. Luther's pretty indignant that someone's dumped a body on his land, but his wife enjoys the excitement."

"I'll be by my phone if you need anything," she said.

"Does that mean you're going to stay home and rest?"

"For the morning, anyway. Then I'll see."

After talking to Jonas, Diane called Andie at the museum and had to tell the whole story over again.

"You're kidding? Why didn't you call me? I'd have come down to the hospital. I'll bet you didn't have any pajamas and had to wear that awful gown with the back out."

"That's true, I could have used a nightgown, but I slept all night and was released this morning, so I didn't need much in the way of clothes."

"Everything's running smoothly here. The herpetologist is installing his friends today."

"I hope I didn't make a mistake by telling him he could exhibit a few live snakes and lizards."

"He did say they would all be small, and nothing poisonous." Andie seemed to be asking as well as repeating what the herpetologist said.

"He gave me a list and I approved it," said Diane. "We'll have to make sure he didn't include anything we can't live with."

"I can handle anything that comes up, so you stay home and rest today."

Diane was beginning to think her presence wasn't needed anywhere. "I may drop in later on today. I'll see how I feel."

"If anything comes up, I can call or E-mail you. Stay home. You'll thank me tomorrow. Oh, you did get a letter from Dr. Ranjan Patel—same guy that sent the fax. It's another copy of the same document—much more readable."

"Thanks. Put it on my desk. Anything else?"

"Yeah, Jonas called with a message. 'Bishop to queen three.' He made me write it down and read it back to him. Is that some kind of code?"

"No. We're playing a game of chess."

"Oh. I wondered."

"That's it, then?"

"Just the usual stuff. Nothing earthshaking. We're getting a lot of people calling about the museum opening. A reporter called wanting to know if we're going to move the museum after we just renovated it."

"What did you tell him?"

"No."

"Good girl. Keep in touch."

When Diane hung up the phone she stretched out on the couch and pulled a throw over her. As she drifted off to sleep, she remembered she hadn't told Frank about food allergies—another long shot, but sometimes they pay off.

She was awakened out of a dream she didn't want to end by a knocking on the door. She was running through the jungle, Ariel in her arms.

Frank, she thought, stumbling to the door. She released the chain and opened it.

Chapter 29

Melissa stood in the doorway, the scowl on her face made darker by the shadows cast from the dim hallway lights.

"You've ruined my life. Who are you to interfere in my life? No one asked you. I hardly know you."

"Melissa? What . . . ?" Diane thought of the visit from Lacy and Emily. "Come in."

Melissa marched in, sweeping past Diane so abruptly she almost knocked her over.

"Where do you get off telling people that Alix is beating me up?"

"I didn't tell people that."

"You did. Laura's a busybody, but she's not a liar."

"No, she isn't, and I doubt she told you that I said Alix was beating you up, because what I told her was that it had been reported to me that she was hitting you and making the bruises. I told her I didn't know if it was true."

"It isn't true. Alix and I are friends. Who are you to interfere in my life anyway? What business is it of yours?"

"I was ready to consider firing Mike Seger because I thought he was abusing you and bringing it to the museum. That made it my business."

"Nobody's abusing me. You've got my parents all worked up over nothing. I'm very active and I get bruises."

"Fine. That's all you have to say to Laura. I have to

wonder at the level of your anger and why you came to my house. That belies your protest that the story isn't true." Diane felt unsteady on her feet, so she went back to the sofa and sat down.

"What's wrong with you? Are you drunk?" asked Melissa.

Diane looked at Melissa for a moment, her angry flushed face, her clenched fists. "No, I was mugged last night in front of the apartment. I just got home from the hospital."

"Oh. Well, I want you to stay out of my business."

No *Oh, I'm sorry. How are you?* Diane was seeing a new Melissa, a very self-centered one.

"Don't bring your personal business to the museum," Diane said.

"I won't. Alix is really hurt. I wish we'd just let whatever was going on happen to you."

"What does that mean?"

But Melissa turned and left, almost running into Frank on her way out.

"What was that about?" he asked.

"It's too odd and convoluted to explain. How's Star?"

"Feeling a little contrite, which is unusual for her. She really is sorry she snapped at you."

"She's right, I'm not her mother." But it had stung, Diane had to admit. Shakespeare knew what he was talking about—"How sharper than a serpent's tooth, it is to have a thankless child."

"You were someone being kind. She needs to respect that. How are you? Tell me about last night. Why didn't you call?"

"You've had enough to worry about. And I can take care of myself."

"Why didn't you call?"

"Just what I said—and I don't want to be dependent."

"Tell me what happened."

Diane gave him a blow-by-blow of the event, along with what she remembered of the attacker's description. "I've been thinking about it. I don't believe it was a random mugging. When he ran, it was down the street and up another street. I think he didn't want his car to be seen on this street, and he wasn't looking for just anyone to mug—I think he was looking for me."

"Because of the bones?"

"That would be my guess. It's been on TV. I think whoever it is, is in a panic."

"Hurting you won't stop the bones from being found—they're already found."

"No. But what if the person thinks that I'm the impetus for connecting the bones with the Boone murders? What if he thinks that if I'm put out of commission, no one else will follow through? The police aren't interested. They want it to be Star. Perhaps he thinks with me out of the way, the digging will stop."

"There's me," said Frank.

"Yes. There's you. I don't know. Maybe they had plans for you too. Maybe I'm wrong and it was a random mugging. Or maybe it was someone who wants me to just leave so the museum can be sold."

"Would Grayson go that far?"

"I don't think so. He doesn't want to go to jail. I think he's a shark, not a maniac." Diane looked at her watch. "I'm going to go to the site and to the museum."

"You're going to do no such thing. If I heard right, you require bed rest."

"That's what people keep saying, but I'm just fine and I've been resting all morning." She looked over at the bags sitting on her coffee table. "What have you got there?"

"I figured you'd need some lunch and you probably wouldn't fix any yourself, so I stopped by a restaurant. How does potato soup and a salad sound?"

"Actually, it sounds good. You brought yourself something, didn't you?"

"A cheeseburger and fries."

Frank put everything out on the kitchen table, and they sat down to eat. She poured the soup into a mug and sipped it. It was warm and soothing going down her throat. The salad was good too; just the right thing. Frank knew just what to do in a crisis. She wondered what he was like on a day-to-day basis, living an ordinary life. She was beginning to get used to him, and that frightened her.

"I wonder how the digging is going?" asked Frank.

"I called Jonas this morning. It was going well."

"Nice to know that Luther and his wife didn't kill the crew during the night."

Diane made a face at him. "Yes, I was relieved to hear his voice."

After eating, Diane felt much better. "I'm going to put in an appearance out at the pit. You can go with me if you like."

"Can I talk you out of it?"

"No."

"Then I'll drive you."

By the time they got to Abercrombie's farm and hiked to the pit, Diane was having serious misgivings about the decision to come. Her whole body ached and her lower back throbbed. It was hotter than she expected, and the sweat trickled down her back.

"Should you be here?" Jonas said.

"Yes," Diane answered. "I won't stay long. I just want to take a look."

After several solicitations from the crew, Whit and the sheriff, and another brief description of the evening's misadventure, Diane set about examining the work in progress.

The crew had actually gotten a lot done. All of the grid units in the pit as well as the outlying areas had some work done on them. The pit looked like a mosaic of bones in relief. The skeletons were brown, like the earth, except for the ones that had been exposed; they were off-white. A few were bleached white.

The human bone she'd seen yesterday was now completely exposed. It was a right humerus. Like the clavicle, it had similar parallel markings on the shaft where rats had gnawed.

"I did a quick measurement," said the woman who'd uncovered it. "It's about thirty-seven centimeters—but that was rough, with a tape measure. I guess you'll use a bone board."

Diane nodded. "I'll have to know the race and have a more accurate measurement, but it looks like we're in the six-foot range. See these muscle attachments? He was a muscular guy."

"You still think it's male, then?"

"I need to see the pelvis, but so far, yeah, it looks male."

"You feeling okay? You look a little pale."

"I'm going to go home, I think. I probably shouldn't have come out here, certainly not hiking in here."

"Dr. Fallon, I think we may have his leg and foot."

Diane looked in the direction of the voice. It was a male crew member standing with the sheriff at an excavation unit several feet away from the pit.

"Looks like the guy's going to be all over the place," said the woman, rising to go over with Diane.

Frank and Whit came over too, and all of them peered down at the excavated leg and foot bones.

"Nice excavation," said Diane.

"Thanks," said the digger.

"Whew," said the sheriff. "Sure looks like you found another part of him."

Diane stooped down, looking at the bones, and raised her eyes to Whit.

"What?" asked Frank, looking back and forth from Diane to Whit.

"Oh, God," Whit said. "Do we have to mention this?"

"You do now," said the sheriff. He was beginning to look at Whit with a measure of suspicion.

"It's a bear," said Diane. "With the claws removed. Poached, I imagine."

"Look, I don't know. The guy brought it in and we mounted it for him. It was a couple, maybe three, years ago, and I told Dad the next time one came in, we needed more information on where it came from."

"It sure looks human," said the sheriff.

"That's because bears, like us, walk on their feet," said Diane.

"Well, what else?" asked the sheriff.

"Deer walk on the tips of their toes, so do horses. Dogs and cats, for instance, walk mostly on their digits, but not on the soles of their feet."

"Well, I sure didn't know that," said the sheriff. "They walk on their toes?"

"Deer have longer and larger metapodials than we do so they can do that. Because the bear walks on the soles of his feet, the bones—without the claws—can look very human."

"You learn something every day," said the sheriff. "Ain't that right, Whit?"

Whit rolled his eyes.

"You look like you're getting tired," said Frank, taking Diane's arm and helping her up.

"I am. I think I'll skip going to the museum and go home," she said. "All of you are doing a great job." She thanked Jonas and the crew and let Frank lead her to the car.

"I'm getting to be such a wimp," said Diane.

"You're not a wimp. Getting beaten up isn't like it is in the movies, where you get the shit beat out of you and get up and go some more. I'm going to take you home, and you are going to stay there."

"You won't get an argument from me."

Diane felt doubly tired by the time she got back to Frank's car. He drove her home. Diane stopped by her landlady's apartment to see if the locks had been changed.

"They just left." She smiled sweetly and handed Diane two keys. "I hope you're feeling better. It's a shame how crime's just moving into a nice neighborhood like this."

Diane thanked her, backed out the door and let Frank see her safely inside her apartment.

"I need to go visit Star awhile. The doctors want to keep her another day. I'll come back and stay the night here."

"I imagine you'll be glad to get back to work so you can get some rest."

Frank smiled and kissed her. "When all this is over,

we need to go do something fun—just the two of us. You like fishing?"

"As a matter of fact, I do. How about you, think you'd like to go caving?"

"Maybe we'll compromise and go to the beach." He kissed her again. "I haven't forgotten your problem with the forgery. I'm checking on some of your employees right now. I'll let you know what I find out."

"You have a lead?"

"Not sure. Get some sleep. I'll be back soon."

Frank left, and Diane settled into the comfort of the couch and dozed off. Hours later she was awakened by the ringing of the phone. She reached over and picked it up and managed a muffled hello.

"Diane? Is this Diane Fallon?" The voice sounded hysterical and came in gasps and sobs.

"Yes. Who is this?"

"It's Star. Please come. Please. It's Uncle Frank. They told me somebody shot him. I'm afraid he might be dead. Please come."

Chapter 30

Diane put down the phone and fell on the sofa, sick, shaking and panicky. She ran to the bathroom and threw up.

"Oh, God, no. Not again, no. Please, no. Please not again."

When she thought she was finished vomiting, she rinsed her mouth and washed her face with cool water. She had told Star she would come as soon as she could. At the moment, she wasn't sure she could even drive. One thing at a time. First, she packed an overnight bag, just in case. *I've got to get control,* she told herself as she tried to calm her shaking hands. Packing done, she raced down the stairs of her apartment and out to her car.

She hardly remembered the drive to the hospital, but there she was, pulling into the visitors' parking. By the time she got inside, she was shaking almost too much to walk straight. She went up to Star's room first and found her sobbing uncontrollably while a nurse was trying to give her a sedative.

"Can you take off these restraints?" asked Diane.

"I've asked the policeman outside and he said no. You'd think he'd have more compassion."

Star cried and pulled at the restraints. Diane stroked her hair as the nurse gave her the shot.

"This will take effect pretty quickly," she said.

"Will you find out for me?" said Star. "Go see him and tell him not to die."

"I will. I'll go right now. I know it's hard, but try to stay calm. The shot the nurse gave you will help."

Diane left the room, sweeping past the guard at Star's door who was reading his Western. She resisted the urge to pull it out of his hands and toss it down the corridor.

The nurse at the front desk downstairs told her that Frank was in surgery and gave her directions to the waiting room. When she got there, Izzy Wallace and his partner were already there.

"How is he?" she asked.

"We don't know. He's in surgery. It didn't look good."

"What happened?"

"He'd just taken some money out of the ATM outside the hospital and was leaving, when this black guy came up, shot him and took his wallet."

Diane looked at Izzy in amazement. "Frank and I are certainly having a run of bad luck, aren't we?"

"We have witnesses to what happened." Izzy sounded defensive. He didn't like Diane, and she didn't care.

"What did the witnesses say?"

Izzy hesitated a moment, as though thinking whether he should give her information.

"A black guy in a cap and dreadlocks came up to within about ten feet of Frank and pulled out a gun and shot him just as he was putting his money in his wallet. The perp grabbed the wallet off the ground and ran. He got lost in the dark. It happened quickly. Two people saw it—well, three, but one was a little girl, a little black girl."

The way Izzy said *a little black girl* made Diane suspicious. "What did she say?"

"Well, naturally, she didn't want it to be a black person. That's understandable. She was just a kid."

"So she said the perp wasn't black?" Diane prodded. She was going to have to pull this out of him.

"She gave a similar description—black skin, dreadlocks, but she said he wasn't really black." He shook his head. "She was only about nine years old. What would she say? Look, I need to ask you—now, don't get mad, but I have to ask. The guy who works for you at the museum. We met him when we were there. He fits the description. Do you know if he has something against Frank?"

"Who?" asked Diane. "Do you have a name?" She knew who, but was going to make him say it.

"He was in the lab, the one he said got broken into."

The one he said got broken into. Damn you, Izzy. As much as she wanted to, Diane didn't voice her thoughts. *If I didn't need information from you, I'd tell you where you can put that tiny brain of yours.*

"Korey, the head conservator?" said Diane. "He hardly knows Frank, and Korey has impeccable credentials. He doesn't rob ATMs."

"I had to ask. He does fit the description."

One good thing about talking to Izzy; the adrenaline rush his conversation gave her was helping with the shakes.

A doctor came out of the swinging doors toward Izzy. Diane held her breath.

"A bullet grazed his heart, and another pierced his lung. He's fortunate he was at the hospital when it happened. Time is everything in cases like this. The surgery went well. We'll know something more in the next twenty-four hours."

"Doc, you haven't told me anything," said Izzy.

The edges of the doctor's mouth twitched slightly upward. "I've told you what I know. I'm cautiously hopeful."

Diane hung on to *cautiously hopeful.* That's what she would tell Star.

"I need to see Star," she said to Izzy when the doctor left. "She's so hysterical they had to give her a sedative. While I'm gone, I'd like you to consider all the coincidences here. George Boone finds a human bone—and before you say anything, I can tell a human bone from a deer bone. We've since found three human bones at a site where George and his son visited a week before they brought the clavicle to Frank. Right after it's known that George has this bone, the whole family is murdered. A week later, as I start investigating, I'm attacked outside my home. The next day Frank is shot. Do the math."

Diane turned and left for the elevator to go to Star's room. A nurse in green surgical scrubs writing something on a pad at the desk turned and laid a hand on Diane's arm. "That was Dr. Sampson. He came to us from Grady in Atlanta. We're very lucky he moved his family here. Your guy's in good hands."

Diane smiled and thanked her. She was a pretty woman in her mid-thirties with a smart twinkle in her eyes and she was good with people. Diane felt instantly better. Grady Hospital has one of the finest trauma units in the country—thanks in part to the frequent gunshot victims they get through their doors.

She found Star groggy, fighting the sedative. Stubborn little girl. Diane stroked her hair.

"Star." Her eyes popped open. "Frank came through surgery fine. The doctor believes that he will be all right." She had put a more positive spin on the doctor's words.

"Are you sure?" she managed to say.

"That's what the doctor said. One of the nurses told me that he is an expert in trauma cases. That means Frank has the best of care."

Star sighed and seemed to breathe easier. She closed her eyes, then opened them again. "Will you stay a while?"

"Sure."

Diane pulled up a chair beside Star's bed and almost drifted off to sleep in it. She didn't leave until the rising and falling of the sheet covering Star was smooth and regular.

She rose quietly and went back down to Frank's floor. Izzy was still there, but his partner was gone. Jake Houser was there talking with Izzy and two men, dressed in suits, that Diane didn't recognize.

"Dr. Fallon. This is just terrible," said Jake. "They put me on the case, and I want you to know we'll get the scumbag who did this. It means I won't be showing up at the museum for a while. . . ."

Diane nodded. She didn't feel like going into lecture

mode again. Frank had a lot of confidence in Jake, so maybe it was good he was on the case. Jake introduced her to the two men standing with them—Frank's boss and his partner from Atlanta. Both were somber and looked like they were at a funeral. She wanted to kick them. She couldn't seem to shake her irritable mood.

"Frank's told us a lot about you," his partner said. "I'm glad to meet you. Frank's tough. I'm sure he's going to pull through this."

"I think he'll be just fine," she said, trying to believe her own words. That's what they wanted to hear too. No small talk, just *Frank's going to pull through.*

"Oh," said Izzy. "We found this in the bushes." He handed her her cell phone. "No sign of your purse."

"Thanks. I imagine it's in a gutter somewhere."

After that exchange, Diane had to explain what had happened to her. The two Atlanta detectives were surprised at the coincidence. Maybe they would give Izzy a nudge, she hoped.

She excused herself and went to the nurses' station to ask if she could see Frank when he was awake.

"Are you a relative?"

"No, a friend."

"I'm sorry, only family members are allowed. His wife is with him now." The nurse was curt, and she started to turn her back on Diane.

"He doesn't have a wife," said Diane.

The nurse stopped and stared at Diane with sparkling black eyes.

"That is probably his ex-wife," continued Diane. "They've been divorced for five years, and she's been remarried for five years. However, they have a son who needs to hear how his father is doing. So it's a good thing for her to see for herself. There's also a little girl upstairs whose whole family has been murdered. Frank is her guardian, and she needs to hear how he's doing. If she had been responsible for what happened to her family, Frank wouldn't be lying in there now."

"Are you Diane?" asked another nurse who had been openly listening to Diane's diatribe.

"Yes."

"He's been asking for you. He's pretty insistent. I think the doctor will allow you to see him." She eyed the first nurse as she spoke.

"If the doctor says so . . ."

Cindy Reynolds came through the double doors from the recovery rooms, and the first nurse frowned at her. Cindy didn't notice. She headed for Diane, and the way her eyes were tearing up, it frightened her.

"How is he?" asked Diane, afraid of the answer.

"He looks so pale. But the nurse says he's doing well under the circumstances."

"And Kevin?"

"He doesn't know yet. He's at my mother's. I didn't want to say anything to him until I . . . I had to see for myself."

"Of course. Star's just terrified."

"That poor child. If anything happens to Frank, it'll be as bad on her as it will on Kevin—worse, in a way. Kevin has family who love him. Star's all alone." Cindy took a breath and bit her lip. "Let me know how he's doing." She dug in her purse and pulled out a card. "Here's my cell phone."

"If there's any change, I'll call."

All animosity that Cindy may have been harboring from their last encounter had evaporated. At least that was one good thing—Diane couldn't handle any more verbal sparring.

She had to wait another hour before she could get in to see Frank. She was tired, and all the adrenaline that had been keeping her pain-free was dissipating and her back was throbbing, as were several muscles that weren't hurting before.

When one of the nurses told her she could see him, she hoped she didn't look like she was on her last legs.

Cindy hadn't exaggerated when she said Frank looked pale. He was so white he could have been dead. Diane held the door frame so she wouldn't fall.

"He's doing much better now," said the nurse. "I've had a chance to work with him for a couple of hours now, and his blood pressure is up to normal. So is his temperature. You're Diane, right? He's been asking for you."

Diane came over to his side and took his hand. It was cold. "Frank, it's me, Diane."

His eyes opened slightly and she thought she saw him attempt a smile. He gave her hand a weak squeeze.

"Don't try to talk. I've seen Star. She's worried, but I told her you're going to be fine. When I leave here I'll go back up and tell her I've seen you."

He nodded his head. "You?" he whispered.

"I'm doing great. Healing up just fine."

"Liar," he whispered.

"Don't try to talk anymore. Just get well. That's an order from Star."

His lips turned upward and he closed his eyes. She looked at the nurse.

"He's fine," she assured Diane. "He's going to be in and out of it. I'll keep him alive. It's what they pay me for."

"Please," she said and squeezed his hand before she left.

She felt she should feel better than she did, but he looked so weak, and the last time she saw him he was so strong. She put a smile on her face and went into Star's room. She was still asleep. Diane sat in a chair and watched her. It was a comfortable chair, and they both needed the rest. She leaned back and went to sleep, not waking up until she heard her name whispered. It was Star, awake and looking at her.

"Uncle Frank. Have you seen him? How is he?"

"I saw him"—she looked at her watch—"an hour ago. He's doing fine. Very weak, but recovering."

"He's not going to die?"

"No." Diane hoped that was true.

Tears welled up in Star's eyes and trickled down the sides of her face. "I don't know what I would have done."

"You don't worry about that now. Get well yourself."

"I'm sorry I was mean to you."

"Don't worry about that either."

"Why did this happen to him? Is it because of me?"

"Because of you? No. This isn't your fault. The police think it was a robbery. He was getting money out of the ATM."

"Yeah, a robbery. First you, and now Frank. Like I believe that was coincidence."

"Neither do I. But don't think about any of that. It would make him feel really good if he came in to see you getting better. Concentrate on that."

Diane left Star dozing and went down to see if she could find Izzy. She caught him as he was going out the door.

"Any more news about Frank?" she asked.

"He's in critical condition. That's all they'll say. How did he look to you?"

"Very pale and weak, but the nurse said he was doing well. I'd like to take her word on it. Izzy, will you give me the name of the little girl who witnessed the shooting?"

"Now, you know I can't do that."

"You've already discounted her as a witness. What's the harm?"

He studied the tile floor for several seconds before he took out his notebook and scribbled something on a page and tore it out.

"This didn't come from me, but if you find anything out, let me know first."

"I will. Thanks."

The sun was setting, and the address Izzy had given her wasn't in a section of town she wanted to visit at night, but she wanted to hear what the little girl saw.

Chapter 31

Diane knocked on the door of a small paint-peeled white house with bright white lace curtains in the window. She saw an older black woman peek out the window before she came to the door.

"Yes, can I help you? Are you out of gas?"

"No ma'am. My name is Diane Fallon." She showed the woman her driver's license. "Is this the Stillwood residence?"

"Who is it, Mama?" A younger woman came into the living room, wiping her hands on a dish towel.

"Some woman who says her name is Diane Fallon. I asked her if she run out of gas."

"I've heard that name, just today. Something about digging up bones. Something about the museum?"

"I'm director of the RiverTrail Museum, and I'm also excavating some bones on a farm outside of town."

Diane thought the best policy was to be as honest as she could. Having some white stranger coming to her house at night wanting to talk with her small daughter would not be something the mother would warm up to.

"What you want with us?" asked the older woman.

"This is rather delicate and I'll understand if you say no, but I was wondering if I could talk with your daughter about what she saw today?"

"You mean at the hospital? I don't know. She was really upset, and the policemen didn't help any."

"The man who was shot was my . . ." Diane hated to use the term *boyfriend*. She felt too old to have a boyfriend, but she didn't know what else to call him—except *friend.* "He was a close friend of mine, and I believe the police are looking in the wrong direction for the person who shot him. I believe your daughter."

The younger woman thought a moment, then relented. "All right. It will be good for her to talk with someone who believes her."

"Come in. Don't stand out there on the porch," the older woman said. "Tamika, will you come here a minute? A lady wants to ask you something."

A young black girl in a pink shirt and embroidered overalls sprinkled with glitter and her hair in a bun on top of her head came into the room and held on to her mother.

"Hi, Tamika. My name's Diane Fallon. Can I ask you some questions?"

"What about?"

"About today at the hospital."

"You won't believe me."

"Yes, I will."

"Let's not stand here in the hallway. Sit down in the living room here." Tamika's grandmother led the way into the living room.

Diane sat on a brown stuffed chair with cutwork embroidery doilies on the arms and an antimacassar on the back. She fingered the needlework.

"This is nice. Did you do it?" she asked the older woman.

"I did those things about twenty-five years ago. Still do it when my eyes let me. Wanted to teach my daughter, but she didn't want to learn."

The younger woman rolled her eyes. "You just wasn't patient enough to teach me."

Diane smiled and turned her attention to the little girl. "Tamika, you told the police that the man who shot Mr. Duncan wasn't really a black man."

"He wasn't."

"Would you mind telling me how you know that he wasn't?"

"When he run, I don't know, he just didn't look like a black man."

"Is there anything else you noticed?"

"His dreads weren't real. They were braids, and way too black. I think it was a wig, and not a very good one. Have you ever seen real dreads? Up close, I mean?"

Diane nodded. "My head conservator has long dreadlocks. He's the guy that restores and takes care of a lot of the museum things."

"He does? You work at the museum?"

"She's head of the museum," said her mother.

"You are? What you doing here asking about this?"

"The man who got shot was my friend. I want to find out who really did it."

"So you believe me?"

"Yes, I do. Could you see his face?"

Tamika shook her head. "I just saw part of his face. Just here." She patted her jaw. "And that was through a window, and he had the collar of his shirt pulled up."

"Thank you, Tamika. I appreciate you talking to me." Diane took out one of her cards she had in her pocket. "Here's my phone number at the museum. If you remember anything else, give me a call, please. If I'm not there, my assistant, Andie, will take a message. And when the museum opens for visitors in a couple of weeks, you and your family can come for free."

Tamika took the card. "Thanks. Can we go to the museum, Mama?"

"Sure, when it opens."

"That'll be in a couple of weeks," Diane repeated. *If I ever get back to work,* she chided herself.

She stood up to leave, but picked up the needlework. "Would you like to teach some workshops?" asked Diane.

"I've never done that."

"Not many people know how to do cutwork."

"You know what that is, do you?"

"Yes ma'am. I do, and I know it's quality work. Think about it, and give me a call. We'll be doing small workshops now and then for the community. I think lots of people will be interested in learning how to do this."

"I'll think about it."

Diane said good-bye to Tamika, her mother and grandmother, thanking them again for seeing her. It was dark when she got back to her car and drove back to her apartment.

She parked as close as she could get and scrutinized the area before she left her car. No lurking shadows or strange noises. However, she hadn't seen the man coming last night. But she wasn't looking for trouble last night.

She walked as quickly as she could to her apartment house without breaking into a run. Climbing the stairs, she yearned for a ground-floor apartment. After letting herself in, she locked and chained the door and collapsed on the couch.

It was much earlier than she usually went to bed, but she ached all over and was bone tired. She made herself get up and go to the bedroom, slipped off her clothes, pulled on a long tee shirt, took one of her pain pills and fell into bed.

Diane thought she would drift off to sleep immediately, but she lay awake thinking. Though her body was tired, her mind raced. It was clear to her that the attack on her and the one on Frank were related. If that was true, then the attack on her probably didn't have anything to do with the museum. But the problem was, if it had to do with not wanting her to find the bones, the attacker was too late. The bones were found, and even if she were out of the picture, someone else would analyze the bones. She wasn't the only forensic anthropologist in the world.

Star was the key. The lead detective, Janice Warrick, thought Star and her boyfriend, Dean, killed her parents. Having put all her money on that theory of the crime, she didn't want a new theory—a new one that would make her look bad—raising its head.

Frank was like the king's pawn, and Star was the king. Take away her guard and she would be checkmated and sent to prison—case closed on the Boone murders. The skeletal remains would be forever separate from the Boone murders—especially if both Diane and Frank were dead. The two of them were the only ones tying the two cases together. It would be forgotten if they were dead and Star was in prison.

But there was the clavicle. Maybe that's what the break-in at the museum was about. Take away the clavicle and it would take away the physical connection Frank and she had with the skeleton. There would be the report, but it would just be a rumored bone coincidentally found by George Boone.

But there was a serious flaw in her argument. Which was the reason she believed the Boones were killed in the first place—so that no one would find out where they found the clavicle, so that no one would find the rest of the skeleton, so that it would never be identified. If Star was in jail and Diane and Frank were dead, the skeleton would still be identified because it was already found. That was a bad flaw, and she was too tired to try to work it out. She finally slipped into a confused, fitful sleep.

Diane awoke in a panic, feeling that she'd forgotten something, something important. Frank was shot. That was it. He was in critical condition. She felt sick. How many mornings had she awakened in the past year with that blank mind, then those thoughts: *Ariel is dead.* She got out of bed and called the hospital.

Critical but stable condition. Critical but stable was good for now. She'd take what comfort she could get. Next she called to check on Star. That wasn't as good. She'd been moved back to the jail.

After a shower, juice and a quarter of a bagel for breakfast, Diane went to the hospital. Frank was still in critical care, but they hoped to move him to a room that day. That worried her. Whoever shot him might try again, and he was completely vulnerable. They let her see him for a few minutes.

He looked better. There was some color in his face. His hand wasn't as cold when she held it. His grip was stronger.

"Hey," he whispered. "Looking good."

"Don't try to talk."

"Star?"

"They moved her back to her cell."

"Call lawyer. See her."

"Who's her lawyer?"

"Serena Ellison."

"I'll call her and make arrangements. Don't worry about anything. Just get well."

He squeezed her hand. "I will."

"Take care."

She kissed his cheek and left. They wouldn't let anyone stay long in ICU.

He did look better. Barring some infection—or attack—he would recover. She allowed herself to be cautiously relieved.

In the waiting room she saw Cindy and Kevin in a knot of people—two men and a woman, all of whom favored Frank. His family. She started to avoid them, but Cindy saw her and motioned her over.

She was being exceptionally friendly since their encounter at the museum. Diane felt a little guilty for coming down so hard on her.

"These are Frank's two brothers and sister. Frank's the baby of the family. Diane Fallon is the new director of the museum in town."

"Frank's said a word or two about you," said one of the brothers.

Diane thought his name was Henry. Frank and Hank. That must have been a kick in school.

He took her hand and shook it. "Rather nice words too."

"How did Frank look to you?" asked his sister, Ava. She had her hands on Kevin's shoulders. Both of them looked at her anxiously.

"He's doing very well. It was good to see him today. He is so much improved over yesterday."

Relief swept across all their faces, especially Kevin's. "But he's still in critical care," said Ava.

"That just means he has good insurance," said Diane, and both of his brothers nodded in agreement. "But I think they might be moving him to a private room soon."

"I heard you had also been attacked," said Cindy.

"What, you too? Were you there?" asked the other

brother, Linc. Frank, Hank, and Linc. Diane almost smiled as the names ran through her brain.

"This was a separate incident. I was mugged outside my apartment. My purse was stolen," she added. The last thing she wanted to do was share her suspicions with his family.

"My God," said Ava. "This must be a crime wave."

"Just unlucky," said Diane, but she could see the brothers looked doubtful. If Kevin weren't there, she felt they would ask her questions.

"How long are you going to be in town?" she asked.

"Long enough to see that Frankie's okay," said Henry. "Mom and Dad don't travel well, and we need to tell them in person that he's going to be all right."

"Please come to the museum. It's not open to the public yet, but most of the exhibits are in place. I'd love for you to see it. We're very proud of it."

"Yes, do," said Cindy. "We've seen some of it."

"That would be nice." Ava looked at Kevin. "Maybe we can go by later on." Kevin nodded.

"The herpetology curator installed some live exhibits yesterday. You might enjoy seeing those. Snakes and lizards," she added.

"Yeah," said Kevin. "Cool."

"I hope," said Diane, and they all laughed, a bit disproportionately to the actual humor of her statement. It was a laugh that gave a small bit of relief from worry.

"I need to get to the museum. It was very nice meeting all of you." She stepped away, wanting to leave before they could think of any more questions.

"I'll walk you to your car," said Linc.

Chapter 32

She wasn't going to be able to make a clean getaway from Frank's family. She smiled, pleasantly, she hoped.

"Are you all right?" Linc asked after they were out the door. "You're pale, and I noticed you're limping."

"Limping? I hadn't noticed."

"Slightly favoring your right side. The others may not have noticed."

Diane remembered that one of Frank's brothers was a doctor specializing in sports medicine.

"You're the doctor?"

"That's me."

She briefly described her injuries, downplayed her pain and added that she was fine.

"You should be home resting. I'm serious."

"I can't now. There's too much to do." She suddenly felt overwhelmed and tired, and the day was just starting. "This is my car." She took the keys out of her jacket pocket and clicked the lock open.

"I wanted to talk to you about Frank away from Ava and the others. I sense that there's more to this. All the police said was that he was held up at an ATM just outside the hospital here."

She pointed to the bank machine to the left of the entrance.

Linc looked the most like Frank, especially the eyes. Frank's eyes were dreamy, amused, sexy, angry, reflecting perfectly whatever mood he was in. Right now, Linc's eyes wanted answers.

"Yes, that's what they believe."

"But you don't."

"No. But I have no proof."

"I know about his friends being killed. Now he's shot and you're attacked. This all seems a little too much for coincidence."

"It does to me too." Diane hesitated.

"Is Frank still in danger?"

"I don't know. But if someone could always be with him for a few days until I can get someone to guard his room . . ." She let the sentence hang.

Linc took a breath and stepped back. "You're serious, aren't you?"

"I'm serious. I just don't know if I'm right. This may be nothing, and I may just be paranoid."

"You've both been seriously attacked. It gives your paranoia credibility. I need to know more about what's going on. Let me take you to dinner."

Diane thought for a moment, trying to organize her day in her mind. "Meet me at the museum this evening— around six thirty or so. We'll have something delivered." She scribbled her cell phone number on the back of one of her museum cards before she handed it to him. "Tell the guard on duty to give me a call when you get there."

He thanked her and opened the car door. Frank had a nice family. She envied him.

"Diane," said Andie. "How is Frank? We just heard. My God, first you, and now him. What's happening?" Andie's perpetual happy smile was turned down in a frown. She stood behind her desk, holding a folder to her chest like a shield.

"Frank's doing well," said Diane. "He's still in intensive care. How are things here?"

Andie's face switched from concern to horror. "One of the snakes is missing."

"Damn. How did that happen?"

"They don't know. He just wasn't in his terrarium or whatever that thing wrapping around the room is. They're looking for him, but the snake guy said he could be holed up between the walls and we may not be able to find him for months."

"What kind of snake?"

"He said a black snake. That's a good kind isn't it?"

"Yes, at least there's that. Damn. Tell him to find that snake. I don't want it showing up and scaring visitors."

"Jonas called. I told him about Frank. He said they had some trouble at the site last night."

"What kind of trouble?"

"He didn't say. He wants you to call."

"What else?"

"That's it for now."

Diane started for her office. "Oh, Andie. Frank's two brothers and sister are in town. I told them they could come see the museum if they had time. I think they may come and bring Kevin. If I'm not here, give them the grand tour."

"Sure thing."

"Have you seen Melissa or Alix?"

"Not today. You want me to find them for you?"

"No. I just wondered if they came by."

"No."

"I'll be in my office. I need some privacy, so if you'll screen the calls?"

"Sure. Why don't you work from home for a couple of days? Have you had any rest at all?"

"I had a good night's sleep. I'm fine."

Diane went to her office and looked up the phone number of Serena Ellison, Star's lawyer. Before she could dial the phone, there was a knock on her door.

"Yes?"

Korey came in and dropped in the chair by her desk. "Can I talk to you?"

Diane had an idea what it was about. "Sure."

"You doing OK? Andie just told me about you getting mugged."

"I'm fine." Diane felt like making up cards about what happened so she could pass them around and not have to answer questions. *People are simply concerned,* she chided herself.

"I'm sorry about that guy you're dating. I hope he's going to be all right."

"I think he will be." She fingered the pages of the phone book on the desk.

"The police came to see me here. They think I shot him."

"No, they don't. They're just floundering around. You're black and have dreadlocks. That's it. I'm so sorry, Korey. I know this is unfair. I've already talked to them once when they asked me about you, and I didn't think they would come talk to you."

"The museum security came to talk to me about it."

"The museum security? Why? They don't have any jurisdiction. . . . You mean Jake?"

"Yeah."

"He was doing his day job with the police department. Apparently, the chief of detectives put him on the case. I would have thought Jake would know better."

"This really pisses me off."

"I know. I'll write a letter complaining to the chief of detectives. They had no reason at all to question you. I don't believe the perp was even black."

"They said he was."

"Some of the witnesses said he was, but there's another witness—that they are discounting—who says he wasn't. She said the dreads weren't real, they were braids, and he didn't move like a black man."

"Didn't move like a black man? What's that supposed to mean? He didn't have rhythm, he couldn't jump?"

"I don't know what it means."

"Why are they discounting her?"

"She's nine years old and black. Not only do they think she's too young, they think she's being protective. But she's very credible and I believe her. I think it was a white man in disguise."

"Some racist." Korey sounded bitter.

"No, I don't think it was that. He just wanted to appear opposite of what he was."

Korey eyed her a moment. "There's something else going on here, isn't there?"

"I think so. But I have no proof."

"I don't like being accused."

"I don't blame you. I don't like it either, and if they try spreading anything around, I'll put a stop to it."

"Fortunately, I was here with three of my staff at the time of the shooting."

"You don't have to give me an alibi, Korey. In my wildest imagination I can't see you holding up automatic teller machines."

Korey almost smiled as he rose from the chair. "Thanks."

He left calmer than when he came in. Izzy certainly wasn't making any points with Diane, and she was really disappointed in Jake.

She dialed Serena Ellison, who agreed to look in on Star at the jail and make arrangements for Diane to visit. Diane emphasized the need to hurry. With Frank in critical condition, Star's fragile emotional state could collapse again.

With that taken care of, Diane changed into jeans, a tee shirt and sneakers.

"You're not going out to the site, are you?" said Andie, looking at Diane going out the door.

"Yes. Call me on my cell if anything comes up. And tell the herpetologist to find that snake!"

"Should you be out here?" Jonas stared at Diane when she emerged from the woods. He was at the tent, taking a break with a few of the crew.

Diane was getting a little tired of people telling her to rest. Yes, she needed to rest, but there wasn't time.

"No," she said, trying hard not to sound snappy and ungrateful. "What kind of trouble did you have here last night?"

"We had some visitors. I guess they must have thought no one was here. They started digging around the pit. One of the deputies yelled at them and they took off."

"Did they do much damage?"

"No. They'd just gotten started."

"They?"

"There were two of them that we saw."

"We?"

"I stayed with some of the guys last night. Thought it might be fun."

"Could anyone get a description?"

"No. It was too dark and their flashlights didn't illuminate them at all."

"I'm glad no one was hurt."

"Andie told me about Frank Duncan. We're all sorry to hear about that. How's he doing?"

"Good. The doctors think he'll pull through."

"That's a relief. What happened? Andie said something about a robbery?"

Diane told them what happened, and like everyone else, they marveled at both of them getting attacked not one day apart.

"We've got something to show you."

"You found something?" she asked, but got no answer.

She followed Jonas and the crew to the site, where a couple of the women were working. They had gotten an extraordinary amount of work done. One entire layer was excavated and they had started down into another.

"We've already taken up the first layer of animal bones. Sylvia came out to help us late yesterday and identified the animals. It was pretty straightforward. No surprises. Deer, fox, racoon, duck. We got a complete list of the ones she identified here. She said that may change when she gets back to look at them more thoroughly."

"Find anything in the screens?" asked Diane.

"A quarter, bone fragments. Mostly just rocks. But this is what we wanted to show you." Jonas led her to the other side of the pit where the two women, Miriam and Ellen, were working.

Diane stooped down and examined the excavation. "Well, finally, there it is."

Chapter 33

Standing out in bold relief, covering two grid units, was a member of the Canidae family. Diane guessed a wolf, judging from the size and low slope of the forehead. And there, peeking through a thin layer of soil underlying the thorax of the wolf, were the ribs and vertebrae of a human. What was so clear about the juxtaposition was the difference between the large arc of the quadrupedal wolf ribs and tightly arced bipedal human ribs—the difference of carrying organs in a horizontal as opposed to a vertical position. But the extraordinary thing was the roots of the sapling that wove down through the wolf and human ribs, supplying at least one end of a time frame.

Someone had dumped the body and covered it with a thin layer of dirt. The Abercrombies tossed the wolf carcass on top of that soon afterward. Sometime later, the seedling began to grow up through the human and wolf bones. Age the tree and they would know the minimum amount of time the bones had been there. Maybe the information would be corroborated by Abercrombie's records.

"Aren't we lucky?" said Diane. "We know the skeletons have been here at least as long as the sapling. Let's put some more excavators here, and I'll want a cross-section of the tree trunk."

She looked for any signs of the skull but saw none. Sometimes skulls are a problem. Being essentially round, they have a tendency to roll away from the torso when the last vestige of flesh lets go. If the body had been buried haphazardly or had been laid over a pile of other carcasses, the skull could have rolled to another location or even dropped to a deeper layer down through cavities made as the carcasses decomposed.

"Very well done," she told them.

"We thought you'd be pleased," said Jonas.

"Have you seen any signs of buttons, zippers, shoe grommets, leather, rubber, textiles—anything?"

"No," answered Ellen. "As far as I can see, he or she was dumped without his or her clothes."

"Too bad. I was hoping for a driver's license."

"Aren't wolves protected or something?" said Miriam, dusting away a layer of dirt from the shoulder girdle.

"Some places," said Diane.

"First the bear, and now this wolf," said Miriam. "I really like the Abercrombies, but . . ."

"We don't know the circumstances of his presence here. For now, let's just be forgiving of what we find. It's my understanding that since Whit started helping in his father's business, he's gotten more strict with his clients. The wolf could be roadkill, after all."

"No," said Ellen. "This isn't roadkill." She pointed to a bullet hole in the scapula.

"I was hoping," said Diane, taking her trowel and starting to work on the human skeleton. "I know this may be going a little fast for your comfort, but I need to get this guy identified."

He's the key, she thought as she started at the first lumbar vertebra and began excavating gingerly around the wolf skeleton. She wanted the juxtaposition to remain as long as possible. Sometimes bones in proximity can reveal surprising information. It looked like there was only a slight covering of soil placed over the human remains, which may mean the wolf was put there fairly soon after the person, before wild animals uncovered the remains, making them noticeable to Luther when he was dumping the wolf.

"We can do this," said Jonas. "Have you rested at all since you were released from the hospital?"

"I'll rest when this is over."

"I don't think it works like that," said Jonas.

"Give it up," said Diane. "By the way, I moved my bishop to queen three."

"I thought you would. Can you remember a king side castle when you get back to the museum?"

"Sure. Maybe we should just play this game with each other in our heads."

"I couldn't do that when I was young," said Jonas. "I'm keeping track of the moves in my notebook." He pointed to his back pocket.

Diane tried out her chess analogy on Jonas as the other excavators listened in. "I think getting Star convicted is the game. Frank was attacked because he was protecting her."

"Like a king's pawn." Jonas nodded.

"With him gone, her position is very vulnerable."

"I thought it was a robbery?" said Ellen.

Diane told them about little Tamika Stillwood, the fake dreadlocks and whatever suspicious thing she saw in his movement.

"I don't know exactly what she meant, but she's a very observant little girl."

"Little kids are like that," said Miriam. "They're like dogs that way. Any change in their environment, they notice. I miss a line from my daughter's favorite story and she gets indignant."

"And they hear everything," said Ellen.

"That certainly puts a different light on things," said Jonas. "What do the police say?"

"They interviewed Korey because he has dreadlocks." Jonas dropped his trowel. "They didn't?"

"As you can imagine, he was upset about it."

"They aren't going to hassle him, are they?"

"No. Fortunately, he was at the museum with half his staff, working, at the time. But the whole idea . . ." Diane stopped and scrutinized the wolf skeleton, running her fingers along a rib.

"He was found shot by a forest ranger," she said.

Miriam, Ellen and Jonas looked back and forth from the bones to Diane to each other.

"Just how do you know that?" said Jonas.

"This is the wolf whose skin is stuffed and mounted in one of our faunal exhibits. A ranger friend of Milo's found it and kept it frozen while he was looking for the poacher. At some point he gave it to Milo for the museum. We have the bullet with the display and a video about dangers to wild animals."

"Whew," exclaimed Ellen. "I was going to ask if you teach classes. I'd sure like to be able to read bones like that."

Diane smiled at her. "It just occurred to me."

"I think this guy ought to be reassembled and exhibited beside his stuffed self," said Jonas. "Bullet hole and all."

"I agree," said Diane.

They lapsed into silence, and there was no sound but the clinking of tools against soil. Digging graves. Dreadful business. The Odells were right. She was a grave digger. A pain in Diane's lower back reminded her that she needed to drink more water. She took a long sip and continued working, for just a foot away from the ribs of the wolf she had uncovered the human pelvis—besides the skull, one of the most important sets of bones to find.

She swept away the dirt from the large flat bones that had collapsed into the dirt. She ran her fingers along the bone looking at the details; no ventral arc, narrow sciatic notch, narrow subpubic angle—classic male. She took a brush and cleaned the pubic symphysis, studying the remodeling of the bone, looking for a sign of the age—when she caught sight of what looked like a healed lesion. She'd seen similar bone formations resulting from inflammation, but mostly in women who had just borne a child.

"Let's photograph and take up the wolf," she said. "I'd like to take the human skeleton with me."

"I have a scapula over here," said one of the male crew members. Diane tried to remember his name—something long or not easy on the tongue. Raedwald, that was it. The scapula was three grids away from the main part of the skeleton.

"This is in bad condition."

"The scapula body's broken, the coracoid process is missing, so is the acromion, the glenoid cavity is badly crushed," she muttered almost to herself. "Have you found all the pieces?"

"No. This is pretty much it."

"Have it photographed and take it up." Her head was starting to ache. She rubbed her eyes.

"I've already sketched it. You want to see the arm you discovered yesterday?"

Diane nodded. She stood, almost too fast, and felt weak on her feet. Fortunately, Raedwald didn't ask her if she was all right. As well-meaning as everyone was, and as right as they were, she wished they wouldn't express it.

She stood for a moment, gathering her wits about her before walking over with him to have a look at the humerus. It was completely excavated and included the forearm bones—the radius and ulna—and the bones of the hand. All neatly sitting on top of the ground as if they had been laid there, but out of place. The radius and ulna were flipped around in their relationship to the humerus. The bones of the hand were off to the side.

"Good job."

"It's really like a work of art," he said. "I mean the bones, not the excavation."

"I've always thought bones are quite lovely. It produces some cognitive dissonance, though, to look at a pit of remains from a mass murder and also see the beauty of the bones."

"I'll bet."

Diane sat down cross-legged to examine the bones as they lay there on the ground. The head of the humerus was crushed. This was the part that would have fit into the crushed glenoid cavity.

"Will you be able to tell the difference between animal activity and, say, an injury?" the excavator asked.

"Probably." She touched the bone lightly with her fingers. "Interesting bones."

The sound of her telephone ringing came from the

pocket of her shirt. She snatched it and pushed the answer button.

"Dr. Fallon, this is Serena Ellison, Star Boone's attorney."

Diane was disappointed. She wanted to hear news about Frank—good news.

"Yes?"

"I've made arrangements for us to see her in an hour. I know this is short notice, but . . ."

"Shall I meet you at the jail?"

"That would be fine. I'll see you there."

Yes, it would be fine, she thought. Then when she saw Frank she could tell him how Star was doing.

Diane stood up. "Can I have your attention?" Everyone stopped and looked over at her. "First, I want to thank you, both for the quality and the speed of work you are doing. I can see you've been putting in overtime to get this done, and I appreciate it. I have to go back into town, but I'd like you to get the human remains drawn, mapped and out today, if you can. Jonas, would you bring them to my office at the museum? And please don't tell anyone what they are."

The excavators looked at each other as if they were all members of a conspiracy.

"Sure thing," said Jonas.

Jonas walked her back to the creek crossing. Diane eyed him as he wiped his neck with a bandana.

"You doing OK?" she asked.

"Me? I think I'm doing better than you are."

"That's not saying much."

"I'm doing just fine. You don't need to worry about me."

"Good. You guys are doing a terrific job."

"We're glad to do it. I'm glad to do it. Thanks for the opportunity."

"That episode last night. Did you get any sense of danger from it?"

"No. I had the idea that whoever it was, was more frightened than we were. For us, it was no more than pot hunters. You think it was the murderer?"

Jonas said the word *murderer* as if he were incredulous over the possibility. She doubted archaeologists ever dealt with murderers.

"I don't know, Jonas," she said.

Chapter 34

Diane crossed the creek and hiked back to her car. Inside she stopped and rested a moment before she put the key in the ignition. What she would have liked to do is go home and sleep. Instead, she drove to the Rosewood jail.

Rosewood's jail was new. The interview room they were allowing the lawyer and Diane to use smelled of paint and disinfectant.

"It seems like it's taking a long time," said Diane, looking at her watch.

"Yes, it does," said Serena Ellison. "I hate it when they have me cooling my heels."

As if someone had been waiting outside listening for the time when Diane and the lawyer were the most impatient, the door suddenly swung open. Star, escorted by the guard, slouched into the room wearing a bright orange jumpsuit. She was pale and looked thin in the baggy, ill-fitting clothes.

"How's Uncle Frank?" she said as she came through the door.

"He's doing well," said Diane. "I saw him this morning and he was much improved from yesterday."

Star came to the table and sat down. The guard looked for a moment like she was going to stay until Star's lawyer shot her a stern glare.

"How are you doing?" asked Diane.

She shrugged. "It's boring and the guards are mean."

"How are they mean?" asked Serena.

"They say stuff to me, like I'm going to hell."

"Are they doing anything else mean? Hitting you, withholding your food?"

"Withholding the food would be a kindness around here. No, they don't hit me or anything. They shove a little, that's all." She looked at her lawyer. "Can't you get me out of here?"

"I'm going to try again today. But you have to have a place to go."

Star looked like she would cry.

"She can stay with me," said Diane. Probably too rashly, but the grateful look on Star's face was worth it.

"That'll be good. Now Star, don't get your hopes up about getting out today or tomorrow. Most likely they won't grant bail, but they might, and I'll keep trying," said Serena.

"The important thing," said Diane, "is that you take care of yourself. I'll come see you as often as I can, but I don't know how often that'll be. I'm making progress with the case, and Frank's getting better. Hold on to that."

Star nodded.

"And be polite," said Serena. "It won't kill you. If you act hard, they'll think you're hard and treat you that way."

"When I get out of here, can we sue them?"

"We'll see," said Serena. "Let's take care of one case at a time."

It was hard to watch Star being led back to jail, and Diane was glad to be rid of the place when she left. She could only imagine what it must be like to not be able to leave. She thanked Serena Ellison and headed to the museum.

When Diane saw her office upon her first arrival at the museum, she thought her private bathroom was nice, but a little extravagant. Lately, she'd been using it as much as her apartment bathroom and was glad to have it. She showered, changed clothes and put on enough makeup to look presentable.

She told Andie to screen her calls, and she settled in to work on her backlog of paperwork. If she didn't get caught up, her detractors wouldn't have to resort to pranks to try and remove her; she'd sabotage herself. First, however, she called the hospital to check on Frank. "Critical" was all they would tell her.

Diane worked on museum business and found it to be a nice break from the past few days. *That's great,* she thought, thinking of her main job as a break. . . . She shook her head as she signed a requisition form.

It was almost two o'clock when she heard raised voices in Andie's office. Andie was trying to tell someone Diane couldn't be disturbed. Diane rose as the door burst open. A woman stood in front of her desk. She was in her early thirties, Diane guessed. Her light brown hair was pulled back into a severe french twist. She wore a brown pantsuit, crisply pressed. Her brow was furrowed into an angry expression.

"Can I help you?" said Diane, sitting back down.

"You can help by minding your own damn business."

Diane's gaze shifted from her desk, filled with piles of paperwork, and back up to the stranger. "I am."

"You know what I mean."

"I'm sorry, I don't. I don't even know who you are."

"Detective Janice Warrick."

"All right, Detective Warrick, what is your complaint?"

"Who are you to mess around with my cases? I doubt you'd appreciate it if I came here and started setting up my own exhibits."

"What cases are you referring to?"

She leaned forward. "Don't act like you don't know what I'm talking about. The Boone murders."

"As I explained to the mayor, I've been engaged to help the defense. I didn't go into your crime scene until it was released. And I did so with permission of the owner. So what are you referring to?"

"The reports in the media about me botching the case and arresting the wrong person—that's what I'm referring to."

"I haven't been watching the media, but surely you

aren't denying the defense the right to have its theory of the crime?"

"No. It's the character assassination, the lies. Do you know how hard it was for me to rise to detective in this town? We have the killer behind bars, and she's going to stay there—despite your efforts to free her. In case you haven't heard, the judge denied her bail again. At least some people aren't buying your hokum." Her lips thinned into a grim smile. "I heard you offered to take her home with you. I guess you can't help taking in strays."

Diane's face hardened. She locked her gaze with Warrick's as she rose to her feet. The image of the mayor came into her mind, as did his mean-spirited insinuations. This woman was like him, even though separated by two levels of bureaucracy—the commissioner and the chief of detectives.

People in leadership gather like-minded people around them—not simply like-minded, but people of similar morality. With good leaders, it can be a good thing. With ill-intentioned ones, it is a nest of vipers. She'd seen it in petty dictators, petty bureaucrats and now here in her hometown's government. She resolved right at that moment to defeat it—to defeat them, to humiliate them, to rub their noses in their own incompetence.

"Andie," Diane called without taking her gaze from Warrick's. Andie hurried into the room, and from the look on her face, she had clearly been listening. "Show this woman out, and she is never to set foot in this private area of the museum again. If she does, call security."

"Ms. Fallon . . ." Warrick began. Her face looked suddenly less angry. "I'm just trying to do my job."

"Anything else you have to say to me is irrelevant. We're finished."

"I can see my way out." She turned on her heels and walked out of the office.

"You all right?" asked Andie. "I heard what she said."

"I'm fine. But I'd sure like to arrange for one of the dinosaurs to fall on her."

A knock on the door brought both their heads around. It was Jonas, looking like he just came in from the field.

"We brought the bones in," he said. "I just left them with Korey, and he locked them in the storage vault."

"Were you able to find the skull?"

Jonas shook his head. "Not yet. But we've got a ways to go to get to the bottom of the pit."

"I really can't thank you enough," said Diane.

"No, it's me who's grateful. My old department wasn't mine anymore. When you retire, they seem to think all your knowledge retires with you. I got hints every day about how they needed office space. This is heaven-sent for me. It's like starting a new career."

"Why don't you spend the night at your house tonight?" said Diane.

"I'm going to do just that. Have a long soak in the tub and then listen to some Bach with a bottle of beer."

"Sounds like something I'd like to do."

After Jonas left, Diane headed for the conservation lab. Korey was still working on separating the papers found in the basement. He had several single sheets laid out on a table.

"You working alone tonight?"

"Yep. Hope I don't need an alibi later on."

Diane smiled at him, as though it was a joke, but she could see he was only half joking. "Anything interesting in the papers from the basement?"

"I haven't read any of them thoroughly yet. A lot are written in this spidery handwriting that's hard to read. But yeah, there's some requisition forms to a veterinary college for a series of calf fetuses, and one to a guy in Utah about some fossil dinosaur eggs. I wonder where those ended up. I guess in someone's private collection. There was a cool 1849 map of the United States. I sent that and an interesting collection of drawings off to be processed at another lab. The drawings looked like they were the original plans for the dinosaur murals in the big rooms." Korey grinned.

"That is interesting. Go ahead and let the exhibit planner—" Diane had gotten into the bad habit of referring to her staff by their titles rather than their names. She needed to break herself of that. "Let Audra know the kind of things you're finding so she can start on some ideas."

"I talked with her this morning."

"Good. Korey, I hope you don't mind if I use the lab here to look at these bones. I was going to set up a separate one on the third floor, but the storage vault in this room is one of the safest places. The last intruders couldn't open the vault."

"You think maybe the break-in was about your bones?"

"Yes, I do. I think they were looking for the clavicle that started all this."

"There's a table in the vault. I can clear it off and you can use it. That way you won't have to keep packing it up and taking it out. It's kind of cool in there, though."

"I'll wear a sweater."

Diane helped Korey rearrange the storage room so she could work. They collected all the measuring equipment Andie had put in the third-floor room and brought it back to the vault.

"Need any help?" asked Korey.

Diane shook her head. "I've already pulled Jonas and Sylvia in. I can't tie up the entire museum staff."

"It's kind of interesting, though."

Korey watched Diane lay the bones in anatomical position on the metal table.

"It's hard to imagine the poor guy was ever alive. You think you can get him to talk to you?" he asked.

"Oh, yes. He'll tell me all about himself. Murderers don't know how eloquent bones can be."

Chapter 35

Most of the bones of the human skeleton were accounted for, with the notable exception of the skull. Even the atlas, the bone that the skull rests on, was there. Diane examined it with her hand lens. She closely inspected each of the other bones of the neck.

"No marks," she said.

"So that means that the murderer didn't cut off the head and take it with him?" asked Korey.

"Probably not. It'd be hard to do it without making cutting marks on the vertebrae."

Her excavators even found the small hyoid bone; the bone that anchors the tongue and the only bone not attached to any other bone. However, most of the terminal phalanxes of the toes were missing, and all of the terminal phalanxes of the right hand were missing. She suspected that many of the smaller bones would show up in the sifted material.

With the bones laid out and the right scapula, humerus and clavicle juxtaposed, there was a clear pattern of damage that she had seen in the collarbone when Frank first showed it to her. The damage included the second, third, fourth and fifth ribs, which were broken where the scapula body would have covered them. At the place where those bones cluster together some force had crushed them.

She examined the scapula with the hand lens. Part of the damage to it had left a straight indentation in the crushed bone.

"That looks like it hurt," said Korey.

"I imagine he passed out, if he was conscious at all."

"Can you tell what happened?"

"Whatever force hit him came from his rear and was focused over the scapula and not distributed." Diane gestured with her hand, pretending to hit the scapula. "It's more damage than a person swinging a weapon could inflict."

"What then?"

"I don't know." She placed the bones back in their place. "He also has a healed break in his left tibia. Maybe he's got an X ray somewhere. It will positively identify him, if we ever get a clue to who he is."

"What else do you know about him?"

"He was muscular." She pointed out the well-developed muscle attachments on his arms and legs. "Bones are plastic and continue to remodel throughout life. Something like hard work or hard exercise shows up on them. Stronger muscles need larger attachments to hold on to."

She told him the results of the stable isotope analyses she'd had done on the clavicle.

"Now, *that* is totally cool. You know, you should add a forensic unit to the museum. We have plenty of room on the third floor."

"One of the board members suggested the same thing. I came here to get away from forensic work."

"Didn't work, did it? Maybe the universe is telling you something."

"Yeah, that I'm an idiot."

Diane would like to have used the skull to determine race. Without it she'd have to use other methods—most of which involve measurement, and all of which are less than precise.

She started with the long bones. She placed the left humerus on the osteometric board—a wooden device consisting of a platform on which the bone is laid, a "headboard" against which one end of the long bone is positioned, and a sliding "footboard" to mark the length. She recorded the measurement on her computer.

"Most of what I'm doing now is measuring," she said. "It's like watching grass grow."

"I was about to get that idea," Korey said. "I'll go out to the lab and work a while. Let me know if I can bring you anything."

Diane continued, losing track of time in the minutiae of the detailed measurements on different parts of the bones. She recorded each of them in her computer program, recollecting Kevin asking her at the party why he would have to learn math. If he could see her now, it would seem that was all she did, but math often gives the best information. Measuring is tedious, but she taught herself to like it for its precision. The math would give her the best guess on the race of the individual, and she needed the race for a good estimation of the height.

The ring of her cell phone made her jump. Perhaps she needed to change it to a melody.

"Dr. Fallon, this is the front desk. There is a Dr. Duncan here to see you."

Dr. Duncan, she thought. *Who's that?* Then she remembered. Frank's brother, Linc. "Would you ask him to come to the second-floor staff lounge? You'll have to give him directions."

Diane left the storage room and locked the door behind her. Korey was still working on the documents.

"I have a guest coming up," she said. "Frank's brother. I'm going to be gone for a while. If you leave, go ahead and lock up. I have a key."

She went into the small bathroom near Korey's office, washed her hands and looked at herself in the mirror. She looked terrible. She ran wet fingers through her hair. It didn't do much good. "Well, he's not here for a date," she told her reflection.

As she left the conservation lab and crossed the lobby to the staff lounge, Linc had just come up the elevator and was walking through the doors to the east wing. He held two large pizza boxes and a bag, presumably of drinks.

"I hope you like pizza," he said.

"I do, but how many people were you planning on feeding?"

He smiled. "You never know."

He reminded her of Frank. Bringing too much food was apparently a family trait. Her eyes started to tear up. She turned her head away and led him into the lounge to a table in the corner.

Linc set the boxes down and pulled out the drinks. He gave her a large bottle of water. "You look dehydrated."

"I'm fine. It's just a bruised kidney."

"No such thing as *just* a bruised kidney. You sound like some of the athletes I've treated. I'll tell you what I tell them. You're not invincible."

"How's Frank?" Linc was silent for a long moment. "What? What's happened?" A sickening panic rose in the pit of her stomach.

"He's developed an infection."

"Oh, God. How serious?"

"Serious enough. They're keeping him in ICU."

Diane stood. "I need to go see him."

Linc took her hand. "He's sleeping. Eat something. You aren't a vegetarian, are you? I ordered pepperoni on the pizzas."

"No. I'm not a vegetarian." Diane got some paper plates from a cabinet in the staff lounge and they settled in to eating the pizza. She was having a hard time keeping tears from forming.

"Frank is always bringing more food than we can possibly eat too. Must be genetic."

"Comes from having three growing boys in the family, I guess. We always needed lots of food on hand."

Diane selected a slice of pizza and took a bite. It was still warm and tasted good. She never realized she was hungry until she ate something.

"Tell me what this is about," said Linc after several bites.

Diane told him the entire story, from Frank first showing her the bone to her possession of the rest of the skeleton, sans skull, in the storage room.

"So you think that what happened to you and to Frank is related to the murder of his friends?"

"Yes."

"What do they have to gain by shooting Frank?"

"Frank and I are the only ones working on an alternate theory of the crime. The police aren't interested. Frank is the only one protecting Star. Without him, she would stand a good chance of getting convicted. There are flaws in my theory, but I have a gut feeling that what's happened to us is directly related to the murder of the Boones."

"It does seem that way. If you're correct, then you're also correct in assuming Frank's still in danger. What were you going to do before we arrived?"

"He's hired security to watch the Boone house—to keep relatives from carrying off Star's possessions. I was going to ask them to put someone outside Frank's room. Frank also has friends on the police force here. I'm sure they would be glad to help."

"Why don't you go home and get a good night's sleep? Have you had one since you were attacked?"

"I want to get the analysis done as soon as possible."

"You and Frank are a good pair. He thinks he's indispensable too. I hope nothing happens to either of you, or the rest of us are doomed."

Diane smiled at him. "I'm not indispensable, but there's no one here this minute to analyze the skeleton but me."

"Yeah, Frank would say the same thing."

"How did he get into learning the accordion?" asked Diane.

Linc grinned at Diane. "Because everyone made fun of it, I think. Frank was a kid totally immune to peer pressure and completely stubborn. He wouldn't let anyone back him down, and he didn't care what people thought."

"That must have made school rough. His peers must have been on to him all the time."

"At first, but Dad taught us to box from the time we could put gloves on and not fall over frontward."

"Boxing? Not some martial art?"

"No, boxing's the best." He went into a boxing posture and punched the air. "Once you get your feet off the ground, you're off balance. We'd love it when the other kids thought they were so cool with their fancy kicks. They were pretty easy to knock down."

"He didn't tell me about the boxing. But I just found out he's pretty mean on a karaoke machine."

"You should see the three of us."

Diane laughed. "How about Ava? Is she into karaoke and boxing?"

"She plays the piano. Quite well. Not into anything physical. She's the older sister and takes her job seriously. Frank's really going to get an earful when he's better."

"You have a nice family."

"We like it." He took a long drink of Coke. "Can I have a look at the skeleton?" he asked.

Diane had finished eating all she could eat, which was two slices from an extra-large pepperoni, mushroom and green pepper pizza. She took a swallow of her water and eyed him closely.

"Frank asked me to keep an eye on you," he said in answer to her silent stare. "He apparently knows you quite well."

"Sure, you can have a look. I'll record a few more observations and go home."

Korey was still there, but was on his way out. Diane introduced him to Linc.

"We're all sorry to hear about your brother," said Korey, shaking his hand. "I'll see you tomorrow, Dr. Fallon. Been finding some interesting stuff in that small stack of papers."

"We have some pizza left," said Linc. "Why don't you take the extra one home with you?"

Korey looked surprised. "Sure. Thanks."

As Korey left, Diane fished the key from her pocket and opened the door to the storage room.

"This is the mysterious guy," she said.

"You don't have a skull?" asked Linc.

"Unfortunately, no. I really wish I had it. We could find out what he looks like. The excavators are still looking for it."

"You think it was removed?"

"The vertebrae don't show it."

"What do you know about him?"

"He grew up in a cool, humid climate, he was a vegetarian but ate fish, he's been missing for about five years, maybe, judging from the vegetation growth over him." Diane told him about the stable isotope analysis.

"I'm impressed."

"You should be. I found that out when we had only the clavicle. With all these bones, you'd think I'd be home free."

"What about his age and condition?"

"He's still undergoing epiphyseal union on all his long bones—from a half to three-quarters fused, including his iliac crest." She ran her fingers along the top of his pelvic bone and picked it up. "Look at the pubic symphysis." She rubbed her thumb over the horizontal ridges and grooves where the two pelvic bones joined in front. "This is a young surface. My guess is he was in his late teens or early twenties."

"My son's that age," Linc said, caressing the bone. "There are some parents somewhere wondering where he is."

"Speaking of his pelvis, this is sort of unusual." She showed him the lesion on the bone near the pubic symphysis. "I usually see this in pregnant women or those who have just given birth. It's caused by the strain on the joint."

"What about his shins?" asked Linc.

"Shins? He has a healed break in his tibia."

"Check his elbows."

Diane raised her eyebrows and reached for the left ulna and examined the proximal end. She raised her eyebrows further and checked the right ulna. However, it had been gnawed by animals.

"The left ulna has a healed lesion. The right might, but I can't tell."

Linc winked at her.

"How about the lower back?"

Diane narrowed her eyes and examined several of the lumbar vertebrae. "One shows some wear on the margins."

Linc grinned broadly, showing a row of even white teeth.

Chapter 36

Diane laid the vertebrae back in place on the table and turned to face Linc, who was still grinning like a Cheshire cat.

"Okay, are you going to tell me?"

"I think your fellow here was a hockey player," he said.

"Hockey?"

"I've seen that cluster of injuries many times in hockey players. Breaks in the tibia are common, so are lower back problems. I've seen olecranon bursitis so bad it'll leave scars on the bone. Groin pain is common in a lot of sports, but the side-to-side motion in hockey puts a strain on the pubic symphysis, causing the kind of lesions you just showed me."

"Possibly a hockey player. Good. In fact, terrific. Grew up in a cool climate, that fits. Surely someone out there will recognize all the information we have and can identify this guy. Thanks."

"Glad to be of help. Now, will you follow my orders as a doctor and go home and get some rest?"

"Sure." Diane locked the vault, turned out the lights in the lab and locked it and the second floor when they left. Their shoes echoed on the marble floor as they walked across the lobby and through the doors to the elevator. Chanell Napier and Bernie Chapman were the two security officers on duty. They were talking to each other at the front information desk. Chanell was inside the semicircular booth and Bernie was leaning on the desk.

"Where's Leonard tonight?" asked Diane.

"He's been sick the last couple of days," said Chanell. "We're filling in for him."

Diane realized how much she'd been neglecting the museum and felt guilty. "Not serious, I hope?"

"I don't think so," said Chanell. "He said he was having migraines."

"You two doing OK?"

"It's real quiet here. Bernie was just about to make the rounds."

Bernie ran a hand through his red hair and put on his security cap. "Just going now," he said, and started off on his rounds.

"Be sure to keep an eye out for that missing snake," she told him. "I want him found."

"Oh, my God," Bernie said. A little tremble went through him. "I forgot about that snake." He watched the floor along the walls and looked under a table in the hallway as he passed. At one point he gave a sudden jump to one side, as if he had seen something, then continued on.

Diane shook her head in bewildered fascination. She hadn't had time to look for a head of security. She was thinking about Jake Houser, but he had a full-time day job. She decided at that moment to give it to Chanell. She had experience at the university before she came here, and Diane could send her for courses at the police academy. Most of all, she'd proved to be reliable and a self-starter.

"Chanell, come by my office when you get in tomorrow."

She looked alarmed for a moment. Diane smiled at her and her face brightened. She felt better having made the decision. It was one she should have made several days ago.

They left the museum in the care of the security guards, and Linc walked her to her car. "Do I need to follow you home?"

"No. I intend to go directly there. I'll be fine. Tell me, is Frank going to be all right?"

"I think so. I won't say it isn't bad right now—it is. But his condition is definitely survivable."

She had never asked anyone at the hospital about the long-term prognosis for Frank's injuries. How he would be when he recovered. She'd been concerned only that he recover. But she thought of it now. Would he have any paralysis? A heart condition? She was afraid to ask. She started to get in her car, but stopped.

"How is he? I mean, when he recovers, will he be OK?"

"I don't know. They repaired all the damage, and he has feeling in his arms and legs. The bullet didn't get near the spine and apparently didn't nick any of the nerves. He'll be weak for a while. Go home and get some rest and try not to worry."

She got in her car and he closed the door for her. She rolled down her window to say good-bye and he handed her a card. "This has my cell phone number on it. Give me a call if you need anything."

She drove home and parked in front of her building. She was getting to feel like she was running a gauntlet in getting from her car to her apartment door, and she was tired of living like this. She hurried to the door, flew up the stairs and opened her apartment door. She flipped on the lights. She expected to feel safe, but didn't. She felt scared.

She stood in the hallway and listened for any sound—creaking, breathing, anything. *This is silly, get a grip,* she told herself. It was a small apartment with very few places to hide. In fact, under her bed and in her closet were it. She quickly checked both places, feeling foolish when she finished. What if she'd found someone? She didn't have a weapon. This was really stupid. She walked back into the living room and was about to turn on the television when she saw a form in the draperies behind her living room chair. Her heart jumped in her chest. She was almost paralyzed in place.

As casually as she could, she moved to the hall and into the kitchen to look for a weapon. What kind of weapon? Her mind raced, trying to think. A knife.

Maybe, but how would she fare in a knife fight with some intruder? She could run but would she make it before he caught her? The best course of action would be to call for help. But her cell phone was in the bedroom, and whoever it was would hear her talking. She could grab the cell phone and lock herself in the bathroom. And then what—hope help arrived before he broke down the door? She heard a rustle and creaking of the floor. No time.

She spotted her cast-iron skillet sitting on the stove, picked it up and stepped out into the hallway. She edged forward until she was almost to the living room. Maybe she could catch the intruder by surprise and knock him out. She raised it over her head as she saw a shadow cast by her lamp. One more second. Now she swung the pan, but at the last moment swerved and hit the wall with a crash, accompanied by a piercing scream.

"Mrs. Odell, what are you doing in my apartment? Do you know I could have knocked your skull in?"

Mrs. Odell, dressed in a pink chenille robe, was holding her chest and breathing hard. Diane led her to the sofa.

"Are you all right? What are you doing in here?"

"Looking." She wheezed. "Looking for the cat."

"Mrs. Odell." She was interrupted by a pounding on the door.

"That'd be Marvin." She was still breathing hard.

Diane went to the door. A man, possibly in his seventies, a little shorter than Diane, was standing at the door with a concerned look on his horselike face.

"Veda, Veda, was that you? Are you OK? What did you do to Veda?"

"I almost knocked her out with an iron skillet. Mr. Odell, I don't have a cat, I've never had a cat here, the landlady doesn't allow cats."

"Veda was sure you did."

"What? She knocked her out with a frying pan?" A voice from the hallway said. The other tenants along with the landlady were murmuring outside her door.

"Is something wrong?" asked the landlady. "Oh, dear."

"Mrs. Odell was hiding behind the draperies in my apartment. I almost crowned her with a skillet until I saw who it was," explained Diane. The last thing she wanted was the neighbors to believe she was beating up little old ladies.

The landlady entered with a justifiably contrite look on her face. "Oh, dear," she clucked at Veda Odell.

"How did you get in?" asked Diane.

Veda cast her husband a guilty glance. "We, uh, well, we just borrowed . . ."

"My key?" said the landlady. "Did you take my key?"

"We borrowed it. Marvin has been having fits with his allergies."

The landlady looked miserable.

"Well, you can't go stealing keys and poking around in people's rooms. Dr. Fallon was attacked in the parking lot the other night. How do you think she felt seeing someone hiding behind her curtains?"

"That was the only place I could hide. She was coming in the door and I was scared to move."

"Marvin, take Veda across the hall—and give me my key." The landlady held out her hand, and Veda dropped the key in it.

Marvin and Veda Odell left, and the other tenants went back to their apartments. There was only Diane and the landlady. Diane gave her the kind of look she did when Ariel got into something she shouldn't have.

"Oh, dear. You know, don't you?"

"I saw the tail the other night."

"She's such a nice cat, and good company. I was hoping. . . . I guess I'll have to get rid of her."

"Maybe you can find the Odells another apartment over a funeral home," said Diane.

"They are such a strange couple, aren't they? They love planning their funerals. Can you imagine? That's such an odd thing to have as a hobby. Two of them. How do you suppose they found each other in the first place?"

"They probably met at a funeral," said Diane.

The landlady shrugged. "You're probably right."

Diane sat on her sofa, suddenly very tired.

"You know they had children," the landlady said. "Seven of them. They all died. Veda showed me pictures of their funerals. Kind of makes your skin crawl, doesn't it?" With that, the landlady went back to her apartment.

Yes, thought Diane, *it does make my skin crawl.* She locked her door, put a chair under the knob, and dragged herself into the bedroom. Before she got in bed she took a pain pill to ease her throbbing back. As she climbed in bed she noticed the light blinking on her answering machine. *Frank,* she thought, and reached for the playback button.

Chapter 37

The message was from Gregory, asking her to call, he had some news. She looked at the clock. Much too early in England to call now, but in a few hours . . . As she was setting her alarm to wake her up in five hours, the phone rang. She snatched it up.

"Diane," said Gregory. "I figured you'd wait until some decent hour to return my call, so I thought I'd call you back."

"Do you ever get any sleep?" she asked.

"I don't need much, really. Four hours a night and I'm fit for the day. I have some news, mostly good. If not good, at least informative."

"I could use some good news."

"The good news is that Ivan Santos and his people are still in Puerto Barquis. No evidence that any have sneaked out of the country or into the U.S. Bad news is they are mounting a successful coup."

"I'm sorry to hear that. The population's been through a lot."

"I'm afraid they are in for more of the same."

"I hate saying I'm relieved he's not here."

"I know. I have some more news too. I've been checking around, and found out that someone in your State Department was discussing the events of last year at a small private party a few weeks ago. I don't think he meant harm, but I chastised him just the same. God

knows they've been giving *me* a hard time. One of the
people at the party was from Rosewood."

"Really? Who?"

"Gordon Atwell. Do you know him?"

"I do indeed. He's on my board of directors and one
of the people siding with Mark Grayson. He also holds
the mortgage on the museum—or, rather, his bank
does."

"Then maybe this news will help."

"It will."

"How is everything else?"

"Are you sure you want to know?"

"Something's happened, I can hear it in your voice.
Tell me about it."

"It's a long story. Will you be able to get your four
hours' sleep?"

"Fire away."

Diane told him the entire story, ending with Mrs. Odell
behind her drapes. That part left him laughing.

"I shouldn't laugh. I'm sorry, but the image of this
woman dressed in what did you say, pink chenille?—
hiding behind your draperies . . . not to mention you
about to club her with a cast-iron skillet, of all things. Is
it an antique?"

"Not exactly. I bake cornbread in it."

"Cornbread? Just that one thing?"

"Yes. It takes several years to season it just right for
cornbread. You don't wash it, so you can't cook anything
else in it."

"You're joking. How do you clean the thing?"

"You wipe it out after you take out the bread. The
next time you use it, you rub it with shortening and put
it in a four-hundred-and-twenty-five degree oven until it
sizzles. That pretty much gets rid of any germs."

"Is that one of those Southern things?"

"Yes."

"I'll have to allow you to bake me a—do you call it
anything special? It can't be a loaf, can it? I remember
hearing something about a pone."

"Some call it that. I simply call it a pan of cornbread."

"You'll have to make me a pan sometime."

"I'd be happy to. Let me know when you plan to come to the U.S. I'd love for you to see my museum."

"Marguerite and the boys would love that. I'm planning a trip in a couple of months. I'll let you know. I'm sorry to hear about your friend Frank, and especially about you. I need to let you get some sleep. It sounds to me like you're still injured."

"A little pain now and then."

"Go to bed and get some sleep. Let me know how things progress. I'm still concerned about you."

"I know. It's good talking to you. It really is." Diane hung up the phone and finally tucked herself into bed. She was glad he called. Gregory had a way of helping keep her feet on the ground.

Morning came too soon. She slapped the alarm off and dragged herself out of bed and into the shower. The warm water felt soothing on her sore muscles. She thought she must be getting better. No sharp pains, and the soreness in her kidney wasn't as acute.

She pulled a pearl gray pantsuit from her closet, slipped it on and grabbed a nutrition bar for breakfast on the way out. The sun was shining. It looked like it was going to be a clear day. A surprise, because rain was in the forecast. She headed for the hospital, praying that Frank was improved.

Diane slowed down as she approached the front desk. Fear was creeping inside her, fueled by the vision of asking to see Frank and being told he was gone—dead. *This is just silly.* She marched up to the desk and asked if she could visit Frank Duncan. As she asked, she saw Linc and Henry in the waiting room and walked over to them.

"He's stable," Linc said before she asked.

"That's a relief."

"You look better too."

"Got a little adrenaline rush last night." She grinned and told them about Mrs. Odell and the draperies. The two of them laughed with her, and it felt good.

"Thanks for your help last night," said Diane.

"I may be mistaken," said Linc, "but I'd be willing to bet he's an avid hockey player."

"I'm going to call Frank's partner today and ask him to put out a missing persons query. Maybe we'll come up with something."

"Would you like to see Frank?" asked Linc.

"Yes. Yes, I would."

Linc led her to the ICU and stayed outside the door as she went in. Frank was awake. He looked so pale. She took his hand.

"Hey," he whispered. "Thinking about you."

"Good, I hope."

"Always."

"Linc's been a big help. Did he tell you?"

Frank nodded. "Interesting."

"I met your partner. I thought I'd ask him to put out an inquiry about our guy."

"He'll do that."

"I won't stay long. I just needed to see how you are. Getting an infection wasn't a good idea."

"No. Seemed like it at the time, though." He gave her a wan smile.

Diane squeezed his hand. "I saw Star yesterday. She's OK. Her lawyer's trying to get her bail. I said she could stay with me."

Frank held tightly onto her hand. "Thanks."

"Get better." She kissed his cheek. "There's something I need you to do for me when you get well."

He attempted a grin. "And what would that be?"

Diane leaned over and whispered in his ear. "Teach me how to box."

"How's he doing, really?" she asked Linc on the way out of the ICU.

"Holding his own. Frank was never one to overuse antibiotics, so that's in his favor. He usually responds well to them. That's always a concern—finding an antibiotic that will work."

"Has there been any . . . other trouble?"

"No. Henry and I are always here. Most of his visitors don't go into ICU. They're content to get information from us or the desk."

"Perhaps I'm just being paranoid."

He smiled. "Maybe, but if you're not, it's good to be prepared. Henry and I don't mind."

When Diane left the hospital, she went to the jail. She didn't expect to be able to see Star, but thought perhaps the person on duty would tell Star she had been there checking on her. She was surprised when they put her in the same room as before and brought Star in to see her. Her bandages were off her arms, and Diane could see the four-inch red scars running up each arm. She also noticed that there were no telltale needle marks on either arm. Whatever drugs Star had been taking were not intravenous. That was something.

"How's Uncle Frank?"

Diane told her about the infection. She feared if Star heard it from another source and she hadn't told her, it would damage the shaky trust Star was building with her.

"He's doing well. His brothers are there. One is a doctor himself and he gives me the real poop on how Frank's doing."

"All this is my fault, isn't it?"

"What do you mean?"

"If Mom and Dad hadn't given Uncle Frank that bone to get the police to look for me . . . that's what started everything."

"First of all, we don't know if the bone is related to what happened to them. Second, and most important, it's the person's fault who murdered them. Don't lose sight of that."

"Still."

"Star, don't borrow trouble. You have enough to deal with. How are the guards treating you?"

"The one on duty now's nice. Her name's Mrs. Torres. She's good to me."

"That's good. Are you good to her?"

"You bet. In fact, she wanted me to ask you if there

are any openings at the museum for a gardener. Her son's looking for a job."

Diane laughed. "What's his name?"

"Hector Torres."

"Tell her to have him come to the museum. I'll give the head groundskeeper his name."

Star grinned. Diane could tell she liked the idea of being a broker from her jail cell. If it kept her happy and made her life easier, a job for her guard's son was a small price to pay. Diane just hoped the guy had something to recommend him.

She said good-bye to Star and got in her car. As she started it up, she realized she was counting on Star's being innocent. What if she wasn't? She didn't want to think about that possibility.

The first order of business when she got back to her office was to call the head groundskeeper and ask him to look positively on Hector Torres when he made an application.

"If he turns out to be a problem, send him to me to work it out."

"Sure thing," he'd told her. "No problem."

Whoever was trying to make Diane look irresponsible should have simply waited a while and she'd have done it herself; they need not have tried so hard forging order forms. Hiring someone just to make Star's life easier, putting both Jonas and Sylvia on the excavation—none of this had anything to do with the museum. She hoped Torres turned out to be a good worker. She shoved her feelings of guilt aside and went up to the second floor to finish with the skeleton.

As she opened the door to the vault, she half expected the bones to be gone, that someone had come in during the night and taken them away.

But the skeleton was there, brown bones laid out in basically the order they appeared in the body, on the table waiting for her to discover something else that would help identify them.

Chapter 38

Before she started Diane gave Jonas Briggs a call at the site to see how they were doing.

"Just fine. Sylvia just identified a *Cebus capucinus*."

"A monkey?"

"We also found a *Sus scrofa*."

"Someone had a pig stuffed?"

"It was hard for me to imagine too."

"Interesting finds. How about a *Homo sapiens* skull?"

"No, not so much as an *H. sapiens* tooth."

"That's too bad."

"We're still looking. Have you made another move?"

She hadn't. She thought for a moment. "King-side castle."

"That's really the most logical."

"Are you going to play both sides now?"

"You're not one of those people sensitive to critique, are you?"

"You're not one of those cocky winners, are you?"

Jonas chuckled. "I E-mailed you my report. Testing this new computer, which the entire crew wants now. It's really nice."

"I'll tell Kenneth. He'll be pleased."

Diane thanked him for the work and started back on those bones of the skeleton that she did have, which was about 86 percent of them. She examined each bone again, looking for any mark that might give a clue as to what had happened to him.

She had found all the healed breaks and lesions already. She didn't find any new cut marks or chipped bones that might indicate if he were stabbed or shot. His hyoid bone was intact, which indicated that he was probably not strangled, but she couldn't rule it out either. There was nothing but the severe injury to the shoulder and underlying bones. Although not a fatal blow in itself, he could have bled out from such an injury, or gone into shock and died. But there was no way to know.

She looked at the gentle curve in the femora. Blacks tend to have straight femora; other races have a slight curve to them. She punched up the measurements in her computer and ran ratios through her program. She knew what they would reveal, but she always liked to check her conclusions against her math. As she thought, the race was probably white.

Comparing the length of his long bones with the chart for white males, she estimated his height to be six feet, two inches. Before she left the vault, her gaze lingered on the skeleton— tall, avid sports player, young, five years dead. She turned and went out, thinking about the parents he had somewhere.

The lab was warm compared to the vault storage room. She pulled off her gloves and washed her hands. Korey's staff was hard at work.

"Any news on the fingerprints?" they asked.

"Nothing yet." Actually, they were still in her office drawer waiting . . . waiting for her to give to Frank.

Korey was in his office on the phone. She poked her head in and thanked him for the use of the storage area. "I'm going to leave the bones out for a while. If you have time later, would you help me photograph them?"

He put his hand over the receiver and nodded. "Sure thing. Let me know."

On her way to the stairs she met Mike Seger. "Mike," she said, "I owe you an apology."

He looked at her for a moment before he spoke. "Thanks. The whole thing's strange."

"Melissa's furious with me at the moment."

"Me too," he said. "But I can't figure out why. I don't understand it. It's too weird for me. I just can't hack it."

"I'm sorry."

"It's a relief, really. You know, I like her music. I wish . . ." He shrugged, letting the sentence go. "I convinced Dr. Lymon of the virtues of her office space."

"I'm happy about that."

"She's not going to be here that much anyway." He paused. "I suppose I shouldn't have said that."

"She does have to be here a specific number of hours, and a curator does have responsibilities that go along with the title, but we'll see how it works out. I'm sure the collection manager will let me know if he feels put-upon."

When Diane got to her office, she found Frank's partner sitting in Andie's office, his legs crossed, reading a copy of *Museum News*. He stood up when she entered.

"This is Ben Florian," said Andie.

"We met briefly at the hospital." She opened her door and motioned him in.

He followed her, holding a cup of coffee in a museum mug.

"Good to see you again," she said. "I was going to call you. I'm glad you came by."

He stood in the middle of the room and looked around. "Nice office."

"Thank you. Have a seat." Diane sat down behind her desk. "I just saw Frank this morning. I guess you know he had a setback, but he's doing well." She kept telling everyone he's doing well—it was as if it was only her positive declaration that was keeping him alive.

He frowned. "I hadn't heard. What happened?"

"Infection."

"Oh, that's bad. My old sergeant got an infection after open-heart surgery. Wouldn't heal. They ended up putting sugar in the wound and it finally healed up. Of course, that was a long time ago. I'm sure they have more modern methods now. Like I said at the hospital, Frank's tough."

"His brother tells me he's responding well to antibiotics."

As she said it, she realized that was not what he said at all. In fact, he hadn't really told her anything—she simply kept pulling positive notes from what he said. The thought alarmed her.

"I'm sure he's right." He must have seen the expression on her face.

Ben looked to be about ten or fifteen years older than Frank. He wore the same gray suit he had worn at the hospital. He ran a hand over his short brown hair and pulled out a small notebook and a sheaf of papers from a pocket inside his coat.

"I suppose this is a smoke-free building."

"Yes," said Diane. "Museums have to be."

He nodded. "I have the results from some tests Frank wanted processed." He handed the papers to her.

They were the test results from the blood analysis and the analysis of the plastic she'd found near Jay Boone. The plastic had powder residue, as she suspected.

"Thanks. This helps."

"Good. I have some information, too. Frank was checking on some falsified documents for you. He asked me to pass along what he discovered." Ben flipped open the notebook. "He was checking the backgrounds of some of your employees. One name popped out and he circled it. You have an employee named Leonard Starns?"

"Yes. He's one of the night security guards."

"His youngest son, Danny Starns, is an agent in the Mark Grayson Real Estate Agency. Are you familiar with them?"

"Yes," said Diane, "I am. Grayson is one of my chief detractors."

"That may be something, then. He said you wanted to handle this in-house."

"I do. Nothing has actually been stolen. But duplicates of some very expensive exhibits were ordered illegally. I appreciate the information. I hope you didn't have to drive all the way from Atlanta just for this."

"No, I thought I'd try to see Frank this afternoon. I

thought maybe he'd be in a private room by now." Ben put the notebook back in his pocket. "Frank said you might have some fingerprints or something?"

Diane took out the envelope of photographs and the fingerprint card from the conservation lab break-in.

"One of the labs was broken into a few days ago. They upset a lot of supplies and emptied drawers, but nothing was stolen, so the police here really can't do much. I took some fingerprints. I was wondering if you could run them for me." She handed him the envelope.

"That shouldn't be a problem. Sounds to me like you have some vandals running around the place. I can't stand people whose only mission in life is to tear up other people's stuff. It's as bad as stealing. Is there anything else I can do for you?"

"Yes. This concerns Frank and what happened to him." Diane laid out the whole story of the skeleton, the Boones, the attack on her and then Frank.

"Yes, you mentioned in the hospital that you were attacked, or someone did. You think all this is related?"

"Either that or a lot of coincidences."

"Yeah, too many coincidences."

"I've analyzed the skeletal remains, and this is what I came up with." She took her laptop and plugged it into its docking station, called up her report and printed it out.

She cast a glance at the laptop Kenneth had sent, which was sitting on the table. She hadn't even tried it yet. In fact, she'd forgotten that Dylan Houser was bringing it over. It must have been brought when she'd been out, which lately was entirely too much. She should at least give it a try. Her absence from the museum was weighing her down.

The page came out of the printer, and Diane handed it to Ben.

"This is what we think we know about the remains. I make it clear in the report what's observation and what's simply possibilities."

Ben read the report and whistled. "This seems pretty

thorough to me. Didn't know you could get this much stuff from bones."

"We haven't found the skull yet, unfortunately. That could tell us a lot more."

"Frank said you're a forensic anthropologist. I didn't know museums had them."

"Many have forensic units. Museums are often repositories of skeletal collections, so a lot of research goes on in them. I'd like to try to match up this information with a missing person."

"I'll put it out. Not every place in the country, or even Georgia, will see it right away, but who knows? We might get lucky."

"I hope so. I think this might be the key to everything."

"All we can do is try." He stood. "Nice museum you have here. I might bring my wife and kids when it opens up."

"Please do. We're very proud of it. Your kids will especially enjoy it. Many of the exhibits are designed for kids to interact with." She rose and shook his hand. "And thanks so much for coming." Diane walked him through Andie's office and to the door, grateful for help.

"I'm going to get some work done," she told Andie. "So unless it's an emergency . . ."

"Sure. I've got a letter from Leonard Starns. He's quit." Andie sounded incredulous, astounded that anyone would quit a job there.

Diane would have smiled at Andie had she not felt so angry with Leonard. She'd be willing to bet it was his key used to gain access to the conservation lab. But if that were true, what was the purpose of the fake break-in? She thought it had to do with the bone, but why didn't they break in the faunal lab? That would be where they would expect bones to be stored—or her office.

"You think he's sick?" said Andie. "He's had to miss work the last couple of evenings."

"Is he due another paycheck?"

"Yes, payroll's going to mail it to him."

"No. Go tell them to call Leonard and tell him he has to come pick it up from you. Then bring it to me."

"Is there something going on?"

"Maybe. There seems to be a lot going on. I want to see Leonard before he quits. Oh, Chanell Napier's going to drop by. Send her in when she comes. She'll need some paperwork. I'm promoting her to head of security. Also find out about training slots at the GBI police academy to send her to."

"Will do," said Andie, reaching for the phone book.

Diane started back to her office. "Oh, Dylan Houser's been assessing our interactive computer needs. How's that going?"

"Well, I think he's been to all the departments. He said sometime next week he'd like to make a presentation to you and all the upper management. Speaking of which, Donald has been looking for you. He's been complaining that you are never around."

Diane sighed. "Next time he comes over, show him in. Has the snake been found?"

Andie laughed. "Donald makes you think of snakes? As far as I know, it's still loose."

"Tell the herpetologist that I've rethought the idea of live examples. I don't care what they've built to accommodate them. We aren't a zoo, and I shouldn't have said yes. Bad decision."

"I'll do it. He's going to be disappointed. He's got this terrarium built that just about encircles the room."

"I know, I've seen it. But I don't want any more live animals. I'm having enough problems with the people."

Diane went back to her desk and pulled out the new computer that Dylan Houser brought from Kenneth Meyers. Fairly soon he'd want a report about it. The computer was a model he called ToughLove DLX. Tough love. She couldn't imagine how guilty Louise and George must have felt, how they must have regretted asking Star to leave home. In her wildest imagination she couldn't see tossing Ariel out. But she had to admit, she'd never walked in the Boones' shoes. But still . . .

She focused her attention back on the computer. She

took it out of its case and opened it up. Kenneth said it was designed for field work. He wasn't kidding. A 3.2 gigahertz processor, shock-protected 120 gigabyte hard drive, global-position satellite receiver, dust- and water-resistant, a ton of software, sleek black, and all in a hardy magnesium case. She turned it on. Fast boot up. She liked it. Kenneth knew how to tempt a woman. She'd have to show this to Frank. *Frank.* She started to reach for the phone and call the hospital to see how he was, but stopped herself. Linc would call if there was any news.

She looked at several of the programs Kenneth had installed—word processing, graphics, maps. There was plenty of room to put her specialized software on it.

She heard Andie talking to someone in her office. She didn't recognize the voice, but someone wanted to see her and they weren't taking no for an answer. She got up to see who it was.

Chapter 39

"I'm sorry, Dr. Fallon," said Andie. "I told him you didn't want to be disturbed."

Dylan Houser stood in front of Andie's desk, arguing with her. "Dylan," said Diane. "I don't have time to talk about the computers now. I realize I've been putting you off for . . ."

He stood with his hands in his pockets, looking sheepish. It was not a look she imagined he had very often. "It's not about that. It's personal. I am sorry, but it won't take long."

"All right, come in." Diane stood aside as he entered. She closed the door behind him. "What's this about?" She hadn't meant to sound short, but she was feeling the need to get some work done.

"It's about Alix and Melissa."

Diane sighed, deeply regretting getting involved. "That's none of my business. I shouldn't have interfered in the first place."

"Perhaps," said Dylan. "Or perhaps not. I just want to set the record straight about Alix. She'd never tell you herself."

Diane waited.

"I know all this sounds strange." He shook his head. "And I know Lacy and Emily told you their version. Maybe they believe it and maybe they don't. Frankly, I don't know them very well."

Diane was wishing he would get to the point, but she

didn't say anything, just waited, unconsciously twirling a pen through her fingers.

"Emily and Lacy are friends, just like Alix and Melissa. The four of them have known each other forever, but they aren't that close and there's some jealousy on Emily and Lacy's part."

"Jealousy?"

"You know how some girls—women—are. Anyway, that's the only reason I can figure they told you a story about Alix. Alix isn't abusing Melissa. The very thought is ludicrous. Melissa's doing it to herself."

"What?"

"Have you ever met Melissa's parents? They've mapped out her life ever since she was born. Parents don't know the kind of pressure they put on a kid. My dad's a great guy and is so proud of me, but I'm telling you, just that amount of pride is hard on me sometimes. Melissa's parents always expected perfection, and they were very controlling. Her response was to abuse herself. She hits herself with things, she's cut herself, sometimes she bites herself—she actually leaves teeth marks. The last thing she did was cut off her hair. Alix trimmed it for her, trying to make it look like that's what she intended. Alix has always been Melissa's protector. And she's really upset that you think she's the one hurting Melissa."

"I don't think anything at the moment," said Diane. "The whole thing is too confusing."

"I agree with you there."

"I was told that Alix hit you."

"No. Was that Lacy and Emily?" Diane didn't respond. "She didn't. I don't know why they said that. Maybe they thought they were protecting Mike. I know you thought it was him."

"He thinks it's her father."

"I know. Melissa needs to get help. I don't think she understands how many people she's drawn into all this. Alix is afraid you're going to fire her."

"As long as she does her job, I have no reason to fire

her. I've already made the mistake of suspecting Mike. I don't intend to compound it. I intend to stay out of it."

"Alix will be relieved. It's not like she needs the job, but she really likes it here. She didn't have an easy childhood either. Her parents were always gone and too busy to pay any attention to her. She was raised by a long string of housekeepers, or stayed with Melissa. I guess that's why they're so close."

"Tell her not to worry."

"I will. I see you're using the computer. How do you like it?"

"So far it's great. I haven't done much. But it's a really nice model."

"It is, isn't it? I'm not fond of the name, but it's a great machine. Do you know you can drop it as far as four feet and it won't sustain any damage?"

"That will be good for field work."

He stood up. "Look, I promised not to talk about computers, so I'll be going. I just wanted to put in a word for Alix."

"Thank you for coming in."

Diane watched him leave. She shook her head. This was what, the third story? Intervention is tricky business. The best she could say about the mess was that she'd learned a lesson.

She pushed her new computer aside and looked at the reports Ben Florian had brought her. Her theory on the plastic had panned out. The plastic was from the kind used for soda bottles. The gunpowder residue on the inside surface was a strong indicator that a plastic bottle was used as a silencer. Frank would be glad to hear it.

She looked at the bloodstain report and compared it to the autopsy reports. No blood except George's and Louise's. Too bad; she'd love to have had some perp DNA.

She matched the identification of George and Louise's bloodstains to the sets of medium-velocity spatters on the walls to see which blow struck George and which one struck Louise. She double-checked it with the autopsy report of the number of times each were struck. It matched with the scenario she laid out for Frank.

She had a lot of information, neatly organized, neatly fitting together, but not enough to clear Star. There was nothing to do now but wait to see if anything came of the missing persons inquiry.

She was about to stop and have some lunch and visit Frank when Andie announced Chanell Napier. Chanell, dressed in a dark green suit, came in and sat down in the chair in front of Diane's desk, clasping her hands in front of her.

"Thanks for coming," said Diane.

Chanell smiled and looked as if she didn't quite know what to say.

"I wanted to know if you're interested in the job as head of security here at the museum. It would mean a substantial raise in pay. It would also mean taking some classes we'd set up for you."

Chanell put her hands to her face. She looked like she'd just won the lottery.

"I take it you're interested," said Diane.

"Yes, oh, yes, ma'am. I'm interested."

"Good. Andie will give you the details and tell you where to go to fill out some forms." Diane stood up and held out her hand. "Congratulations."

Chanell took her hand and shook it. "Oh, thank you, Dr. Fallon. I'll do a really good job for you. I will."

"I'm sure you will. You can start today."

As she was congratulating Chanell, Diane heard Leonard Starns in Andie's office through the crack in the partially open door.

"Payroll called and said I had to pick up my check from you."

"Yes," said Andie. "This way." She led him into Diane's office.

"How you doing, Leonard?" said Chanell.

He looked from Diane to Chanell. "What's this about?"

Diane picked up the envelope with his check in it.

"I've just made Chanell head of security. One of the things she'll be investigating is who's been forging my name to order over a hundred and fifty thousand dollars worth of supplies and exhibits."

Andie and Chanell were both completely caught off guard. But not Leonard. He stood, stiff and frowning, in front of Diane's desk.

"Was anything actually stolen?" he managed to say.

"An attempt was made to steal over a hundred and fifty thousand dollars from the museum through fraudulent purchases. That carries with it more impact than simple mischief. I intervened in the middle of one attempt and prevented it. I suspect the purpose was actually to deprive me of my job."

"Do you have my paycheck?" Leonard's lower lip stuck out like he was about to pout. Diane smiled. "You think that's funny?" he said. Leonard was becoming belligerent.

"Considering I was paying you to guard the place, yes, I do. Were you also involved in the break-in of the conservation lab?"

"You can't prove anything."

"I just sent a set of fingerprints off to the crime lab." Leonard grinned broadly. "You can't prove anything."

To Diane, that was like an admission of guilt. But, unfortunately, an inadmissible one. She opened a drawer to her desk and pulled out a pair of surgical gloves and pulled one on over her hand and held it up.

"What I think, Mr. Starns, is that you made those fake orders, and you did it for your son, who works for Mark Grayson. Were you helping him get some brownie points?"

Leonard's attention was focused on the gloved hand.

"I think you were involved in the break-in," said Diane. "You used the master key to let whoever it was in. If you were alone, you wouldn't have bothered to wear these gloves. You could just say you were checking things out if we found your prints. Was it your son?"

"You can't prove anything." He was sounding like he was caught in a loop.

"Did you know that this kind of glove fits so tight it can leave fingerprints through the latex? I lifted some from the break-in, didn't I, Chanell?"

"She sure did. Nice clear prints too."

Leonard's smug expression started to collapse.

"If your son's prints are anywhere on file and there's a match, I will prosecute, vigorously."

"You think this place is so important. It's just a collection from somebody's attic. There's other things more important, and you're too stubborn to see it."

That was quite a long speech for Leonard. And another bit of admission.

"Like the bonus your son would get if he brings Mark Grayson my head on a platter?"

Diane could see the uncertainty in him. The snide facade was cracking under the gentlest pressure she was putting on him. She could almost read his thoughts in his eyes as his gaze darted from one point in the room to another. Indecision—say something to defend his son, or stay quiet until he could get advice? Leonard was a follower, not a leader, and she suspected it was his son who was doing the leading.

"You going to give me my paycheck?"

"Yes, Leonard, I am. We'll just see what happens when the report on the prints gets back. Don't think for a minute I won't follow through."

"What do you want?"

"I want to know why the conservation lab was broken into."

"You'll have to ask Mrs. Grayson."

"Signy Grayson?"

"You'll have to ask her. I don't know anything and neither does my son."

"How about the attempted break-in at the faunal lab last night?" asked Chanell.

This time Diane was caught by surprise. So, it seemed, was Leonard.

"What? You can't pin that one on me or my son. I don't know anything about that—I don't. Maybe Mrs. Grayson knows about that too."

"Would you mind holding out your hands and arms so that I can see them?" Diane said.

"What?" Leonard pulled his hands to him reflexively and seemed to step back on his heels.

"Whoever attacked me three nights ago received considerable damage to his hands and his arms. Could I see yours, please?"

Leonard pulled up his shirtsleeves and held his hands out before her, turning them palms-down and then palms-up for her to see. "I didn't have nothin' to do with no attack on you."

He had no swollen fingers, and there were no bruises or bite marks on his arms that would be on her attacker. Diane handed him the check.

"Chanell, I want you to start changing all the locks in the museum." She spoke to Chanell, but she didn't take her eyes off Leonard Starns. He turned abruptly and left the room.

"I know it's going to be a big task," she said. "But I'm sure he made copies of the keys. From now on, I want you to work up a plan to coordinate the night security with the custodians. But get your paperwork done first. You want your paycheck to reflect your new job."

"Sure will. I'll get to everything right now. You want me to see about the faunal lab, too?"

"Tell me about the faunal lab."

"We had someone try to break in. Bernie scared him off."

"Bernie?" said Andie. "I'd have thought they would have scared *him* off."

"Bernie's not as wimpish as he looks. He's just scared of the primate skeletons and the snakes."

"You have any idea who it was?"

"He didn't get a look at him. He knocked Bernie down and started to kick him. Bernie pulled his gun, and whoever it was ran off. Bernie said he was dressed in black and had a ski mask."

"Was he white or black?"

"Bernie said he was white."

"Did you call the police?"

"Sure. They took our statement and said they'd get back to us. Me and Bernie's holding our breath. We were going to call you, and I . . ." She hesitated. "We handled it, and you were already handling so much, I just thought I wouldn't disturb your sleep since I was coming in to see you this morning anyway."

"Looks like you and Bernie had everything under control. Call one of the temporary security companies and get some extra people for the night shift."

"OK."

"I've given you a lot of work for your first day as the new head of security."

"You won't be disappointed." Chanell left smiling.

Andie stood in Diane's office with her hands on her hips. "I feel as though there's a lot of stuff going on in the museum that I don't know about."

"There's stuff going on here that I don't know," said Diane. "But I'm going to find out. Send a message to all the departments telling them that no one is to be working alone. And if anyone wants me, give me a call on my cell."

Diane ran up the stairs and stopped midway when a sharp pain shot through her lower back. It was acute enough to deliver a wave of nausea. "Shit," she said and tried to remember if she'd been drinking enough liquids, or too much. Probably not enough rest. She waited until the pain subsided and continued up to the lab at a slower pace.

Korey was in his office on the phone. Barbara, one of his staff, came up as she entered.

"Korey told me to help you photograph the skeleton."

"Good. It shouldn't take too long."

They went into the vault where Barbara or Korey had already set up the camera equipment on a long arm so it would reach over the bones.

"I heard someone tried to break in the faunal lab," said Barbara. "What's going on?"

"I'm not sure," said Diane. "Security's working on it."

"We seem to be generating our own crime wave. Who'd've thunk it in a place like this?"

"It's going to stop," said Diane. "I believe some of it has to do with this guy here."

They set up a shot of the shoulder girdle.

"You think someone's looking for him? His murderer?"

"Maybe. I've just promoted Chanell to head of security, and I'm going to hire extra people. I don't want anyone to work alone at night until this is solved."

They photographed the entire skeleton, including close-ups of all the remarkable characteristics. As they worked their way around the bones, Diane explained the history of the skeleton and the steps they'd taken to discover its story.

"Cool stuff. You know, some museums have a forensic unit," Barbara said.

"So I've been told," said Diane.

She packed up the bones and labeled the box. Just for added security, she put the box in a large empty supply box, taped it up and stored it next to the excess supplies apparently ordered by Leonard Starns. She wrote the initials J. D. on the outside of the box.

When she left, Korey was still on the phone.

As she got back to her office, Sylvia Mercer darted through the closing door.

Chapter 40

"Hi," she said breathlessly. "Is there such a thing as a forensic zoologist?"

"A forensic zoologist? Is that what you've become?" Diane showed her faunal curator into her office. Sylvia sat down at the table under the Escher prints and began spreading out her papers. Diane pulled up a chair, sat down beside her and picked up one of the sheets of paper.

"This looks like a copy of the Abercrombie taxidermy records."

"It is. I've been looking at the animals directly under and over the main part of the human skeleton. We have a *Canis lupus* directly above, and on that same level we have a *Vulpes fulva* and four *Odocoileus virginianus*. Below we have a *Sus scrofa* and two *O. virginianus*."

"Wolf, fox, deer and pig?"

"Right. That was lucky, really lucky. It could have been nothing but *O. virginianus* above and below, and that wouldn't have given us much to work with. I've been working with Whit Abercrombie on his father's records. They're a bit difficult to read." She paused and looked over at Diane. "By the way, Whit's a babe. I don't like what he does for a living—the taxidermy stuff." She shrugged. "But then again, I collect roadkill."

"He's also the county coroner."

"There's that too. You know he carves the taxidermy armatures himself from wood? He's really an artist. He gets all the musculature beautifully. I told him it's a shame to cover them up with the animal skins."

"I didn't know he carves. Sounds like you two had a good time."

"We did, actually." Sylvia sounded surprised. "Anyway, the wolf wasn't a problem. They mounted only three in the past six years. Of the two most recent, one was mounted last winter and the other one just last spring. So, thinking that the one we found was the one mounted for the museum, we looked up the date it was mounted: June 6, 1998."

"So we know the human bones were dumped no later than that date," murmured Diane.

"Right. Now *S. scrofa* was a bit of a problem."

"How's that?"

"One, the skull was missing."

"I understand that problem."

"Yeah, Jonas said they're still looking for your skull. I can see how that makes identification harder."

"It'd certainly be nice to have it."

"Another problem is that they mounted several pigs in the target years. Some were feral pigs shot by hunters, and some were pets."

"People mount their pet pigs? People have pet pigs?"

"I found it hard to believe too. A couple just last week had their pet potbellied pig mounted. Whit said he and his dad have done several potbellies. Some were in our time frame, but, unfortunately, Luther recorded only pig or deer or whatever, the name of the client, the date, kind of mount and what he charged. He didn't differentiate by genus and species and certainly not subspecies." Sylvia seemed to think that it was amazing of Luther not to include that information. "And, of course, he didn't include where he dumped the carcass."

"So what did you do?"

"Went on a road trip with Whit." She grinned. "First, I identified the subspecies of *S. scrofa*—the pig bones. I had to take them to the university's faunal collection for that. We have a more complete range there for comparison. One of the things I'd like to do here is increase the collection of reference skeletons for the lab."

"I think that's a good idea."

"From the bones we recovered, we identified our pig as a potbellied pig. So we went to visit all the people on the taxidermy list to look at their stuffed pigs to see which ones were potbellies. Interesting—of most of the pigs that were hunted, only the heads were mounted. The people with pets had the whole animal done. That should have given us a clue in the records, but we were having a good time and didn't stop to make that deduction. Only two on the list had a stuffed potbellied pig. One was significantly larger than ours. The other one looked right. The date was March 1, 1998." Sylvia had a look of triumph on her face.

"Excellent," said Diane. "You've impressed me."

"Jonas said your skeleton is young—late teens, early twenties, maybe?" Diane nodded. "I was thinking. Between March and June lies the dates of spring break for some schools, ours included."

"Damn, Sylvia, you're right. Good thinking. You've got a knack for this."

"I thought so. Go figure."

Sylvia left her notes with Diane. She also left an evidence bag filled out by Jonas with a cross-section in it of the tree whose roots skewered both the wolf and the human skeleton and, as it turned out, the pig. She took it out and looked at the rings—four years. Another verification. The skeletons were there before four years ago, or else the tree could not have planted its roots between their ribs.

She very nearly had a date. After calling Frank's partner, Ben, and leaving a message about the time frame that Sylvia had discovered, Diane took the evidence up to the conservation lab and slipped it in the box with the bones. In just a few days she had amassed quite a bit of information. She had no doubt she could find out whose bones they were, and for the first time she felt really close to a breakthrough.

"Is Korey around?" she asked his assistants on her way out.

"Somewhere. He's been acting kind of strange all day," said Barbara.

"Been on the phone all day talking to a string of people," said another assistant.

"I hope everything's all right. Tell him I was looking for him."

"Sure thing."

Diane walked down to the first floor. While she was in the main lobby she decided to go talk to the herpetologist to see if he was any closer to finding the snake. It made her shiver just thinking about it. She had these visions of opening a cabinet somewhere and having the snake fall out on her.

As she walked through, going to the west wing of the museum, she stopped by the museum store to welcome the owners and to check on their progress in getting ready to open. The proprietors, owners of a gift shop in town, were busy shelving merchandise.

They had a huge variety of items, including books, dinosaur replicas, museum kits and tee shirts, and several shelves of toys. She really loved the museum, but any joyful thoughts about it were always followed by sadness that Ariel wouldn't be here to share it with her.

As she crossed the second lobby with the huge high ceiling that was off the dinosaur room and was the twin of the Pleistocene room, she spotted Korey sitting alone on a bench. She went past the twenty-five-foot-long *Albertosaurus* skeleton greeting people at the entrance with its mouthful of sharp teeth and sat down beside Korey under a Pteranodon suspended above, its wings spanning almost the width of the room.

"Are you all right?" she asked.

"Fine." He was smiling.

"I was looking for you. I got a lead on who may be involved in the lab break-in."

"Mrs. Grayson," he said.

"Yes. How did you know?"

"Deduction."

"There seems to be a lot of that going around among my staff."

He didn't ask what she meant, but continued to stare at the wall, looking like the cat who had just found the source of all cream.

"Are you going to tell me?" she said.

"Yeah." He turned toward her and grinned.

"You going to make me drag it out of you?"

"Just enjoying the moment. You remember when I was showing Mrs. Grayson the papers we found in the basement?"

"Are you telling me they turned out to be valuable?"

"They're not particularly valuable, no. Well, some are, but what Mrs. Grayson feared was that they might have certain valuable information that she didn't want to fall into our hands. And as it turned out, she was right. Fortunately, I locked them in the vault and either she or whoever she got to break in couldn't find them.

"I believe it was Leonard Starns and his son. His son works for Grayson Real Estate."

He nodded. "That makes sense. I've been calling people all day to make sure that I found what I think I did, and I also took the liberty of inviting an expert out to the museum—I'm flying her in from New York."

"New York?" She almost gasped. It was not like Korey to do such a thing without asking her.

"I also know what this moving-the-museum thing is all about."

"You do? You know why Mark Grayson wants to sell the museum?"

"I know why he wants to buy it. Those." He nodded his head toward the wall murals. "It turns out they were painted by a relatively little-known artist named Robert Camden, who died at the turn of the century at the age of ninety-one. The tiny unicorns in his paintings were one of his trademarks. He may have been little known then, but like our friend here . . ."—he pointed to the pteranodon above them—"the value of his paintings has soared. They're now selling for several million dollars apiece." He turned his head again to Diane. "And we have twelve of them."

Diane stood and walked over to the painting—a huge brontosaurus, head held high on his long neck, walking and dragging his tail. Between his front feet, almost obscured by the dust he created with each step, was a small unicorn. The detail of the painting was remarkable. The brontosaurus' hide was painted like the skin of an elephant, with all the lines and wrinkles and shades of gray. The distant mountains had such clarity and distinction that Diane thought she could probably find them somewhere if she tried.

Korey joined her standing by the painting.

"You're not joking, are you?" she asked.

"Nope. I found the initial sketches of the paintings and a reference to the painter in the material we gathered from the basement, and, I don't know, something just clicked in my head. Wouldn't it be interesting to find out about him, you know, have an exhibit of the drawings and the man? I made some calls to friends in art conservation and they referred me to several other experts, who were all quite excited, let me tell you. A woman is coming down from the Metropolitan Museum of Art tomorrow to have a look at them."

"It's a good thing we built a railing to keep wandering hands off the walls," said Diane.

Korey nodded. "I think we'll have to do more. I was thinking a Plexiglas wall, so no one can get under the railings."

"I can't believe this," said Diane. "When they were found, didn't anyone investigate their origin?"

"From what I can find out, Milo asked someone from the art department at Bartrum University to come over and have a look. He declared them interesting."

"But Signy Grayson recognized them." Diane recalled the snatch of conversation she heard between Signy and her husband—"If it weren't for me, you wouldn't even know about them."

"Yes," Korey said, "I think her husband was going to buy the museum building through one of his companies. I believe when you sell buildings, certain things always go with the building—like the walls and anything attached to them. At any rate, he'd have the contract written so he'd get the paintings for a fraction of their value. And if it was true about the golf course . . ."

"You know about that rumor?"

"It's hard to keep secrets in a place like this. Everyone's been worried about their jobs."

"I'm sorry about that. I never had any intention of selling the museum."

"Some were afraid you'd be forced to."

"It would take some serious errors or malfeasance on my part for them to be able to unseat me. They were trying. That's what all those extra supply orders were about."

"How far did they expect to get, ordering extra paper clips?"

"They also sent orders out for a duplicate set of these guys." She pointed at the dinosaurs.

"That'd be a lot of money, but as soon as the Bickford called . . ."

"Exactly. The person who did the ordering didn't understand the process. He didn't know they would have to call about details of the order."

"This campaign doesn't seem well thought-out on their part," said Korcy.

"I believe that's because it was carried out by several people. The extra orders, I think, were done at the instigation of someone who worked with Grayson. I believe Grayson and his cronies were doing other things that might very well have had an impact."

"Like what?"

Diane went back to the bench and sat down. She was silent for a long while. Now that she had shared Ariel with Frank and Andie, perhaps it was time to share her with other people. She told Korey a shortened version of her daughter and what happened to her—and the music.

"That was cruel and sadistic."

"Yes, it was. And it had an effect. This past year I was a mess. I couldn't even work. I think they wanted to send me back to that black place I just climbed out of."

There was something else that had been bothering

Diane. Something Melissa said: "I wish we'd just let whatever was going on happen to you." She mentioned it to Korey, explaining only that Melissa was angry with her when she said it.

"That's an odd thing to say. I wonder what she meant."

"I don't know."

"How's Frank?"

"He picked up an infection. They're treating it. You haven't been visited again by the police, have you?"

"No."

Diane looked around at the murals. "I wonder how much money we're talking about."

"A lot. The last painting sold a year ago for 7.4 million in Paris."

"So if Grayson could buy the museum, he could take the paintings out, do a little remodeling and resell the building to cover his cost and still come out with almost—what?—ninety million dollars? Not counting the property that goes with the building, which he could sell to the Japanese."

"That's a lot of money," said Korey. "I'm surprised he hasn't tried to kill you."

Chapter 41

Diane stared at Korey.

"Maybe he has tried to kill me," she said. "I thought it had something to do with the skeleton, but it doesn't have to, does it?" She shook her head. "The person who tried to break into the faunal lab was dressed just like the person who attacked me. That suggests that my attack had something to do with the skeleton."

"The faunal lab? I hadn't heard."

"Last night. Bernie scared him away."

"Bernie?" Korey laughed. "Good for him."

"By the way, Chanell Napier is the new head of security, so if you have any questions or suggestions, you have someone to address them to. I should have hired a head a long time ago."

"Don't let all this get you down, Dr. Fallon. It's just stuff. This is a great museum, and I can only see it getting better."

Diane stood up. "Now I have to figure out what I'm going to do about all this."

"Do you reckon he told all his cronies about the paintings, or was that just between him and the flashy Mrs. G.?" asked Korey.

"Interesting question. Probably just between the two of them, I'd think. I imagine they just tossed the others enough of a bone to get them on their side." Diane looked at the paintings again. "Korey, you've certainly made my day."

Korey's gleaming smile lit up his face. "This is something, isn't it?"

"Keep this quiet," said Diane.

"Sure. I hope it was all right to have the expert come down."

"Of course. You did absolutely right."

Diane decided to forgo a visit with the herpetologist. Instead, she went back to her office and called Vanessa Van Ross.

Diane told her about the paintings and their probable value. The other end of the phone was silent for a long while.

"Doesn't that explain a lot? That little worm. Well, Diane, you have some decisions to make."

"Yes. I was thinking about how much we could do in the museum for that amount of money. On the other hand, what a treasure they are for people to visit. That's why we're here. We suddenly have something unique and unbelievably valuable. Should bring in a much larger audience."

"You have plenty of time to make decisions. It's good to have choices. And it's good to find out what that weasel and his floozie wife are up to. Korey sounds like a bright young man."

"He is. I'm pleased with the entire staff of the museum."

Diane hung up the phone and sat staring at her Escher prints, in particular at the tessellation of angels and devils. Her mind went back to her attack. What if that was Mark Grayson? But why was Frank shot? Of the things going on lately, it was hard to separate which of the acts went with which motivations.

That amount of money was indeed great enough to kill for; if they couldn't make her leave, then they could make her gone for good. But his attempts to discredit her were poor at best. The fake orders were a joke, the music was cruel, but surely they didn't think it was sufficient to make her quit.

Her mind went to the skeleton and the faunal lab break-in. Someone close knew she was trying to identify the skeleton. Close. How close? Could they have a job in the museum?

She called up on her computer a list of people hired in the last week. There were several: one custodian, the exhibit designer hired a carpenter, Donald hired an assistant, she'd hired Melissa and Alix, and two of the curators brought in graduate assistants. That was it. But anyone could come in and not be noticed. Because of all the work there was a lot of temporary help coming and going, not to mention the people working on the restaurant. Diane closed her eyes and tried to think. She didn't really know where to begin, nor did she want to investigate her employees—sneaking around in Donald's office had left a bitter taste in her mouth. On the other hand, checking out her employees had turned up Leonard's connection to Grayson.

She turned off her computer and told Andie she was going home to get a good night's rest.

"Good. I've been concerned about you."

"I'll get plenty of sleep tonight. Provided my neighbor doesn't try to search my apartment again."

"What?"

"Didn't I tell you about that?" Diane related the story and had Andie in stitches.

"What strange people. So it's the landlady who has the cat?"

"Yes."

"Nice of you not to squeal on her."

"I think she's going to give it away."

"If she can't find a home, I'll take it."

"Are you serious?"

"I love cats."

"I'll let her know."

Before she went home, Diane went to the hospital. They had put Frank in a private room. Linc was there reading a newspaper when she entered. Frank was asleep. Diane tiptoed in.

"How is he?"

"Better," said Linc.

Frank opened his eyes. "Hey. I was wondering when you were going to come see me."

Diane kissed him on the cheek.

"You can do better than that. You want to give my brother the wrong impression about us, after all I've been telling him?"

Diane kissed his lips. "I just didn't want to get you too excited."

"I could use a little excitement. The hospital's a drag. What's new?"

"Quite a lot. My head conservator's solved the Mark Grayson mystery." She told him about the paintings.

Linc whistled. "Damn, brother, we could go over with a chain saw tonight and make out with a bundle."

"I'm surprised Mark hasn't resorted to that. What are you going to do about it?"

"I don't know yet."

"That's a lot of money," said Frank. "You think Grayson is behind the attack on you?"

"I've thought of it, but we had an attempted break-in of the faunal lab and the guy apparently visits the same tailor as my guy—mask and all."

"That's interesting. What do the police say?"

"They'll get back to us."

"I'll talk to Izzy," said Frank.

"He was the one who took the call."

"I'll talk to him anyway. He may not have put the two together."

Diane didn't say anything. She glanced at Linc, who met her eyes.

"How are you feeling?" asked Linc.

"I'm going home to get a good night's sleep."

"I think that's a good idea."

"How's Star?" asked Frank.

"She's doing better. She's brokering jobs for the guards."

"What?" asked Frank.

She told him about Star's guard's looking for a job for her son. "It's not a big job, and if it'll get Star better treatment . . ."

Frank took her hand. "You're a jewel, Diane. Go home and take care of yourself. I've got plans when I get out of this joint."

Diane kissed Frank again before she left. "You take care of yourself, if you plan to carry out your plans."

She was tired—a soft bed would feel good. She pulled out her car key, said good-bye to Frank and Linc and walked outside, glad to get away from the sterile smells of the hospital.

Approaching her car, she frowned. Someone in a van had parked so close to her driver's side it was going to be a close fit getting in. She squeezed between the vehicles and clicked her car door open just as someone grabbed her from behind and pulled a hood over her head. She heard the side door of the van slide open.

Chapter 42

Diane fought hard, grabbing at the hands restraining her and tried to scream. A sharp blow from something hard as steel to the back of her head caused an overwhelming pain inside her skull, and everything went black for several seconds. She was stunned nearly to unconsciousness, and she collapsed but didn't pass out. She could feel herself being dragged into the van. The door slammed closed, and they tied her arms behind her and then her feet together. She prayed someone in the parking lot saw what happened to her.

The van started moving. Backing out of the parking space, then forward. She listened to the road sounds. They were going slow through the parking lot, bumping over the speed breakers. She counted them. Four before they turned left out of the lot. She knew which exit they took. Maybe that would help later—if she got out of this.

"What do you want?" she asked, and was met with silence.

They weren't going to let her hear their voices.

Left turn—about five seconds and a left turn. She listened. A helicopter overhead. That would probably be a traffic chopper, or maybe one carrying someone to or from the hospital. She could find out. What time was it? She left the hospital about 4:15—it was now probably 4:25.

The van stopped. The engine idled, traffic sounds passed. Red light. About thirty seconds after, they started again. Definitely a red light. They speeded up, then slowed. Another red light. It had probably just turned yellow.

"Careful," someone whispered. Male.

There were at least two of them. One was warning the other not to get stopped.

They drove for another minute and stopped again. Another traffic light. Three so far. In her mind's eye she could see the route they were taking. This time they turned right. They were taking a route that was on the way to the museum. Abruptly, they turned left and stopped.

Where was this? She tried to think of what was here. Houses?

They started up again, turned right and onto a rough road and stopped again. She heard doors slam. They were leaving her here?

Diane lay there for what seemed like hours and listened. She heard faint road noises, but nothing else. She shifted her position until she was sitting up, leaning against the side of the van. She wished she'd gone to the bathroom before she left the hospital.

Who is it, she wondered. *Grayson?* Or the killer of the bony remains sitting in her vault? Or maybe someone else she'd managed to really piss off. Maybe it was the Odells. She tried to smile, but even the Odells didn't seem the least funny right now. Concentrating on remembering the turns and stops kept her mind busy early on, but now fear welled up inside her, threatening to overwhelm her. What were they waiting for? Was this some kind of torture? Softening her up with the dread of waiting? Waiting for time to pass? Waiting for someone?

She worked at her bonds but they were tight; she kept pulling at them anyway. She was growing hot and sick from the hood over her face. She inched her way to where she thought the rear of the van was. She raised her legs and dragged her feet along the back, feeling for the handle. She found it and tried to manipulate it with her feet. It was locked or she was clumsy. She started beating on the door with her feet as hard as she could. Nothing, no one came, and her legs were getting cramped.

OK, she needed another plan. She scooted toward the front until she ran into the back of the seats. Now, to work her way into the front seat. She stood and hopped through the opening between the seats and tried to feel with her fingers behind her for the keys. She found the ignition, but the keys weren't there.

Hopping and turning around, she tried the front visor with her head. She found it, but couldn't get a grip on it. She wedged her nose between the visor and the ceiling but couldn't get the visor to budge. She gripped the edge with her teeth and pulled and was rewarded with a clink of falling keys.

Now, to look for them. Squatting, she felt the front seat with her face. Good. The keys were there. She was too frightened to feel any joy. For all she knew they could be watching her through the windows. She stood again, turned with her back to the driver's seat, squatted and felt for the keys with her fingers.

They . . . no, it . . . was in her grasp. Thank God there was just one key on the ring, and she didn't have to worry whether or not it was right-side up. She maneuvered until she fit the key into the ignition.

She hesitated. What would be the best thing to do? Get out and run—blind? Or try to drive the van blind? She opted to stay in the van and turned the key. The van started.

She grasped the gearshift lever in her hands and tried to pull it into reverse. It wouldn't move. She tugged at it. Nothing. What was she doing wrong? She envisioned herself in her car, putting it in gear. The brake pedal. The damn safety mechanism. The vehicle won't let you take the gearshift out of park until the brake pedal is pressed. Her feet were tied together, and her hands were tied behind her. She couldn't sit and reach the brake pedal and still reach the gearshift.

She inched her toes backward, wedging herself against the steering wheel until she felt her heels touch the brake pedal. Shifting the gear with her hands in this position was impossible. She caught the shift with the front of her arm, pushed her shoulder forward and down. She felt a slight bump as the transmission slipped into reverse. Now, for the moment of truth. She twisted herself around and sat down in the driver's seat and pressed the accelerator with both feet. As the van darted backward, she questioned her sanity. But she hadn't hit anything yet.

A sudden crash slammed her farther back into the seat. Pain shot up both arms to her shoulders. "Damn," she shouted.

She maneuvered around until she was in the passenger's seat. She opened the door and hopped out into a fist in the stomach.

She passed out. When she regained consciousness, she'd wet herself. Damn them to hell, whoever they were.

The sudden voice in her ear made her jump. "You have one chance." It was a hoarse whisper. "Do what I tell you and live. Don't and die."

"What?" she said, and gagged like she was going to throw up.

Her captor lifted the hood up just past her mouth. As she was trying to control her gagging reflex, he whispered to her, "When it's dark, we're going to the museum. You're going to tell me where the bones are. That's all I want."

"Bones? We have hundreds."

"You know which ones I mean. Don't play dumb." He slapped her on the side of the head. "I'm already pissed about what you did to the van. Don't make it worse."

"I don't have the bones you're talking about."

He slapped her head again. "Don't lie. You have everything but the skull."

He pulled the hood down and retied the rope around her throat. He half lifted her and then dragged her for a ways, scraping her feet on the ground. She heard more noises that she recognized and dreaded. They were the noises of a car trunk being opened. She was suddenly lifted off her feet and tumbled, headfirst, into the trunk.

"Wait," she called out before he slammed the trunk.

"What? Begging won't work." His words were barely above a ragged whisper.

"Unless you want me to suffocate, I need more air than this hood allows me."

She heard rustling around as if he were fishing inside his pocket. She felt a tugging at the hood and heard a ripping sound. She could breathe. The trunk slammed shut. It was suddenly very quiet, and she knew without moving or touching the top or the sides that she was in a small, dark, enclosed place. It didn't smell like a new car.

Doors slammed. The engine started. The car was moving. They were going again. She was on her side. She started working to get her hands down and around her feet so they would be in front of her. It was a painful strain on her shoulder joints, made many times worse by the bruising and soreness that had not yet healed from the last attack. But she shoved the pain aside and worked.

It took her less time than she had imagined. She could reach the ropes on her legs. It was a small-diameter hard rope, probably nylon. No chance of breaking it. Nothing to cut it with. She found the knots and started working at them with her fingers. Someone knew how to tie knots. They held if she strained against them, but were relatively easy to untie. Obviously, they wanted to be able to get the rope loose when they got her to the museum. With her feet free, she worked on her hand restraints with her teeth. That took even less time because they had used the same knot and she knew how to untie it. She pulled loose the rope that held the hood closed around her neck and jerked the hood off her head.

It didn't help her vision, but she breathed more freely. She felt around inside the trunk. It was mainly empty. A spare tire, rags. She felt along the edges, in cracks. Her fingers wrapped around something metal wedged between the floor of the trunk and the side. It moved when she pulled at it.

It was too hard to get out, it wouldn't come loose, it was taking too much time. The car was bumping down an uneven road. She could hear the sounds of the tires on gravel. She started to panic. She wanted to cry. Finally, the object slipped free. It was metal and felt like the blade of a screwdriver. No handle, but good enough. She wrapped the cloth hood around the shank of the screwdriver to improve her grip, felt with her fingers along the back ledge of the trunk lid until she found the hook that held the lid shut, pushed the screwdriver tip into the hook and pulled hard.

The screwdriver slipped, her knuckles hit hard on something sharp. It hurt like hell. Her fingers throbbed. She couldn't tell if she was bleeding. She felt with the tips of her fingers and found the latch again, wedged the screwdriver tip in tight and pulled against it with all her strength.

Chapter 43

The trunk lid popped open. The first thing she saw was the tree line streaming by against the twilit sky. She didn't stop to think; she lunged out the back, landed on the dirt road, rolled, scrambled up and ran into the brush. The car hadn't been going fast, but it didn't matter; she would have jumped anyway. Better to get killed on your own terms. She had no doubt they'd kill her once they got what they wanted.

Tires crunched on gravel as the car slid to a halt—car doors slammed, muted shouts. She kept on running. Adrenaline must be deadening the pain, for she felt strangely invigorated. And she knew where she was: the back approach to the museum, going toward the loading docks. She stayed in the woods, running alongside the road.

A frightening thought—the museum was locked. Even if she got that far before they caught her, she didn't have a key and there was no time to wait while she banged on the door, hoping the security guards would hear her. They could be on the third floor or in the basement, and she would be overtaken before they could get to her. She was close to the nature trail and she knew it like the back of her hand. There was a toolshed on the trail. If she could get to it, she could find a weapon.

They'd be looking for her near the roadway. She veered further into the woods. The trees broke into an open field; she sprinted toward the nature trail on the other side. Damn, she heard shouts behind her. Had they seen her? Her heart felt like it was going to explode.

She crossed a path. *For heaven's sake, don't stick to the paths.* She stayed to the woods. The shed was near the pond, and the pond was the center of the ten acres of trail. She wanted badly to stop and rest, but all she allowed herself to do was to slow. It was like running in the jungle, looking for Ariel, running from Santos' men. Hate welled up inside her and she ran faster. Just ahead was the pond. There was a bridge over part of it. That gave her an idea.

As soon as she reached the edge of the pond, she quietly slipped into the water, ducked under and swam, coming up only briefly to fill her lungs with air until she got to the pilings that held up the bridge. She stopped behind a piling and rested, propping herself against a crossbar, holding herself still. Her lungs wanted desperately for her to gulp in air, but she forced herself to breathe slowly and silently. Sound travels over water.

The water was cool and it eased her aching body. Beams from flashlights swept through the undergrowth. Ariel. Where was Ariel?

"No," she whispered out loud, and got a mouthful of water and choked. *Shit, don't cough, and don't start having some kind of flashbacks. Not now. They'll find you.*

Calm down. Calm down. You can stay here until daylight if you have to. They won't hang around that long. Someone will find the crashed van unless they move it. Someone will find the car on the road to the museum; they'll have to leave to move it. Just stay calm and wait them out.

Sudden footfalls resounded across the wooden bridge and echoed across the water. She almost screamed, but remained quietly bobbing up and down behind the piling. The footsteps pounded overhead and turned toward the feeding dock, a walkway perpendicular to the bridge with a deck for watching the swans.

It was too dark to recognize anything but outlines. The flashlight beams searched for her like silent hounds on the hunt. They darted across the water, and she ducked under the surface as they sniffed under the bridge. She held her breath for as long as she could. She was pretty good at holding her breath. One of those fantastic esoteric talents, like being able to guzzle a quart of beer at once, that served no useful purpose other than to impress her friends when she was in college—until now, and now it might save her life. She stayed underwater to the count of 120. Two minutes. She forced herself to let her eyes come up slowly to make sure . . . Good thing she was a caver. It made her strong. She needed physical strength right now. Emotional strength too. That was a lot harder.

They crossed the bridge again and again. Searched the toolshed, broke in its door. She waited. The water was cool and seductive. She could see how easy it was for people to drown themselves. *Just slip under and breathe, let the water fill your lungs and take you to a place where there's no pain or grief. But not me.*

Diane never wanted to die, even in the depths of her grief for Ariel, cursing God and man, throwing up until her ribs ached, crying until her eyes were so swollen she could hardly see. All that, but she never wanted to die. She didn't want to die now, and she wasn't going to. She would kill before she would die. She waited.

She knew patience. Anyone who could take weeks to excavate a mass grave of murdered innocents, map miles of unexplored caves, take eight hours to climb twenty feet up a rock face was patient. She could wait.

He, the raspy voice, knew about the missing skull. The thought had struck her as he said it, but now she had time to think about it. How did he know? It wasn't a secret, but he had to be close to her investigation to know. Who was the secret enemy in her camp?

The cool, soothing water was feeling colder, but she didn't think she was in danger of hypothermia. She pretended she was in a cave. She'd traversed many a waterway colder than this. There was nothing more serene and lovely than an underground lake. Cave ethics dictate that you remove your dirty clothes and stuff them in a waterproof bag to keep the pristine waters of an underground

lake or stream as unpolluted as possible. She thought
about how the cool cave waters felt on the skin, how she
felt like an otherworldly creature slipping through the
still waters of a deep, dark chamber. She pretended the
piling was a stalagmite, one she could touch—another
principle of caving is to not touch anything that has taken
eons to form and could be destroyed by careless touching, but this one she could touch. This one was life-
giving.

She'd have to do a cave exhibit at the museum. Take
visitors on an underground adventure beneath the earth,
give them a new view of nature. She could do that in
the basement—create a cave environment. She wondered
if Mike Seger, the geology student, knew anything about
caves. She planned the entire project in her head as she
waited and listened, trying to hold at bay the feelings of
terror inside her.

No more light hounds, but can't trust them to be pre-
dictable. They may have been crouched in the dark, waiting for her to move. She'd wait all night until her staff
arrived, until the groundspeople arrived. In the meantime, she'd continue planning exhibits and try to figure
out who might be doing this.

Korey thought Frank's attacker was a racist. She didn't
think so. He just wanted to look the opposite of what
he is. People would see the dreadlocks, the dark face,
and think African-American; they wouldn't think white.
But where did that get her? She had already guessed
that.

Better to go back to planning exhibits. She could handle concepts, but her brain was having a hard time with
deduction. What she would really like to do is sleep.
Perhaps it might be safe to move now, to get out of the
water. She quietly moved away from the piling and
scanned the distance around the pond. No lights; everything was quiet.

Something, perhaps fear, told her to stay with her plan.
She felt physically unable to deviate from it. She went
back to her place just as a flash of light swept through
the woods. The hounds were still there.

She began planning an attack on Jonas' chess pieces, forcing her brain to plot moves, anticipate responses. By the time the sun was beginning to show through the trees she'd planned a campaign against his black king, and designed an underground adventure exhibit for the museum. Perhaps all she needed to be able to get her museum work done was to become stranded overnight in the swan pond with murderers on shore searching for her.

When the road noise picked up and she saw the movement of the groundskeepers, she swam out from under the bridge for shore and climbed out, frightening one of the gardeners, a young Hispanic man, heading for the toolshed. She must look like the swamp creature.

"Lady, what you doing in the lake? You shouldn't be there. You hurt?"

"What's your name?" Her words came out in a hoarse whisper.

"Hector Torres, ma'am."

"Hector Torres, I'm very glad to meet you. I hired you. I'm Dr. Diane Fallon, the director of this museum. I know that appears unlikely at the moment, but could you help me get out of here?"

"Hector? What's going on?" Luiz Polaski, the head groundskeeper, was driving down the trail in a golf cart.

"This lady says she's the director of the museum. She walked out of the lake."

"Dr. Fallon, what happened to you? My God, sit down."

Diane let them lead her to the golf cart.

"I was attacked." She didn't want to get into the details. It would take another night.

"Again?"

"Yes, again. Will you take me to the museum, please?"

"Of course."

"Dr. Fallon, thanks for the job," yelled Hector Torres as they drove off.

"How is he working out?"

"So far he's found you, so I guess he's doing pretty good. He says his mother is a women's guard at the jail?"

"Yes. She said her son was looking for a job."

"I know there are some interesting stories here," he said as he drove the cart up to the rear of the museum. "Can I help you inside?"

"If you don't mind walking with me. I've been in the water all night."

"All night?"

"I know this must all sound incredible, and when I can I'll tell you all about it."

They walked down the hallway past the restaurant to the mammal exhibit, where she cut through to the Pleistocene room and to the lobby just as Andie, Korey and Mike Seger entered through the large double doors.

Chapter 44

"Dr. Fallon. Oh, my God, what happened to you!"
Andie came running and grabbed her around the waist
just as her knees were giving way.

Diane could only imagine what she must look like, not
to mention smell like. She felt like a wet cat, standing in
her bare feet, dripping water onto the marble floor. The
initial relief of getting out of the lake was wearing off,
and now she felt herself sinking against Andie, unable
to stand. Several more staff arrived and they all gathered
around, some helping Andie support her, others mumbling and asking questions. She felt suffocated—and
afraid.

Donald was among them. He elbowed his way through
the crowd, his features tight and his face pale. "Diane?
What happened?"

"You need to go to the hospital," said Korey. "I'll
take you."

"You need to take care of our arriving guest. Andie,
you're in charge for a while—and I need you to get me
another cell phone."

"I'll take you to the hospital," said Mike.

"I can drive."

"No, you can't," they all said simultaneously.

"You're right—my car's at the hospital," she said.

Mike picked her up. "My SUV's just outside."

Diane didn't remember ever being carried by a guy.
Even as a child, she didn't remember her father picking
her up. It was an odd feeling, a very vulnerable feeling.

"I'll call the hospital and tell them you're on the way," Andie called after them.

Mike put her in the passenger's side, got in and drove her to the hospital.

"Thank you," she told him.

"I owe you."

"For what? Not unjustly firing you?"

"No. Melissa told me something a while ago. Things seemed to be all right and I was in my usual mind-my-own-business mode, so I didn't mention it. But now I see I should have."

Diane had been about to drift off to sleep, but she was now wide awake. "What was it?"

"It happened at that party you had."

"The contributors' party?"

"I suppose. The one where the quartet played. They saw some woman in a slinky red dress switch drinks with you."

"What? Signy Grayson? She did what?"

"Alix saw it, and she and Melissa switched them back. Not because Alix was feeling righteous. The woman was hitting on Dylan and it pissed her off. Melissa said they made quite a show of it. She said neither of you suspected a thing."

Diane remembered talking to Signy at the giant short-faced bear exhibit. Signy spilling, then catching her drink, before the whole glass spilled. Diane had turned her back to clean it up as Alix and Melissa came over, talking to each of them—distracting each of them. Slick. And the next day, finding Signy disoriented upstairs, having slept all night on the sofa in the boardroom. So Signy had tried to slip her a Mickey. She must have guessed right away she'd gotten the wrong drink and went somewhere where she wouldn't be discovered. What was the purpose? To make Diane pass out? What would be the point?

Perhaps the point was to make a fool of her. They could have slipped her something like Rohypnol—odorless, tasteless, metabolizes in forty-eight hours. A small amount mixed with wine, and Diane could have seemed drunk or worse. She could have made an absolute fool of herself and wouldn't have remembered a thing. At the contributors' party, that would have gone a long way toward ruining her credibility. Those sons of bitches.

"Thanks for telling me, Mike."

"I should have when Melissa told me. I'm sorry. I really thought it was probably nothing."

"Dylan came to see me the other day. He said Melissa is hurting herself. Alix is her protector."

"Some of that's probably true. Melissa can be self-destructive, but I've also seen Alix hit her."

"That's so odd. Why is Melissa friends with her?"

Mike shrugged.

They arrived at the hospital. Mike parked, went around and picked up Diane when she got out.

"I can walk," she said.

"And I can carry you. You really don't look too good, Dr. Fallon."

"I don't imagine I do. Do you know anything about caves?"

"Caves? Yes. In fact, I'm an experienced caver."

"So am I. I've got this idea for an exhibit."

"You can tell me about it as soon as you're fixed up."

He carried her into the emergency room, where they immediately took her into the examining room. Diane asked if Dr. Linc Duncan was in the hospital. She had to explain that he was a visitor of Frank's, but he was also a doctor and she wanted him.

After she changed into the dreaded bare-butt hospital gown, she lay back on the bed and drifted off to sleep. She was awakened by someone taking her hand. She jerked it back and tried to jump off the bed.

"Hey, it's me."

"Oh, I'm sorry, Linc. Thanks for coming down. How's Frank?"

"Better than you at the moment. Are Henry and I going to have to move down here and watch the two of you?"

"Looks like we need some kind of keeper. Someone

attacked me here in the hospital parking lot as I was getting in my car."

"Last night? Where have you been? They told me your clothes were all wet."

"In the lake behind the museum."

"In the water all night? They threw you in the lake?"

"No, they didn't throw me. I escaped from them and hid there."

"Are you in pain?"

"Yes. My head hurts, so do my back and abdomen."

"Did you get hit in the head?" He looked at the chart where the receiving nurse recorded her blood pressure and pulse.

"Yes."

"Were you ever unconscious?"

"Briefly—I'm not sure. If I was, it couldn't have been but for a few seconds."

"Any nausea?"

"A little."

"Vomiting?"

"No."

"Let me know if this hurts." Linc lifted her gown. Diane groaned and put her arm over her forehead. "Are you in pain?" he asked.

"Just embarrassed. I should have thought of that before I called you."

"Is this the first time you've ever been examined by a doctor?"

"By one that I knew."

"What? You change doctors after you see them once? That must get tiresome."

"You know what I mean."

He smiled. "Tell me if this hurts." He palpated her abdomen. "Any tender spots?"

"No. Yes, there."

"How about when I release pressure?"

"A little."

"And your shoulders?"

"No. I'm sore, but no specific pain. Why?"

"Organ injuries sometimes cause referred pain in other

areas of the body. OK. I'm going to ask them to order some tests. And I want you to listen to me very carefully, not like you did before, when you didn't take my advice at all."

"All right."

"You could have an injury to your spleen, liver, or reinjured a kidney. The thing about organ injuries is that they can bleed slowly or stop—only to bleed again days or weeks later. This is serious. You are going to have to rest."

"How's Frank?"

"I answered that. Don't avoid the subject."

"I'm not. I was just thinking, maybe you shouldn't tell him."

"He'll find out."

They wheeled Diane for yet another series of X rays and scans, to the surprise of the X-ray technician, who was the same one she had before. He admonished her to be more careful. When she came out, Linc was waiting for her.

"Can I go home now?" she asked.

"No, you may not. You're going to stay here at least for tonight."

"I'm feeling much better, and I've got a lot to do."

"Did you think that by asking for me I'd stick on a Band-Aid and send you home?"

"No. Not at all, I . . ."

"Good. I've reserved you a room across from Frank. That way, Henry and I can keep an eye on the two of you. That'll be much easier on the two of us."

"I didn't realize you're so tough when I asked for you."

"You're pretty tough yourself."

Diane's first visitor was Frank, wearing a dark green-and-navy plaid robe and smelling of cologne. He came in under his own power, looking pale but better than he had in several days. Diane was so relieved to see him up, she almost cried.

He leaned over and kissed her mouth gently.

"Smells good. Is that for me?" she asked.

"Yeah. It's hard in a place like this, but I'm trying to make a good impression."

"You've already made a good impression."

"I'm so sorry I got you into this."

It pained Diane to see the worried look in his eyes.

"I'm not. This is no one's fault but whoever's doing this. We must be really close for them to take these kinds of chances."

"What exactly did happen? Linc only knew you'd been attacked." He pulled up a chair by her bed and sat down, making a pained face as he settled on the chair.

"I hate being in bed," she said. "It makes me feel weak." She found the controls for the bed and put herself into a sitting position.

"I know what you mean. I'm ready to go home."

He took her hand as Diane told him her story, from the time she was dragged into the van at the hospital to Hector Torres' surprise at finding a woman walking out of the pond. When she finished, Frank sat open-mouthed.

"Diane. Damn. Diane, I had no idea. I thought it was something like the other evening—not that that was a piece of cake, but damn. You spent the night in the water? You must have been terrified."

"It kept my heart rate up."

Frank shook his head in amazement.

"I didn't want them to kill me."

He caressed the top of her hand with his thumb. "So the attack was about the bones."

"Yes, definitely. Their entire focus was on getting them."

"Have you talked to the police yet?"

Diane rolled her eyes. "I'm sorry, Frank, but I'm so tired of hearing that they can't do anything."

"You need to tell them about this. This is assault and kidnaping."

"I think the hospital called. Someone will wander in in a few hours, or days, and take my statement and that will be it."

"No, it won't. I'll see to it. Have you called your family?"

"No."

"You want me to call them?"

"No. My family isn't like yours. We aren't speaking at the moment."

"I'm sorry, but they might be a comfort if they know you're injured and in the hospital."

"I don't think so. My father would say something like, 'Well, what do you expect,' and my mother's a lot like Crystal McFarland."

"I didn't think there could be two of them."

"Mother's more refined, but the sentiment's the same. When I told them I was adopting Ariel, Mother's comment was 'Is that wise?' My sister, Susan, suggested that perhaps it was for the best when I told them she'd died. She couldn't quite understand that I loved Ariel. To Susan, she was like a stray cat I found by the side of the road that was going to be nothing but problems. So no, my family isn't a comfort. They certainly wouldn't go to the lengths your brothers go to for you."

"I'm sorry."

"Me too. I think the concept of family is a good one."

Frank managed a laugh, though she could see it hurt him. "Actually, my brothers—they're great guys, but they aren't usually this attentive."

Diane didn't say anything. He'd probably send them home if he knew she'd asked them to stay and keep a lookout. On the other hand, she doubted they could be run off very easily. She envied Frank for his family.

"How are you? I mean really, how are you?" she said.

"I'm lucky. It could have been much worse, but both bullets managed to miss important nerves and organs—if you don't count my lung. The repair work the doctors did will take some time to heal, and I'd be out sooner if it weren't for the infection. But that's under control."

Frank sat with her until a nurse ran him back to his bed.

"I'll visit later," Diane called after Frank.

"Get some rest," he said.

Diane slept for about an hour, until Andie came in with an armload of shopping bags. She'd brought pajamas and a robe, a change of clothes, cosmetics and various other sundries, the ToughLove laptop, a new cell phone and flowers.

"Andie, you're worth every penny I'm paying you, probably more."

Andie went about the room, putting things in drawers, while Diane showered and changed into the pajamas and robe. The peach-colored silk nightgown was sexier than she would have bought for herself, but it was soft and did have a back to it.

"This is much better. Now I don't have to go around with my butt hanging out."

"How's Frank?"

"He's doing well. He's across the hall, if you'd like to peek in."

"That's convenient. You can have a midnight rendezvous."

"His brothers keep a pretty close eye on him."

"He has brothers? Do they have his eyes? Are they married?"

"Yes, yes and yes, with children."

"Too bad."

"What's going on at the museum?"

"You're the big topic of conversation. Donald is really upset. It's strange. I've never seen him like this. Do you think he had something to do with this?"

"I don't see how. It was about the skeleton."

Andie looked alarmed. "Oh."

"Any museum business?"

"Korey went to the airport to get some mysterious guest. I called Jonas at the site and told him what happened. He's very concerned."

"I don't think we'll ever get our chess game finished. I don't suppose he mentioned finding the skull?"

"No. Still no sign of it. Do you think the murderer cut it off?"

"No. I think it probably got carried off by some animal. It could be somewhere in the woods."

Andie shivered. "Gruesome."

"Have Korey call me when he knows something."

"What exactly is he supposed to know?"

Diane grinned. "I think it'll be a surprise, a really big surprise. One that'll get the Graysons off our backs."

"OK, you got me hooked."

"Ms. Fallon, I need to talk with you about your attack."

In the doorway stood Janice Warrick. She wore the same pulled back hairstyle, but its severity was softened by the white blouse, blue blazer and skirt. Her face was smooth, free of the angry lines from their last encounter, but she seemed as reluctant to speak with Diane as Diane was to invite her into her room.

Chapter 45

Diane mentally braced herself for another unpleasant conversation.

"I wonder if we might speak privately," Detective Warrick said, looking at Andie.

"This is Andie Layne, my assistant. You met her earlier in my office. I trust her with very sensitive museum business. I can trust her here."

Andie made no move to leave. Diane knew she wouldn't. Andie could be as stubborn as she, and from the way her chin jutted in the air, she was in full stubborn mode.

"Very well. We're very concerned, of course, about these attacks on you. But your insistence on linking the attacks to the Boone murders is not helping our efforts. It's giving people a false impression and, unfortunately, whatever hoodlums are attacking you are giving your theories a false credibility."

Diane watched Detective Warrick's eyes as she spoke. They were on her, then they shifted to Andie and back to her. Now she glanced down at her expensive Italian leather shoes. She was worried. Her first murder case and it was a biggie, the kind they write books about. She could go down forever as a hero or a bungler.

Diane heard laughing across the hall and glanced over. Jake Houser was visiting Frank. It gave her a sense of well-being to know that Frank was laughing.

"Has Jake Houser made any progress finding out who shot Frank Duncan?"

"I'd prefer not to discuss an ongoing investigation with a civilian."

I'll take that as a no, thought Diane. "Are you saying the attacks on me are random?"

"Yes, they do appear to be."

"How strange it is, then, that all the attackers wanted was for me to give them the skeleton we excavated from the Abercrombie farm. They abducted me and were taking me to the museum for that purpose."

Gotcha. Diane watched Janice Warrick's face change from that blank expression she was trying to maintain to surprise to unease in just a few seconds.

Before Detective Warrick responded, Jake had left Frank's room and walked over to Diane's.

"Dr. Fallon," said Jake. "I'm sorry about this. I feel like if I'd been at the museum, maybe this wouldn't have happened." He pulled up a chair and sat near the bed.

"It's not your fault," she said. "It started here in the hospital parking lot, not at the museum."

"Here? And you ended up at the museum? Are you saying someone grabbed you and moved you to another location?"

"Yes."

Jake frowned. "This is more serious, Janice," he said.

"Yes. I see it is. We can't have people snatched in parking lots. Tell us what happened, and I assure you we'll look into it," said Warrick. She pulled up a chair beside Jake.

Diane told the story from beginning to end without interruption. As she finished, her phone rang. It was out of reach, and Andie handed it to her. It was a reporter from the *Rosewood Herald* asking about the skeleton and the attack on her.

"I'd prefer not to discuss the attack right now while the police are investigating," Diane said. The two detectives nodded.

An idea occurred to her as she listened to the reporter ask about the skeleton—an idea that might take focus away from her, but she had to word it carefully. Jake would ask her about it, and she couldn't lie to the police.

"The skeleton is in Sheriff Canfield's jurisdiction," she told the reporter. "Yes, I think the break-ins at the museum are related to the skeleton, but whoever it is won't find anything. I've done all I can do with it. I believe it would benefit from having other experts look at it, so it's been boxed up and is being delivered to a nationally known forensic anthropologist for a second opinion." She listened for a few moments. "No, I can't comment on who or where." She ended the conversation and hung up the phone.

The terrible thought had occurred to her that whoever wanted the bones could call her up and threaten Frank, Kevin, Andie or anyone, unless she gave them the bones. The skeleton put everyone at risk. But if the perpetrator thought it was gone, the threat to her and those she cared about would be gone with it. She hoped the perps would read the papers or hear it on the news.

Gregory always said it's only a secret if you are the only one who knows about it. That was the tricky part. Keeping it only to herself. It meant misrepresenting its whereabouts to the detectives here, to Frank, to everyone.

"I suppose that's just the beginning," she said, closing her eyes to avoid looking at Jake and Janice Warrick until she could internalize her lie.

"Reporters are a bitch," said Jake.

"Just because someone is after the remains," said Warrick, "doesn't mean that the remains are related to the Boone murders."

Diane opened her eyes and gave her a long look. This woman was going to hang on to her theories to the bitter end. "That's a true statement," Diane said. "The fact that George Boone had one of the bones in his possession before he died could be just a bizarre coincidence."

"Star Boone and her boyfriend could have something to do with the skeleton and didn't want it to be discovered," Warrick said.

Jake, Andie and Diane stared at her for a moment.

"Yes," conceded Diane. "Star and Dean could have killed the victim and dumped his body on the Abercrombie farm. If I were you, I'd find out if either of them knew how to drive at age eleven."

"Eleven? Are you saying the bones were buried out there, what, five years ago?" Warrick looked uncomfortable. "Sheriff Canfield hasn't shared any information with us. I didn't know. We'll catch whoever did this." Warrick left, and it was a relief to Diane to see her go.

"I'm sorry, Diane," Jake said. "We're all pretty wound up these days. Crime was supposed to go down and suddenly it's shot up, and I'm kind of caught between a rock and a hard place. I may have to resign my night job at the museum."

"I understand."

"Is there anything you can tell me that might lead to whoever nabbed you?"

Diane shook her head. "They were pretty good at making sure I didn't see much."

"You're sure it was more than one?"

"Yes. I'm sure of that. I'm sorry, even the van was just a white van. I didn't really take notice before it happened."

Jake nodded and closed his notebook. "OK. Look, ladies, from now on, if a van or something like it is pulled in beside your parked car, don't go near it. Get someone to walk you to your car. Get in on the passenger's side if you have no choice. Don't get between the van and your car."

"I know that," said Diane. "I just wasn't thinking."

"It's not that you haven't had things on your mind. I'm going to say good-bye to Frank, then get on this. I'll find out what's going on. Try not to worry."

When Jake left, Diane sent Andie on her way too. The stark hospital room was depressing—so were her thoughts. She could win all the small verbal sparring battles with her adversaries, but winning the war seemed beyond her reach. Right now, unconsciousness was inviting. She closed her eyes and went to sleep.

The ringing telephone didn't sound like hers, and for a moment Diane didn't know where she was. She was reluctantly pulled awake, still groggy. She reached for the phone.

"Diane. I'm so sorry to call you at the hospital."

"What's wrong, Andie?"

"Mark Grayson. He's called a board meeting for this afternoon. He says he has all the figures. Donald said they were very persuasive. I've called Mrs. Van Ross, and she's going to come to the meeting. What do you want me to do?"

"When is it set for?"

"Three o'clock."

"I'll be there. But don't tell anyone."

"Are you sure you can? I mean, you didn't look too good."

"Will you ask Mike to come pick me up?"

"Sure."

Diane got out of bed, put on some makeup and packed. She took the laptop into Frank's room.

"I have something for you to try out. Kenneth Meyers gave it to me. It's his new field computer. You can drop it from a height of four feet and it won't break I think it's one he wanted you to look at and recommend for the police department."

The three Duncan brothers looked at her, dressed, with suitcase in hand. She noticed that their expressions of astonishment made them look almost like triplets. Linc was the first to find his voice.

"What do you think you're doing?"

"I have to go to the museum."

"Absolutely not. What did I tell you about rest? That's not like, take an aspirin and call me in the morning. It's like, you may have internal hemorrhaging if you don't."

"Diane," said Frank, "listen to him."

"You're a good one to talk," said Henry. "You'd be going with her if you could."

"Look, Frank," she said, "I wouldn't, but Andie just called. Mark's called a board meeting. I think he's cooked the numbers, but I can defeat him."

"Diane, you told me you have unilateral power."

"I do, but with everything that's been going on, if he has compelling figures—" *Anyway, I want to see his face,* she thought. "I have to do this. After it's over, I'll come back here and rest."

Linc was looking really angry. "You are without a doubt the worst patient I've ever had. At least when I put athletes in the hospital, they stay there until they're released."

"I'm sorry. I have to do this."

"Come back here. I'll . . . ?" He threw up his hands. "Fix it with the hospital."

"Thanks." She kissed Frank. "You doing OK?"

"Yeah. Fine."

"He's had some bad dreams," said Henry.

"Just reliving the shooting," said Frank. "It's nothing. Do what Linc says. He really is a pretty good doctor."

"I know."

"I'll walk you downstairs," said Linc.

Diane didn't dare refuse, and he kept muttering his displeasure all the way down to the ground floor. She was relieved when they arrived.

"If you don't behave yourself when you get back, I'll have the hospital put you in restraints." His face softened into a smile. "But I suppose someone's already tried that."

Diane had to wait a few minutes outside the hospital. There was a constant stream of people going and coming, an ambulance sped to the emergency entrance, someone was changing a flat tire in the visitors' parking lot. *Hundreds of dramas constantly being played out,* she thought, as she saw Mike's Explorer drive up and stop.

"What's up?" he asked as he helped her in.

"Board meeting."

"Couldn't you just skip it?"

"Not this one."

"I didn't realize being a museum director was so demanding."

Diane laughed, and it hurt.

When they pulled up in front of the museum she was out almost as soon as he stopped.

"Take it easy, Doc," said Mike.

"I'll be fine. Thanks for the ride."

She went straight to her office. Jonas was with Andie. He was writing her a note.

"What are you doing out?" he asked.

"Very long story." She turned to Andie. "I'll bet Donald has an advance copy of Grayson's figures, and I want to see them. Go to his office and tell him you're delivering a message from me, but don't tell him I'm here in the museum."

"Sure."

"Tell him it's time for him to choose whose side he's on."

Diane turned to Jonas. "Anything new?"

"Yes. I have something I need to show you. I'm not certain, but it may be important."

"Let's go to your office. I want to hide out for a while."

"Not only do I sense a long story, but an unusual one."

"Andie, have you heard from Korey?" asked Diane as she was leaving.

"No. You want me to call him for you?"

"When you find him, send him to Jonas' office."

Chapter 46

Diane led Jonas from Andie's office through a private door into the Pleistocene room, across the mammal exhibit to the set of elevators that ran up the middle of the museum and opened at Jonas' office. She managed to traverse the whole area without being seen.

"Who knew this job would call for this much stealth?" said Jonas.

"I know this must seem very bizarre."

"Yes. Why are you hiding from your staff?" Jonas pulled out a chair, one of the comfortable stuffed ones at the chess table, for Diane, and he took the other one. "Of course, I've known a department head or two who've hidden out from the faculty."

"We're having a board meeting."

"Ah. They must be like our faculty meetings."

Diane managed a laugh. "This involves the man who's been after me to move the museum. I don't want him to know I'm here until it's time for the meeting. He thinks I'm in the hospital. We're at the endgame."

"I see. Who's going to win?"

"We'll see. What do you have to show me?"

He handed her an arrowhead. "Do you remember Rick finding this?"

"At the pit?" Diane thought a minute. "Yes, I remember. They all thought it was rather ironic."

"He didn't notice when he picked it up, but after he cleaned it he found a number on it."

Diane looked at him, not understanding the significance.

"It's been cataloged. It has provenience," he said.

"You're going to have to spell it out for me." She paused. "We know where it came from. Oh, if it happens to have belonged to the perp or the victim, we know where he got it."

"That's our thinking. Rick didn't notice the number at first. Someone's tried to scratch it off, which means it's probably stolen. Makes sense—it's a nice stemmed point. I'd say Laurentian, from around New York, but I'm not sure. I thought we could look at the number through the microscope."

They took the arrowhead to his workroom, where he had a dissecting microscope sitting in the corner. Diane looked at the table covered with potsherds and at his small amount of space.

"You need a better lab, don't you?"

"This is fine for my needs. As I understand it, this is the largest office space in the building."

"Still, if you ever need more room . . ." She put the dark gray chert point on the stage and looked at a strip of partially scratched-off white paint with fine writing on it in black ink. "I see a one and a nine—and what looks like a B or an E."

"Nineteen. That's Massachusetts." He went into his office and came back with a book. "The possibilities are Barnstable, Essex, Berkshire and Bristol."

"What are you looking at?" asked Diane.

"A map of Massachusetts—these are counties that begin with B and E. Do you have any clue what the second letter might be? The county designations are like the postal abbreviations for states—GA for Georgia, TN for Tennessee. Same principle. The second letter might be a clue as to which county in Massachusetts."

"No. It's gone."

"There should be a third set of numbers after the letters. They reflect the site number within the state."

"Maybe the first digit is a . . . could be a zero, or

maybe a nine or an eight. It could possibly even be a two or a three. Only the portion between the cap line and the X line are there."

"Which means?" he asked.

"The bottom of the number is missing. The second number is a four, I think. There aren't any more on that line."

"There's another row?" Jonas said. "That may be an artifact number. Can you read it?"

"No. It's just white paint now. They were successful in scratching it off."

"I'd vote for zero or three on the first digit. I don't think Massachusetts has that many sites, but I may be wrong. I'll make some calls, if you like."

"That would be good. Thanks for doing this."

"Because the site is in Massachusetts, doesn't mean the person got the point from there. University of Arizona, for example, could have excavated the site and stored the artifacts there. But I'll start with the Massachusetts state archaeologist and see if he'll fax me a list of their sites and site numbers."

Jonas went into his office to make his calls. Diane stayed in his workroom and called Frank's partner, Ben Florian, on her cell phone. He picked up his phone immediately.

"Hi," he said. "I got your message about the missing persons query and passed it along immediately to the police in Rosewood."

"What do you mean?" Diane had a sinking feeling.

"My boss thought it would be better if Rosewood handled sending out the query. It's not an official case for us, and he likes to maintain good relations with the surrounding jurisdictions."

"They won't do anything with it."

"Sure they will. . . ." He hesitated.

"No, they won't. They'll sit on it. That's why Frank was doing it himself. They have their theory of the crime and that's it for them. Besides, the skeleton wasn't found in the city of Rosewood's jurisdiction, but in the county under Sheriff Bruce Canfield's jurisdiction. They don't like him either, so they'll have given it to some secretary and told her to put it on the bottom of her to-do list. The sheriff won't get it probably for a few months."

The other end of the line was quiet for several long moments. "I'm real sorry, I didn't know."

Suddenly Diane wanted to cry. She bit her lower lip and tried to keep her voice from quavering.

"We've only lost a couple of days," she said. She told him about the artifact number she and Jonas were trying to translate. Trying to express as clearly as she understood it what the site number meant. "I'm going to call some of the Massachusetts universities and ask if they've had any students go missing in the past five years. I'll give Sheriff Canfield the information too, so he can send out a query." Diane wondered if she sounded bitter—at that moment her voice reminded her of her mother's "well, if you can't do it, I'll have to do it myself" voice.

"I'll call a few people and see if I can hurry the process along," said Ben. "How's Frank doing?"

"Getting better. We have rooms across the hall from each other."

"You're in the hospital too?"

"I was." She told him about her kidnaping and the desire of the kidnapers to get their hands on the remains. "I've got out to go to a board meeting, but I had to promise the doctor I'd come back."

"This isn't good," he said. She could hear the regret in his voice. "Look, I'm real sorry about the misunderstanding." Diane could hear from his tone that he was, but the anger still sat in her stomach like undigested food. She was working as hard as she could to solve this, and the people in authority—even the friendly ones—did nothing but throw up roadblocks. When she hung up, she wanted to put her head down and cry. She was so tired and her body ached all over.

Instead, she called the sheriff. To her great surprise and relief, he had sent out a query as soon as he heard about the results of the stable isotope tests, making updates when he found more information. Diane thanked him so profusely it seemed to confuse him.

"Just doing my job. I heard something else happened to you."

Diane related a quick version of the incident.

"Whoever did this is here and desperate. You take some serious precautions, you hear?"

"I am."

"I'll get on this new Massachusetts information right away. Who knows? We might come up with something in a hurry."

Diane thanked him again and pushed the disconnect button.

"They're going to fax my computer with a list of sites," said Jonas from his office. Diane went back and sat in the comfortable chair, closing her eyes, grateful that the sheriff, at least, knew what his job was. "You need someplace to rest."

"I . . ." She was interrupted by a knock on Jonas' door. "I hope that's Korey."

Jonas opened the door slightly as if checking credentials before letting anyone in. It was Korey and a petite woman with short salt-and-pepper hair and a face much younger than her gray hair suggested.

"This is Dr. Allison Onfroi, an art historian from the Metropolitan Museum of Art."

Diane rose and greeted her. "We're glad you could come to look at our murals."

"I am just mesmerized by them."

"So they are authentic Robert Camdens?"

"Oh, no question."

Diane and Korey grinned at each other.

"These are those wonderful dinosaur and Pleistocene paintings?" asked Jonas. "I go in the rooms sometimes and just sit and look at them."

Dr. Onfroi nodded. "I find his work, though some of my colleagues disagree, similar in mood to William Trost Richards. Of course, they both were American Pre-Raphaelites. Richards created such emotion with his realism. Camden does the same for me. Most people don't know him—he was never in favor in his own time, partly because of his rather strange insistence on inserting those whimsical unicorns in his paintings, juxtaposing the utter realism with the utter unreal. Now people identify with that."

"Were wall murals his usual work?" asked Diane.

"It turned out that way. He had to make a living painting illustrations and murals for buildings. Most haven't survived. And there weren't that many of his other works. Your paintings are the best I've seen. I'd love to work with Korey on protecting them for you."

"Allison had another interesting tidbit of news," said Korey. "It seems that several months ago, someone from the Heron Museum of Art was asked to have a look at a collection of Camden murals for a museum."

"It was all very secretive, as a lot of our work is."

"Grayson," said Diane.

"I'm sure," said Korey. "I told Allison about the secret plans to buy the museum building and move us somewhere else."

"I wish I could say I was shocked," said Allison Onfroi, "but I've seen a lot of underhandedness going on in the art world. I'm sure the Heron thought it was on the up-and-up. I deal with them a lot, and they'd be shocked to know what they were a party to."

"I've booked Allison into a Sudwith's bed and breakfast," said Korey.

"Oh, you'll like that," said Diane. "Thanks again for coming. I look forward to working with you on this project."

Before they left, Korey handed Diane a piece of paper. It was Dr. Onfroi's appraisal of the monetary value of the paintings. Diane stared hard at it for a moment and put it in her pocket.

Chapter 47

Andie arrived on their heels, carrying a folder. "Donald made his decision," she said, handing Diane the folder. "I also brought you the original museum budget for comparison."

"Thanks, Andie. How is Donald?"

"Odd, even for him. I gave him your message and he sat for the longest time, stroking that desk of his. I thought maybe he'd been going quietly nuts all this time and this was somehow the final straw." Andie shook her head. "I don't know. He really took your attack hard. Hard enough it made me suspicious of him—but if the attack on you was about the skeleton, I don't see how that makes any sense."

"It might, if he thought it was connected with the Graysons." Diane told Andie what Mike had related to her about the switched drinks.

"Why, that flashy, trashy bitch," said Andie. "Can't you have her arrested?"

"For what? Apparently, she's the one who ended up with the drug."

"Serves her right. Why would they go to such lengths?"

"This." Diane handed her the paper Korey had given her. Jonas looked over her shoulder. She watched both their eyes widen until they were almost round. Andie, with her remarkably curly hair, looked like Little Orphan Annie.

*   *   *

Between the sheriff and Korey, Diane was feeling optimistic for the first time in a while. There were still a couple of hours to go before the meeting, so she sat down and relaxed with Jonas and their game of chess. It was a lot more fun sitting at the chess board than E-mailing moves back and forth.

Korey knocked on the door and came in just as Jonas captured Diane's queen with his rook.

"Looks like you're in trouble, Dr. F.," said Korey, looking at the chess board.

"It's not over until it's over," said Diane.

"Andie sent me to escort you to the meeting," he said.

"Escort me?"

"You're supposed to be in the hospital."

"OK. It's time, then." She turned to Jonas. "Well, I suppose the endgame is starting."

"You talking about the museum or chess?"

"Both."

Jonas chuckled. "For our game, you could resign now."

Diane smiled and left with Korey to go up to the third-floor meeting room. In the lobby they met Mark and Signy Grayson, who both looked surprised and a little disappointed at seeing her.

"You must not have been as bad off as people have been saying," said Mark.

"I'm very sorry to disappoint you. I'm injured but not dead. And how is your cold, Signy? I've been concerned about you after that strange episode after the party. I hope you've changed your cold medication."

"I'm fine, thank you." She gave a thin smile, and Diane noticed that both she and Mark eyed her closely.

"I'm going to the meeting room," said Mark. "I'll see you there, Diane. Glad you could make it."

Diane watched him stride confidently to the conference room. She started to follow, but the elevator doors opened and Vanessa Van Ross stepped into the lobby.

"Mrs. Van Ross," acknowledged Signy. "You're looking well. I've seen your limousine at the hospital more than once. I feared you were ill."

"No. I've just been visiting the Center for Research on Aging there at the hospital."

"Looking into the latest research on longevity?" Signy gave her a bright smile.

"My dear, are you hoping I'll hurry and move on to the next world and make space for you and your husband?"

"Nonsense. Why would we want that?"

"You think if I were gone, Diane would be more vulnerable—in fact, you think many of Mark's other real estate ventures would be easier. I've been a thorn in his side for quite a while, opposing all those zoning changes he wants."

"I think you're just oversensitive. We don't wish you ill."

"Good, then you'll be happy to know that not only is my mother still alive and kicking, so is my grandmother."

"Your grandmother? That's not possible," said Signy.

"Yes, dear, it is. If you and Mark weren't so self-absorbed, you'd know that my grandmother is the second oldest person in the United States. So, dear, when you're my age I'll probably still be alive and going to those city council meetings to oppose Mark and his self-serving projects."

Diane and Vanessa left Signy standing openmouthed in the lobby. "The herpetologist is putting in an interesting exhibit," she heard Korey telling Signy.

Almost everyone was in the meeting room when Diane entered. They all greeted her with surprise and sympathy. Her usual seat was vacant, and Craig and Mark had taken up their positions on either side of her.

She sat on one end; Vanessa Van Ross on the other. If it were chess, Vanessa would be the queen defending her king—the museum. She was the one who wielded the greatest power for Diane's side. Diane wasn't sure what she was—a pawn, perhaps. No, a knight. A good guard with power to move in creative ways.

She looked at the faces of her board members as they studied Mark's figures.

"Good to see you," said Kenneth. "How's that computer working out?"

"Great," said Diane. "I love it. I loaned it to Frank. I told him his unit should get some."

"That's my girl," said Kenneth. "It's a honey of a computer."

Laura entered, out of breath. "Diane. I went by the hospital and they told me you'd left temporarily. Are you all right?"

"I'm doing fine. The doctor wants me to spend the night there, so I have to go back. He suspects I have internal injuries."

"Should you be here at all?" said Harvey Phelps. "You look pale."

"This won't take long," she said.

She met Gordon Atwell's gaze. He held hers for a moment and looked back down at the figures Mark had handed out. Diane wondered if it was he or someone he told who requested "In the Hall of the Mountain King" at the reception.

"Are we all here?" she said. "Mark, I believe you have a presentation."

He stood and cleared his throat. "I have the figures Laura asked for at the last meeting. I think the numbers speak for themselves, and the museum would indeed come out ahead making a move to the Vista Building. I'll be glad to answer any questions."

"Are these figures accurate?" said Harvey Phelps. "How much were the original renovations?" He looked at Diane.

Laura frowned; so did Kenneth. His numbers did look good, but Diane had no doubt he'd fudged some of them. Only Vanessa's eyes twinkled as she fanned herself with the budget.

"I have a question," said Diane.

"All right," answered Mark.

"I don't see any mention of the museum's one hundred million dollars' worth of assets in paintings reflected in these figures. Nor do I see how you plan to accommodate them in the new building. You know, of course, I would expect to remove them before this building is sold to your investors."

Everyone except Vanessa and Mark looked, bewildered, at Diane. Vanessa still fanned herself. Mark had turned several shades of red.

"What's she talking about, Mark?" Craig Amberson frowned as he looked at Mark across the table.

"A hundred million dollars?" said Gordon Atwell. "Mark, do you know what she means?"

"Well, *I* don't know," said Kenneth Myers and Harvey Phelps together.

Madge Stewart kept flipping through the pages of the budget. "I don't understand. There's nothing here about paintings. Isn't that a lot of money for paintings?"

Donald, sitting by Madge at the end of the long table, looked relieved. Diane supposed it was because in the end he'd chosen his side correctly.

"You didn't tell them, Mark?" said Diane. "You weren't going to share all that profit, were you?"

"Shut up, you fucking bitch," Mark exploded, standing up, red-faced, staring down at Diane, looking like he wanted to strangle her.

Madge audibly sucked in her breath.

"Here, here," said Kenneth. "Mark, I think you have some explaining to do."

Diane didn't take her eyes from Mark. "In case you were wondering, Signy wasn't incompetent the night of the reception. She successfully slipped me the glass with the—was it Rohypnol?—but someone saw her and switched the glasses back." She looked at the group. "That was what that strange episode was about at the last board meeting. Signy got the drink meant to make me look like a drunken fool in front of all the contributors."

"I didn't sign on for that," said Craig Amberson, rising to face Mark.

Gordon Atwell nervously tapped his fingers on the table.

Mark took another look at Diane. She saw in the depths of his gray eyes that she'd made an enemy for life. They were so filled with hate that she wondered if it could have been him behind her attacks—just diverting attention to the skeleton because it was a handy red herring.

"Do you have anything to add to your report before we vote?" she said, not unlocking her gaze from his.

He turned and left the room.

"I'll take that as a no," said Diane after the door slammed behind him.

The remaining board members seemed to be stunned into silence.

She turned her attention to the other conspirators. "What I want to know, Mr. Atwell, is was it you or someone else who requested 'In the Hall of the Mountain King' at the reception?"

He said nothing, but she could hear the labor of his breathing.

"You have grandchildren. So do you, Craig. You know how cruel that was. Is this the kind of men you are? If so, I want your resignations from the board."

"I told Mark that was perhaps unwise," Atwell said finally.

"Perhaps unwise. Yes. Perhaps it was."

"Will someone tell me what's going on?" said Harvey Phelps.

"The paintings on the wall in the Pleistocene and dinosaur rooms are remarkably valuable. We had an expert from the Metropolitan Museum of Art come in today and appraise them."

"The ones with the unicorns?" said Madge.

"Yes. Mark apparently had them appraised several weeks ago by someone at the Heron Museum of Art. He knew their value. That's when he got the idea of buying the museum building and the paintings and moving us out to that second-rate Vista Building."

She hoped she was sufficiently rubbing Craig's and Gordon's noses in it.

"Korey and Dr. Allison Onfroi from the Metropolitan Museum of Art are working on protecting them," she added.

Craig Amberson and Gordon Atwell looked defeated. Apparently, Mark Grayson hadn't told them about the paintings.

"I think this meeting is adjourned. We aren't selling the museum. For our next board meeting we need to get down to the business of the museum, and put this mess behind us."

Diane sat back in her chair, exhausted. Just as soon as she talked to Jonas about the provenience of the arrowhead, she was heading back to the hospital. Vanessa Van Ross smiled at her as she continued to fan herself with the budget figures.

Diane got the room across from Frank again. She didn't think she'd ever be glad to be in the hospital, but the bed felt good, and all she wanted to do was sleep. Even though Jonas hadn't yet received the fax about the sites where the arrowhead may have come from, she felt optimistic. The last thing she did before getting Laura to take her back to the hospital was to fax the sheriff all the information she had on the skeleton. Surely, someone somewhere would recognize the description.

Getting Grayson off her back and rooting out the vipers among her board members was a major relief. And although Jonas didn't know it, she was going to beat him at chess with her queen sacrifice. Adding to all of that, Frank was much improved—and it was only five thirty. Now all she had to do was wait for the sleeping pill to kick in. She didn't even know it when she fell asleep.

She dreamed of snakes. Black snakes crawling across the table in the boardroom. The boardroom was ankle-deep in them, with no place to step. Diane jerked awake. She hated snakes.

The hospital was quiet. She looked at the clock next to her bed. Three thirty-two in the morning. That was a long sleep, and her bladder was full. She went to the bathroom. When she came out, she felt like she needed to walk. She put on her robe and walked out into the dimly lit hallway. At the far end of the corridor two nurses were chatting at the nurses' station. She walked across the hall and peeked in Frank's room.

Henry was dozing in a chair. Frank was asleep. Her presence roused Henry, and he came out to talk to her.

"How are you feeling?" he said.

"Better. Restless. I imagine you and your brother are pretty restless yourselves."

"We're doing OK. Actually, it's hard to get Linc to take a vacation. He tends to be a workaholic. Now he has nothing to do but rest. His wife told me to keep him here for as long as I can." He and Diane laughed together.

"I haven't seen your sister lately."

"She went home to see Mom and Dad."

Diane shook her head. "All this must be really strange to you and your brother."

"Well, yeah, it is. I feel like I got dropped into a Sam Spade movie."

Diane and Henry talked a while. She enjoyed getting to know Frank's family. She'd have liked to get to know his sister too.

"You look like you need to get back to bed," said Henry after a while.

"You're right. Thanks for the company." She walked back into her room and climbed in bed and went to sleep. She could see Henry standing outside Frank's door. For the first time in a long while, she felt safe.

Diane dozed for a while and then jerked awake. She wished she had another sleeping pill. An uneasy feeling that there was something she should know stood on the edge of her dreams like an apparition shaking her awake every time she slipped into comfortable sleep.

The clock in her room said it was five twenty. She tried to go back to sleep, but it was no use. She got out of bed and went to Frank's room. Henry was sound asleep; so was Frank. She picked up the computer by Henry's chair and went back to her room. There was a chair in the corner of the room near a phone jack. She

pulled another wooden chair up and sat the computer
on it as if it were a desk. She plugged in the computer,
booted it up and connected the phone cord to the jack.
She'd remembered that missing persons for each state
are posted on the Internet. Why hadn't she thought of
that before? She could look herself. But instead of going
to the missing persons site, she went to the Google Internet search engine and typed in the words *missing,
male, hockey, spring break, 1998.*

It occurred to Diane that people oftentimes put up
Web pages seeking help in finding a loved one—a way
of tacking up missing persons posters across the world.

She got 1753 hits on the first search. Too many. Glancing down the list, she saw that one hit was about a missing male cat whose owner played field hockey. She
needed to tweak her search parameters. It was amazing
how many hits she got with what she thought was an
unusual selection of key words. She got short stories and
lots of hockey sites. On her third tweak of the parameters, she realized she should put quotations around
"spring break" so that it would be read as a phrase by
the search engine. That cut the number of hits down to
512. After almost an hour of looking at Web pages, she
was about to give up and go through missing persons
records, state by state. It would take a while, but the
current strategy was apparently turning into a wild goose
chase. Before she gave it up, however, she added *vegetarian* and *archaeology* to the search criteria. This time
there were four hits. The title of the first hit was: "Will
you help me find my son?"

Chapter 48

Diane's hands were shaking as she clicked on the link to the site. Immediately, a photograph of a young man, smiling, wearing a blue oxford shirt came up. He had dark hair and eyes, a bright smile and even, white teeth. He looked so young; maybe nineteen. His name was Aidan Kavanagh.

Reading about him was heartbreaking. The site was put up by his parents. They described his physical appearance, his height and weight. They told about his interests, what a good hockey player he was, how he broke his shin but made a winning goal just the same. He was from Washington State, had lots of friends. There was a picture of him with his girlfriend. He was majoring in business at Harvard but flirted briefly with archaeology.

The saddest thing was a message from his father asking that if his son was somewhere reading this to please come home because they loved him. She wondered if there were some issues between him and his parents.

He disappeared after March 28, 1998. His girlfriend had spoken to him on the phone that evening. He had decided to stay at school during spring break and study. After that phone call he wasn't heard from again. His SUV was in the driveway of the house he shared with three other male students. They had gone to Fort Lauderdale during spring break, leaving him alone. No one saw him leave; no one saw anyone come to the house. He just vanished without a word to anyone, without a trace.

Until George and Jay Boone found his collarbone.

There was a number to call if anyone had any information. The instructions on the answering machine were to leave a message and number where the caller could be reached. Diane imagined they had to put in a special phone line. She wondered how many crank calls they got each month.

She looked at the clock. It was a little after 6:00 A.M. The hospital had been waking up for about half an hour. The hallway had grown steadily noisier as the sounds of the breakfast carts rattled down the hallway.

She dialed the number from the computer screen. One ring, then the answering machine. A voice with the same instructions.

Diane hesitated for a fraction of a second before she introduced herself to the machine.

"Hello, my name is Dr. Diane Fallon. I'm a forensic anthropologist and director—"

There was a sudden click on the other end and a mature male voice spoke. "Did you say you're a forensic anthropologist?"

"Yes. I got your number from your Web page."

"Is this about Aidan?"

"Possibly."

"I'm his father, Declan Kavanagh. Have you found my son?"

"I don't know for sure. Can I tell you what I've found?"

Diane explained only that skeletal remains were found in a remote area of a farm and that she had analyzed them. She told him that analysis of the remains suggested that the bones belonged to a young male, six foot two, who grew up in a cool climate and was basically a vegetarian, but ate fish. She wondered if perhaps he had a childhood allergy to beef. He'd had *osteitis pubis,* possibly from the side-to-side movement of playing hockey, and he should have had considerable groin pain from it at one time. He had olecranon bursitis that should have given him elbow pain, and a broken left tibia—shin. There was a possible archaeology connection. He disappeared probably between March and June of 1998—about the time of spring break for many schools. The sheriff of the county where the remains were located recently sent out queries across the country. She had plugged key words into an Internet search engine and came up with the Web page.

Diane had laid out all the findings briefly and clearly, as if she were giving a report. When she finished she heard a low groan on the other end that turned into a deep wail. She understood. She had taken away all his hope. She wanted to cry with him.

When he came back on the line, his voice was calm and emotionless. "You have described my son completely. Tell me where you are. I have X rays, dental records."

Diane didn't tell him the skull was missing. She thought it would sound too gruesome over the phone. She gave him her address.

"How did he die?" he asked.

"I haven't been able to establish the cause of death. The severe injury to the shoulder could be the cause, but there is no way to tell. Nor can I say for certain the manner of death."

"But it looks like murder to me. Is the sheriff looking for the killer?"

"First the remains had to be identified. We hope that will lead to the story of what happened, and that will lead to the killer, if it was murder."

"You seem to be skirting around the issues."

"No. I'm simply not going beyond what I know."

"Yes. I'm sorry. You've obviously gone to great lengths to find out where the remains of my son belong, and I thank you. I'll be leaving as soon as I can make arrangements."

Diane gave him the name of the sheriff and his phone number.

Linc came in and looked at her chart. "You're up and working. I thought I was a workaholic. How are you feeling?"

"Much better. I slept for a long time."

"Good. Get back into bed and let me see if there's any swelling. Your chart looks good. Any pain?"

"No. Just soreness."

"I think you'll have that a while."

Diane got back into bed, and Linc felt for any swelling of her organs.

"So far, so good." He listened to her heart and her lungs. "You're doing better than I thought, with all the coming and going you've been doing."

"How's Frank?"

"He's doing well. I'm pleased. Looks like the two of you will pull through."

"I suppose you and Henry are anxious to go home."

Frank laughed from the doorway. "Half the nurses think he's a new doctor here." Frank came in and took a seat beside Diane's bed. "How's she doing?"

"I think you can stop worrying, at least about this current episode."

"I've put you through more than you bargained for," Diane told Linc.

"It's been good for me. I've enjoyed visiting with Frank. I've gotten to spend some time with Kevin. I just wish it were under better circumstances."

"You look good," Diane told Frank. "Your color's back." She gave his cheek a gentle pinch. "You growing a beard, or going for the rugged look?"

"I'm feeling better every day. I think they'll let me go home in a few days."

Diane looked up at Linc. "Can I go home?"

"You think one night's rest does the trick? You can go home if you only go home and not to the museum. Will you do that?" Diane stared at him, and he shook his head. "You know, I can see it in your eyes. You have no intention of staying home."

"I've identified him," she said.

"Who?" Linc hesitated a moment. "The remains? You know who he is?" He pulled up a chair. "How? When?"

"Just now."

"You figured it out from your hospital bed?" Frank

grasped her hand and held it tight. It felt good that his grip was strong again.

"Actually, from that chair over there. I searched the Internet for missing persons."

"Good idea. What made you think of that?" said Linc.

"Lying here with nothing to do but think. I have to look at the X rays, but he fits everything—he's a hockey player, had all the symptoms we saw in the bones. He even dabbled in archaeology."

"I don't remember that," said Linc. "How did that show up in his bones?"

Diane told him about the arrowhead with a site number on it. "I called the father and he's flying down from Washington State with X rays. He's coming to the museum. Can I go, huh, can I?"

"You're really impossible. You think you can stay out of trouble?"

"Sure. We're sliding home now. If we can solve this, things can get back to what passes for normal."

"All right. But listen to me. No running, jumping, lifting, getting into fights, no late hours. I want you in bed, asleep, early at night and set up regular appointments with your doctor for a few weeks. We have to watch for any internal bleeding."

"I can do all that."

"I'll see to your release. Don't make me regret it." Linc left the room, and Diane turned her attention to Frank.

"I was thinking, when you're ready to go home, why don't you stay at my place a few days? We can take it easy together."

"Or you can stay at my house. I'm not sure I want to stay across from the Odells."

"Linc told you about them?"

Frank laughed and held his chest. "God, it hurts to laugh. Yes. Strange people. Ben Florian, my partner, called. He apologized up and down for sending the information to the Rosewood police."

"It's all right now. I really think we've found the guy, and I think he'll lead us to the murderer of your friends."

*　　*　　*

Diane drove her car and parked in front of the museum. It looked like home. She was getting to love it more every day. Now that the problems with the Graysons were over, there'd be only the normal problems of museum life. Not that they couldn't be difficult, but it wasn't like dealing with snakes in the grass. *Snakes*. She wished she hadn't thought of snakes.

Mike was there changing a flat tire on his SUV. He had the flat off and was about to put on the spare.

"Looks like I picked up a nail somewhere," he said. "You look much better than the last time I saw you."

"I'm doing good. Thanks for the information you gave me. It helped." Diane looked at the brake disc exposed by the missing tire and rim. Her gaze shifted over his heavy SUV and back down at the disc. "That's a heavy vehicle."

"Yes. It is."

"If the brake disc fell on you, it would do some damage, especially if you were on a hard surface."

He looked up at her. "Is that a threat?"

Diane looked at his puzzled face and realized she was thinking out loud and he had no idea what was running through her mind. She had to laugh.

She squatted down beside him and put a hand on the disc. "This is what caused the damage."

"My Explorer? What damage?"

"No. Not yours, but one like it." Diane was thinking about the damage to the shoulder girdle on the bones of the skeleton. "Before you put your tire on, will you make me a cast of the bottom part of the brake disc?"

"Sure. I can do that. It's a little weird, but that's what I've come to expect."

"There should be some quick-drying stuff in the museum."

"I've got some in the geology lab. I'll get right on it."

They walked into the museum together. Diane went to her office, Mike to the second floor.

"Diane, you look great!" Andie gave her a hug. "How are you feeling?"

"I'm fine. Just have to take it easy."

"Anything you need, just ask. By the way, Donald was very relieved when he discovered your attack was about the bones. He thought it was Mark Grayson and the real estate business. He is really being nice. I hope it sticks."

"It will for a while anyway."

"I can't believe what Signy Grayson tried to do to you. What if she'd gotten away with it?"

"She didn't."

Things seemed back to normal at the museum. It was a comfort. Andie and the staff had done a good job keeping up with things. She called Jonas' office.

"Hi. We found the skull," he said when he heard who it was. "I have it here. It had fallen through empty cavities in the pile, like you thought. The team is wrapping things up. Oh, and I got the correct site number."

"I'll be right up."

The skull was resting on a doughnut ring on Jonas' desk. The mandible was beside it. Diane picked it up. It was a typical male skull: prominent brow ridges, large nuchal crest at the back of the head to hold the heavier male neck muscles, large mastoid process, square jaw. Not that females couldn't have these characteristics; they sometimes do, and some male skulls downplay the characteristics most often consistent with maleness. The skull also had typical Caucasoid characteristics. It was nice when everything fit.

However, the feature that was the most prominent was the angle shaped compression fracture on the frontal bone over the right orbit and another similer fracture higher up on the parietal. She now had the cause and manner of death: blunt force trauma to the head— murder.

She told Jonas who he was.

"I'll be damned. Good girl. You can turn everything over to the sheriff now and be done with this. No one will have a reason to be after you."

When he said that, Diane realized she wanted to finish it. She wanted to be sure the person was caught. "Where was the site?" she asked.

"The site was in Massachusetts, like the nineteen indicated, near the border with New York. It was excavated about twenty years ago by the archaeology department at Harvard."

"Twenty? That long. So it might not have been associated with Aidan Kavanagh at all?"

"Twenty years doesn't change anything. It was probably stored in the department, and he could have somehow gotten his hands on it."

"He dabbled in archaeology."

"So that fits."

"Yes, it does. He later switched over to the Harvard Business School." Diane was struck by a sudden insight. "Oh, my God," she said. "That's not possible."

"What?" Jonas looked at her with concern. "Sit down, you look pale."

"Jake's son, Dylan Houser, also went to Harvard Business School around the same time."

Chapter 49

She picked up the phone book and looked up the number for the city jail. She dialed and asked for Star Boone, telling them it was an emergency. She knew that would scare Star to death, but if she was right, she wanted to act quickly. It took about ten minutes, but Star came on the line.

"Is Uncle Frank all right?"

"Yes, he is, Star. This is Diane Fallon. He's fine. I'm sorry to have frightened you. I have an important question I need to ask you. It's important," she said again. "Did Jay know Dylan Houser?"

"Sure. They went hunting and fishing together with Dad and Mr. Houser. Jay idolized him."

"What did you think of him?"

"I thought he was an arrogant prick. Mom and Dad thought he hung the moon. What's this about?"

"Right now it's confidential, so don't tell anyone about this conversation. I mean it."

"OK. I can keep a secret. You don't think . . ."

"Don't think about what I just asked. Forget about it. OK?"

"You'll tell me later?"

"Sure. I'll tell you everything later. I talked to Frank this morning. He's up and around and looking really good."

"When they called me to the phone and said it was an emergency, I was afraid . . ."

"I know. It is an emergency, just not with Frank. I'm sorry I scared you."

"They told me you were in the hospital too."

"You have a pretty good grapevine going there."

"If it's something that tortures me, they tell me about it. Actually, Mrs. Torres told me about you. She said her son found you in the lake and you were OK."

"I was in the hospital, but I'm fine now."

"Is everything going to be all right?"

"Yes, Star, it is. I don't think you'll be there much longer."

Diane got off the phone just as Jonas was opening the door for Mike Seger. He had a semicircular cast in his hand. "OK, you going to tell me what I'm doing with this?"

Diane took the cast from him. "This is great. Thanks. Now, would you mind getting your tire iron for me and meet us in the conservation lab vault?"

Mike looked at Jonas, who shrugged at him.

"Sure. Be right back. I have to say, you're the most unusual boss I've ever had."

"Why, thank you, Mike." She smiled at him.

Mike went on his errand. Diane and Jonas went to the conservation lab, carrying the skull and the cast.

"You found the skull," said Annie. Several of Korey's staff followed her and Jonas into the vault.

She opened the double boxes and took out the right scapula, the one with the damage, and aligned the cast of the brake disc with the straight indentation in the crushed bone.

"Not an exact match, but close—it's a good possibility."

Mike came in with the tire iron and laid it on the table. "So that's why you wanted the cast. You think a jack slipped."

"He'd have to slip too," said Diane. "And somehow end up with his right shoulder under the disc."

"That hurts just thinking about it," said Mike, rubbing his own shoulder.

Diane set the scapula down and gently picked up the

skull and tire iron, fitting the curved heavier end into the compression fracture. It was a good fit.

"What happened?" asked Mike. "The guy has a car fall on him and somebody caves in his skull with a tire iron? That's a bad day."

"Perhaps the car falling was afterward, to make the murder look like an accident," said Diane. "But then why dump the body someplace else? I don't know. I'll have to think about it."

Diane put the scapula back in the box. "Look, guys, don't mention the bones are here in the vault to anyone. I'd rather people not know it."

"Sure thing," they all agreed and went back to work, muttering about the undesirability of having a car fall on you.

"Can I put my tire on now?" asked Mike.

"Yes. You're a good sport, Mike. I appreciate all your help."

"Anytime you need something really odd done, just give me a call."

Diane carefully packed the skull and taped the box closed. She turned to Jonas. "Let me call the sheriff, and then I'll beat you at chess."

"You're going to have to work hard to win. You're in a bad situation."

"That makes it interesting."

The sheriff wasn't convinced right away to investigate Dylan Houser.

"I know it's a stretch, Sheriff. But bear with me. Both Dylan and the victim were in Harvard Business School together. There was a good chance they knew each other."

"So did a lot of people. That's a big school, and they may never have met."

"I know. I don't have anything in stone, but you could at least ask if he knew the guy."

"I could do that. Do you have anything else?"

"Not a lot. I believe that whoever killed the Boone family was afraid that if the bones were found and identified, the identity would lead us to them. The only way that would be true is if it could be proved that the killer and the victim knew each other or had some association with each other. The fact that the bones were here in this county, all the way from Massachusetts, suggests that the victim may have been visiting someone he knew. If the killer was a random stranger, why would he care if the bones were identified or not?"

"I don't have any quarrel with that, but it's a long way from the Houser boy."

"I know. Dylan was idolized by Jay Boone according to Star. He's one person who could have lured Jay out of the house, even asked him to bring a gun to him. The person who killed Jay was taller than either Star or her boyfriend, Dean. He was about Dylan's height."

"Being tall isn't rare among young men these days, even young men with a Harvard education," he said.

"I know. George Boone may have hit his attacker with a bat. Dylan has a bruise."

"How do you know?"

"I was told by someone who knows him," said Diane.

"That's something, but not much. He's an active boy."

"Whoever kidnaped me knew the skull was missing. It wasn't a secret, but not many people knew. One of the people who was in a position to know was Dylan's father."

"Now, hold on here."

"I know, Sheriff, but just listen. You can tell me I don't know what I'm talking about later."

"I'll do that."

"Jake Houser also knew that the bones had been there for several years. Not many people knew that either. And before you ask, that's very tenuous. It's based on a reaction he had."

Diane explained about Janice Warrick not knowing how long the bones had been dumped, but Jake did.

"I know that's very little, but why didn't Warrick know? She's been following everything I do, and Frank's partner sent her the report on the bones. There's a possibility that the report was intercepted so no one would query missing persons."

"So you think Jake's son, Dylan, for one reason or another killed this Kavanagh kid and dumped the body. George finds evidence of it, and he and his entire family have to be killed because any member might know where the bone came from. One thing led to another, and Dylan had to go after you and Frank to keep his secret. Jake found out and is trying to help his son cover everything up. Is that about it?"

"I know the whole argument leaves a lot to be desired. But what if Dylan was friends with Aidan Kavanagh, and Kavanagh just happened to disappear in his hometown?"

"I'll grant you, flimsy though your argument is, it makes a kind of sense. But why go to all that trouble to kill the Boones when he could just deny knowing anything about Kavanagh?"

"I don't know. That's a good point. It might be that he's going into a career where there can't be a hint of scandal. Will you talk to Dylan?"

"I'll talk to him. I'll confirm first that they did go to the same school at the same time with the same major. That's enough right there. As for the rest, well, we'll see."

"One last thing, Sheriff. When I was attacked the first time, I jerked one of my attacker's fingers back really hard, left a bad bruise on one of his arms where I bit him and kicked his shins half a dozen times."

"That ought to be pretty easy to spot," he said. "You're a damn tough woman."

As Diane and Jonas sat playing their game of chess, she tried out her reasoning again with him. He looked as skeptical as the sheriff had sounded.

"I know it's a terrible thing to accuse someone of anything they didn't do, especially something so dreadful as a multiple murder."

"I'm not saying your logic, as far as it goes, isn't sound. But it's the 'as far as it goes' part that's troubling. You're right. It's very tenuous."

"I know. There's no proof. Do you want to resign?"

Jonas looked startled. "What?"

"You can't win. I've got you beat in five moves."

"Oh, you scared me. I thought this was a side of you I hadn't seen. The woman who can't handle disagreement." He chuckled and scrutinized the chessboard.

"I don't believe it. You're right. There's no way I can get out from under all the ways you have me pinned and forked. How did this happen?"

"When you fell for my queen sacrifice."

Jonas met her gaze. "You are a devious woman."

"I didn't have a lot to do when I spent the night in the lake, so I worked out my chess strategy. Too bad I can't apply that to this case." She thought for a moment. "Perhaps I can. I need to call up the sheriff and ask him if he's talked to the Housers yet."

Chapter 50

Diane sat in her office looking over exhibit proposals. She'd sent Andie on an errand and told her to just go home after she was finished. Her hand shook as she took a sip of hot tea, and she almost jumped when the knock on the door finally came.

"Yes?"

Jake Houser stood in the doorway with his gaze on Diane. She took another sip of tea and forced herself to be steady.

"Jake. How's Frank's case going?"

"Dead end," he said.

"You mentioned you may be quitting the museum. Are you here to resign?"

"Partly. It's not working out for me here."

"I'm sorry to hear that," said Diane.

Jake sighed. "I did like it here." He paused. "You had a daughter, I understand."

"Yes. She was murdered."

"A terrible thing. Our children are our heart. There's just nothing we wouldn't do for them." He fingered the geode on her desk.

"Almost nothing," Diane agreed. "Do you need a letter of recommendation?"

There was another knock on the door. Both of them started. Diane looked at her watch. "It's getting a little late for visitors," she mumbled. "Come in."

Vanessa Van Ross, dressed in a white knit pantsuit that matched her hair, came into the room accompanied by her driver. "There you are. I didn't expect to find you working. You haven't been here the last three times I've come to talk with you."

Diane stood up. "Mrs. Van Ross, I'm so sorry. Things have been . . ."

"I really don't want to hear excuses." She turned to Jake. "Young man, will you wait in the other office?"

Jake looked a little confused and reluctant. He shrugged and walked into Andie's office. He didn't look good, and Diane was worried about him.

"Diane, Milo really thought you had potential. So did I, frankly, but this episode with the bones and the publicity, the fiasco with the Graysons. The board can't get rid of you, but I can. I don't want to. I wish I didn't have to. I like you. But . . ." She shook her head. "You have a week. I'm putting Donald in charge until we find a replacement."

"Mrs. Van Ross, what are you saying? You can't just fire me without some kind of . . ."

"Yes, I can. Read your contract."

"I know things have been a little rough lately. But I think if you'll just let me show you what I've done here, you'll see the museum is doing well. Why are you doing this?"

"Have you seen the newspapers? The museum doesn't need that kind of publicity. We haven't even opened our doors yet and I'm already getting calls from contributors asking what the hell's going on here. And the museum isn't doing well. My God, you almost lost the damn thing. No. I'm sorry. I'll give you a good severance package, but I want you out."

Vanessa Van Ross turned and left. Jake reentered before she was completely out of Andie's office. Diane stood behind her desk, watching some empty space. "I don't understand this," she muttered. "Look, Jake, I can't talk with you now. You can just deal with Donald. I'm sorry."

"My business isn't with Donald, it's with you. I have my gun. Don't make me take it out. There's lots of people still here in the museum. I don't want to hurt any-body, I just want those bones."

Diane looked startled. "What? Jake, are you crazy? What's the matter with you?"

"Don't play this stupid. I really don't want you to get hurt. That's the God's honest truth. This can be played out easy or hard. You're one tough woman, I'll give you that. You don't need to be tough now. All your proof is in the bones, and I want them. Now get up and let's go up to the vault where you keep them."

"They're gone. I sent them . . ."

"No, you didn't. The sheriff told me. That was a good little ruse, I'll hand it to you. Now get up and let's go. When I'm gone, you can do all the talking you want, but I have to tell you, nobody in this county's going to be-lieve you or even listen to you, and it will be your word against mine. The mayor and the whole police depart-ment will back me up."

Diane rose. As she walked past Jake he grabbed her upper arm. "Don't do anything fancy," he said. "Let's just go to the elevator and go upstairs. We'll cross the mammoth room and use the center elevators. That way we can avoid getting into a conversation with Chanell."

They crossed through the exhibit rooms to the center elevators and went up to the second floor.

"There will probably be someone in the lab," said Diane.

"There's not. I checked before I came down to your office. Let's go."

Diane led him to the lab and into the vault.

"Jake, don't do this."

"I just want to save my kid. You understand that."

Diane got the box and set it on the table. "I under-stand wanting to save your kid, but, my God, Jake, look at what he's done. You knew George and his family. Frank is one of your best friends."

A wave of pain spread across his face. "Open it up," he said. She began tearing the tape from the box. "Dylan panicked and let things get out of control. I know he did some terrible things, but I'm setting them back to zero. He can start with a clean slate. Without these bones, there's nothing to connect him to any of the deaths. You're the only one who will know."

"If you kill me, my death will be investigated."

"I'm not going to kill you. I said a clean slate. We can handle accusations. That's the great thing about this country and its legal system. You need some kind of proof, and you have nothing but these bones. You don't even know who they belong to and you are not likely to find out. There'll be just this tale you tell people, and right now you're lacking in credibility. I have to tell you, the mayor hates your guts, so does the chief of detectives, and the sheriff thinks you're nuts. Janice Warrick's ready to arrest you for messing in her case. Your best bet is to move on."

"There's Frank."

"Frank only knows what you've told him."

He reached in the box and unwrapped a couple of bones from the soft cotton material. Diane glanced at the door.

"Don't try anything. You're home free if you just play it safe."

He took out a sack and looked in it. "Those are the bones of the hand," said Diane. "They're packed separately, left and right."

"All nice and organized."

"This person has family somewhere who want to know where he is."

"I'm sure he does, and that weighs on me, like all of this. But they will just have to go on wondering. Taking Dylan down's not going to bring this boy back."

"Why did he kill this young man?"

"He didn't mean to—he panicked. You don't need to know. The less you know, the better. Dylan's got a bright future ahead of him. I'm giving him a chance to start over clean. Now you're going to see me out the door."

"It sounds like Dylan panics a lot. Look, Jake. I examined the crime scene. Will you let me tell you what I found?"

"I don't see any use in that."

"He was in a frenzy when he killed them."

"Just don't say anything else."

"I think he has a mean streak that's going to get worse, especially since he's hooked up with someone with her own mean streak."

"What are you talking about?"

"His girlfriend."

"Alix? She's a nice girl."

"Is she? I have it on more than one authority she has a mean temper, just like Dylan."

"Dylan doesn't have a temper. Not like you're talking about. He gets scared sometimes. If George hadn't found the bone, none of this would have happened. I'm not blaming George. It was just bad luck. Dylan was protecting himself."

"Have you really talked yourself into believing this? Are you listening to what you're saying?"

"Let's get going."

"Just listen to me, Jake. Dylan is going to continue making mistakes. There was no reason to kill the Boones. Let me show you something. Dammit, set the box down. It won't hurt to listen."

He set the box on the table and Diane took out the scapula and showed it to him. "This entire area is crushed, including the head of the humerus and the adjoining ribs. It's my opinion that an individual couldn't have caused that kind of damage. See this straight line in the damaged area here? I think the disc brake of a jacked-up car fell on him. It looks like an accident. Why in the hell did Dylan dump the body and kill the entire Boone family? He needs professional help, not a clean slate to start over."

"Don't tell her, Dad."

"What're you doing here, son? I told you I'd take care of this."

"You're going to just let her go."

"Yes, son. There's no reason to kill her."

The Dylan standing in the doorway of the vault could have been an evil twin of the one she knew. He had the same features, but his eyes were as cold as death. This was a mean young man, and Jake couldn't see it.

"Dylan, listen to me. I have this under control."

"No, Dad, you don't. This will always follow me unless something is done with her. I think she's already guessed it was the two of us who snatched her. She probably saw us when we were out on the dock looking for her. Sooner or later she'll convince someone. I'm right, aren't I?"

Diane didn't say anything for a long moment. "Dylan, all this was so unnecessary."

"Unnecessary? You don't know his old man." He gestured toward the box of bones. "Do you know, when he was five years old a kid accidentally ran over him on his bike. He wasn't even hurt, just a few cuts. His old man made sure the boy's father was fired from his job. They ended up on welfare."

Diane looked puzzled.

"Don't you get it? His dad was as vindictive as hell, and he was proud of his father for it. I asked him to come home with me for spring break on the spur of the moment."

Diane ignored Jake and focused her attention on his son. "His dad was vindictive? That's your excuse for this crime spree? I think you just enjoyed killing."

"Don't tell her, son. Don't give her any information she can use to identify this person."

"Why not? I want this bitch to understand. She thinks I'm some kind of maniac. We were in my SUV and had a flat. It was raining, and he wouldn't get out and help. He'd rather sit and drink. I was jacking up the car in the rain and he was bouncing up and down, harassing me, laughing at me. I pulled the son of a bitch out of the car, we got in a fight and he fell under the truck and knocked out the jack. He screamed like a pig. I got the jack from under the truck and jacked it up and pulled him out. Was he grateful? No, the SOB screamed and cursed me, telling me what his old man would do to me. Me, the policeman's son who somehow made it to Harvard."

"Son."

"Shut up, Dad. Let me do this. I want her to understand this wasn't my fault. I knew if his father got even with the boy on the bike for nothing, he sure as hell would get even with me for this." He put a hand on the box of bones. "He was really fucked up—couldn't even move his damn arm. He passed out a couple of times. I didn't know what to do. Every time he came to, he'd start screaming. So I hit him. And he stopped. We weren't far from where we used to go on old Abercrombie's place, so I put the spare on, dragged his sorry ass in the SUV. God, do you know how hard that was? I took him to where Luther dumped his carcasses. I thought that'd be a fitting grave. I took his clothes so he wouldn't be identified easily. He'd still be there if George hadn't found that damn bone and taken it."

"I can see that you were caught in a bad situation," said Diane.

"You still don't see. It was my first year at Harvard. His old man would have gotten me thrown out. In a flash, my whole career gone because of that stupid, drunk son of a bitch. It was his fault. Why should I have to pay for it?"

"Taking the bones won't clear you. They aren't the only evidence."

"What do you mean?"

"There's your fingerprint on the silencer you used when you shot Jay."

"No. You're lying. Dad said they just had a partial that they couldn't match."

"You didn't read the report closely, Jake. It was the opinion of that expert that *he* couldn't get a match because of the recent court decisions. There's a good chance they can get enough points of comparison by using another expert."

"Damn, this isn't happening." Dylan slammed his fist on the table. "This isn't happening."

"Son, it's not happening. I can fix this. I can make everything right. You can come out of this and the rest of your life will be good. I promise."

"Listen to yourself, Jake," said Diane. "You're a cop. You've seen killers before. He's a killer."

"No. He was just defending himself. Everything he did was tied to that one mishap. It won't happen again."

"Jake . . ."

"Dammit, he's my son."

Diane glanced at Dylan. He'd quit listening to his father. His eyes were darting back and forth, searching for some way out.

Diane wondered at the wisdom of talking about the fingerprints. This wasn't going exactly as planned. She wasn't counting on Dylan being such a loose cannon. *But why not?* she asked herself. *He's already killed four people. It would have been five if Frank had died.*

The plan was straightforward. Everything was being monitored and recorded through a device in the vault. The sheriff and deputies were less than a thousand feet away, sitting in their cars in the museum garage, listening. As soon as the incriminating statements were made, they were supposed to be there to make the arrest. A simple, elegant plan. Vanessa thought so anyway. It was Diane's version of a queen sacrifice, in which she was the queen. It was good on paper. She'd convinced the sheriff it would work.

If things got a little sticky or out of control, as they now appeared to be heading, she was to use the "safe word," the word that would summon help immediately. If possible, she was to stay in the vault and lock herself in and wait for the sheriff to arrest them. A simple matter of closing the door. But the execution of it was going awry. With both of them there, she couldn't figure out how to get them out the door.

She had no doubt about the part of the plan where they would be caught and arrested. But she feared they would kill her before that happened. She didn't want it to be a real sacrifice.

"Son, they can't do anything with the partial. Besides, I can get it from the property room. It won't be a problem. Let's just take the bones and go. She won't say anything. She's just been fired from her job here—no one will believe her."

"Who fired her?"

"Old Mrs. Van Ross."

"She likes her. Why would she fire her?"

"She didn't like the publicity she's been generating."

"The old lady fired her? I don't think so, Dad. The old lady dotes on her . . . Damn, you said Sheriff Canfield gave you the photographs of the bones and told you she had the real skeleton in the vault after all, that she'd lied to the press."

"Yes. Canfield said Janice Warrick wanted to look at the photographs."

"Shit, Dad. We've been had."

Shit is right, thought Diane. She was in trouble now.

Jake pulled out his gun and pointed it at Diane. "The boy's right. I wasn't thinking clearly. Now, I'm sure you're making a tape somewhere, so give it to me."

"Jesus Christ, Jake. Put the gun away. You don't want my murder on your hands. This other can be handled, but not if you kill me. Think about the road you're heading down, for Christ's sake." There. She'd said the safe words twice. Help should be there in less than a minute.

Dylan grabbed Diane and ripped her shirt, looking for a wire.

"It's not on me," she held her torn shirt together. "You're too late. You know how a wire works."

"You bitch."

"You murderer." She stepped back and maneuvered behind the table as Dylan tried to slap her. It was then that she noticed his finger was taped up. He was the one who attacked her in front of her apartment. "Guys, give it up. Aidan Kavanagh's father is already on his way."

Dylan froze. Diane used that second to push the heavy table into them. Linc's words, *No heavy lifting, no fights,* ran though her brain. Shit, he was going to be mad.

Dylan and his father were knocked off balance, but not down. Jake fired his gun. Like a funky jack-in-the-box, Korey, wielding a knife, jumped out of a large supply box and lunged onto Dylan, grabbing him around the throat from behind with his arm, holding the knife in the air, ready to strike. Diane was as shocked as Dylan and his father.

"Drop your gun or so help me I'll cut him. Questioning me when it was your sorry-ass son who shot Frank and you knew it."

Dylan started fighting hard, breaking Korey's hold. None of this was going down the way Diane had envisioned. Korey had no intention of killing Dylan, but Jake didn't know that. Jake aimed his gun at Korey.

"No, Jake, don't!" screamed Diane, lunging at him. There was a deafening explosion. "Oh, God, Korey," said Diane.

But it was Jake who slumped over, a pool of blood spreading on his chest.

"Dad!" cried Dylan. He pulled away from Korey and went to his father.

Diane was shocked to see it was Frank in the doorway holding a gun. The sheriff came running in with a deputy, pulling Dylan away from Jake and cuffing him.

"Frank? What are you doing out of the hospital?" Diane ran to him, putting an arm around his waist to steady him.

"The sheriff called and told me what you had planned. What in heaven's name possessed you?"

"How did you get past Linc?"

"I didn't. I got past Henry," said Frank as he walked over and knelt by Jake. He felt for the pulse in his neck. "Dammit, Jake," he whispered.

Korey picked himself up off the floor and stumbled over to Diane.

"Are you all right?" Diane asked him.

"Sure. Just fine. Scared shitless. That's the last time I do anything like that."

"How . . . ?"

"Jonas was worried about your scheme. He didn't think a lot of it either."

"You could have gotten killed."

"Don't I know it. We all need our heads examined."

Diane stood on the third floor of the west wing of the museum in the middle of her new forensic lab. Laura and Vanessa Van Ross had insisted she get back into forensics. It didn't take much convincing. She really had missed it in the past year. Digging the animal pit was a help in a strange sort of way. So was being able to give the Kavanaghs back their son—and getting Star out of jail.

Adding a forensic unit to the museum turned out to be a popular idea. Aidan Kavanagh's father had made a large donation to it; so had Vanessa. It was stocked with the most modern equipment, and Diane had renewed her forensic affiliations, resubscribed to her forensic journals. She wished Ariel was with her, but the pain of her absence wasn't as sharp and the memory of her face brought a smile before it brought a tear, and that was a welcome improvement.

Diane sat down at her desk in the lab and reread the letter Frank and Star sent her from Hawaii. His gift to Star for going back to school. Frank sent a picture of Star and Kevin on the beach. Diane wondered if Star would recover from the loss of her family. Frank was trying so hard to give her a life.

The phone on her desk rang and she looked at it, surprised. As far as she knew nobody had the number.

"Diane Fallon," she said into the receiver, expecting it to be the telephone company checking up on the connection.

"Dr. Fallon. This is Sheriff Tucker over at Cherokee County. We've found some bones here and need your help."

Diane felt herself smiling as she reached for a pen and paper.

Also Available from

BEVERLY CONNOR

Dead Guilty

A Diane Fallon
Forensic Investigation

In the shadow of Diane Fallon's new forensic
lab in Georgia, a land survey crew has
discovered three bodies hanging in an isolated
patch of woods. The sensational case has
aroused the interest of the media, unnerved the
locals—and inspired a gruesome game
between the killer and Diane. It begins with
taunting emails and chilling phone calls. Where
it leads is a dangerously personal investigation
as each bizarre clue brings Diane closer to a
heartless betrayal and a desperate man's
obsession for justice—and revenge.

**Available wherever books are sold or
at penguin.com**

Also Available from

BEVERLY CONNOR

Dead Past

A Diane Fallon
Forensic Investigation

As a child, Juliet Price witnessed the bloody
slaying of an entire family. Then the killer
chased her down, brutalized her, and left her
for dead. The police were never able to find
the man responsible. For years, Juliet's
traumatized mind hid the events from her.
Then she sees a television show featuring the
unsolved cold case, and the horrors come to
her in her nightmares. She shares her fears
with Diane Fallon, who realizes that Juliet's
shattered visions recall not one, but two
intertwined crimes—crimes that Diane intends
to uncover.

**Available wherever books are sold or
at penguin.com**

Also Available from

BEVERLY CONNOR

Dead Hunt

A Diane Fallon
Forensic Investigation

Clymene O'Riley is in prison for killing her
husband—though Diane Fallon is sure she
killed another, and suspects she may have
left a veritable graveyard of dead men in her
wake. Either way, Diane was happy to help
put her behind bars. So when Clymene informs
her that one of the prison guards may be in
danger from a serial killer, Diane is suspicious.

And when Clymene escapes from jail,
Diane becomes the prime suspect in a bloody
murder that puts her in the path of an angry
killer who wants her dead...